A Tortuous Path

Molly, aged 87, has had an unconventional life as recorded in her memoirs, *Of Such Things*. She grew up in war torn Bromley, was evacuated to the country to escape the flying bombs, and returned at the end of the war. She read History at Bedford College, then did a Postgraduate Diploma in Archive Administration and worked as an Archivist in the India Office Library where she made many Asian friends. Marriage, the arrival of children, and the purchase of a derelict oast-house, led to community activities. In 1972 she started lecturing, then taught in a secondary modern school in an Urban Priority Area, while doing a Master's Degree in Education. After thirteen years she left to become the Appeal Organiser for a hospice project, raising £1.5 million to build a hospice for Maidstone. Aged 60 she retired, and embarked on fund raising for mediaeval churches in Kent as well as organising many community and church activities. In 2019 she was awarded a BEM in the Queen's Birthday Honours List.

A Tortuous Path

Molly Poulter

Arena Books

First published by Arena Books in 2021

Arena Books
6 Southgate Green
Bury St. Edmunds
IP33 2BL.

www.arenabooks.co.uk

Molly Poulter

A Tortuous Path

British Library cataloguing in Publication Data. A Catalogue record for this book is available from the British Library.

ISBN 978-1-914390-06-7

BIC categories:- FA, FJH.

Cover design
by Jason Anscomb

Typeset in
Times New Roman

PROLOGUE

The full moon, straight overhead, cast an eerie silvery light on the huddled trees of the forest as two boys, hoods pulled down tightly to conceal their faces, pedalled their bicycles slowly and silently along the rutted paths covered with the red and gold leaves of autumn. The heavy packs on their backs rattled each time they encountered a pothole. In the half-light they didn't notice the path had recently been trodden.

They came to a small clearing where a fallen tree trunk barred their way 'We're well off the main path now, Kev. This place'll do. The ground looks soft and the tree will help us find it when we come back. But we'd better hide our bikes just in case.'

They put down their rucksacks, untied the spade which was strapped to Kev's bike, and looked round for a suitable hiding place. There was a large clump of blackberry bushes nearby and Sid said, 'Put the bikes in here, Kev. No one's gonna want to get tangled up in them thorns.'

They pushed their bikes into the middle of the clump, then Sid picked up the spade, handed it to Kev, and pointed to a spot near the roots of the fallen tree.

'Start digging here, Kev. 'Dig the hole deep. We won't be coming back for the goods for a couple of years. By then everyone'll have forgotten all about it, and we can dispose of the goods safely.'

Kev nodded agreement, and started digging. The hole got deeper, and sweat began to pour down his face. 'Your turn now,' he said.

Sid threw away the cigarette stub he'd been chewing and took up the spade.

He dug steadily for ten minutes then suddenly cried out, 'Holy shit!' His face was ashen.

'What is it?' asked Kevin anxiously.

Sid pointed down the hole. Kevin looked, and saw a face staring up at him from the bottom of the hole.

'Jesus! It's a body,' he said, awed.

He went white and started retching. The next minute he was violently sick.

'Oh, for Christ's sake, don't be such a wimp,' said Sid.

'I've never seen a dead person before!' He wiped away the vomit and looked down the hole again. 'We'll have to tell the police.'

'Don't be stupid. We can't tell anyone about this.'

'Why? We can't just leave it there.'

Sid snarled, 'Don't be a fool. If we tell the police, they'll think we did it.'

'I never thought of that,' said Kevin miserably.

'Christ, you're thick! Just think about it. We'll have to keep this to ourselves. We must never tell anyone – especially not your family.' He looked so menacing that Kevin took a step backwards. Then he asked, nervously, 'What are we going to do then?'

'Just shut up and let me think,' said Sid

Kevin nodded - then offered, 'We could dig another hole somewhere else.'

'No, there's not time. We've got to get back before it gets light. It's already three o'clock.'

They sat a little longer, thinking, then Sid said, 'We'll just have to dump the goods in the hole and fill it up. No one'll ever think to dig here again.'

They undid their packs, and a quantity of silver - clocks, dishes, christening mugs, flasks, candelabra, and cutlery - tumbled into the hole. After looking at it for a moment, they quickly covered the hole with earth, dumped the spade in the bushes, recovered their bikes and set off for home.

Reaching the main road, they skulked in the shadows until they reached the estate where they lived. Sid put his hand round Kevin's throat and said, threateningly, 'You must never, ever, tell anyone what we found. No one would believe we didn't do it – and we'd end up in prison. Understand?'

Kevin nodded miserably. They cycled on a little way, and as they passed the newsagents they saw the previous night's newspaper hoarding still standing outside. 'Daring robbery in Lyndwell. Jeweller's shop emptied of all its silver.'

The boys looked at the notice for a moment, took in a deep breath, then cycled on and parted.

-1-
The Appeal

As he'd stood in the line-up, waiting for the arrival of Royalty for the formal opening of the hospice, David had looked round at the assembled company and realised that very few of those present – staff and local dignitaries – had any idea of the five tortuous years that led up to this moment.

They'd started out as a group of ordinary people wanting to provide a hospice for the town. There was nothing extraordinary in this. The hospice movement had steadily gained ground since Dame Cecily Saunders first built St. Christopher's Hospice in Sydenham in the 1970s, and hospices were springing up all over the country. But what was extraordinary was that a group of very ordinary people, coming from different walks of life, and for very different motives, should be drawn into a drama of national proportions which changed the course of a number of lives.

David realised he'd been involved almost from the beginning of the enterprise.

-2-
The meeting at the hospital

One evening in early October he was sitting at his usual table in the hospital's staff dining room, trying to will himself to get up and go home. The evening was always the worst part of the day for him. The thought of going back to an empty house always depressed him. When Joanna, his wife, left him, she'd taken more than half the furniture, and the house always seemed empty and echoing. It accentuated his loneliness and he craved for company.

He remembered the details of that particular evening well. As none of his usual companions were in the dining room he'd picked up a newspaper from the pile near the till and his eye was caught by an article on loneliness. He was surprised to read that 34% of the population lived alone – some from choice, but more from marriage break up, bereavement, job loss, and homelessness,. 'That's me,' he thought, acknowledging that he was suffering from a sort of bereavement himself. The article said that research showed that the people who coped best were those who took up new hobbies or got involved in charity or community work. The article made him think.

David managed to keep his feelings of depression to himself and few at the hospital realised he was depressed. He did confide in his friend Stuart who'd been partly responsible for Joanna's desertion. When David had told him about her serious sexual hang-ups, Stuart had suggested that she saw a sex therapist. It all backfired when she and the therapist ran off together.

David not only felt a deep sense of loss, but was also very angry about the therapist's unprofessional conduct. He was frustrated because he felt he could do nothing about it. Fortunately he enjoyed his work at the hospital as its senior administrator. The job was interesting and demanding, and he met lots of people during the day. But the minute he was alone, misery flooded back.

After Joanna left, he'd discreetly taken out a number of hospital nurses, but the only one he felt really attracted to was Kim, the senior oncology nurse at the hospital. She was an extremely attractive woman with a mass of red curly hair, a superb figure and a vivacious smile. She was very popular with the men at the hospital but managed to keep them all at a distance while retaining their friendship. She was in her late twenties and the fact she'd never married puzzled David. He'd hoped to develop a relationship with her, but although she said she was very fond of him, that was as far as it went.

David often visited her on her ward and poured out his misery and frustration. She was always sympathetic and gave him practical advice and encouragement. Recently he'd noticed a change. He'd heard via the hospital grapevine that she and the American doctor, Jamal Khan, had been seen together on several occasions. This made David feel even more depressed.

On this particular evening, David finished his meal and started walking along the half lit corridor when he was surprised to see a man leaning against the wall, talking on a mobile phone. The man was shabbily dressed and smoking a cigarette which was not allowed within the hospital building. He looked a little uneasy when he saw David, who asked him why he was there at that time of night. 'Thanks mate, I'm just waiting to take my wife home.'

'Well,' said David, 'visiting time's over now so I suggest you wait in the entrance hall. There are people on duty there who can help you find her if she's lost– and, incidentally, smoking isn't allowed in the hospital building.'

David waited while the man, reluctantly it seemed, stubbed out the cigarette, picked up the rucksack which lay on the floor at his feet and moved slowly towards the entrance hall.

He watched him walk away. He thought it a bit odd, but decided to do nothing about it.

A TORTUOUS PATH

David then walked on a few yards down the corridor and was surprised when he heard voices coming out of one of the small side rooms. These rooms were never used in the evening. It didn't occur to him that there was any connection between the two incidents, and he opened the door to investigate. He found a group of people sitting at a table surrounded by glasses and bottles of wine. One of the group was his friend Kim.

They all looked uneasy when he opened the door but relaxed when they saw it was David. He was very popular in the hospital and not known as a stickler for petty rules. Kim got up and came forward. 'Hi David,' she said. 'We're talking about our new hospice charity. Do come and join us and have a glass of wine,' David was interested.

His mother had died in a hospice and the care was so exceptional that he'd vowed he would do all he could to help the growing hospice movement in the country. Such vows are easy to make- but then came Joanna's desertion, together with the time consuming nature of his hospital responsibilities, and David had almost forgotten about his vow.

He accepted the glass of wine Kim held out to him, and enquired what had brought them together. 'Well,' she said, 'we all feel a hospice is needed in our town, and Dr Khan has persuaded us all to join him in raising the money to build one.'

David looked round to see who'd embarked on this project. There were seven people in the room and all but one were members of the hospital staff: Dr Jamal Khan, a junior consultant at the hospital; Kim; Tracy who worked in the accounts office; Mick, the senior hospital porter; Betty the kitchen supervisor and union rep; and Maud, David's secretary. The seventh person was a man David didn't know, yet who looked vaguely familiar.

David was a little surprised to see Kim there. She was studying for an MA in her spare time and had spent a lot of time discussing with David whether or not she should do it as her role as the senior oncology nurse was so demanding. She'd just embarked on the course and had to travel to London twice a week.

Dr Khan walked over to David and said, 'You haven't met my friend Al Mercer. We were room-mates at university in America, and Al is staying with me while he's in England.'

David shook Al Mercer's extended hand. He tried to remember why the man was familiar but memory eluded him. He noticed that, though Dr Khan was happily sipping a large glass of wine, Al Mercer was sticking to orange juice.

They all sat down and Khan brought the gathering to order. He said Maud was going to take the minutes. 'To start with, I must tell you that my friend Al has very generously offered to give us a donation to get the appeal started.' Everyone gasped when he revealed the amount. He said that Tracy had agreed to be Treasurer of the Appeal, and that she and Al had already been working together to set up the necessary accounts. Tracy looked very pleased with her new role, but David wondered whether she was really competent to take it on. Working in the accounts office as she did, David saw her almost daily, but she was not over-bright.

However, he kept his thoughts to himself, wondering what motive Al had for being so generous when he didn't even live in England. David felt there must be some very strong bond between him and Dr Khan.

Dr Khan said that fund raising for the appeal would be a crucial element and that Betty had agreed to take on that role. David thought that was a very good choice. Betty was the hospital's Catering Supervisor - a formidable lady in her mid-fifties

Maud, one of David's secretaries, was to take on the secretarial role. She worked in the registry and should have retired a couple of years before but David kept her on out of compassion.

The other member of the group was Mick Ellison, the hospital's senior porter. Like Betty, he'd been at the hospital for years. He was in his sixties, and nearing retirement – although David hoped they could find a way of keeping him on. Mick was quiet and gentle, and was much loved by everyone on the staff.

Mick said he would act in a support role, and would get involved wherever needed.

While Dr Khan was talking David watched the group sitting round the table. Tracy and Maud couldn't take their eyes off Dr Khan, and David knew, from hospital gossip, that he had all the younger members of the female staff flocking round him.

David noticed that Al Mercer was observing the group with some amusement.

Khan's presentation over, Betty turned to David and said, 'Kim told me your mother died in a hospice a couple of years ago. Can you tell us about it?'

David felt cornered. He liked Betty and didn't want to seem churlish, but felt reluctant to talk about it. The loss of his mother was still raw. But he was deeply appreciative of the care his mother received in the hospice so took a deep breath and said, 'Well, my mother had terminal cancer and was suffering a lot of pain. My sister in Scotland managed to get her into their local hospice where she spent the last three weeks of her life. It was a great relief to us all. The hospice gave her wonderful care, and managed to get her pain under control. They included us in their care and helped us to talk about what was happening.

We, Mother included, made plans for our father's future. Mother died peacefully with all the family round her.'

David near to tears, finished his account with relief.

Khan touched David gently on the shoulder and said, 'Thank you very much for sharing that. I know how difficult it must have been to talk about it,' and he gave David a warm smile.

Then Khan said, 'Back to the appeal. We are planning a public meeting in a month's time when we hope to recruit more helpers. Perhaps you would like to come along to it, Mr Gardner. In fact, I wonder whether you would consider joining our committee? Your experience would be invaluable.'

David said quickly, 'I'm afraid I'm far too busy to take on anything new. But I might be able to come to the public meeting. It would be interesting to hear the public's response to the idea of a hospice.'

The meeting ended and everyone started collecting their belongings. David found himself standing next to Al Mercer. 'Are you a doctor too?' he asked,

'No! Just a businessman. But I'm interested in this project of Jamal's.'

'Are you planning to stay in England then?'

'No. I do a lot of travelling. I've just come from visiting a kibbutz in Israel. Absolutely fascinating! Makes one think! But I'm often in England and always stay with Jamal when I'm over here. We were flat mates in the USA.'

David looked surprised.' So is that why you've offered to fund the appeal? What did you study?'

'Economics.'

Before he had a chance to ask any more questions, Kim came up to David, thanked him for staying and telling them about his mother. Then she gave him a brief kiss on the cheek and told Al Mercer it was time to leave.

David watched miserably as Kim left with Jamal and his friend and felt more alone than he had at the beginning of the evening.

-3-
Reflections on the meeting

When he got home David poured himself a whisky and sat down to analyse the evening. He thought about Khan's friend, Al, and felt puzzled. Al was American and, despite his name, probably of Asian origin. David couldn't understand why he wanted to get involved with an English charity. He'd indicated that visiting a kibbutz had been the motivation, but that hardly seemed a relevant reason to support a hospice charity in a foreign country.

'David suddenly remembered where he'd seen him. He was waiting for his friend Stuart at the Tandoori Restaurant in London – a restaurant he always visited when in town because he liked the décor and its restful low lit atmosphere. He'd arrived early. He sat down and looked around and noticed a group of men sitting at a table the other side of the restaurant. The group intrigued him. They seemed to be holding a meeting. It was an all-male group, and, as far as he could see, they were all of Asian extraction. There were no glasses or cutlery on the table but a pile of documents. The dominant member of the group seemed to be the man in a red jacket whom David, now thinking about it, realised was this Al Mercer. Then, to his surprise, he saw Dr Khan arrive and join the group. He didn't see David.

Stuart arrived and they had their meal. From time to time, David glanced across at the group which seemed to be having a furious argument. As he watched, Dr Khan leapt up angrily and left. The waiter came along at that moment with their bill, and they left for the concert. David forgot all about the incident and never discussed it with anyone.

The mystery solved, David thought about the rest of the group at the meeting. Maud had been his secretary for several years. She was extremely competent but quite devoid of initiative. An elderly rather grey lady, he had not been surprised when her husband walked out on her. But he'd left her in financial difficulties, and David, feeling sorry for her, managed to keep her on after retirement age to help with her financial problems.

He sighed when he thought about Tracy. Her scatter brained attitude to work would, he was sure, be a liability to the group. He couldn't see how she would manage the accounts – even with Al Mercer's help.

Mick, the hospital's senior porter was one of his favourite people. Like Kim, he was very popular with all the staff, but was nearing retirement. David hoped he would stay longer as he valued both his care and his advice. He'd missed him when he'd had two month's compassionate leave to look after his dying wife. David regarded Mick as his 'eyes and ears', and relied on him for all the hospital gossip, knowing that people often failed to notice the humble porter standing nearby, listening in to conversations. Though Mick was very caring, David couldn't see him being an active member of the group.

Then he thought about Kim. Her role as sister on the oncology ward was not an easy one. David felt she was really suited to that branch of nursing. It needed someone compassionate as well as efficient. The morale on her ward was always good, and she was supportive of the younger nurses who often found it emotionally difficult coping with terminally ill patients. But he knew that, studying for an MA, she would have little time for the appeal.

As he lay there analysing the group, he suspected that the only one who would have any clout would be Betty, the catering manager. She was a formidable lady in her mid-fifties. Large, with grey untidy hair and a florid complexion, she was the union representative for NUPE and was a tough negotiator as David knew to his cost. But he'd discovered over the years that, despite her manner, she had a kind heart and was amenable to compromise if treated with respect. Apparently she was destined to be the fund raiser.

He decided that, with so many of his staff involved, he ought to find out more about Dr Khan and his friend, and needed to talk to Kim as soon as possible.

With that thought, he drifted into an uneasy sleep.

-4-
The Lambert's dinner party

Arriving at work a few days later, David found a formal looking envelope sitting on his desk. When he opened it, he was amazed to find an invitation to dinner from Sir James Lambert, the hospital's Chairman. They'd been working together for a number of years, but though they got on well, they never socialised. Sir James came from a very different social background. He lived in a gracious Georgian house in one of the more attractive villages in the area, and his family was long established in the community.

David felt both puzzled and intrigued by this sudden and unexpected invitation. Every day, on his way to the hospital, he would pass Sir James' house, nestling on top of a grassy hill, and had often wondered what it was like inside.

Being unsure of himself socially, he consulted his friend, Stuart, about what he should wear. Stuart told him that an invitation from the Lamberts always meant a black tie.

He set out feeling apprehensive, but was re-assured by the warmth of the welcome he received from Lady Lambert.

'It's good to meet you, David. May I call you David? I've heard such a lot about you and all the good work you do at the hospital.' She was a striking woman, well-groomed, with dark hair turned gently under, just above her shoulders. David immediately recognised the poise and confidence which comes from private schooling and affluence.

Lady Lambert waved him into the drawing room and introduced his fellow guests. David was relieved to see Andrew Johnson, the hospital's cancer specialist, whom he knew well, and his wife Rachel. The others were strangers: the Lambert's daughter and her barrister husband, and Sir Anthony Pender Jones and his wife. David had read a lot about Sir Pender as he'd been involved in one or two parliamentary commissions on medical and political matters, and his name had hit the national press on several occasions. Looking round to see who else was there he noticed a very attractive young woman and found he'd been placed next to her at the dinner table. She introduced herself as Samantha, and told David that Sir James was her uncle.

To his surprise he was enjoying himself. The food and wine were excellent, conversation was lively and ranged from music and theatre, to books and the current political situation. He suspected he was the only Labour voter there, and that the rest would always vote Conservative, but they seemed to acknowledge that conservatives didn't always get things right. David usually found at dinner parties that political discussion often became either partisan or heated, but the people at the dinner party had, refreshingly, given objective thought to the current state of the country, and the discussion was measured.

When the ladies departed, a decanter of port did the rounds and the conversation moved on, but the atmosphere changed when Sir Pender turned to face David and said, 'Tell us, Mr Gardner, about your Dr Khan.'

Surprised, he asked how he knew Dr Khan. 'Oh, Sir James often talks about the staff at the hospital. Khan's involved in this hospice project isn't he? I gather you are involved too.'

David wondered what on earth had given Sir Pender that idea. He disclaimed any involvement and said he'd just happened by chance on a meeting at the hospital the previous week and had been told about the project. That was all.

Sir Pender said, 'Khan's a Muslim isn't he? A curious project for a Muslim to take on!'

David felt uneasy at the implied racism but didn't want to upset Sir James who was listening intently, so said, 'Khan's an idealist. He's talked about doing a spell with Medicins sans frontieres, and he often talks about the needs of the Third World.'

'What does he think we should do about it?'

'Well, he's quite angry about the west's attitude to it – doesn't think we do enough to help.''

'But what has a hospice to do with that?'

David shrugged his shoulder. 'I really don't know. It puzzles me too.'

'He's American isn't he?

'No. He told us at his interview that he was born and bred in England – but educated in America.'

'Curious,' murmured Sir Pender.

'Not really. He told us his father's business collapsed, and relatives in the USA offered to finance him through university.'

'But Dr Khan wasn't the only Asian at the meeting was he?'' said Sir Pender.

David was amazed by the question. The meeting had been low key and unannounced so how did Sir Pender know it had taken place? But for some intuitive reason, he felt he couldn't ask, so said, 'Well, yes. Dr Khan's American friend was there as well. He'd just arrived in England. Said he'd been visiting a kibbutz and was interested in the hospice project.'

'Unusual. What was his name?'

'Al Mercer.'

'An American name. But he's a Muslim too, isn't he?'

David felt irritated. 'I really don't know. He may be.'

At this point Sir James intervened and said, 'You mustn't harass poor Mr Gardner.'

Sir Anthony seemed annoyed at the interruption but Sir James said, 'You know, David, there's no way the NHS can afford to support an in-patient hospice unit. It's in serious financial difficulties'.

'Yes, of course,' David acknowledged.

'I'm told there's to be a Public Meeting about the project. Adverse publicity's not going to help the NHS. Regretfully, I can't go but it would be good if someone in authority went,' and with that he looked straight at David.

Everyone round the table nodded. Someone said that the public meeting had been advertised in the press and needed someone to 'speak up' for the day-care idea which the Health Authority was prepared to support. It seemed obvious to David who they had in mind for the task and was one of the reasons he'd been invited to the dinner party. He felt annoyed, but not wanting to create a fuss, said, 'I've already promised to go to the public meeting so I'll try and promote the idea of a day hospice.'

Sir James looked pleased, and as they walked to the drawing room to join the ladies, put his arm across David's shoulder and said, 'You and Samantha seemed to be chatting happily. She's with us for a week and I'm afraid we're so busy we can't entertain her properly. I don't suppose you could show her a bit of the countryside?'

David was surprised by the request but had found Samantha so attractive and interesting that he said he'd be happy to do so. Sir James looked pleased and propelled David towards his wife who was sitting alone at one end of a large and comfortable looking sofa.

She welcomed David with a smile and patted the seat beside her. 'I've been looking forward to having a conversation with you. James has told me so much about you and your work at the hospital.'

David smiled, and looking round said. 'What a beautiful place you live in.'

Lady Lambert smiled. 'We've been so lucky to inherit this house and all this lovely antique furniture which we'll pass on to our children when the time comes. Do you have children, David?

'No. Sadly. My wife left me before we had any – which I suppose is a blessing. And you?'

'Yes. We've been very fortunate. We have three - all married – and six grandchildren. Sadly two are abroad and the other lives in Scotland so we don't see much of them'

Then, with a warm smile, she looked towards her niece who was talking to Sir Anthony Pender Jones and said, 'Go and relieve Samantha. She doesn't want to spend the rest of the evening with old fogies like us – and I'm dying to hear about Anthony's latest revelations on the health authority! Samantha's staying with us while her flat's being re-furbished. Her father has asked James and me to entertain her, but we're so committed we're not going to have much time to look after her. Do be a dear and show her some of our beautiful countryside.'

That was the second time he'd been asked to look after Samantha but it seemed such a simple request that David said he'd be very happy to take her out at the weekend. Looking back, he realised there was no hint whatsoever that there was an ulterior motive in bringing them together.

He walked across to where Sir Pender was talking to Samantha and David told him that Lady Lambert wanted to talk to him. Sir Pender looked reluctant but said to Samantha, 'It was good talking to you. Come and see me soon.'

Samantha's welcoming smile as David sat beside her, reassured him. 'Sorry to interrupt your conversation. I hope it wasn't important.'

'No, just chit chat.' She smiled.

'Lady Lambert says you're staying with them while your flat's being re-furbished,'

'Yes, I live in London above the Art Gallery. It's all such a mess I had to move out.'

'Tell me about your work.'

'Well. I run the gallery which means I have to travel a lot.'

David expressed surprise that that she hadn't decided to take a holiday abroad.'

'Well, I've recently ended a long-standing relationship and wanted a quiet time to think in peace.'

He didn't think to question her story. He was, however, a little surprised when she asked what they'd been talking about after the ladies left the table. When he said they'd been discussing the hospice project and Dr Khan's involvement, she surprised him again by asking what Dr Khan was like.

'Well, he's a very good doctor. He's come over from America, but he's only been with us for a year.'

'He's a Muslim isn't he?'

'I don't really know. He never talks about religion. Why do you ask?'

Samantha thought for a moment, then said she'd had Muslim friends at school, and had always been interested in how they lived and in what they really believed. David accepted the explanation at face value and then tentatively mentioned the weekend.

'Lady Lambert's suggested you might like to see a bit of the local countryside at the weekend?'

'That's a great idea. I'd love to see the area. And dinner afterwards?'

David accepted the suggestion with alacrity and arranged to collect her the following Saturday afternoon.

They spent the rest of evening together. Samantha sent out strong sexual vibes, flirting outrageously, and David was bowled over by her beauty and vivacity. He knew he could easily fall in love with her.

When he got home, he couldn't sleep. The whole evening had been curious. He'd gone there feeling uneasy because of his background, and though his anxiety had been put to rest by Lady Lambert's warm reception, he'd come away with the niggling feeling that the invitation had been made with an ulterior motive – something to do with Dr Khan. He wondered how on earth Sir Pender had got hold of the idea that he was involved with the hospice project. Who could have told him that he was at that meeting. He'd told no one, so how did they know he was there? Then there was Samantha. He couldn't understand why she seemed so interested in Dr Khan. But then the thought of an evening with Samantha excited him, and he took a long time to get to sleep.

-5-
First date with Samantha

It was a busy week at the hospital but that didn't stop David worrying about his forthcoming date with Samantha. He couldn't get her out of his mind but realised their very different social backgrounds made any development of the relationship unlikely. Late on Friday he had a phone call from her saying that something had come up and she couldn't manage the afternoon tour of the area, but would still like to go out to dinner. She suggested he collected her from the Lambert's house at seven so they could have a drink before setting off.

David spent a restless afternoon on the Saturday, and when the evening came, dressed very carefully before setting out. He realised ruefully that if anyone had known his state of mind, they would have thought he was a young man about to go out on his first date.

Arriving at the Lambert's mansion, Samantha greeted him warmly and said that Lady Lambert had asked them to stay for a drink before they set out. David was surprised the Lamberts were still there as Lady Lambert had told him they were going to be away most of the weekend.

Sir James shook David's hand and said, 'Enjoy your dinner. I look forward to hearing about Khan's public meeting when next we meet,' said Sir James'

He hadn't been there long before Samantha linked her arm through David's and said, 'We must be going.'

David took Samantha to his favourite country pub which was very old with low ceilings, dark beams, and a glowing log fire even though it was August.

Samantha's comment that this was just her sort of place set the evening off to a good start. Conversation flowed easily and David quickly realised that Samantha was very intelligent. But when he asked which university she'd been to, he was surprised to discover she'd not been to university. 'It may sound odd,' she said wryly, 'but girls from my background are still sent off to finishing schools in Switzerland.'

She told him about the Art Gallery she worked in and said ruefully that it was full of abstract paintings by modern artists, 'I much prefer the classics. That's why I love Italy. But modern artists are my bread and butter.'

David discovered she also liked classical music, but said, 'Though I do enjoy musicals as well. They're so full of life and colour.'

'I like some,' said David cautiously.

'Such as?'

'*Les Miserables* for one.'

'O goodie! One of my favourites. I'll try and get tickets for it when you come up to London.'

Surprised at the implication of this remark, David began to relax, and felt flattered when she asked him to tell her about his work at the hospital.

He started giving an outline of what his job entailed, but she interrupted. 'No David, it's your hospice work I'm really interested in. It's so good of you to give up your time when you've got such a responsible job.'

David felt deflated and exclaimed, 'But I'm not involved with the hospice charity. I don't know why people think I am.'

She looked surprised. 'But you do know Dr Khan. Tell me about him.'

'Again,' he thought, rather irritated, but did his best to answer. 'I don't know much about him. He's been at the hospital since January. He came over from the USA with excellent references. He's a very good doctor – but not very popular with his fellow doctors.'

'Why's that? Because he's a Muslim.'

'Of course not! We're multi-cultural at the hospital. More than half our staff are from overseas. No, it's because he's arrogant – and very popular with the ladies. I think some of the young doctors are jealous.'

Samantha laughed. 'So he's not married! I'd heard he was an interesting person!'

'Where did you hear that from?' David asked.

'My uncle, Sir James, He's always talking about him.'

David thought back to the conversation at the dinner party and asked, 'Why's your uncle interested in Dr Khan?'

'Oh,' she seemed to search for words, then said,' 'I think he must have met him several times. I'd like to meet him too. Perhaps you can introduce us when you take me round the hospital.

Surprised that she was expecting to visit the hospital, he felt pleased. But, knowing how attracted the young women at the hospital were to Dr Khan, decided then and there to do all he could to prevent Samantha meeting him.

But she wouldn't let the subject of Khan go, and asked about his Muslim friends. David said that, apart from an American friend whom he'd met once, he didn't know anything about his friends – Muslim or British!

At the mention of an American friend, Samantha leant forward in her seat and asked 'What's the name of the American friend? Is he a Muslim?'

'I'm not sure. His name's Al Mercer. That's not a Muslim name is it? I never really think about people's racial background. As I said nearly half the hospital's staff are from overseas and they all blend in well. Why do you ask?'

'Oh. Just interested,' she replied, and dismissed the subject.

They stayed talking in the pub till closing time, and it was very dark when they set out for home. As they neared the Lambert's mansion it was shrouded in darkness. Samantha said she had a key to the servants' door and told David to drive round to the side of the house. 'This is it,' said Samantha, and before David had turned off the ignition he felt Samantha's hand wandering suggestively along his thigh. 'Why don't you come in. My room's nice and comfy.'

He'd never before received such a direct proposition and was excited at the thought of making love to Samantha. He couldn't hide the erection her exploring fingers had discovered. But he knew it wouldn't be a good idea. This was the home of his boss, and he suspected Sir James wouldn't approve if he found out. So, very reluctantly, he said, 'Much as I'd like to, I don't want to upset Sir James. He's my boss, and this is his home.' He quickly got out of the car before he could change his mind, walked round to her side and held open her door.

Samantha shrugged her shoulders and got out. 'Next time,' she said as he kissed her chastely on the cheek. 'I'll ring you when I get back from the continent.'

With that, she walked to the door, unlocked it and went in.

David returned to the car and set off for home. He was in a state of arousal and found it difficult to concentrate on driving. He didn't know what to make of her. He'd never been propositioned so directly before. She was beautiful and intelligent, yet he realised she'd spent most of the evening quizzing him about the hospice and his contact with Dr Khan. It was all very puzzling.

-6-
The Public Meeting

On the Monday morning when he arrived at the hospital, he was confronted by Dr Khan who wanted to know whether David had decided to go to the public meeting. Curious about who was likely to be there, he asked Khan who'd been invited. Khan reeled off a long list of people and organisations and David realised that if they all came it was likely to be a lively meeting.

During the week several colleagues popped in to his office to ask David what he thought about the hospice idea. He was non-committal.

When he got to the meeting the following week, he found a crowded hall. Members of the general public were there in large numbers. He also saw a number of G.Ps who were normally difficult to persuade to attend meetings after seven o'clock, There were members of the health authority, and people from the social services department as well as many who were not involved with the health authority. David realised Khan had trawled his net widely. The local press was well represented with reporters and photographers from both local newspapers.

On the platform with Dr Khan were Maud looking important, her pen poised ready to take the minutes, and Tracy who sat the other side with a couple of collecting boxes in front of her. On his right David was surprised to see Martin Allardice, the local Borough Councillor. He was not one of David's favourite people as he was always criticising the local health service.

Looking round, he spotted Kim in the middle of the hall and made a bee-line to her. She introduced David to the lady she was sitting next to 'This is Mary, an old friend of mine. I'm trying to interest her in our charity.'

'Hello,' said David politely, and shook her hand. Then, ignoring Mary, he sat down next to Kim and asked 'Why aren't you sitting on the platform with Dr Khan? I'm sure it's your baby as much as his!'

'You know me, David! I prefer to keep out of the limelight, especially as I'm involved with so many terminally ill patients at the hospital.'

'Yes, that's probably wise,' said David, and started telling her about the dinner party and the guests' curious interest in Dr Khan and Ali Mercer. He didn't mention Samantha.

Kim looked annoyed, 'It's all racial prejudice. It makes me so cross.'

David asked, not expecting a reply, whether Al Mercer was coming to the meeting.

'No. He's on his travels again. He won't be back for some time.'

While they waited for the meeting to begin David thought about Kim and what a special warm and caring person she was. He still regretted she had responded negatively to his overture, suspecting that this new relationship with Samantha would develop.

His reveries were brought to an end when Khan opened the meeting, welcoming everyone and explaining that he and his friends were keen to raise money for a hospice in the town. He talked about what hospice care entailed, its value to those who were dying, and also to those who were caring for them. David was impressed with his presentation. It was lucid and not too long, and it soon became clear that many of those present were in sympathy with his aims.

He introduced Maud and Tracy and said they both worked at the hospital and had agreed to become the charity's' secretary and treasurer. Then he turned to Martin Allardice who, he said, needed no introduction. He was well known as their Borough Councillor and for his championing of better health care in the area.

David smiled to himself at this. Martin was a Labour Councillor and had been a thorn in the flesh of the local health authority, raising time and again at Council meetings the inadequacies of the local health service. He was surprised to see him there and whispered to Kim 'Why's Allardice here?'

She whispered back, 'He's going out with Pamela Litchfield'

That was enough to satisfy David. He knew Khan had just recruited Pamela to the committee and presumed he'd recruited Martin at the same time.

David returned his attention to the meeting. Khan was introducing the speaker. 'Mrs Giles has a very special knowledge of hospices as she's been responsible for setting up the hospice in Beetson. She's very kindly come tonight to tell us about her own hospice and how they set about fund raising.'

Mrs Giles got to her feet. She described the services her hospice offered, talked about the benefits of hospice care to both patients and families, spoke about the sort of fund raising activities they'd organised, and urged the people present to give their support to Dr Khan's project.

It was then that the fireworks started. Mrs Giles was questioned by officials from the health authority and by the G.P.s about costs. At first she tried to concentrate on the capital cost of the hospice - and spoke enthusiastically about the dedication of the fundraisers and how the £900,000 needed had been raised in three and a half years.

This was not what the medical people wanted to hear. They pointed out that costs had risen hugely since her hospice had been built. They were more interested in the running costs of a hospice than the capital cost of a building, but found it difficult to extract precise figures from Mrs Giles who repeatedly said the money needed always came in. Pressed to explain how, she insisted that when something was right, then the necessary funds would somehow be found. David thought it was almost as though she felt she had some magic wand at her finger tips, and her comments enraged the medical people there. Pressed further, she told them about the three hospice shops in the towns that her hospice served and said proudly that they brought in an income of £90,000 a year. There were derisory laughs from the health authority representatives who stated that, on the basis of their calculations, at least £900,000 would be needed to run the hospice each year - not taking into account inflation.

One consultant from the hospital, who was always crying for more funds to carry out his orthopaedic work, got up and indignantly said that if money were poured into hospice care, all those patients who were on waiting lists for operations would once again lose out. He pointed out that many of these were unable to work until they'd been operated on; that the state was paying them sickness benefit to which everyone present was contributing; and it was a nonsense to divert money to the dying who could perfectly well be looked after at home by their relatives. That had always been the norm until these new-fangled ideas started being bandied around.

At this, there was pandemonium in the hall. Everyone wanted to speak at once, and Khan had great difficulty in getting the meeting under control. Eventually, a woman got up and spoke quietly but passionately about the trauma she and her family had been through when her husband was dying. She said the consultant didn't know what he was talking about. Had he ever nursed a dying patient in such pain that the family felt desperate and the children wouldn't come home at night because they couldn't bear to hear their father cry out in agony? Had he ever had to suffer the frustration of dealing with a thick-witted doctor who refused to give enough morphine to cure the pain of a dying patient in case the patient became addicted! Had he ever had to stay up night after night nursing someone because the health service couldn't afford to provide night nurses, and the family couldn't afford to employ private nurses? Did he know about the extreme tiredness that carers suffered after weeks of sleepless nights? Did he have any idea of the fear that patients suffered? Did he know what it was like to have to time visits to the shops in the brief intervals when the tablets were working? She started to go on - and then burst into tears and those round her rushed to comfort her.

This story was taken up by many in the hall with similar tales to tell. One woman spoke about the care her husband had received in a hospice in the West Country, and talked movingly of how much she and her family had been helped.

It seemed the meeting was moving in the right direction when Dr Peter Langton, a friend of David, got up to speak. He was a large man with a commanding presence, and was well known in the community. It was clear that what he had to say would command respect. He started by acknowledging as true all that the first lady had said; that there were indeed major gaps in health and community care in the town which he, like everyone there, wanted to remedy. But he didn't think putting up an expensive hospice building was the answer. He said this had been the pattern for hospices in the pioneer days in the seventies, but times had changed and ideas had moved forward. He said that the most useful and cost effective form of hospice care was a home-care service.

He then explained how this worked - with a team of people ready to go into homes and deliver hospice care on the spot. He said this sort of care had already been developed in a number of areas with great success. He'd visited some of these projects, seen them at work, and had spoken to many of the families enjoying the benefits. He said this was the pattern of the future, adding that if people went that route, he knew they would get all the help and support needed from the local health authority.

David breathed a sigh of relief. Dr Langton had said exactly what he would have said had he found it necessary to keep his promise and speak up for day care. He hoped that Langton had swayed the meeting, but Khan got up and started talking. He'd come prepared for this argument and was armed with statistics. He said he too had visited a number of day-care projects as well as a number of hospices throughout the country and agreed with Dr Langton that hospice home care teams were doing a great job for the terminally ill - but he didn't agree that they were a substitute for a hospice building which offered not only terminal care but also symptom control and respite care. He declared that both aspects of care were desperately needed. He produced figures for the number of people dying in hospitals, and the number of people he'd spoken to who couldn't cope at home with the nursing required during the last stage of illness. He felt that the people of the town wanted a hospice they could be proud of.

Things suddenly got nasty. A woman from the audience shouted out that it was all wrong dumping people in a hospice when they were dying. 'I nursed my husband right up to the end. He was an old so and so - but I wouldn't have deserted him. It's just like putting an old dog down when you can't be bothered to look after it anymore.'

Someone else got up and asked whether they could be sure that the money raised would stay in the country. 'Look,' he said, 'pointing at Dr Khan, 'at who is leading the project. How can we be sure the money raised isn't going to some God-forsaken Muslim country?'

Despite exclamations of horror from many in the audience at such blatant racial prejudice, several people applauded and another man from the audience cried out, 'Yes. How do we know the money you raise will go to a hospice,' and another said belligerently. 'What's a Muslim doing putting his nose into our affairs? Why don't you go home and leave us to look after ourselves!'

Then Jane Masters, a lady, whom David had met once or twice before, stood up and speaking quietly said, 'I'd like to think we are both a Christian and a tolerant nation. I think the gentleman who has just spoken should apologise for what he's said. It demeans him, and creates entirely the wrong impression of our country which is noted for its tolerance.' At this there was applause in the hall.

This quietened some of the protesters, and Khan tried to explain that, though the charity had a wide remit, its first project was a hospice for the town. David noticed a number of people shaking their heads and muttering.

Then someone who obviously knew nothing about the way hospices operated, said, 'Why should we put our hands in our pockets to raise money for something only the rich can afford?'

Trying to regain control, Khan explained that hospice care would be free to all. Then he brought the meeting to a close, saying that if anyone would like to help him with the project, they should stay on and give him their names.

David stood up and looked towards the platform to see if anyone was responding to Khan's call for volunteers. He saw there were several middle aged ladies and a few men talking to him. Among them was Jane Masters, the woman who'd chided the speaker for his intolerance; his bank manager's wife, Margaret; and a man who'd recently set up a very successful photocopying business in the town.

David decided to make a point of speaking to Khan at the earliest opportunity, and was on the point of re-joining Kim and her friend when he saw a reporter from the local paper coming towards him. David could see he was looking gleeful, confident that he'd got hold of a good story for that week's paper. David tried to dodge him but was unsuccessful.

'Well, Mr Gardener, what do you think the Health Authority's going to make of this malarky? They're short of money at the best of times. They're not going to like this.'

'I think that's something you've got to discuss with the Health Authority. I can't speak for it.'

'Oh, but I'm sure you have your opinion about the idea.'

'I've nothing to say,' said David and walked away.

He looked round for Kim and her friend, intending to ask them to join him for a drink, but discovered they'd already left. He was on the point of leaving as well when he saw Pamela Litchfield. She was an old friend. They'd met at Oxford where she was studying for a doctorate in sociology. They'd spent a lot of time together until Joanna came on the scene. David had enjoyed her company and felt she was a woman he could talk to on equal terms, but he was never in love with her. She had a lot of men friends at Oxford but as far as David knew, there were never any romantic attachments. He and Pamela had lost contact when David got married, but their friendship resumed when she turned up at the age of thirty-three as the number two in the town's large Social Services department.

Joanna, David's wife, never really liked her, but David insisted Pamela was invited from time to time to their dinner parties so she could meet people outside her work. His friends liked her and she became part of their social circle. During the last stormy year of his marriage, when entertaining came to an end, it seemed natural for David to turn to Pamela for advice.

'Where've Kim and Mary gone?' she asked. 'I saw you sitting with them.'

'They must have left,' he replied.

'A pity! They could have joined us for a drink.'

'How do you know them?' he asked, curious.

'Oh, I know Kim through work,' she replied.

He nodded, but didn't bother to ask her about Mary. They found a corner in a nearby pub, and sat down to discuss the evening's meeting.

'I gather you've joined Dr Khan's committee,' said David. 'Do you know much about hospices?'

'Yes. I visited St. Christopher's hospice in Sydenham several times when Jeanette was there.'

'Jeanette? You don't mean Jeanette Macauley?'

Pamela nodded.

'I didn't know she was ill!''

'Yes. She had breast cancer. She died in St. Christopher's Hospice in Sydenham.'

David shook his head in disbelief. 'But she was only our age!'

Jeanette had been one of their crowd at Oxford, and Pamela's news upset him badly. He realised he'd been so preoccupied with his own miseries he'd lost touch with his old friends.

'Jeanette received wonderful care in the hospice, and they supported her family as well. They were devastated by her death as you can imagine. I met Dame Cecily Saunders while I was there, and she was a real inspiration to talk to. She told me why she'd started St Christopher's and how the hospice movement had grown rapidly both in this country and in the rest of the world. I found her a formidable but inspiring woman.'

'So that's why you've got involved?'

'Yes. I determined to help if ever anyone set up a project to build a hospice in this area.'

'So what do you think are the chances of getting a hospice here?'

Pamela thought carefully before answering. 'Not very great. As you know well, the health authority is strapped for cash so it will want to go for the Day Care idea. On the other hand, there's likely to be a strong emotional response to the idea of a hospice from the general public. I think it depends partly on the sort of support that comes out of tonight's meeting.

But then there's the problem of who's leading the appeal. Jamal Khan's a very determined character but the appeal would stand a much better chance if he wasn't a Muslim.'

David was shocked. 'I didn't think you were racist.'

'I'm not,' protested Pamela, 'I like Jamal. But I'm a realist. There's a lot of prejudice out there. And I think, despite what Jamal says, that there's more chance of getting a day hospice. I know that's what Andrew, our cancer specialist, thinks,' she added.

'I must have a word with him sometime.' said David. 'So what do you think of Dr Khan?'

Pamela surprised him. She seemed to know far more about him than David did, even though he and Khan worked in the same building. David thought how curious it was that women seemed able to glean information about people in a very short time. It confirmed his belief that men and women differ in far more ways than their physical characteristics - and thought that, if he was a chauvinist, he would find that a very good argument against sexual equality!

David realised that Pamela found Dr Khan attractive, and when she said she was worried about Kim's involvement with him, wondered for a moment whether it was jealousy rather than concern for Kim. But he retracted the thought when she said, 'It's not because I don't like him. He's a nice guy. But he's a Muslim and in my experience mixed marriages often ended up in disaster.'

David had to agree, and they both hoped all would go well for Kim.

'So what about you?' David asked, 'knowing that she and Martin Allardice were going out together.

Pamela looked at David and laughed. 'Yes, well you've obviously guessed about Martin and me!'

David felt rather sad for Pamela, but didn't say anything. He'd always disliked Martin. Over the years he'd had to fend off his criticisms of the hospital and local government in general, and found him pompous and opinionated.

They finished their drinks and the clock ticking midnight, they arranged to have dinner in a fortnight's time. David gave her a fraternal kiss on the cheek and they parted.

The local press had a field day reporting the Public Meeting. On the Friday, the local paper sported a front page story headed *Overseas doctor in clash with the health service*. In typical journalistic fashion, the reporter had picked out all the less pleasant comments, as well as stating that 'local consultant, Mr Derek Stoneham, declared that a hospice project would seriously jeopardise the chances of those waiting for a hip operation'. The article ended by saying, 'Does this town really need a hospice when our citizens are already being short-changed on health care.'

-7-
David takes Dr Khan out to lunch

Returning to the hospital the day after the Public meeting, David knew he would soon have Sir James questioning him about the Public Meeting and Dr Khan. He also had the uneasy feeling he might also start asking questions about Samantha.

He decided to invite Khan out to lunch and engineered a meeting in the corridor. 'Lively meeting last night! It would be good to talk about it. Are you free for lunch sometime?'

Dr Khan looked a little surprised but said, formally, 'Well, thank you. That would be very pleasant.'

They arranged to go out for lunch on the eleventh of September. David decided to take him to the same country pub he'd taken Samantha to.

They found a table and sat down. David didn't know what to expect when he asked Khan what he would like to drink. He knew most Muslims didn't drink and couldn't remember whether or not he'd been drinking at the hospice meeting. But Khan quickly put David's mind at rest when he said he'd like a beer. But when Khan searched the menu for a vegetarian dish, David felt confused and asked whether he was a vegetarian. He denied it with a laugh, and said 'I just like vegetarian food – and beer.' Seeing that David looked puzzled, said, 'Does that surprise you? Though I'm a Muslim by birth, I'm afraid I don't follow strict Islamic tenets. I eat and drink what I like!'

David laughed and then said, 'Tell me about yourself. What made you come to England?'

'Because I'm English!'

'I know you were brought up in England. But you've done most of your training in America, haven't you? How come?'

David expected him to be evasive, but he was quite open about his story. 'I've lived in America, but was brought up in Bradford. When I was sixteen I went to visit my aunt and uncle in America, and while I was there my parents' business crashed and they lost everything – including our home. They had to move to rented accommodation, and my aunt and uncle offered to keep me in America so I could finish my studies. I went to high school there and on to Berkeley where I did a degree in economics.'

'That was very generous of them,' David observed.

'Yes. I owe them a lot. But when I got my degree, I felt I should come home and help my parents with their business – but they'd got back on their feet quickly and didn't need me.'

'Shame!'

'Well, no! It was fortunate for me because they said they would support me while I got the necessary science qualifications.

'But you studied medicine in the USA.' David was puzzled, as he'd seen his medical certificates.

'Yes. But my first degree was in economics. My aunt and uncle financed me through both my economic and medical studies.'

'How very generous! You were very lucky.'

'Yes. I owe my aunt and uncle a lot. Not like my friend Al.'

'Tell me about him. He seems an interesting man.'

'Yes, he is. We met at university and shared a room for two years. He was very bright – studied economics and agriculture and came top of his year at the university. He was an idealist, and, because his parents were very wealthy, had the idea of setting up a sort of Kibbutz in Uganda. When he told his parents about it, they were horrified. They were hard headed businessmen and said they didn't want to see their money squandered on the down and outs. So they cut him off altogether and said he would have to find his own way of making money. Al was very bitter – but determined to carry on with his ideas.'

'How did you feel about it?'

'Well, you only have to look at all the suffering in the world – the starvation, the conflicts, the dispossessed – to know that Al is on the right lines. I've often thought of volunteering for Medicine Sans Frontieres myself – but I don't think I've got the guts to do it. But I do admire those who have gone out.'

David agreed that it was a very worthy organisation, but then moved on and asked him about his hospice charity and what he was hoping to do first.

'Well, as I said at our meeting at the hospital, Al has donated money for office equipment and the printing of stationery.'

'I find it difficult to see why your friend should be so interested in a project over here when he doesn't even live in England.'

'Well, that's Al's strength. He's always been very generous, and his business has been going extremely well in the last two years.'

'But surely,' said David, puzzled, 'it's unusual for someone to give away money just at the beginning of a career – however successful.'

Khan laughed and said, 'Well, that's Al all over! And though he won't be in the country often enough to take on the role of treasurer, he's offered to be the advisor to whoever takes on the task.'

Khan then asked David about the hospice his mother had been in, and David couldn't help but be enthusiastic about the care it had given to him and his family, and about the philosophy of the hospice movement.

David felt this was the opportunity to ask what he thought about day hospices. Khan replied emphatically, 'They offer a very good service, but we need residential care as well. Day hospices are excellent but they can't operate effectively without the back-up of an in-patient unit.'

David realised that Khan was quite fixed in his views and there was no point in taking the discussion further.

Food arrived and they spent the next hour in relaxed conversation about the state of the health service, hospitals, hospices and their families. They returned in a happy mood. On the journey back Dr Khan insisted there was no need for formality, and asked David to call him by his family name – Jamal. A little surprised, David agreed.

Their mood was shattered when they got back to the hospital. They were greeted by the news that the twin towers in New York had been deliberately destroyed. The news was so horrifying that little work was done in the various offices in the hospital, although work on the wards and in the operating theatres went on as before. Whenever they could, staff and patients crowded round television sets to watch, incredulous that such an atrocity could be planned in cold blood. Throughout the rest of the afternoon, phones kept ringing with friends and relatives asking if they'd heard the news.

For most people their feeling of security was shattered. Some of those who had been through the rigours of the Second World War, said that they hadn't felt so uncertain about life since the dropping of the atom bomb on Hiroshima – an event that had made them realise man's potential for destruction.

By the end of the afternoon, it was known that it was an Islamic terrorist attack, and there were mutterings among the staff about their Muslim doctors. David wondered how Khan was going to react to the news, knowing he'd always kept himself rather aloof from his colleagues. As he walked round the hospital that afternoon David sensed a feeling of hostility developing towards the Asian doctors and just hoped it wouldn't escalate.

In the late afternoon, David was not surprised to find Khan knocking on his door. He looked very angry. 'What a crazy thing to do! This won't do the Muslim cause any good ...,' then, seeing David's look of consternation, he changed tack and said, 'What I mean is that it will just exacerbate prejudice. Race relations are already bad enough – even in this country.'

David raised an eyebrow, and Jamal continued, 'It's the most appalling atrocity – inflicting death and injury indiscriminately. The people who thought it up have no heart – no compassion. My heart bleeds for all the suffering. I just don't believe this is the way to world peace.'

'You're a Muslim,' said David. 'What's the motivation for this?

'Jihad – and world domination!' he said curtly.

David couldn't help but agree with him, though he felt he had to ask whether Jamal had experienced any hostility because of his Muslim background. 'No, I can't say I have'' he replied. 'But I think that's because of my professional background. It's very different for the man in the street.'

They talked on for a long time, and moved to the staff common room where they watched more of the unfolding events on television. David found Jamal's attitude puzzling. At one moment he seemed to be justifying the event by trying to explain how badly Muslims were treated across the world, and the next moment expressing horror at the enormity of the attack. He talked about the plight of the wounded and bereaved, and the aid effort that would be needed. He said he would like to go out to help, though he suspected there would be enough American doctors on the scene very soon. David didn't really know quite what to make of him.

David and several of the staff decided to go off to the pub for a quick drink on their way home – feeling that might ease the horror of the event a little. Khan declined to go with them.

The pub was full of people, but instead of the usual cheerful chatter, there was an uneasy atmosphere of gloom - and even of fear.

After such an eventful and horrifying day, David expected not to sleep. But for once he fell asleep as soon as he got into bed.

-8-
Visit to Samantha

The morning after the Twin Towers everyone was still talking about what had happened, and there was a heavy feeling of gloom in the hospital. When the phone rang, the last voice he expected to hear was Samantha's.

'Hi. It's me. I expect you're all feeling as gloomy as we are here in London, but I've got a bit of news that might cheer you up. I've managed to get us two tickets for *Les Miserables* on Saturday. Why don't you come up after lunch and then stay the night. We can try and forget what's going on in the world!'

David really hadn't expected to hear from her again and was both surprised and delighted – especially at the invitation to stay the night. David accepted and it was only when he'd taken down all the details of where her gallery was, that he realised he'd already accepted an invitation to dine with Stuart.

He felt embarrassed when Stuart asked teasingly what was more exciting than an evening with him and his wife. When David told him about Samantha, Stuart's only response was 'Take care, David. She's not all she appears to be.'

Believing Stuart was referring to her social background, David said, 'Yes. You're right. I'll be careful.'

He set off for London on the Saturday in a mood of happy anticipation. When he got on the train he was surprised to find that, instead of the usual silence with people minding their own business, everyone was talking about the twin towers. All barriers seemed to be down, and people were talking about what the event meant for the future. People's sense of security seemed to have been shattered by the atrocity.

When he got to London he took a taxi and went straight to the gallery, expecting to find Samantha there. Instead, he was greeted by a confident well-dressed man who asked David if he could help.

'I've come to see the manager,' said David. 'She's expecting me.'

The man replied, 'I am the manager.'

Puzzled, David blurted out, 'But I thought Samantha was the manager!'

'Oh!' He looked at him sideways. 'Well, yes. She's part of the organisation. She lives over the gallery. But she's hardly ever here. She travels a lot. But I think you'll find she's upstairs today.'

David thanked him, and feeling an inexplicable nervousness said, 'Well, now I'm here I might as well look at the exhibits first.' He was not impressed. The paintings were modern - not very much to his taste - and he remembered that Samantha had said they were not really to her taste either.

Saying goodbye, he made his way to the door of Samantha's flat and pressed the remote control button on the door panel. His heart lurched when he heard her laughing voice saying, 'State your name and number and have your passport ready.'

She opened the door and stood looking at him for some minutes, before pulling him into the hallway and taking his bag. A little smile hovered round her lips as she bent towards him and kissed him. Then, taking his hand, led him into the living room.

'Come and see my pad. The decorators left last weekend and the furniture came back on Wednesday. I've been in one hell of a mess, but it's all straight now, and I've been dying to show it to someone. You're my first official visitor.'

With that she took David on a tour of the flat. He'd expected it would smell of paint as the decorators had left so recently, but it looked as though it hadn't been touched for years. He felt puzzled, but said nothing.

The flat, though not large, gave an impression of luxury and stylish living. The living room spanned most of the Gallery below. The decor was subtle and restful, and the room contained what David suspected were valuable antiques - a rosewood bureau, a beautiful folding table with four chairs to match which David thought were late eighteenth century, and a cabinet full of china animals. There were two wing armchairs and a comfortable sofa with loose covers toning in subtly with the pale blue velvet curtains. Two alcoves were fitted with bookshelves, which David made a mental note to rummage through later. He always found people's books revealing. There were pictures everywhere - some of which he suspected had been painted by the artist whose pictures were on show in the gallery below.

'This is my den,' Samantha said opening the door into a tiny room with a divan bed, a desk with a computer on it, and bookcases lining the whole of the side wall. The divan was piled high with books and papers, and the possibility of anyone sleeping in it seemed remote. 'I'm afraid it's not much use as a bedroom. My guests have to sleep elsewhere,' she said, giving him a half teasing, smile. David thought about that comment later when things began to go awry, and wondered how many 'guests' had enjoyed the luxuries of her bedroom!

A TORTUOUS PATH

The bathroom was spacious and luxurious. A large kidney shaped bath with gold taps occupied one corner, with a washbasin and bidet alongside, while the lavatory was discreetly hidden behind draped curtains. The suite was a delicate shade of peach with towels and drapes to match. Many mirrors reflected the concealed lighting, which Samantha switched on as they entered. Inset shelves contained statues and vases, and here and there, trailing pots of variegated ivy. It was the sort of bathroom David had only seen on film-sets, and for a moment he had a feeling of unreality.

Moving down a short corridor, Samantha opened the door into a feminine looking bedroom, with a dusty pink carpet and luxuriously draped curtains patterned with flowers. The room was dominated by a very large double bed with plush coverings and a beautifully carved mahogany headboard.

Samantha, seeing David looking at it, put her fingers to his lips and whispered, 'Later'.

David's pulses quickened, and he wanted to take hold of her, but she led him gently out of the bedroom and into a tiny galley kitchen. 'You've had lunch,' she stated as she collected a bottle of champagne from the refrigerator.

Returning to the living room, he saw that she'd put a tray with glasses on the low marble coffee table in front of the sofa. She passed him the champagne bottle, saying 'Open it.' David picked up the bottle and wrestled with the cork till it flew across the room. He filled the glasses, and handed one to Samantha. She twined her arm through David's, lifted her glass and said, 'It's good to see you David.'

She sat down on the sofa and patted the space beside her. 'So what do you think about this atrocity in America? It must have made things a little tense at the hospital,'

David told her about the reactions and said he hoped it wasn't going to spoil the racial harmony that he'd worked hard to establish at the hospital.

'And what did your friend Dr Khan say?' she asked.

'Well, he seemed as horrified as the rest of us – but he was worried about what it would do to people's attitudes to the Muslims over here. When I asked whether he'd personally suffered any racial abuse, he said no – but he thought that was because of his profession. He knew Muslims who had.'

As they sat drinking their champagne David was startled when he found her hand moving up his thigh. He knew he would have an erection at any moment and was wondering what to do when Samantha stood up and pulled him to his feet. 'Come! Let's not waste time.'

David was amazed at her directness, but let Samantha lead him to her bedroom.

His amazement continued. Though he'd slept with a number of women over the years, he'd never before met anyone who'd propositioned him as directly as Samantha. He felt excited but anxious about his performance, knowing he'd been celibate for many months. She seemed to have no inhibitions at all, and held out her arms for David to undress her. As he peeled off her clothes, his senses quickened. She stood before him, naked, uninhibited, and with a quizzical expression on her face.

Trembling, he pulled her into his arms and they fell on the bed. His pleasure was intense. For him it was a new experience. He hadn't realised a woman could be passionate and felt he was drowning in a sea of delight from which she brought him back to consciousness with laughter, only to encourage him to explorations which took him down avenues he'd never known existed.

'That was fun,' she murmured as she stroked his face

The comment perplexed him. Fun was not the word he would have used to describe such an intense experience. He realised he knew nothing at all about this woman who'd just come into his life.

They surfaced late in the afternoon, and he felt ravenously hungry, but Samantha said, 'We must get going. There's no time to waste. I've booked a table for six o'clock and *Les Mis* starts at eight o'clock.' She phoned for a taxi and said, 'The Tandoori restaurant please.'

'The Tandoori restaurant!' David exclaimed, 'It's my favourite restaurant. I always go there when I'm in town.'

'Good,' she said. 'I like it because it has such an interesting menu.'

Samantha had booked a table at the side of the room - 'Where we can be private,' she said, but David noticed it had a good vantage point, overlooking the whole of the restaurant. He ordered – insisting that he paid for the meal. He chose an expensive bottle of wine (wanting to impress Samantha, but knowing it was far more expensive than he would normally have ordered) and they settled down to look at the menu.

As they were eating their first course, Samantha suddenly stiffened, and sat up straight. David saw her looking towards the far side of the room, and to his amazement, saw Al Mercer sitting at a table in the corner with another Asian.

Samantha heard his gasp and, looking at him keenly, said, 'Who have you seen?''

'Al Mercer, the American friend of Dr Khan.'

'The Asians?' she asked, pointing to the corner of the restaurant.

'Yes. How did you guess?'

'Do you know them?'

'Oh no! Just Al Mercer. And I've only met him once.''

'Which one is he?' she asked - an intent look on her face.

'The one sitting on the left – the short one in the maroon jacket.'

What do you know about him?' She watched his face intently.

'Very little, as I told you when you asked before. He seemed very pleasant – was interested in the hospice project. Has provided some of the money needed to launch the appeal

'Has he now! That's very generous.'

David agreed.

'So what does he do for a living?'

'I don't really know. Khan says he's a businessman. I gather he travels overseas a lot.'

'What sort of business?'

'All I know is what Dr Khan told me. He's American, studied economics - and has just been visiting a kibbutz.'

'Has he a home in England?'

'No. I don't think so. I believe he stays with Khan when he's over here.'

'Where does Khan live?'

'Somewhere in town,' David said curtly, by now irritated by Samantha's interest in Al. He changed the subject to *Les Miserables*. 'How on earth did you manage to get tickets at such short notice? It's such a very popular show.'

'Ah! It's who you know that counts!' she said laughing.

She looked at her watch and realised they would have to leave straight away if they were to get to the show on time.

Exhausted by the afternoon's love-making, David dozed off in the second act and woke to the sound of applause. He felt embarrassed, but Samantha just laughed. 'Come on. Let's get a drink. Then you can enjoy the second half.'

To David's annoyance, when they got to the bar they found two of Samantha's friends, standing there. They came over and joined them. David immediately felt ill at ease – and far from happy when Jane eyed him up and down and asked Samantha 'And where did you find this handsome man?'

'Oh, we met at my aunt's,' replied Samantha airily. 'Aren't I lucky!' and she tucked her hand into David's arm to reassure him.

Back at the flat, they had a night cap, and returned to bed. Though David was exhausted from the afternoon's exertions, Samantha made it quite clear she was expecting him to make love to her again. David obliged but afterwards fell into a deep sleep.

He was woken by the sound of a doorbell. The next moment a young man entered the room and stood at the foot of the bed, looking at them with a grin. He was so like Samantha that there was no mistaking he was her brother. Samantha sat up, and though she was naked, made no attempt to cover herself up. David felt embarrassed, and even more so when the stranger said, 'Do introduce me to your latest.'

David tried to snuggle under the bedcovers, but Samantha laughed and said, 'You don't need to worry. This is my brother Daniel. Take no notice of him. He's been trying to put me down ever since he was a teenager. He's quite harmless really.' Turning to Daniel, she said, 'You can go and cook us breakfast while we have a bath.'

David hadn't realised that she meant the 'we' literally, and felt more than a little embarrassed when she dragged him into the bathroom with her. She seemed quite unconcerned at her brother's presence, and once in the bath there was no way David could resist her exploring fingers.

When they emerged, Daniel had breakfast on the table, and looked as though he regarded what had just happened as an everyday occurrence. It was all so far removed from the conventional environment he'd been brought up in that David had a feeling of unreality. Moreover he'd picked up Daniel's words 'your latest,' and felt a twinge of unease. But the pleasure had been so intense that he tried to kid himself that he was special.

Breakfast was almost over when the phone rang, and Samantha left the room to answer it. When she came back, Daniel asked who it was. 'Father's been trying to get hold of you.'

'I know,' she replied. 'That was him on the phone,' Then, turning to David she said, 'Fancy coming with me to Kew Gardens?' He felt a little surprised at the suggestion, but as he hadn't been to Kew for a long time, and the weather was fine, the idea of spending a day at Kew with Samantha was very attractive, so he agreed.

'Well, if you're off to Kew, I'll be on my way. When are you going down to see the parents?' Daniel asked.

'I'm waiting for instructions,' she replied, 'but probably when Miranda gets back from Hong Kong.

'Who's Miranda?' David asked.

'Didn't Samantha tell you? Miranda's our big sister – very staid and proper. She's been living in Hong Kong for two years, and is coming back with Peter, her husband and their son, Bobby.'

'Bobby's lovely. You'll like him,' said Samantha in a matter of fact way. But her comment gave David a thrill because it indicated the continuation of their relationship.

Breakfast over, Daniel left and Samantha called for a taxi to Kew Gardens. David was surprised when she asked the taxi driver for a receipt, but didn't like to ask her why. Another surprise was to find that Samantha was well informed about the gardens. She told him about the rare plants they had in their garden at home, and said that her father was something of an expert - collecting rare plants while he was abroad and sending them home quickly via the diplomatic bag. 'Home' was in Wiltshire, and she told him that her family had a substantial house there, with large grounds. When David asked what her father did, she changed the subject, and started talking about some of the plants her father had brought back.

As they wandered round the gardens and the great glass houses, David was amazed by Samantha. She seemed such a complex character - beautiful and intelligent, yet at the same time with a sexuality so powerful that he sensed it wasn't quite natural. He tried to put this thought to the back of his mind as they wandered round, hand in hand, taking in the sunshine and the relaxed atmosphere of the gardens.

David was feeling happier and more relaxed than he had for a long time when he suddenly caught sight of Jamal Khan the other side of the garden, deep in conversation with Al Mercer. The coincidence of seeing Al twice in one weekend seemed amazing, but the last people David wanted to see were the people Samantha had been so interested in. He tried to steer her in another direction before she saw them, but he was too late.

'That's the man we saw at the Tandoori restaurant – the one you called Al – isn't it?' she said.

'David agreed, 'Yes, but let's get away quickly. I don't want to get involved with them just now.'

'Ok. But who's the man with him?'

'That's Dr Khan – Jamal. They're friends. I told you.'

'Why don't you want your doctor to see you?' Samantha persisted.

'Well,' he paused, 'I don't want to share you just yet with anyone. Let's get away before they see us.'

She nodded, and said 'OK. But before we go, I must just take a photo of this beautiful plant,' and with that she held up her camera. David felt almost certain she pointed it in Dr Khan's direction but when he asked to see it, she said, laughing, 'No. You must wait till I print out a set for you!'

David felt irritated, but said nothing. The whole incident seemed so odd - seeing Al twice in one weekend. It was almost as if Samantha had orchestrated it. But he dismissed the idea as stupid – even when Samantha persisted with her questions about Al.

'What's an American – and an Asian at that – doing financing a hospice?'

'I really can't say,' David replied. 'But I do agree it's odd.'

'What's his business?' she asked.

'As I said yesterday, I really don't know. Jamal tell me he travels a lot, especially to Pakistan. I think he's even been to Afghanistan – very brave – but I don't know what he does there.'

'He's a Muslim isn't he?'

'Well, yes. I gather from Jamal that he's a fairly strict Muslim – goes to the mosque regularly, doesn't eat pork, doesn't drink – all the usual taboos. But he seemed to me, on the occasion I met him, to be a pleasant chap.'

'Did he talk about the twin towers?'

'No,' said David irritably. 'As I said, I've only met him once.'

'And what about Jamal?'

'What about him?'

'What does he do apart from working at the hospital?'

A little reluctantly, David told her what he'd heard from Pamela about Khan's family life. What he didn't mention was his suspicion that it was the charity that had been indirectly responsible for bringing Samantha into his life because of the Health Authority's interest in the hospice project.

'I wonder what your Mr Mercer thinks about the twin towers.

'Oh, I don't know. Let's change the subject.'

She wasn't prepared to let the subject drop. 'What's Jamal's relationship with Al? Jamal's not gay is he?'

'Far from it,' David laughed. 'He seems to have had a fling with most of the nurses at the hospital.'

'But they're good friends are they?'

'I suppose so. Jamal shared a flat with Al in the States during their last year of study. He obviously admires Al for his charity work and business expertise. But now,' he exclaimed, 'for goodness sake, let's change the subject!'

Samantha looked a little reluctant but gave in with a good grace when he steered her in the other direction.

David was puzzled to see Jamal at Kew. He remembered one occasion when Jamal had expressed astonishment that people should waste their spare time gardening - a view David certainly didn't share. But thinking about it, he realised that Kew was as good a place as any to pass the time with friends in London - after all, that was exactly what he and Samantha were doing.

Any hopes of avoiding Jamal were dashed when, about an hour later, they came face to face with him in the tea-rooms. He was by then on his own and came straight across to their table.

'What a surprise to see you here! Who's your lady friend?' he asked, giving Samantha an appraising stare.

'This is Samantha Lambert,' said David. 'Samantha, my colleague - Dr Jamal Khan.' They shook hands.

'Where's Al gone?' David asked.

Jamal looked startled. 'Al? What do you mean?'

'That was Al I saw you with earlier, wasn't it?

'Earlier? What do you mean?' he repeated. Jamal's expression changed, and he looked worried. He seemed to be thinking rapidly, and collecting his thoughts.

A TORTUOUS PATH

'We saw you by the tropical glasshouse. Surely that was Al Mercer you were talking to?'

'Oh no,' Jamal replied quickly. 'It definitely wasn't Al. He's gone back to the States.'

Now David knew how easy it was to mistake people, but was absolutely certain it was Al Mercer that Jamal had been talking to. He was one of those people it was difficult to mistake.

'Then who was it with you? Al must have a double.'

Jamal thought for a moment, then said cautiously, 'That was my cousin Danni. He had to dash off, as he had a train to catch back to Scotland.'

Samantha said, with a teasing smile, 'With a name like Danny I'd have expected your cousin to be catching a plane to Ireland, not a train to Scotland!'

Jamal seemed nonplussed, but pulled himself up straight, and went into an elaborate, explanation about his cousin's career which David felt was totally unnecessary. Then he rapidly changed the subject and asked, 'And where did you two meet?'

'Oh. We met at my aunt's home when David came to dinner,' said Samantha without any hesitation.

'Lucky David,' said Jamal. This irritated David who could see that he appreciated Samantha's beauty from the smile on his face, and he wasn't too happy with Samantha's response to his appraising looks. But he tried not to let Samantha see that he was jealous. It was far too early in their relationship for him to become possessive. He sensed that Samantha would hate it if he tried.

Fortunately, after a few pleasantries, Jamal said he, too, had to dash off as he was on call that evening at the hospital. When he'd left, Samantha commented that she thought he was a very interesting man, and wanted David to tell her more about him.

'I think I've told you all I know about him,' said David a little curtly. 'Isn't it time we were getting back?'

'Yes. I think we've done all we set out to do. Let's go back to the flat for some supper.'

They took a taxi back to Samantha's flat, and David reluctantly declined her invitation to stay for supper as he had a very early start the next morning. Kissing Samantha goodbye he got back into the taxi and set off for the station.

On the journey home he reflected on what had been an amazing weekend. All his senses were awakened by the sheer abandonment of their love-making. In his wildest dreams, he'd never imagined sex could be so exhilarating and passionate.

Joanna, his ex-wife, had been so different. He'd admired her from a distance for several months before plucking up courage to ask her out, and had been amazed when she agreed to marry him. It was quite early in their marriage when he realised she had serious sexual hang ups. She'd refused to sleep with him before they married but David had put it down to her strict religious upbringing and accepted it reluctantly. Once they were married, he realised she had a real problem. She would never undress in front of him, and always insisted they made love in the dark.

The contrast with Samantha was amazing. But David was also puzzled by the weekend's encounters with Al and Jamal, Samantha's obvious interest in them, her comment about doing all they'd set out to do. He knew he hadn't been party to any discussion about doing anything special at Kew. That was a mystery. And then he recalled her comment about their love making – that 'it was fun.' It was hardly the expression he would have used to describe something that meant so much to him.

-9-
Social Gathering of new committee

A few days after the public meeting Khan buttonholed David and persuaded him to come to a social gathering at the home of Margaret, the wife of David's bank manager. 'The objective,' said Khan, 'is for the new volunteers to meet the original members.'

David was interested in group dynamics - how new groups of people either jelled and became effective or ended up quarrelling and dysfunctional. He agreed to go.

He was the last to arrive. Looking round the assembled gathering in the drawing room, it struck David once again that Khan had got together a group of very disparate people.

The first to greet him was Al Mercer who came over with outstretched hand. 'It's good to see you. David. We need people like you on board.' David warmed to him, while protesting that he'd only come out of curiosity.

Looking round, he hardly recognised Betty who looked very smart in a navy blue suit with a frilly white blouse. David was surprised to discover she was a blonde. He'd always seen her in her catering clothes and never without a white cap which covered her hair completely. He realised that, had he not been expecting to see her, he wouldn't have recognised her.

Mick was, as always, sporting a yellow buttonhole, while Maud had obviously done her best to make herself look younger than she was by wearing a full skirted white dress with huge red polka dots. David felt it had the effect of making her look a little like a circus clown. Sitting next to her was Tracy Pilkington who was heavily made up, with her blond hair tied in a pony-tail.

Most of the others were strangers to him and he was pleased when Jamal opened the meeting with a special welcome to the newcomers. He said he was going to ask them all to introduce themselves and tell everyone their reason for wanting a hospice for the town.

'I'd better start by introducing myself properly,' he said. 'My name is Jamal Khan and I'm a doctor at our local hospital. I trained in the USA but I was born and bred in England. Maud, perhaps you'd start the ball rolling by telling us why you've joined the appeal.'

Maud beamed and David realised her reason for joining the appeal was her personal devotion to Khan. She started telling them about a friend who worked in a hospice shop in Bristol, but Jamal cut her short and moved on to Tracy. It soon became obvious that she knew very little about hospices, and, like Maud, the motivation was Khan's personal charm.

Mick told them about his wife's illness, how, as the illness progressed, he was beginning to feel the strain, and wished there'd been a hospice locally. 'After my wife died, I heard that Dr Khan was starting a hospice project and I thought I would offer to help. Even though I hadn't been able to benefit from hospice care, I knew it would help others.' Everyone nodded sympathetically.

Khan then turned to Margaret, one of the newcomers. David was curious about why she was there. He had preconceived ideas about her as he knew his friend Stuart couldn't stand her which had made their social contacts a little strained. She was about fifty, well preserved, and was always extremely well dressed and carefully made up, with dark red lipstick and blue eye shadow. Her short blonde hair, not her natural colour David was sure, was immaculately styled. She exuded confidence, and David suspected she would be a useful and efficient member of the committee.

'My sister died in a hospice in Devon. She had wonderful care as did my bother-in-law and the children. I think everyone should have access to the sort of care a hospice offers.' Again, everyone nodded approvingly.

Alec Williams was next. David knew he had a thriving computer business in the town. He was in his early forties, had a confident manner, and, like Margaret, was expensively dressed. An extremely good looking man, David noticed the women eyeing him and wondered what sort of marriage he had. He suspected it would be very easy for him to stray!

'My mother-in-law died of cancer last year, and my wife nursed her for the last five months. The strain was great, and the situation would have been much easier if a hospice been available.' Alec didn't tell them then, but David learnt later from Stuart that his wife had had a breakdown after her mother died, and was still in and out of the local psychiatric hospital.

Khan then turned to the attractive blonde. David noticed her the minute he came into the room. She said her name was Alice and she was a nurse in the town's private hospital. 'I've always wanted to work in a hospice so thought I'd better get involved with this project.' She had a sort of translucent look, which made her seem fragile. Her fair hair framed her face and emphasised her expressive brown eyes. David realised that, had he not met Samantha, he might have been attracted to her, especially as she was a blonde.

Khan then turned to Martin Allardice who was one of the few Labour members on the local council. He was very critical of both the government and the Liberals. David had hoped to see the Liberals and Labour members getting together, and ousting the complacent Conservatives who'd dominated the town's council for many years. He always felt that if someone less abrasive than Martin had been the main spokesman, a Lib-Lab pact might have emerged. As it was, the whole council was polarised, and party politics, instead of the town's welfare, was the dominant theme of all council meetings

David was sorry to see Allardice there. He always tried to dominate a meeting and had a habit of interrupting whoever was speaking, and would put down anyone who was shy or timid, with scathing comments. David felt sad he'd been asked to join the hospice committee.

Henry Winchester introduced himself as a gentleman of leisure. He said he was a retired businessman and knew everyone who mattered in the town – a remark that didn't go down well. He said he'd lost his wife two years before which had knocked on the head all their plans to live abroad. He was now at a loose end and thought this hospice project was something he might get his teeth into.

Alison, one of the nurses on Kim's ward, got emotional, telling them about her bad experiences with dying patients in a hospital. She nearly broke down in tears, and Jane Masters, who'd stood up at the public meeting and rebuked the man making racist remarks, leant forward to comfort her. 'You're working in one of the most difficult branches of nursing,' she said. 'It's natural to get upset when you talk about it.' She gave Alison a warm smile.

David had been watching her while the others spoke, and took an instant liking to her. She was in her sixties - with a slender figure and brown hair which was beginning to turn grey. She was attractive in a quiet way, although her clothes were rather old fashioned. David realised it was her face that had drawn his attention. She had a beautiful smile, and she'd looked directly at people when they spoke, managing to convey that she was interested in what they were saying. He thought that if eyes can smile, hers did. David knew she was the sort of person he would be able to talk to in a crisis, confident she would listen to his troubles. She said she and her husband, a clergyman, had been involved in the local hospice at their previous church, and she'd been a volunteer there. She didn't say in what capacity, but David suspected, from what she said later, that she'd been a counsellor.

Khan then turned to David and asked him to tell the meeting about his experience of hospice care. He still found it difficult to talk about his mother without getting emotional, but managed to repeat all he'd said at the previous meeting in the hospital. He wanted to say that he was not planning to get involved with the project, but somehow couldn't bring himself to tell the group and deflate expectations.

'Thank you David,' said Khan. 'I know that was difficult. You're probably wondering why Kim isn't here. As some of you know, she's studying for her Master's Degree and has had to attend a seminar this evening. She's our senior oncology nurse at the hospital and knows an awful lot about palliative care. The only other members who are not here are Pamela Litchfield and Mark Dedham, the editor of our local paper. He's coming later. Pamela, a social worker and is at a conference in Manchester, so can't be here

Now I'd like to introduce my friend Al Mercer. He's from America. We shared a room for two years when we were studying at Berkley University. Al has agreed to act as financial adviser and help the treasurer. He's very generously donated the initial cost of launching the project.'

Mercer stood up and said, 'Hi folks. I think this hospice idea is great so I'd like to help it along. It's so good to find you people prepared to devote time and energy to such a wonderful cause.' He smiled approvingly at the assembled group. People nodded their approbation but Martin, never one to hold back an abrasive question, said 'How come you've got involved? Has Jamal put pressure on you?'

'Not at all. I'm helping finance the start of the appeal because I've made a personal commitment to help people in need throughout the world, and I think this hospice project is very worthwhile.'

'That's wonderful,' said Jane, 'especially in a world where so many young people don't seem to be interested in helping society. I think we should all thank you.'

Al Mercer acknowledged Jane's endorsement with a smile, while Martin, with a big scowl on his face, grunted but said no more.

This was the last of the introductions and David realised that neither Jamal nor Al Mercer had revealed any personal reasons for joining the committee. This he found a little puzzling. He couldn't help remembering the racist comments at the public meeting about foreign Muslims sticking their noses into English affairs, and wondered whether these racist comments had substance. Was Jamal Khan really the idealist he portrayed or was there more to it?

Looking round the group, who all seemed to have good reasons for wanting a hospice, he chided himself for his uncharitable thoughts, and turned his attention back to the meeting.

Jamal said, 'Although the project's been going for quite a time, we haven't yet raised much money. We've now got to develop our fund raising strategy. We need people to take on responsibility for various tasks; going out and speaking to groups, publicity, editing a newsletter, developing a network of supporters, and setting up a marketing team. I'd like everyone to think about what area they'd like to get involved in - and then give me a ring before the next meeting so I can begin to make some plans.'

When asked about Local Health Authority help, he said the Authority was not at this stage prepared to entertain an in-patient hospice with all its financial implications, but he intended to keep battling on and hoped eventually to persuade it to change its mind.

David realised this was his opportunity to put in a plea for hospice home-care instead, but he did so in a half-hearted way because he felt the battle was already lost.

Just as the meeting was nearing its end, Mark Dedham walked in, apologising for being late, saying there'd been a crisis on the paper. Everyone in the room knew him. He was the editor of the local rag and was a controversial figure in the town. He was outspoken, like Martin Allardice, but unlike Martin had a wonderful sense of humour which allowed him to get away with outrageous comments. He had a bit of a reputation as a playboy but David knew that in reality, he was a sober family man, and the playboy image was just a publicity gimmick.

Jamal thanked everyone for coming, fixed a date for the next meeting, and waved them to the food which had been waiting on the side table. Small groups formed round the room and soon there was a buzz of conversation. David moved over to greet Mark and was soon joined by Henry Winchester who told them that Jamal had asked him to head up fund raising. He seemed confident about his abilities to raise the money needed, that as a widower he had time on his hands. David felt that was a curious comment because it seemed he was a member of all the male clubs and organisations in the town.

Then Alec Williams and Al Mercer came over and joined the group and soon Al had them all laughing as he told them about some of his adventures during his travels.

Looking across the room he noticed that the original group from the hospital were huddled together, looking uneasy and a little suspicious. It didn't surprise him. The social divide between the two groups was obvious. He felt a little sorry for them, and so did Jane Masters, for he saw her looking towards them and, after observing them for a few moments, moved over to join them. She very quickly had them laughing and joking. Realising she was going to be a great asset, David determined to get to know her better, and walked over and joined them too.

As they left and thanked Margaret for her hospitality, David felt that the evening, despite a slightly frosty start, had been a success and he felt hopeful the appeal would start moving on successfully. He even felt he might join the committee if he could sort out his personal life which he didn't feel exactly confident about.

-10-
Samantha visits the hospital

His unease about his relationship with Samantha was confirmed when, hoping she felt as he did, he phoned her to arrange a meeting the following weekend. Her response was disappointing. 'No darling. I'm afraid I'm tied up with the gallery all weekend.'

'Can I come along too?' he asked.

'Sorry. It's one of those occasions for just the professionals. I'll be in touch. Have a good weekend!' and she hung up.

The fact that she called him 'darling' was a slight consolation, but he spent a miserable Saturday on his own. On the Sunday morning he decided to go to the local pub where he found Stuart, just back from church. It wasn't long before David was telling Stuart about Samantha.

Anxious about David getting hurt again, Stuart said, 'David, don't rush into this relationship. Samantha's from a very different background, you know. Sir James has told me quite a bit about her. She's always globe-trotting. Her father's a very wealthy man.'

'What does he do?'

'I think he's been an ambassador – somewhere in the middle-east. But I believe he's retired now. I don't really know much about him, but Sir James always mentions him with awe.'

Stuart's comment left David feeling more discouraged than before, but it didn't stop him trying the following week to make another attempt to meet up with Samantha. Despite repeated phone calls, he got no reply. He berated himself for being obsessive about her after such a short acquaintance, but he couldn't get her out of his mind.

When, the following week, he received a call from her saying she was coming down to see the Lamberts at the weekend and would like to see him, he felt reassured. She said she could come down on the Friday, if he liked, and 'visit his hospital so she could picture where he worked'. She said she'd love to meet some of the people involved in the hospice project – especially Dr Khan.

Though David liked the idea of showing her round the hospital, the last thing he wanted was for her to meet Dr Khan again. But he didn't tell her that. He said he'd be delighted to show her round, and would meet her at the station. She said that wouldn't be necessary, as she'd be driving down from London.

On the Friday, he was like a nervous child, his heart beating fast with excitement as he waited for Samantha at the hospital. She arrived just before five, and gave him a passionate kiss which reassured him.

Although David had every intention of avoiding Jamal, they met him in the hospital's restaurant where he'd taken Samantha for a drink. He'd forgotten Jamal was on call that night He was alone, and David knew they had no option but to join him.

There was an immediate frisson between them, and David felt uneasy. She told him she'd heard a lot about him and wanted to know more. 'Your hospice project! How wonderful of you to get involved. Tell me why.'

Jamal responded happily to Samantha's flattery, and explained what he was planning to do.

Samantha nodded. 'But it's going to be very expensive to build. How are you going to finance it?'

David was surprised at her question because he'd already told her about Al Mercer's involvement. However, he said nothing.

'Fund raising. Hard work!' Jamal replied.

'But surely you'll need finance to get it going?'

Jamal took, what David realised later, was the bait and told her about Al's involvement.

'Al. He's a friend of yours?'

'Yes.'

'Where did you meet him?'

Jamal explained that they'd studied together at Berkeley University in America.

'Oh,' said Samantha, looking interested. 'I wonder if you ever came across Suleiman Patel? He must have been at Berkeley the same time as you.'

Jamal looked surprised at the question. 'Suleiman Patel? Yes, I met him once or twice, but I didn't really know him. He was in the year ahead of me.'

'He was interested in politics like you – and a member of the university's debating club. You were its President weren't you?' she asked

Jamal looked surprised. 'Yes, I was. But how did you know?'

'Oh. David told me,' she said airily.

David was amazed. He was quite sure he hadn't told her that much about Jamal. But then, he thought, perhaps he was so smitten with Samantha, his memory had become addled.

'But how come you know Suleiman?' asked Jamal.

'Oh, we met at an international conference in Chicago. He seemed an interesting man – very passionate about the Third World and Islam.'

'I wouldn't know about that,' said Jamal sharply. 'Our paths hardly ever crossed.'

Curious, thought David. If Jamal was President of the Debating Club and Suleiman a member, surely he'd have known a bit about Suleiman's interests. However, he couldn't pursue this because Samantha then turned to Jamal's life at the hospital.

'I suppose, being on call at times, you have to live near the hospital?'

Jamal said he had a flat less than a mile from the hospital, just off the local park.

'So, what time do you get home when you're on call?'

'Oh! Soon after eight. I'm on call this evening – that's why I'm eating now – otherwise I'd be home by now.'

Feeling anxious that Jamal might be tempted to ask them back to his home, David felt it was time to move on. He said, 'Let's go, otherwise I'll never be able to show you all the hospital.'

Samantha seemed reluctant to move, but turned to Jamal. 'It's been good meeting you. I hope we see you again.'

With that, Jamal stood up and acknowledged her comment with a formal little bow.

They set off on the tour, but it wasn't long before Samantha said, 'Well, it's a marvellous hospital, but I think I've seen enough to know what you do. Let's go back to my hotel.'

'But I thought you were staying with the Lamberts,' David said, astonished.

'Yes, tomorrow. But I wanted to spend the evening with you so I've booked into the local hotel.'

He drove her to the hotel just outside town. After signing the Visitor's Book, they went straight up to her room to refresh themselves before dinner. That that was not her intention was soon obvious to David.

David found her as passionate as before, and convinced himself that Samantha was as much in love with him as he was with her. It was some months before he realised how naïve he'd been.

They had a leisurely dinner before returning to the hotel room for a further session of love making.

Next morning he was amazed to find her up and dressed before seven.

'What's the hurry?' he asked.

'Oh, I've got to dash off. I've just had a call from my boss.'

'I thought you were the boss,' he said, questioning, but she didn't respond, only saying, 'Sorry darling. It was a great evening. I'll be in touch', and with that gave him a swift kiss, and left the room.

Totally bemused, and at the same time feeling a little foolish, he showered and dressed, and went down to Reception where he discovered Samantha had already paid the bill.

When he got home he felt so puzzled by the whole encounter that he decided to phone the Lamberts on the pretence of making an arrangement to meet up. He left it till the late afternoon to phone, and Lady lambert answered and said, 'Oh, no! Samantha's not here. She's had to dash off somewhere on business.'

David expressed surprise, and she said, 'I'm afraid our Samantha has a reputation for dashing off at a moment's notice.'

'Why? Surely the art world's not that hectic!' he exclaimed.

'No. I agree. But I think Samantha has other interests as well. But don't ask me what. I never ask questions!' Then she asked him how he was keeping, how the hospice appeal was developing, and said she hoped to see him again before too long. With that, she hung up.

Frustrated once again by Samantha's erratic behaviour, David spent the rest of the weekend in a state of misery.

-11-
The Appeal committee gets to work

The exciting but disturbing contact with Samantha left David with a feeling of insecurity, but the contact with the hospice charity was proving fascinating and helped him avoid depression.

He listed reasons for joining the hospice group.

There was, first of all, his half commitment to Sir James Lambert and his friends to infiltrate the charity and try and channel its energies in another direction. He'd agreed, but was more than a little puzzled about the motivation for such a request.

He knew he would enjoy the opportunity of studying a newly formed group with such a diverse range of people.

He began to find Jamal more intriguing. He liked him but realised he was rather arrogant. It didn't surprise him that he was unpopular with his male colleagues, though he was very popular with the female members of staff. He never talked about his Muslim background and David had no idea whether or not he was a believer. And now there was this friend, Al Mercer, who'd turned up out of the blue.

As so many of his staff were involved, David's paternal instincts came to the fore and he felt he should keep an eye on them.

So,when Jamal, for a second time, asked him to join the committee, he agreed – little knowing what he was committing himself to.

A TORTUOUS PATH

Jamal arranged for the new committee to meet at the office of Alec Williams. The array of computers and photocopiers in the hall that met him made David realise that the rumours that Alec was running a very successful business were true.

They were shown into an elegant room with a large mahogany table in the centre. Jamal welcomed everyone and said that he was pleased that he had managed to persuade David Gardner to join the committee. They all knew him and his reputation for getting things done, and knew he would be a great asset. Then he turned to the woman who was sitting beside Kim, and said how delighted he was that Kim's friend, Mary Gilburn had also agreed to join the committee. David remembered she'd been sitting next to Kim at the public meeting.

Jamal said, 'Several members of the committee are unable to come today, but everyone has been in touch with me since the public meeting and roles are beginning to be defined. Henry has offered to take on fund raising, Alec marketing and Alice to make contact with local organisations.' This, thought David, was a good choice. She was eye-catching enough to attract a lot of support from all the men's organisations in the town, and he'd already discovered what a pleasing voice she had. He had to admit that had he not been bowled over by Samantha, he might well have made an effort to get to know her better.

'Jane has offered her services in preparing a newsletter.'

Margaret said, 'That's a wonderful offer. Jane knows all about newsletters. She's the editor of her own parish magazine.'

David thought that editing one newsletter is bad enough, but taking on two was more than anyone should do. It struck him that clergy wives had a difficult role - still expected to be unpaid curates despite the fact that two thirds of the female population were now in full time employment. However, Jane gave a quiet smile when Jamal mentioned her offer, and it was obvious she was the sort of person who would get on and do something without making any fuss.

Mark Dedham, as was to be expected, said he would take on the media coverage, and Martin said he would be happy to assist. Mark didn't seem to welcome this offer with any enthusiasm, but Jamal, detecting this, passed on rapidly. Margaret Thompson went on at length about the very busy social lives she and her husband led, but said she would be happy to take on any entertaining needed.

Tracy Pilkington was already settled into the role of treasurer, which left four members of the committee without a role - Mick and Betty Andrews from the hospital, Mary Gilburn, and David. Betty said she would help with fund raising, and talked about some of the things she'd already been organising – coffee mornings, jumble sales and raffles.

Then Alec made a remark which started a fracas in the group. He said, 'We don't want to be footling around with jumble sales and brick-a-brack stalls. What we need to do is concentrate on getting 'real' money from the well-to-do in the town rather than waste time and manpower on trivial events.'

Knowing Betty, David knew she would feel angry and intimidated by Alec's comment and would realise immediately that she would have no part to play in his sort of world. She was the salt of the earth, and if treated with courtesy, would do anything for anyone, but she was very aware of class divisions and was always the first to point out the 'them and us' syndrome, and made no bones about the fact that she thought the 'them' factor totally lacking in courtesy and consideration.

Had Alec not prefaced his remarks with the words 'footling around', David thought it was just possible Betty would have kept her thoughts to herself. But those words were, to Betty, a direct insult. She'd been doing small scale fund raising since the very first meeting, and she turned on Alec with blazing eyes, 'Are you suggesting that footling around is all that we've been doing all this time?'

Alec looked a little surprised at being challenged. He conceded that it had been all right to start that way, but added with a superior air, 'I want the hospice built in the twenty-first century, not the twenty-second!'

This was adding insult to injury. Betty looked thunderously at Alec and said, 'And don't you think we all want the same? We haven't been working hard all these months for a hospice that will only be of use to our grandchildren. Just because ...' and her voice began to rise, 'I work in the kitchen and not in one of your plush offices, doesn't mean I haven't thought about what we're doing.'

Alec, with what David thought was a contemptuous lift of his eyebrows - a gesture which Betty couldn't help noticing - said, 'Let's not argue about it. I'm sure everyone wants to get on with the job instead of wasting time on trivia,' and he looked round the room with a glance that seemed to indicate that everyone but Betty was of the same mind.

David expected Henry to say something, but he sat there with an anxious look on his face, obviously torn between backing Betty, and offending Alec. The latter won, and he said nothing. Betty would have exploded then and there if Jane, who was sitting beside her, hadn't put a restraining hand on her shoulder. David was about to say something when a quiet intervention came from Mary Gilburn. 'Surely there's room for all approaches in a big enterprise like this?'

'Depends what you mean by 'all approaches'. The public's not going to think much of an organisation that wastes it's time on jumble sales and sunflower seeds. It's all a question of PR and manpower. The effort involved in raising £30 at a jumble sale is enormous, and a tremendous waste of people's time.'

'Our jumble sales bring in well over £100,' said Betty, angrily defensive.

'But my dear lady,' said Alec in an unctuous voice, 'we've got to think in terms of thousands, not hundreds.'

David knew Alec was in essence correct, but it was not tactful to say this at the very first meeting. He expected Jamal to try and placate Betty. Instead, making his second mistake, he turned to Henry and in one sentence, negating his tactful opening, said, 'Well, Henry, this is something that needs to be thrashed out by the Fund Raising Committee. As you are the Fund Raising Chairman, perhaps you would organise a meeting in the near future.' Henry agreed.

Betty sucked in her breath as the penny dropped that, in addition to having her efforts belittled, she had also been replaced. David knew Jamal had lost Betty's support even before she got to her feet.

'Well, it's quite clear there's no room on this committee for the likes of me, if that's what you think of all the 'footling around' we've all been doing the last six months. You don't need me now you've got a new Chairman. And I'm not going to go poncing around your county toffs. They've got more money than they've any right to, and I'm not at all sure that they'll part with it as quickly as you think, however much you sweet talk them. I'm off,' and with that she stalked out of the room.

There was a stunned silence for a minute, then everyone started talking. Most of the men were critical of Betty, expressing the view that she was a stupid woman. David could see this didn't please Mick who'd known Betty and her warm heartedness for too long to be happy at such comments. It didn't surprise him when Jane expressed concern for Betty, and said she thought she'd felt hurt and isolated by Alec's comments.

Then Mary Gilburn spoke up. It was the first time David had really taken notice of her. 'Alec's ideas are good,' she said, 'but they're limited. It's a shame we've lost Betty. I think you should try and get her back. If the fund raising is to be really successful, it has to touch all sections of the community, and Betty's efforts would bring in a substantial amount over the years, especially if we all backed her. You can never really count on the richer element, especially in these days of recession. We must go after the pennies as well as the pounds. And it's not a good idea to alienate anyone at this stage. We need all the help we can get.'

Mary spoke confidently and with a certain authority which David had certainly not expected when he first met her. They were all impressed, although Alec expressed the view that they'd be better letting Betty go rather than risk having a trouble-maker on the Committee. 'If someone offers their resignation I always accept it. I don't believe in trying to woo people back. It's only blackmail - and is a sure road to further problems.'

But Alex's views were over-ruled, and Henry said he would talk to Betty and see what he could do. He mentioned his long experience of working with unions and militant people like Betty, and his 'reputation' as a peacemaker. 'I'm sure I'll be able to get her back with a bit of sweet talk,' he said, in what David thought was a rather self-satisfied voice, but everyone else reacted warmly to his offer.

Henry asked if anyone knew where she lived or where she worked and David made his first contribution, by offering to arrange a meeting with Betty and Henry in his office. He felt sorry for Betty, and was not happy at the way Alec had handled her. Moreover, he still had to work with her and didn't want to alienate her. His relationship with the kitchen staff at the hospital had always been good, and he didn't want to spoil it. Impressed by Mary's contribution to the little fracas they'd just had, he turned to her and said, 'Perhaps you would like to come along as well?'

'I'd be happy to,' she replied, 'provided you fix it up at a time when I'm free. Perhaps it could be during the lunch period?'

He agreed to see what could be arranged, and they exchanged telephone numbers so he could make the necessary arrangements.

The incident had cast a shadow over the meeting, and after a few minor matters had been discussed, Jamal brought the meeting to a halt and fixed another a month ahead.

As David was walking out of the door, Alec grabbed him and suggested he joined him for a drink at the pub opposite. David agreed, saying he'd join him in a few minutes as Jamal had signalled that he wanted to talk to him. When they were alone, Jamal asked whether he should have a word with Betty as well, but David replied that it was better for the moment to leave it to Henry because he would be the person Betty would be working with.

When he got to the pub he was surprised to find Mary and Alice sitting with Mark and Alec. Then he remembered that Mark said he knew Mary. Inevitably, once they were all settled with a drink, the discussion focused on Betty's behaviour.

'I must say, Alec, you were a bit rough with her,' said Mark. 'But you always were an insensitive swine.'

'Thanks, friend. I appreciate the character reference!' These two were old sparring partners, but David could see that Alec didn't like Mark's censure in the hearing of the two women. 'It's no good taking on people like Betty if we really want to move forward. An organisation can't afford sentiment. People like Betty are a drag and would divert us from the real task. I say good riddance,' said Alec defensively.

'I'm afraid I don't agree with you,' said Mary. 'It's not sentiment or even compassion that makes me say that. We're in a task of networking. People like Betty will bring in others, and somewhere along the chain of contacts there'll be people with money. And I don't think you should sneer at these small scale events. Added together, they will bring in quite substantial sums - and, again, it's a way of widening contacts.'

Mark nodded agreement giving Mary a warm smile. Then they started talking about the members of the group, and Alec expressed his amazement that the whole project was being led by a Muslim doctor who came from overseas. 'I wonder what motivates him? He's obviously gathered together a lot of information about the hospice movement, and is very enthusiastic. But it's all a bit odd. He comes from America, doesn't he?' he asked, turning to David.

'No,' David replied. 'He's actually British though he was educated in the USA from the age of sixteen.'

'Why has he come back to England, do you think?'

'Probably because his family are still over here.'

'Well, that makes sense. But I still think it's a bit odd. Though,' Alec added hastily, 'I do like him. I think he's a good egg.'

With that, Mark started talking about the PR aspect of fund raising, and said he would be promoting the charity in his local rag in the weeks to come. He said that it would be important to focus the charity on one or two people who would become known as the charity's representatives, and turned to Alice, and said he hoped she would allow herself to be used as one of these people as she was so photogenic. This prompted Alec to make enquiries about the economics of the local paper, and the conversation soon drifted into local politics, of which all the group seemed to have a pretty good grasp. They parted just before closing time, and said they were all looking forward to their next meeting.

-12-
David asks Mick about Mary

When David returned to the hospital the next day the first person he saw was Mick who'd obviously come to his office talk about the previous evening's meeting. He was clearly upset about the way Betty had been treated and wanted David to see her as soon as possible. 'There was no need for that hostility,' he said. 'Betty's got a heart of gold and she would bring in a lot of supporters. She's very popular with a lot of people despite her forthright manner.'

David agreed and promised to see her as soon as possible. 'I'll have to find a time when Henry and Mary Gilburn are free.'

'Well, don't leave it too long,' advised Mick.

'What did you think of this newcomer - Mary Gilburn?' David asked. 'She was quite forceful.'

'Oh, I've met her before. She's one of Kim's friends.'

'How did you meet her?'

'Here in the hospital. Mary brought her over one day to show her round the hospital and give her lunch. I met them in the corridor and Kim introduced us. She said that Mary was her oldest and closest friend and they'd known each other since childhood. Kim was waylaid by one of the doctors for quite a long time, so Mary and I sat down and chatted. I told her what a very special person Kim was and that everyone loved her. Mary said she wasn't surprised to hear that – even as a child Kim had been very popular – she was so kind and sensitive.

When I asked Mary how she'd come to know Kim she told me that when she was six, Kim and her parents moved into a house at the end of the road she lived in. As the little girl looked as though she was the same age as Mary, her mother called and invited them for tea – and that's how their friendship began. Mary said they were inseparable and spent most of their time at her house because Kim's mother wasn't very fond of children. They often went up to London to stay with Kim's Aunt Judith, her godmother, in the holidays. It was the highlight of their holiday.'

At that moment there was a knock at the door and Mick left.

-13-
David's Father

David had found the appeal meetings more interesting than he'd expected. He'd anticipated that Khan would have difficulties in melding the old and the new groups, but he hadn't expected such a strong reaction from Betty. Kim's friend Mary had impressed him with her forceful comments, and he felt she was going to be a good addition to the team and that with her help he might be able to persuade Betty to come back.

On the whole, he felt more optimistic about the people Jamal had got together but was still very doubtful about Tracy. He knew Jamal's friend, Al Mercer, had promised to help her, but he was already out of the country and David wondered how often he would be in England to assist.

All thoughts of organising a meeting between Betty, Henry Winchester and Mary Gilburn went right out of his mind when, a few days later, he got a call from his sister in Scotland saying their father was seriously ill in hospital. She said he should get up to see him as quickly as possible

His father lived with his sister and her family near Perth in Scotland. They had a large house with an annex and when their mother died, their father, a retired university professor, moved into the annexe. Over the years, David had been so busy, and Scotland so far away, that he hadn't seen as much of his parents as he would have liked. It had been an enormous shock when his mother died in the local hospice of breast cancer, and he had resolved to get up to Scotland more often to see his father.

He'd seen his father only a few weeks before. David's brother-in-law, James, had brought his father down for a long weekend, and David took him round the hospital. In the corridor they'd bumped into Dr Khan and just as he was introducing them, David received an urgent message to go to the orthopaedic ward. Khan had said, 'Don't worry. I'll look after your father till you come back.'

David was gone for longer than he'd expected and when he came back, anxious about the time lapse, he found the pair comfortably ensconced in Jamal's room drinking coffee and engaged in animated conversation. His father looked up and said, 'Well, thanks to Jamal I've had a really interesting time. He's told me all about the hospital and a lot about America that I didn't know.' Turning to Khan he said, 'I hope next time I come down we'll be able to meet again. Perhaps we can persuade my son to take us out to lunch together.' With that, he shook hands with Khan and he and David went on their way.

'What an interesting man,' said David's father, 'and so compassionate. You're lucky to have him on your staff.

David didn't feel it appropriate to tell him how the other doctors viewed Jamal

'Jamal tells me you are greatly respected by all the staff and that you're an excellent administrator. I'm very proud of you, son.'

He then asked David whether the Muslim doctors on the staff were really integrated into the medical fraternity or whether it was just a facade. It was a question David couldn't really answer, but promised his father he would try and observe what was going on. Until he worked at the hospital David had always lived in areas where there were so few black and Asian people that the issue of racial inequality and prejudice had never arisen

David and his father were rather alike –quiet and reserved. Before his mother died, David had never had any in-depth conversations with his father, but making visits to Scotland every two months enabled him to get to know his father better. He would stay with him in the annexe where they talked endlessly about the government, world politics and the environment which he was passionately interested in - a natural follow-on from his work at the university.

His father told him he'd been writing his life story as a way of coming to terms with his wife's death while David found he was able to talk about his difficult relationship with Joanna and her sexual hang-ups. He knew his parents had had a happy marriage, but it had never occurred to him before that his parents had continued to make love right up the end of her life. His father said with a chuckle, 'most children think their parents are too old for sex. Little do they know! Good sexual relations are very important in a marriage – just as important as is the ability to talk and share ideas and activities.'

David realised this had not been the pattern in his marriage to Joanna.

Another topic of conversation was hospital management. When a few years earlier, David's father had spent a short time in hospital with a prostate problem, he'd expressed his concern about the dirty state of the wards and bathrooms. He said he couldn't fault the care given by the doctors and nurses, but felt their time was not being organised properly. 'Get the Matrons back' was his cry.

The news of his father's illness was a great shock and he immediately made arrangements for cover at the hospital and set off for Scotland the next morning.

Mick, the hospital porter, drove him to the main line station. They left in good time which was fortunate because they were held up by a major traffic jam. They were stopped just outside a mosque that had been built a couple of years before. As David sat there feeling impatient, he peered vacantly out of the window and noticed four Asian men walking towards him – two older men and two youths of about seventeen. The four were talking animatedly, and the older men had their arms familiarly round the shoulders of the two youths. It seemed somehow inappropriate.

Mick said, surprise in his voice, 'Isn't that Dr Khan's friend Mr Mercer?'

David looked closer and agreed. Then he remembered that Jamal had told him that Mercer had gone back to the States.

The traffic started moving, and David thought no more about it. It was not till many weeks later that he remembered the incident

It was a comfortable journey, but though he took plenty of reading matter David spent much of the time thinking of his mother's last weeks, and praying that he wouldn't be losing his father as quickly.

When he got to Perth, James, his brother-in-law, was waiting for him. 'How is he?' David asked anxiously.

'Well, he's in hospital. The doctor, a friend of dad's, called this afternoon and thought he would be better in hospital where they can make a proper diagnosis.'

'Diagnosis? I thought they know already it's a prostate problem.'

'No, the prostate's OK. It's his breathing that's worrying them. They don't know what's causing him to be so breathless.'

This was something new. Alison hadn't said anything about it when she phoned, and his father had seemed fine when he last visited.

James told him they were investigating a number of possibilities – heart problem, lung cancer and asbestosis.

David was puzzled. 'Why asbestosis?' he asked. 'Surely Dad's never been in contact with asbestos?'

'That's what Alison and I thought. But, apparently, he worked for a short time in an asbestos factory while he was waiting for call-up.'

'But that's nearly fifty years ago!'

'I know. We couldn't understand why they're considering the possibility, but the doctors say asbestos can lie dormant in the body for many years.'

David was appalled at the thought. He was familiar with asbestos and mesothelioma, its deadly form, but it had never occurred to him that his father might be a victim.

'It's open visiting on your father's ward,' said James, 'so I can take you to see him first thing in the morning.'

That night, thinking about his father, David didn't sleep till the early hours, but, as so often happens, when morning came he was in a deep sleep, broken only when Alison came in with a cup of tea.

After breakfast, James drove them to the hospital. 'He's in a side ward – a special privilege as he's well known in the town. He's trying to be cheerful, but I know he's very worried about his illness.'

He stopped the car at the hospital entrance and told David to phone him when he was ready to leave. 'Say 'hi' to him for me', said James, and then drove off.

David found the ward easily and introduced himself at the nurses' desk. 'How is he today?' he asked, and one of the nurses told him they were waiting for the doctor's round later that morning. She pointed him to a small side ward where he found his father, propped up in bed with an oxygen mask attached to an oxygen cylinder. It was a shock to see him like that, after leaving him looking so well only a few weeks before, but he managed to control his tears as he bent over to kiss him.

'Good to see you, son. I'm so glad you've come up. I hope it hasn't interfered with your work too much,' and he held out his arms for a hug. David was shocked to find how much weight he'd lost in the last few weeks.

'I'm afraid I'm in a very sorry state. I can't breathe properly without the oxygen. They're beginning to think I have asbestosis. I've had a biopsy and they hope to give me the result this afternoon.'

'But dad, you didn't work with the asbestos itself. James said you were just in the office.'

'I know. But there was a cloud of asbestos dust everywhere. It even came into our little office. I often went home smothered in dust, and I used to take my clothes off as quickly as possible, have a bath and put on clean clothes. Then I felt human again. But now, let's change the subject. Tell me what you've been up to. How's the hospice project going? And how's your romance with Samantha? Still going strong?'

David told him he'd visited Samantha in London but didn't tell his father how uncertain he was about the relationship. His father, sensing his son's doubts, he said, 'Well, David, just take care. I'd hate to see you hurt again.'

David told him about the hospice appeal and the traumatic meeting they'd had the previous week.

'Well, I thought Jamal was a very interesting man. I liked him and felt he was very genuine. I'd looked forward to meeting him again, but it doesn't look like we're going to get that pub lunch we talked about.' David felt like crying, but knew he must keep up a brave face, so told him about Jamal's romance with Kim, and the different reactions from the hospital staff. 'I think it's going to be a long time before mixed marriages are really accepted by society,' said his father.

'Don't you think that attitude is a bit old hat, Dad? I think mixed marriages are much more widely accepted nowadays.'

'Well, may be in the world you live in with so many doctors and nurses from abroad. But in smaller towns and in the countryside, seeing coloured people is a rare occurrence. I think you'll find there is still prejudice and anxiety about mixed marriages. And then there's the problem of the cultural differences which often come to the fore once the knot is tied. I've seen it happen in my work over the years.'

'Perhaps you're right,' said David, not wishing to argue with his father. 'But, despite what I've just said, I do hope that if Jamal and Kim do get together they don't get too much stick.'

'I hope so too. I think Jamal will make her a good husband. Kim's a lucky girl'

'So is Jamal,' thought David wryly. He was surprised by his father's admiration of Jamal – especially as he'd always been a good judge of character.

David had been with his father for about an hour when he began to look tired and had a nasty coughing fit. David said he would leave him for a while so that he could have a little sleep, and promised to be back in an hour. He wandered round the hospital grounds for a while, but they were not particularly interesting and it was quite cold, so he went back in and took himself off to the hospital canteen where he had a coffee and a piece of cake. Then he went back to the ward and found his father in a deep sleep. One of the nurses said he was likely to continue to sleep for at least another hour, so David phoned James to come and collect him.

Alison had lunch ready as she wanted to visit the hospital in the afternoon. When they got back to the hospital, the doctor was there. He beckoned them in and said he had just got the test results back on the biopsy they'd taken earlier that week. 'It's not good news, I'm afraid. Your father has mesothelioma. He knows what that means. What we have to decide is where's the best place for him to be.'

Alison burst into tears. David heard a voice in his head screaming 'No! No! No!' and came to in time to hear his father asking how long he'd got.

The doctor said it was difficult to predict but, once the mesothelioma showed itself with breathlessness, it was usually a matter of months. They were shocked, but their father said, 'Now don't cry. I've always known that this might happen. Since retiring, I've read a lot about asbestosis and mesothelioma. I always hoped that if it happened to me, I would get the milder version,' and he gripped their outstretched hands and held them tightly.

The doctor said he'd be sending along one of the staff, Rosemary, who specialises in terminal cases. She would talk their father through his options.

The doctor's use of the term 'terminal cases' seemed to be really rubbing it in, and David had to hold back his tears

'He must come home. We want you home, Daddy. I'm sure that's what you want, isn't it?' said Alison.

'Why don't you wait until your father's seen Rosemary and then you can make a decision,' said the doctor. 'I'm so sorry to be the bearer of such bad news. I've heard a lot about you, and I know about all the good things you've done for this town. It's a privilege to look after you,' and with that he shook their hands, and left.

They sat for what seemed a long time in silence, then their father said, 'I'd like to come home, but Alison, I'm afraid that will be difficult now you're a headmistress. I had a golfing friend who had mesothelioma and I know how much care it entailed. Your mother and I often visited, and his wife was exhausted.'

'But she was older; I'm still young and energetic!'

'Well, I'll only come home if you promise to get me transferred to the hospice when it gets too difficult.'

'No, no, you must come home,' said Alison.

'Ok, if that's what you want,' said their father, then he continued, 'Let's talk about something else. How did your concert go? I hope that a lot of your parents turned up,' and with that, he managed to get them both telling him about their activities.

The supper trolley arrived, and he told them to go home and get their own supper. 'Now don't fret yourself too much. We've all got to die sometime, and I've had a good life. And who knows, I might meet up again with your mother.' He grinned, knowing that David wasn't a Christian and didn't believe in an after-life. 'Give me a hug and then go home.'

The next few weeks were traumatic. Their father came home and Alison set about organising cover, and time off from the school for herself. She was a greatly respected head, and the local authorities were helpful – allowing her to work only mornings so she could be at home for the rest of the day to look after her father.

David scooted back to London to sort out some outstanding problems and made plans to take some of his annual leave and go up to Scotland every other Thursday for a long weekend. Being part of the medical world he had no illusions, and realised it would only be a matter of time before his father died.

When the hospital sent his father home, saying they could do nothing more for him, Alison and James moved him into the main house and installed a television set which he could watch from the bed, while James erected bird feeders just outside the bedroom window so he could watch his beloved birds.

Friends popped in for short visits and kept him up to date with news. They said afterwards what a lovely man he was, always keen to know about their families and their activities. Some of the most caring visitors were young people who'd known him in their student days. The family hadn't realised how popular he was. They were impressed with the help afforded by the NHS. Health visitors who came in every day – and as their father's health deteriorated, they came more frequently. Carers came in to help him wash and shave, and other carers came and sat with him, while Alison popped out to do grocery shopping.

The four grandchildren reacted differently. Jenny, aged fifteen, became very quiet and withdrew into herself. Steven was twelve. He and his grandfather were very close and shared an interest in bird watching, spending many Saturdays holed up in a hide with binoculars. Steven started by asking his parents dozens of questions about his grand-father's illness, and then, dissatisfied with their answers, started questioning his grandfather himself. It was a good move. His grandfather answered all his questions while at the same time managing to reassure Stephen, insisting he'd had a good life and it was time for him to 'move on'.

Susie, aged eight, would only go and see her grandfather if someone was with her – and then she would hold tightly onto their hands and look at him as he lay in bed with a very frightened expression on her face. She didn't say anything or ask any questions, but was clearly sensitive to the situation – and frightened by it.

The youngest, Jack, aged four, seemed oblivious about what was going on and would bounce in and out of his grandfather's bedroom as he'd always done. He would hurl himself onto his grandfather – until they had to dissuade him from doing so by telling him 'grandpa has to be treated very gently because he's not very well.'

David went up to Scotland every other weekend – hoping that the between weekends would be spent with Samantha. But that proved a forlorn hope. Each time he tried to organise a date, she said she had to be away on 'business.' It seemed to David curious that the work of an art gallery should take her away so often, but she assured him that was the way of things. She did come down one weekend to stay with the Lamberts, and booked a room in the same hotel they had visited before where they spent an afternoon in what David could only describe as an orgy of love-making.

Then they went on to see a James Bond film which, looking back, David thought was curiously appropriate. He tried to kid himself that she was as keen as he was - though knowing in his heart that she was somehow using him.

David knew instinctively that he wouldn't be able to discuss his father's illness with her, but found it deeply comforting to be able to talk about it with Stuart who'd known his father for many years. He knew Stuart admired him, and David was able to pour out his feelings of distress at the fact he was soon to lose him.

Stuart and his wife were very supportive. They would invite him over for Sunday lunch after they'd been to church. If it was fine, they would go for long walks before returning for a light supper. David realised how lucky he was to have such close friends. He'd always been able to talk freely to Stuart and had told him all about his troubled relationship with Joanna. Now David confided in him about this new relationship with Samantha. Stuart cautioned him – saying that from the little he knew about her, David shouldn't get himself in too deep.

One person who, unexpectedly, was very supportive was Jamal. When he heard the news of David's father's illness, he came straight to his office to express how sad he was to hear the news. Thereafter, he popped in frequently to discuss what seemed trivial matters, but, David soon realised was his way of giving him support. This he much appreciated.

On one occasion David mentioned to him that, on the day he'd had to rush up to Scotland, he'd taken a taxi to the station and had seen Al and a friend, with two young men, going into the mosque. Jamal looked puzzled. 'You must be mistaken,' he said. 'Al's been in the USA for the last three months.'

'He looked so like Al I was sure it was him.'

Jamal shook his head. 'No, it couldn't have been. He doesn't get back to England for some time.'

David didn't argue, but was not totally convinced and felt puzzled.

David found it a help being busy. There were several meetings of the hospice appeal committee which David attended – largely to take his mind off his father's illness. Of all the people on the committee the most caring was Jane, the vicar's wife, who invited him to her home for a meal on several occasions and encouraged him to talk about his father. Her husband, Colin, was equally welcoming. They both knew David was not a Christian, but never alluded to the fact, and he felt totally comfortable with them.

Alison coped well for the first four months – and then their father's health began to deteriorate rapidly, and the nurses from the Health Service started coming in twice a day to make him as comfortable and as free from pain as possible. Alison got more and more exhausted, and they all felt, their father included, that the time had come for him to go into the hospice. He was quite happy to go because he realised how hard it was for Alison.

It was at this stage that David felt he should spend more time with his father and Alison. With the journey to Scotland taking nearly a whole day each time he visited, he decided to take leave. He worked hard, tying up as many ends as possible, and then handed over to his deputy.

It had been a hard decision because he'd been hoping to invite Samantha to go on holiday with him, but knew he would regret it if he sacrificed the little time he had left with his father to be with her. He'd hoped to explain all this to her the weekend before he went up to Scotland – but it was not to be. It was one of the many weekends which she said was already booked. He knew, but wouldn't admit it, that the relationship was going nowhere despite the ecstasy of their love making. But his anxiety about his father was such that he managed to put the thought to the back of his mind.

He didn't regret his decision. His father spent ten peaceful days in the hospice before he died, with his pain under control.

David and his sister took it in turns to be with him, and when his father was sleeping, David spent time observing all that went on in the hospice. There were activities available for those well enough to enjoy them – art, creative writing, craft, and board games. Some patients were encouraged to write their memoirs for their children. Counsellors were on hand to help with relationships – more complicated than in the past because of family break-ups and second marriages. David was told that not everyone in these situations was tolerant, and the hospice staff had to work out carefully the timing of the visits of different family members.

Hairdressing was on hand for the women. Food was always of the highest standard and as tempting as possible, while meals could be accompanied by alcohol if patients were strong enough to enjoy it.

There was a lot of music with people coming in to play quiet music in the background. Either the hospice chaplain or his assistant were always on hand, and there were daily services in the little chapel. David felt it was strange to say it, but felt that in many ways the hospice was a happy place with a lot of laughter. He even heard some people said it was like staying in a luxury hotel.

David and Alison knew, when he was admitted, that their father only had a few weeks of life left, but realised that the hospice staff were helping them to come to terms with their father's impending death.

The ten days were very peaceful, and Alison and David stayed at the hospice for the last few nights, and they and James were with him when he died. He said 'goodbye' to each of them and then drifted into a coma and died a few hours later. David was grateful his death was so peaceful because he knew the dying process could be very distressing to watch.

They managed to arrange the funeral fairly quickly, deciding on a private burial service followed by a Memorial Service. The latter was attended by a large number of people from the town as well as by many friends and relatives. The many tributes to him were heart-warming and David and Alison agreed that the Memorial Service had been a great comfort. David had often been told before about the importance of the funeral service for the grieving process, and he found this to be true, as they experienced the love and support of so many friends and acquaintances.

They all agreed the children should attend the service, and talked later about their very different reactions. There were curious questions from little Jack who kept asking where his grandfather was. Susie, at eight, became more clinging than before and wouldn't go anywhere near his bedroom in the annexe. Stephen adjusted best of all. He said that his grandfather had spoken to him about his impending death, and had told him not to be worried because it was as natural a thing as birds mating, flying and dying. It was Jenny, at fifteen, on whom it seemed to have the most dramatic effect. After the funeral she went completely silent for a few days, then started railing about a God who could allow such a thing to happen. She asked what was the purpose of life if they were all to die, and she began behaving badly. Alison was worried, but the hospice chaplain persuaded Jenny to go to the local Young People's Fellowship. It was actually an offshoot of the local Baptist church, but Jenny didn't realise this, and agreed to go along. It was, said Alison, a life saver for her.

David stayed on for a week to support Alison and help sort out his father's many possessions. They were all neatly organised, and he'd labelled what he wanted to go where. Many of his papers went to his university. They cleared out some of the furniture from the annexe and the rest they left until such time as Alison and James could decide what to do with it.

David went back south to the hospital, wondering whether he would be able to slot back into his old life in quite the same way.

-14-
David returns to the hospital: Kim's 30th Birthday Party

When he returned to the hospital David was encouraged by the warm welcome he received from everyone. He had the impression that people were relieved to have him back. Jamal was one of the first to welcome him and showed an empathy with and understanding of bereavement which made David realise why he'd embarked on the hospice project. He told David they would love to have him back on the appeal committee, but he was to wait until he felt ready.

He'd already given the matter some thought knowing that hospices didn't let volunteers return to work after bereavement. But this was different – an appeal - all about raising money in the initial stages. He felt it would help take his mind off his father's death and be a good way of filling up his spare time, so he told Jamal he'd be happy to remain on the committee.

Mick was another early visitor. As he'd nursed his wife until she died, he was very sympathetic without being sentimental. He brought David up to date with hospital gossip and said that Kim and Jamal were now accepted as an item. He expressed his unease about the relationship, though added, 'I've nothing against Dr Khan. He's a good man. It's just his different background.' David nodded, though didn't have the strength to embark on the same conversation he'd had with his father a few weeks before. However he made a mental note to take Kim out to lunch and find out how the relationship was progressing.

Before he could do so, Kim popped into David's office with an invitation to her thirtieth birthday party. 'It's rather a milestone,' she said, 'so I've decided to celebrate rather than moan about old age coming on! I know it's rather soon after your father's death but I hope you'll come – and do bring your new girlfriend along – I'd love to meet her.' David wasn't at all sure Samantha would come but said he would ask her. As he'd expected, she declined the invitation saying she was off to a conference in the north that weekend, though added that 'I'll get in touch directly I get back.' David was not re-assured.

David arrived at the party on his own and looked round to see who was there. He noticed Jamal and his friend Ali standing in one corner who looked as if they were having a serious conversation. Kim was on the other side of the room, talking to her friend Mary, and David heard her ask, 'Is that Al Mercer?'

Kim nodded and said, 'Yes. He's just got back from America. I'll introduce you later.'

David saw Andrew Johnson and his wife, and Pamela Litchfield and Martin Allardice talking together and went over to join them, but when they eventually sat down to dinner he found himself sitting next to Kim's friend, Mary.

Mary had hoped to be sitting with Pamela and was disappointed to find she was seated next to David. She hadn't taken to him, mainly because she'd heard nothing since the hospice meeting from him or Henry Winchester about her offer to try and help persuade Betty back on the committee. She felt disappointed that David hadn't taken up her offer, knowing how well respected he was in the community, and suspected he thought she'd have little to contribute. She admitted to herself that her pride had been hurt.

She was also sad because she knew the longer the time passed, the more difficult it would be to get Betty back. She felt the group had lost someone who would have been a very useful member as she would have tapped a different social group in the community.

She sat down determined to be sociable for Kim's sake, but before she could say anything David said, 'I must apologise for not doing anything about bringing Betty back to the appeal committee. You may not have heard, but my father died recently and I've spent much of my time with him in Scotland.

Mary felt mortified she had misunderstood him and said contritely, 'I'm so very sorry.'

They discussed Betty's resignation and agreed that, though Alex had been very tactless, he'd put his fingers on the main areas they needed to tap – the business and moneyed community, though it was obvious community fund raising was very important. That was where Betty could have been so useful. They agreed that now David was back at the hospital they would try and get Betty back.

As the wine flowed he told her a little about his domestic circumstances and said that his girl-friend was unable to come as she was at a conference. Then, looking towards Kim sitting next to Jamal he said 'I believe you knew Kim as a child.'

'Yes, we met when we were six. Kim and her parents moved into a house at the end of our road and my mother invited them to tea. From then on we were inseparable and spent all our spare time together. We went to the same school, went to Sunday school together, and spent our summer holidays in London with my Aunt Judith. We even shared the same boy-friend, Patrick.'

'That must have been difficult,' said David laughing.

'Not really. We both decided he wasn't for us!'

'But I've not heard Kim talk about you before. How come?'

'Well, we've only just got together again. We both went abroad and studied and lost touch – you know how it is.'

David was eager to learn more about Kim. Mary told him that Kim wanted to be a doctor but failed to get the required grades so abandoned the idea and went into nursing instead. 'Kim was very clever and I blame her parents for her poor exam results. They split up the very week she started sitting her A levels. I think they were very selfish. They sold the house and moved away – her mother to Devon and her father to New York. Kim's mother was a very cold woman. I never liked her. Her father was different – warm and very kind – but he was hardly ever there.'

'Poor Kim!'

'Yes. But she has an amazing capacity for forgiveness. Instead of blaming her parents, she blamed herself for not working harder. She said her parents had never been happy and hoped they'd find happiness elsewhere. Despite what she said, I think Kim was far more hurt than she ever let on.'

'I've often wondered about Kim. Underneath that lively exterior there's a sort of sadness.'

'Yes, you're right. But I think the sadness comes from what happened to her in Africa.'

'What happened there?'

'Well Kim went to the Congo to help in an orphanage. While there she fell head over heels in love with the Director of the project. She wrote to me and said he was everything she'd ever looked for in a man. They planned to marry when they came back to England at the end of her time with VSO. She sent me photographs of the two of them together outside the orphanage, and another with the orphanage children clustered round them. They all looked very happy. Paul seemed quite a bit older than Kim and I did wonder at the time how he'd managed to stay single for so long.'

'So what happened?'

'Kim had it all worked out. She said Paul insisted she did her nursing degree as planned and that he would try and get a job nearby so she could live at home. It all sounded as though they'd sorted out their future together. But, just before the plane touched down at Heathrow, Paul announced that he wouldn't be coming to London with her because he had a wife and family living in Chester and he'd decided to go back to them.'

David sat stunned for a minute, unable to say anything.

'I just hope she doesn't get hurt again,' said Mary looking towards Jamal. 'He seems very nice but they're from such different backgrounds I worry about them.'

'Me too,' said David. 'I'm very fond of Kim,'

'I know,' said Mary giving him a sideways look.

David was so upset by what Mary had just told him that he quickly changed the subject to the hospice appeal and never thought to ask Mary about her own life.

They were called to order by Andrew Johnson who tapped his glass and said it was time for a speech. First he wished Kim 'happy birthday' saying he refused to believe she was thirty. She looked far too young! Then he said that Kim was a very special person, that she was much loved by all the hospital staff, and there were many patients and their families who had reason to be grateful to Kim. She was a wonderful person and they all wished her every happiness in the future.

They stood up to sing 'Happy Birthday' and then settled down to more conversation till the early hours.

-15-

Kim and Mary discuss the party and the guests

David would have been surprised to know that he was the main topic of conversation when Kim and Mary met soon after the part. Kim was enthusiastic about how well the party had gone, and asked Mary whether she had enjoyed talking with David Gardner.

'Yes, we had a good conversation. What's he like?

'David's a good friend and I'm very fond of him. He's an excellent administrator, and greatly respected in the hospital. It was good he came to the party. He's had such a difficult year what with his divorce and his father's death. And now he's got involved with the niece of Sir James Lambert. I just hope he doesn't get hurt again.'

'Why are you worried?'

'The Lambert family's really out of David's league. They are part of the county set and I can't see Sir James's niece settling down with David.'

Curious, Mary asked, 'What was his wife like?'

'She was a beautiful woman – but very cold. I met her several times at hospital parties, but I never really liked her. She ran off with the man who was her marriage counsellor which, as you can imagine, upset David both from a personal and a professional point of view.'

'So, what about this new friend, this niece of Sir James. Have you met her?'

'No, no one has.'

They moved on to talk about Pamela whom they'd both known for a long time.

'It seems she and Martin are an item,' said Kim. 'Such a shame! He's self-opinionated, makes heavy pronouncements about the state of society, and as far as I can gather, does very little in a practical way to help the community. And he's still married!'

'Yes,' said Mary. 'She deserves better.'

Mary had often wondered about Pamela and her single situation, and before she got tied up with Martin, had thought of trying to bring Pamela and her old friend Patrick together. She said to Kim, 'I used to think of introducing her to Patrick. You remember him?'

'Of course. You're forgetting I knew him long before that. Don't you remember? We argued about him when we were both teenagers! He's a lovely man – very kind and caring. I used to wonder whether one day he might be a replacement for Ben. He's obviously very fond of you.'

'No!' Mary shook her head vigorously. 'He's one of my closest friends, but I could never think of marrying him.' She laughed. 'You know, before you met Jamal I had thoughts of trying to pair you up with Patrick.'

They both burst out laughing and agreed that matchmaking was not their forte!

They chatted about the charity and the members of the committee and were intrigued by Alice and Alec because they had both, on separate occasions, seen them together in situations that didn't seem to have any relevance to the charity. Mary said she felt rather sorry for Alec's wife who was just emerging from depression after the death of her mother, and hoped her suspicions were unfounded.

'And what about Al?' Mary asked. 'I tried to get into conversation with him. I wanted to find out what it was about him you disliked. But it almost seemed as if he was avoiding me. I got the impression he preferred male company.'

'I think, maybe, you've hit the nail on the head,' exclaimed Kim. 'Perhaps I don't like him because he doesn't seem the least bit interested in me either.' She paused for a while, and then said, musingly, 'But that's not all. There's something different about him, something I just can't pin down.' Then she shook her head and said, 'Not to worry. He lives abroad and is only an occasional visitor, and Jamal always has warning when he's coming.'

A TORTUOUS PATH

After the birthday party, Mary met Jamal a number of times and bit by bit, got to know him better. Kim told her about his American connection and why he'd studied medicine over there. She said he must have done very well because he'd done some research and had a paper published which was very well received, and was one of the reasons he'd got his present job at the hospital.

Mary was very fond of Kim and though she liked Jamal, felt uneasy about their relationship. Kim sensed this, and on one occasion, when just the two of them were having lunch together, she challenged her. 'I know you don't really approve. But you don't know Jamal. He's such a lovely man.'

'It's not that I don't approve,' Mary hastened to say. 'It's that I'm worried for you. He's a Muslim and the cultural differences are so great that I'm afraid of you getting hurt again.'

'What if he is a Muslim? That shouldn't matter. I didn't think you were prejudiced.'

'I'm not,' Mary replied indignantly. 'I have several Muslim friends. But I do know there are lots of problems with mixed marriages. The cultures are so different – and many Muslim women are not free in the way European women are.'

'Well,' said Kim, 'Jamal is very Westernised. In fact, I feel he's really a Muslim only in name. He's not what you would call a practising Muslim. He doesn't pray every few hours, and he eats and drinks just as we do. As for Ramadan and fasting, I don't think he ever observes it. I know he's read a lot about comparative religions. I think he's sympathetic to them all.'

'Well, that's reassuring,' Mary responded, knowing that Kim was a committed Christian, but she couldn't help adding, 'You do seem to choose much older men! I wonder how Jamal's managed to remain single for so long? He's so very good looking.'

'Oh,' said Kim, eager to move the subject on, 'I think that's what brought us together. He had a girl-friend in America and wanted to marry her. But she was American and a Christian, and all his Muslim relatives were against it. They told Jamal's parents, and they went rushing over to America to put a stop to the marriage. The girl got cold feet, and although Jamal said he would have gone through with the marriage, despite his parent's opposition, she called off the whole thing. He said he was devastated and wanted to get right away. That's why he came back to England. And that's why,' she added, 'Jamal and I have so much in common. We've both suffered loss.' ('And so,' thought Mary, 'have I.')

'And what do Jamal's parents say to his relationship with you?'

'Well, I think they've now realised that he's not going to accept an arranged marriage, and I think they're bowing to the inevitable – that he's going to make his own choice.'

'Have you met them?'

'No. Not yet. But Jamal's driving me up to meet them soon.

'That should be interesting. I hope it goes well.'

Whenever the opportunity arose, Mary observed Jamal closely. She found him charming, and could understand why Kim had fallen in love with him. They talked about the hospital, about his life in America, and about the hospice project. They also talked about friendship – Kim and her long-standing friendship, and his and Al's. Jamal said that friendships were so important that one must never let go of old friends.'

One evening, Mary had gone to dinner with Kim and found herself alone with Jamal while Kim was cooking. She decided to take the bull by the horns and ask Jamal how he felt about marrying someone who was a committed Christian, while he was a Muslim.

'That's a question people often ask me. I don't see any problems at all. In the first place, I'm a Muslim because I was born a Muslim – not because I have any strong belief. I suppose I'm what some would call a 'universalist.' I think all the main religions seek a path to God. Islam and Christianity have a great deal in common, you know.'

'Such as?' she asked.

'Well, Islam has the same roots as Christianity. Muhammed was well versed in the Jewish scriptures. Have you ever read the Koran?'

'No,' she admitted. 'It's something I've intended to do, but I've never got round to it.'

'That's what so many people say,' said Jamal smiling. 'I think you'd find it quite instructive. There are hundreds of references in it to the Old Testament – to the creation and Adam and Eve, to Abraham and Moses, to King David, the prophets – it's all there. And of course, there are many references to Joseph and Mary and to Jesus.'

'Then why are Muslims so opposed to Christianity?'

'Because they believe that Christians have strayed from the will of God. They have disobeyed him by worshipping Jesus as divine. God's command is to worship only him – and that in calling Jesus the son of God they are blaspheming. The Koran says that men must be brought back to the right path – absolute submission and resignation to the will of Allah.'

'So what does the Koran actually say about Jesus?'

'It says that Jesus was just a prophet – a Holy man whom Allah favoured and endowed with the Holy Spirit. But it lists him among the Old Testament prophets – not on his own.'

'A prophet. Not the Son of God? That's quite a difference.'

'Yes. I agree. But I personally still find it difficult to see Jesus in that light. I have no quarrel with what Jesus taught. His tenets are wonderful. If everyone lived by them the world would be a different place.'

'Don't you think that that's where the problem is? Christianity is all about love. But I don't see much love in the attitudes of many Muslims. Muslims seem to me to want to take over the world.'

'That's another issue altogether. The Koran preaches the oneness of God - His divine mercy and forgiveness – the compassionate one. It talks about justice, fair dealing, kindness to orphans and widows, charity to the poor –the same things that Christianity preaches - but it also talks of a stern God who will exact retribution on evil-doers.'

'You seem to know your Koran very well! Mary said dryly.

'Inevitable! I was brought up on it – and many of its tenets are totally acceptable – but not all.'

'Such as?'

'Punishment, for example – a hundred lashes for the adulteress, lashes for slander and defamation, cutting off of limbs for theft, crucifixion for the apostate – some horrendous things alongside compassion and love.'

Mary shuddered.`

'Sadly,' said Jamal, 'though most Muslims want to live a quiet life of prayer and obedience to Allah, there are now more and more militant Muslims who are picking out the violent bits of the Koran to promote their political beliefs – Jihad.'

'Jihad?' Mary asked, not having heard the word before.

'Yes. Jihad is a political not a religious movement – though it carries with it the name of Islam. Jihad does huge damage to the Muslim community.'

At that point, Kim came into the room and said, 'Is Jamal on his pet hobby horse? Tolerance? That's why I love him.'

Jamal looked a little embarrassed by Kim's declaration, but managed a smile.

Mary left for home feeling less anxious than before about Kim's relationship with Jamal.

-16-
Jamie ill. Kim tells Mary of her engagement

It was not long after questioning Jamal about mixed marriages that Mary was called home in the middle of the day by the nanny who said Jamie was very unwell. She'd taken him to the doctor who said he should be taken straight to the hospital and he would arrange for someone to see him as soon as they arrived.

Celia drove them there and Mary held Jamie in her arms all the way. She knew she was breaking the law, but felt Jamie was far too sick to be strapped into a baby seat, so they sat huddled together in the back seat.

As soon as they arrived at the hospital they found a doctor waiting to see them, and Jamie was put in intensive care where he remained for well over a week. The doctors suspected meningitis but, despite numerous tests, couldn't diagnose what was wrong with him and Jamie wasted away before their eyes. They were warned to expect the worst, and Mary was frantic with anxiety. The thought of losing Jamie and her last contact with Ben was more than she could bear and the tension took a toll on her health

She was allowed to stay at the hospital with Jamie all the time, and Celia and Dan came over each day to be with them. Colin, their Rector, and his wife Jane came over to the hospital on several occasions to pray with them, as did the hospital chaplain. Looking back, Mary thought that people who criticise hospital chaplaincy have no idea of the value of this ministry. After a week, Jamie rallied and came out of intensive care and they began to feel hopeful that he might recover. He spent another week slowly making progress before he was allowed home.

Mary took unpaid leave from the office and didn't go back to work until the end of August. The nanny was very supportive throughout the crisis and seemed as traumatised as Mary, Celia and Dan. After Jamie had been home for a week, they sent the nanny off on a fortnight's leave as a thank-you for all her support. Colin held a brief service of thanksgiving in the church for Jamie's recovery

Mary didn't think about the appeal at all during Jamie's illness. Though Kim kept in touch with letters of prayer and encouragement she was tactful enough not to mention either the charity or Jamal. Another person whose help they valued was Patrick, Mary's childhood friend, who came over to stay with Ben and Celia to give them support. Mary was very conscious of the fact that, however much the media and others criticise society as being selfish and uncaring, there were many who receive nothing but love and care in times of crisis and illness. She thanked God every day for Jamie's recovery and for all the support showered on her during his illness.

Things were getting back to equilibrium when Kim invited her to supper and told her that she and Jamal were going to get married. 'I wanted you to be the first to know.'

Kim looked so happy that Mary suppressed any anxieties that still remained and gave her a big hug, saying she was happy for her, and truly hoped it would all work out well.

'Have you met his parents yet?' she asked.

'No. Jamal has decided he doesn't want me to meet them until we've made all our plans. He's determined not to let them influence him again.'

'How does Jamal get on with them now? Does he have anything to do with them?' Mary couldn't stop herself from asking.

'Oh yes, of course. Jamal's very fond of them. He sees them occasionally, but they live miles away, and his father's very frail, so they seldom come down.'

'Has Jamal any brothers or sisters?'

'No. But he's got cousins – quite a number of them – and they all live nearby. I gather it's quite a close-knit community.'

'And what about Al?'

Kim pulled a face. 'He's a bit of a problem. We've decided to move in together straight away, but I'm going to keep on my flat because of Al (and Jamal's parents if ever they were to come down). As you've probably gathered, Al's a strict Muslim and doesn't approve of people living together before marriage. Jamal doesn't want to upset him, so we're not going to tell him.'

'A bit difficult,' Mary observed.

'Yes. But, when he comes to stay, I'll decamp to my own flat.'

Mary didn't say anything but thought how difficult that would be for Kim - having to take all her belongings away each time Al came to visit.

'I don't think Al really approves of our relationship,' said Kim reflectively, and added, 'I don't really like him. I can't say why. But he and Jamal have been friends for so long, I can't say anything.'

This was not the first time she'd told Mary she didn't like Al. She admitted that Jamal's relationship with him had been the cause of one or two arguments – 'the only time we ever disagree,' she said emphatically

Mary asked when they planned to get married, and she said it would be as soon as she finished her Master's degree the following May. She said she and Jamal were going to announce their engagement at a small party they were having in a fortnight's time and hoped Mary would be able to come.

Mary wondered what sort of wedding they would have, knowing from conversations with Jamal that he was not a practising Muslim. She couldn't see how they could get married in church. 'We've thought about that,' said Kim, 'and though I'd love a church wedding, we've decided it would be best to get married in a registry office and perhaps have a blessing in church.'

'Why don't you ask Colin, Jane's husband?' suggested Mary. 'I'm sure he'd be very sympathetic to your situation.'

Kim was delighted at the idea, and Mary was surprised she hadn't thought of it herself as she knew Jane both as a friend, and as a fellow professional. 'I'm hoping they'll come to our engagement party. Perhaps I'll sound him out then.'

'I'm sure he'd be very sympathetic to your situation,' said Mary.

Kim took up Mary's suggestion and contacted Colin who readily agreed to conduct a service of blessing for them.

-17-
David's weekend at Samantha's country home

After his return from Scotland, David heard nothing from Samantha and only got the ansaphone when he telephoned. He was beginning to try and convince himself that the relationship was at an end when hope was rekindled. He received a call from Samantha apologising that she hadn't been in touch. She was sorry to hear his father had died (David wondered how) and then invited him to go with her to her parent's house for the weekend.

'My father's just got back from America and would like to meet you – and, of course Daniel will be there – and my sister Miranda is back from Hong Kong - so there's going to be a bit of a house party.'

It was a slightly ambiguous invitation, but David was so happy at the thought of being with Samantha that he didn't query it.

He took the Friday afternoon off, drove to London, and collected Samantha from her gallery. He couldn't help noticing it was still open and the man showing people round was the same person he'd seen on his previous visit. He felt curious, remembering Samantha had told him at their first meeting that she ran the gallery. He wondered how she was able to get away so often.

It was a beautiful sunny day as they drove down to Hampshire, arriving just after six. David had imagined Samantha's home would be large, but wasn't expecting a mansion. The drive up to the house was lined with beech trees with an open aspect to fields full of deer on either side. The house itself was Georgian with a white facade and delicate pillars on either side of the doorway.

As they got out of the car, Samantha's father came out to meet them – giving Samantha a warm hug before turning to David with his hand held out in greeting. 'Good to see you. We've been hearing a lot about you from Samantha.'

'It's good to meet you too,' said David, not quite knowing what to say next as he was still reeling from surprise at the size of the house.

'Come on in. Daniel's already here. He got away at lunch time so had a very speedy journey down.' With that, he put his arm round Samantha and led them to the house.

David hesitated, wondering about their luggage, but Samantha's father waved him on saying 'Nelson will see to the cases. It's too late for tea, so I suggest you go up to your rooms and change – and then come down for a drink. Your mother's still upstairs– but you'll see her when you come down.'

David hadn't thought to ask Samantha what her parents' names were, nor how to address them. With people he was used to meeting, there was usually such informality that, more often than not, they got on to Christian name terms immediately. But he knew that some of the older generation, particularly those from what he regarded as 'the upper classes', resented this informality, and felt it was an intrusion. He remembered a neighbour in his home town being deeply offended when one of the locals called her Emma instead of Mrs Stevens, and she was even more offended when she broke her hip and found all the nurses and doctors in the hospital calling her by her Christian name. He'd always felt this supposedly trivial matter delayed her recovery.

He kicked himself for not thinking about names on the journey down but thought he'd have a chance to discover them as he followed Samantha upstairs. However, Nelson preceded them and showed them to separate rooms, and Samantha gave a cheerful wave, and disappeared round the corner while Nelson opened the door to his room.

It was large and gracious, and overlooked a lake. It had its own en-suite bathroom and David decided he would have a quick shower before dinner. Fortunately, Samantha had warned him that his parents always dressed for dinner, so he'd packed his dinner jacket.

Twenty minutes later, there was a knock at the door. David expected to see Samantha, but it was Nelson. 'Miss Samantha asked me to tell you to come down as soon as you're ready. They're all in the drawing room.'

'Thank you,' he said, feeling he'd been left in limbo. He'd expected Samantha to pop in and take him down herself when he could have asked her the questions he realised he should have asked on the journey. From his very brief encounter with her father, he realised that they came from the same stable as her aunt and uncle, Sir James and Lady Lambert, at whose dinner party he'd first met Samantha.

There was no help for it. He knew he would have to go down alone, and realised he was well out of his comfort zone. He hoped and prayed he wouldn't make a hash of it.

He found the drawing room, expecting to meet just the family, but the room was full of people. Nelson pointed him to Samantha who was standing by the window talking animatedly to a lady who, he was quite sure, was her mother. Seeing him enter the room she beckoned him over and said, 'This is my mother, Lady Julia. I've told her all about you.'

Taking her extended hand he realised immediately where Samantha got her good looks from. She was almost the double of Samantha except for a few lines round her eyes, and her silver hair which seemed to shimmer in the light streaming through a side window

'I'm very pleased to meet you,' said Lady Julia in the gentle clipped voice which David always associated with the gentry. 'You must tell me about your work and this hospice project while you're here. Samantha has told us all about it – but first you must have a drink.' She beckoned to a maid. David took a glass from the tray and turned to see who else was in the room. Lady Julia immediately noticed his glance and said, 'We must introduce you to the rest of the party. You know Daniel. He's always late for everything - and Miranda's putting the children to bed so she'll be down later. Peter, her husband, is over there talking to my husband. You've met him already, I know. He's looking forward to having a good talk with you later. But you must come over and meet our other guests.'

With that, she drew him across the room and introduced him to an elderly couple. 'Sir John and Ann are our oldest friends. You'll enjoy speaking to them.' Then she left them and moved across the room to talk to someone else. David looked round for Samantha, praying she would join him, but she'd already joined her father and brother-in-law on the other side of the room.

'I understand you're a hospital administrator,' said Lady Ann. 'That must be an interesting but demanding job. I know a little about hospitals as I'm on the board of our local hospital.'

That decided the topic of their conversation for the next ten minutes or so. Lady Ann proved knowledgeable about the way hospitals worked, and they were engrossed in arguing, or rather agreeing, about the need to bring back matrons, when Lady Ann suddenly stopped and said 'Ah, here's Sir Ralph coming across to join us.'

David turned round and saw Samantha's father walking across the room towards them. He mentally thanked Lady Ann for getting him out of the embarrassment of not knowing his name.

At that moment, the butler ushered them to the dining room. He was relieved to find he was placed next to Samantha. Opposite was a man whom Samantha introduced as Stephen. 'He's a colleague of my father,' Then Daniel, who'd arrived just as they were going into dinner, joined them and David felt able to relax as he knew Daniel had a great sense of humour.

Conversation was lively and Samantha and Daniel did a sort of double act, telling stories of their somewhat bizarre activities as children. It was obvious they both loved their home and had enjoyed a happy childhood, but they made it clear that they hadn't enjoyed their boarding schools, and would make sure that any children of their own would be educated locally.

Lady Julia heard this part of the conversation from the other end of the table and clearly didn't agree. 'One of the great things about boarding schools is that they make children learn to stand on their own feet, as well as helping them to make contact with the right people. I used to hate the beginning of term, especially when they were little - waving them good-bye at the station, usually on my own because your father was always away. I used to miss them dreadfully, but we both thought we were doing the best for our children.'

Samantha and Daniel smiled at her. It was obvious they'd heard this before, but David's heart quailed. The product of a very ordinary middle class family, he'd been educated at the local grammar school and then gone on to Oxford. He hoped the Oxford part of his life would make him acceptable to Lady Julia

Half way through dinner Stephen stood up and gave a' welcome back' toast to Sir Ralph. When David asked Daniel where he he'd been, he said 'The USA.'

The conversation turned towards hospitals, and immediately David was in the thick of a discussion about public financing and the private sector. He realised he would have to be a little careful because it quickly emerged that they would all be using the private sector if they became ill. David tried to steer the conversation to the less tendentious topic of matrons – and discovered they all thought that matrons should be brought back.

Then, to his surprise, Stephen Maitland suddenly said, 'Tell us about your hospice project, David. It sounds interesting.

David was taken aback and wondered how on earth Stephen had heard about it when he was living so far away in Hampshire? It didn't seem to him to be worthy of the interest of the gathering, but Samantha nudged his arm and said, 'Yes, do tell them. It's such an interesting and worthy enterprise.'

With no option but to respond he took a deep breath and began by telling them about the basic hospice philosophy – that people should die with dignity with their pain controlled as far as humanly possible, their affairs put in order, and their relationships healed.

They all nodded. Samantha said, 'And both his parents died in a hospice.'

There was a murmur of sympathy and Samantha touched him lightly on the shoulder as a gesture of support.

'What surprises me is that you have a Muslim leading the campaign. What's his motive?' asked Stephen.

David was struck again with amazement. How on earth did Stephen know about Jamal? Was it so very strange to have a Muslim leading a charity? There were a number of Muslims in public life – so why not in a charity? And why should this be of interest to this little group here in Hampshire.

'And I gather he's got another Muslim who's helping him,' went on Stephen. David saw Samantha shoot a warning glance at him, and he immediately shut up. But the Muslim theme was taken up by some of the other guests, who expressed anxiety about the threat that Muslim extremism was now presenting in this country – and indeed in the world. Discussion inevitably turned to the twin towers, and David realised, with a shock, that Stephen had been in New York at the time. Having witnessed the horrors of the event fully explained his comments about Muslim involvement.

But, after everyone had expressed their anxiety about the growing threat of terrorism, the conversation reverted to hospices. Stephen took up the thread by saying, 'Samantha told me all about your hospice project when I was telling her about my aunt's distressing cancer. She suggested I should look out for a hospice for her.'

David told them that the hospice project was at the very earliest stage, and that a proper committee was only just being formed. He explained that Jamal wasn't really a foreigner; that he'd been born in England, and then studied in America – coming back to England when his parents fell on hard times.

Stephen wondered how Jamal had got interested in the hospice movement.

Not wanting to put Jamal in a bad light, David invented a reason, saying that Jamal got interested after reading a book by Dame Cecily Saunders. He made a mental note, when he got home, to check that such a book existed!

This seemed to satisfy their curiosity, and the conversation covered a whole range of subjects, many of them political, following a similar pattern to the Lambert's dinner party where he'd met Samantha - the ladies leaving the table while the men stayed behind with their port. Daniel and David found themselves in conversation, and talked about Samantha's art gallery – and the awful pictures she had on display at the moment. They both agreed they wouldn't give any of them house-room.

The men didn't stay in the dining room very long, but soon joined the ladies in the drawing room where David was introduced to Miranda, Samantha's sister. It was difficult to believe she came out of the same mould as Samantha and Daniel. She was plump and matronly, and had short curly dark hair. She struck him as a warm, outgoing, person. She said how nice it was to meet Samantha's latest. She blushed as she said it, realising she'd made a gaffe, and quickly asked if he'd met her husband, Peter. David told her he hadn't had a chance to talk to him – trying to put behind him the implications of her insensitive remark.

'I'm sorry,' she said. 'I'm always putting my foot in it. But Samantha's talked about you a lot – so it's nice to meet you,'

When, he wondered, had Samantha had the opportunity to discuss her love life with Miranda, when Miranda had only arrived from Hong Kong the day before? It was a mystery, but he determined to put it out of his mind, and they spent a pleasant hour talking about Hong Kong which he'd visited just before graduation.

Just before eleven, Lady Ann and her husband got up to go to bed. Everyone stood up to say goodnight, and soon after, by mutual agreement, they all decided it was time to retire.

David kissed Samantha goodnight just outside his bedroom door, knowing there was no chance whatever that they would get together that night.

He slept well and came down to breakfast to find just Sir Ralph and Daniel at the table. The breakfast food was set out on a side table. Sir Ralph pointed to it and said, 'Just help yourself. Tea and coffee's on the table.'

Sir Ralph was reading *The Times* and Daniel was looking at a racing magazine. It didn't surprise David that he was interested in horses, and he suspected he was somewhat of a gambler.

When he'd helped himself to bacon and egg, Sir Ralph passed him the coffee pot saying, 'The ladies are all going shopping this morning and Daniel is leaving us to go shooting, which means we'll have a little time to ourselves for a nice chat. There are one or two things I must do first, so perhaps you'd join me at about eleven for coffee? My study's in the east wing – the fourth door along. So do, please, make yourself at home. There are quite a few recent books in the study – or you might like to walk down to the lake. It's very beautiful at this time of year.'

With that, he got up and left the room.

'You've got your marching orders then,' laughed Daniel. 'No one's been able to say no to the Pater! But he's alright, really.'

David wanted to ask Daniel to tell him about his father, but the maid came into the room at that point, so he lost the opportunity.

David spent the next two hours walking down to the lake and round the estate. It was very beautiful with distant views but he felt a little miffed that Samantha had gone off without him. He couldn't help feeling apprehensive about the forthcoming meeting with Sir Ralph, suspecting that he was going to be grilled about his 'intentions'. He thought that, as a recently divorced man, he wouldn't be seen as much of a catch for Samantha.

Eleven o'clock came. David decided to be a few minutes late before finding Sir Ralph. It was a ploy he'd used when he wanted to get something important through at a meeting. He thought the gesture would let Sir Ralph know that he was not a weakling, ready to jump at his slightest word.

David found the room easily. Sir Ralph was sitting at his desk, reading some official looking papers – but he got up directly David walked in and ushered him to one of the two large leather chairs placed in an alcove with a low table between.

Sir Ralph was tall and aristocratic looking with an abundance of neatly styled silver-grey hair, piercing grey eyes, an aquiline nose, and a clean-shaven face. His voice was pleasing and he had an air of authority. David could imagine him addressing large audiences with ease.

When David sat down, Sir Ralph poured out coffee and asked if he'd enjoyed walking round the lake. It's one of the many joys of coming home.'

David raised his eyebrows as though to question him, hoping he would say more about his travels, but he immediately began talking about the house and the grounds. 'I've been very fortunate living here. I inherited the estate from my father when he died in the nineteen-seventies. I was born here – as were Miranda, Samantha and Daniel. It will, of course, go to Daniel when I die, but there are several outhouses which I'm leaving to Miranda and Samantha should they wish to come back and convert them.'

'Converting old buildings is all the rage now, isn't it? So many old farm buildings – oast houses and windmills - are being turned into very desirable residences. My house is next door to an old stone barn which has been made into a three-bed-roomed house. I thought of buying an old property once but, sadly, my ex-wife wouldn't hear of it.' There, David thought, I've been open about my ex-marriage.

'You met Samantha at my brother-in-law's house,' he said. 'It was so good of you to take her under your wing. I know she had a very enjoyable time in Berkshire – thanks to you.'

David nodded. Here comes the questioning about my prospects, he thought. The next question took him by surprise.

'What I'd really like to talk about is this hospice project of yours. I'd like to pick your brains a little as we have a similar project going on here, and we are having difficulties.'

Then followed a whole host of questions about costs, whether the Health Authority had endorsed the project, had they found a site, what sort of people were involved in the project – all straightforward and the sort of questions one might have expected. But then the questioning focused on Jamal, which, when he thought about it later, was puzzling. Sir Ralph wanted to know where he came from, how long he'd been in England, what was his background - and when David said 'medical', he said 'No, I meant religious'.

Once again, surprised by this rather intrusive interest in Jamal, he replied, somewhat curtly, that though was brought up as a Muslim but didn't seem very devout.

'How so?' asked Sir Ralph.

'Well, he never talks about Islam. Drinks alcohol freely. I've never heard of him going to the mosque - or praying. He's very westernised. But for his skin, you wouldn't think he was any different from anyone else,' David finished lamely.

'Married?'

'No,' he replied. 'He's been very popular with the ladies but he's now got himself involved with one of our senior nurses. I think it's serious.'

Sir Ralph reflected for a moment, and then, to David's amazement, said, 'And what about his sidekick, Mr Mercer?'

David was astonished that he knew about Al, but, recovering his equilibrium, said, 'I hardly know him. I've only met him a few times. He seems quite agreeable – tells amusing tales about his travels. He and Dr Khan met at university in the States, and they shared a room for two years.'

'I gather you've seen him twice in London?' David was surprised and beginning to feel uneasy. Obviously Samantha had been talking to her father about their relationship, and he wondered why Sir Ralph was so interested in Jamal Khan and Al Mercer. Sir Ralph sensed David's unease and turned the conversation to theatre and politics. When they got into the sensitive area of party politics, he decided to be brave, and revealed his left wing inclinations. Sir Ralph made no comment!

The shopping party returned and Sir Ralph rose from his chair in what David took to be a gesture of dismissal. The conversation had gone in an entirely different direction to what he'd expected – and he still hadn't discovered what Sir Ralph did for a living. Stuart had told him that he thought he'd been an ambassador. David realised that if he really wanted to know about Sir Ralph, he'd have to ask Samantha - but he suspected she wouldn't be too happy about him asking such personal questions.

After a light lunch all the guests scattered - the older ones going for a nap, while Samantha gathered together Stephen and his wife, Jennifer, Miranda and Peter and little Bobby, Daniel and David, to go and view a National Trust house which was within walking distance. David felt it was all very pleasant apart from the fact that he wanted Samantha to himself.

After dinner that evening the guests were entertained by Miranda and Peter's photographs of Hong Kong and China. They were very good and surprisingly, everyone enjoyed seeing them and hearing about their life in China where they'd been posted for the last three years.

Next morning Samantha said she would be going to church with her mother and asked David if he would like to come. David surprised himself by saying 'yes'

His feelings towards Christianity had always been ambivalent. He knew he couldn't call himself an atheist because he could never rule out the possibility that there just might be a God. But he couldn't envisage what this God might be like. And if He was a God of love as so many of his friends said, how could He have allowed the horrific wars that had taken place over the centuries, or the complete devastation of the school in Wales, or the destruction of the twin towers, and the awful disasters occasioned by hurricanes, tsunamis, volcanoes, floods and earthquakes which had taken so many thousands of lives.

But, on the other hand, David loved the peace one finds in a church. He enjoyed the singing of good choirs – especially those in England's great cathedrals – and he loved the beautiful words of the Prayer Book.

So, when Samantha asked him if he would like to accompany them, he said 'yes' – somewhat to her surprise. But she seemed delighted to have him along. Sir John and Lady Ann Mackintosh joined them, and they set off for church on foot. It all seemed a bit like a cameo from one of Jane Austen's novels.

David was glad he'd agreed to go. It was a perfect summer's day, and the bird and wild life around was beautiful. The little village church was delightful, and the choir, despite having only six members in it, was excellent. To top it all, the vicar's sermon was well crafted, and touched on the international problems that were calling on everyone to re-evaluate their lives.

They returned to an excellent lunch, and after a leisurely coffee in the sitting room, they all prepared for departure. Lady Julia kissed David goodbye which he felt was a good sign, and Sir Ralph shook him by the hand saying he looked forward to a further chat the next time they met.

They set off for London and Samantha asked him if he'd enjoyed the weekend. David said he had, but grumbled that they hadn't had any time on their own. They got caught in a terrible traffic jam, and arrived in London very late. Much as he would have liked to, he couldn't stay. He had to be off very early next morning as he was taking a colleague with him to a meeting in Manchester.

So, after a hasty farewell to Samantha, he set off for home, turning over in his mind all the discussions of the weekend, pondering why on earth there seemed to be so much interest in the hospice project, and asking himself why he'd expected Sir Ralph to quiz him so soon about his intentions for Samantha. Above all, he realised that through his relationship with Samantha he'd entered a rather different social milieu to the one he was brought up in, and didn't feel altogether comfortable about it

-18-
Kim and Jamal's Engagement Party

David returned to find an invitation awaiting him from Kim and Jamal to an engagement party.

The party was held at Jamal's flat but the same group of friends who'd been at Kim's birthday party a month or two earlier were there - Alan Johnson, the oncology consultant, and his wife Rachel, Pamela Litchfield and Martin Allardice, Geoffrey and Eric, doctors from the hospital, Jane and Colin Masters, Kim's friend Mary Gilburn, and Mick, the hospital's porter who seemed quite at home in the gathering. Another guest was Al who was in England on one of his many business trips.

Mary couldn't understand why Kim didn't really like Al. He seemed very friendly and kept them all amused and interested with tales of his many excursions abroad. But she had to admit that she'd not had an opportunity of talking to him alone, so was no nearer than before to knowing what he was really like nor what he did for a living.

Mary was again placed next to David at dinner and told him she'd just been through a trauma with Jamie.

'Your husband?' asked David.

'No! My son. He's only two.'

'I didn't know you had a son. What a terrible time for you. Which hospital were you in?'

'Yours,' she said with a smile. 'But it must have been when you were in Scotland.'

'Were you happy with the care you received?'

Mary laughed. 'A professional question! Yes, the care was absolutely marvellous – by both the doctors and the nurses. I can't fault the hospital at all. I stayed there all the time, and I was also extremely well looked after. I think you can be proud of your hospital.'

'Thanks for that,' said David. 'It's good to get some direct feedback. People are quick to criticise but they don't always remember to give praise!'

Mary asked whether he enjoyed his work at the hospital and he told her that though he found it very demanding, he loved it, and wouldn't want to do anything else. He asked her what her husband did. Mary was so taken aback she replied, 'He's dead,' and wondered why on earth she hadn't told him the truth.

'I'm so sorry,' he said quickly, but seeing her closed face decided to ask no questions. Mary turned the conversation and asked about his wife –

knowing full well from that he'd had marital problems. 'Oh, we're divorced.'

'I'm so sorry,' she said, and realised she'd echoed his words. 'That must have been very sad. Do you have any children?'

'Fortunately, no! That would have made it more difficult.' Establishing where they each lived, Mary asked whether he knew Stuart Wilson. She realised she was being devious, as she knew he was a friend of Stuart, but didn't want him to think they'd been talking about him. He acknowledged that he knew Stuart well, and that he'd been a great support during his divorce. He made a mental note to ask Stuart about Mary next time they met.

Before the conversation could go any further, they were stopped by Alan Johnson calling for a toast. He said how delighted they all were to hear the news, and hoped Jamal and Kim would be very happy. He thought they were very well suited. He said, 'I looked up the meaning of Jamal's name on the internet. It means 'beautiful'.

They all laughed.

'Well, I think we can safely say he's very handsome and distinguished – and I feel sure,' he said, amidst laughter, 'that Jamal has a beautiful character as well. And we all know what a lovely person Kim is.' Then he added, on a warning note, that, society, being what it was, they might encounter some criticism. He told them they must take no notice of it. He went on to say that after all her hard work, it was important that Kim got her Masters qualification before embarking on 'the matrimonial boat' – an allusion apparently to an old letter he'd come across in his family archives written to a bride in 1922. He added that he hoped marriage wouldn't take Kim away too soon from her work in the hospital – but realised the advent of children might!

Kim laughed and said they hoped to have children – but not too soon. 'We want to enjoy a little time to ourselves first.'

Jamal then stood up and made an emotional speech. 'Thank you all for coming to help us celebrate our engagement. It's great to be among such good friends – some going back a very long way,' and he gave Mary a special smile. 'And I've been very grateful for the new friends I've made and for your support since I've been back in England. I feel truly blessed that Kim has agreed to be my wife. You all know what a wonderful person she is – so loving and caring – and yet so full of fun. I feel I'm a very fortunate man,' and he raised his glass and said,' To Kim, the love of my life and my future wife.'

Everyone raised their glasses to Kim, and then burst into spontaneous applause. Mary was not the only one to have tears in her eyes.

David Gardner reached out and put his hand on Jamal's shoulder. 'I hope you'll be very happy. You're both lucky people.'

Looking at Kim and Jamal, Mary couldn't help feeling a slight twinge of envy. They looked so very happy, and made such a handsome couple – Kim with her bright auburn curls and vivacious smile, and Jamal with his dark good looks. She was not sure whether it was respect for their guests or a cultural thing on Jamal's part, but she noticed they didn't touch each other in public – but there was no doubting their love for each other.

They didn't leave the dinner table till eleven – but the party went on till well after midnight. Jamal ushered them into the lounge while Kim made coffee. Mary hoped to get a chance to talk to Al when they left the dinner table, but it was not to be. He sat with a group of men in one corner of the room from where gales of laughter came wafting across the room.

As they left, Mary felt happy for Kim and Jamal, confident they had a good relationship, and that they'd be well supported by their colleagues at the hospital.

-19-
Visit of Jamal's cousin

Kim moved in with Jamal and blossomed. Mary hadn't seen her looking so happy since their teen years. Reactions to the engagement, outside her close circle of friends, were, as Alan Johnson had predicted, mixed. There was still quite a lot of prejudice about, and some shook their heads solemnly and said 'mixed marriages never work.'

Not long after the engagement party Mary and Kim spent a pleasant evening together in her new home. It overlooked the local park which was very beautiful with a lake and some lovely trees. Jamal had furnished the flat tastefully, rather to Mary's surprise, and Kim had put her own mark on it by introducing pictures and ornaments from her own flat.

Jamal was on call so they had an opportunity to spend what Mary thought of as 'a gossipy evening' together. Kim was enthusiastic about how well the party had gone and Mary commented on what a lovely group of friends Kim had – apart from Martin Allardice.

Then they turned to David Gardner. Kim said how much she liked him – but was rather worried about him because of his friendship with the niece of the Chairman of the Health Authority. 'I invited her to our engagement party but she couldn't come as she was abroad. David hardly ever sees her she's so often abroad which seem odd when she's supposed to be running an art gallery. David's a good friend, and I'm very fond of him. I just hope he doesn't get hurt again.'

'That would be sad. I thought he was a very nice man,' said Mary

'And what about Al?' Mary asked. 'I tried to get into conversation with him. I wanted to find out what it was about him you disliked. But it almost seemed as if he was avoiding me. I got the impression he preferred male company.'

'I think, maybe, you've hit the nail on the head,' exclaimed Kim. 'Perhaps I don't like him because he doesn't seem the least bit interested in me.' She paused for a while, and then said, musingly, 'But that's not all. There's something different about him, something I just can't pin down.' Then she shook her head and said, 'Not to worry. He lives abroad and is only an occasional visitor, and Jamal always has warning when he's coming.'

Before they could gossip any further Jamal returned and the conversation became general.

Mary spent several evenings with Kim and Jamal, and each time she met him she warmed to him more, and felt very confident that they would have a good marriage.

It was, therefore, a great surprise when one evening, just after eight, the phone rang. It was Kim. She was crying, and said, 'I've just got to talk to you. Something terrible has happened and I don't know what to do.'

'Where are you?' Mary asked.

'I'm in your village. I didn't know where to go.'

'Come straight over. I'll be waiting for you.'

A few minutes later, she arrived, looking distraught.

'What on earth's happened?' Mary asked, 'Have you had a row with Jamal?'

'No,' she said, and burst into tears.

Mary took her up to her flat, made her a cup of coffee, and sat her down by the fire. 'Now, tell me,' she said.

Between tears, she said, 'Well, I was in the kitchen clearing away dinner - Jamal was working - when there was a knock at the door. He went to open it and brought in two men. He didn't look too pleased to see them, but said to me, 'These are my cousins from Leeds.' Before he could introduce them, one of them said, pointing to me, 'What's that woman doing here?' Jamal said, 'This is Kim, my fiancée.' Then the older one said menacingly, 'Your whore you mean.'

Jamal was very angry and said 'How dare you speak like that.'

'Well,' said the other man, 'that's what your father thinks. You've shamed our whole community, and disgraced your father. We've come to tell you to get rid of this woman (he pointed at me with a threatening look on his face) and bring you back to the true path'

Jamal exploded and told them to get out, but they wouldn't budge. I thought they were going to attack him, and felt that if I stayed, he might be in more danger. Moreover, I realised that if I stayed, they would discover I was living with Jamal, and be even angrier. So I decided to make a quick exit.

I said to Jamal, ''Ok, Jamal, I've finished the job, so I'm off. See you tomorrow at the hospital.' I didn't give him any time to try and stop me, but just ran out and jumped into my car. I didn't really know what I was doing. All I wanted was to talk to somebody – and that's why I rang you.'

'I'm glad you did. But how awful! You say he said they were cousins?'

'Yes. I knew Jamal had some cousins, and I met two of them when we went up to see his parents, and they were very nice. But Jamal did tell me he had some very militant cousins who were likely not to approve of the marriage, so he didn't want us to meet them.'

'Very wise too,' Mary observed. 'But what are you going to do?'

'I just don't know. I'm frightened for Jamal. They seemed so hostile.'

'You could try and phone him and see if they've gone.'

'Yes,' said Kim brightening up. 'I'll do that now. Can I use your phone?'

'I'd leave it a while. Give them a chance to go. If you ring straightaway they may still be there.'

'Yes, I suppose you're right,' agreed Kim. 'But what am I going to do? What if Jamal decides to give me up.'

'He won't do that,' said Mary soothingly. 'I'm sure he loves you too much to give in to a couple of thugs.'

Kim looked doubtful. Mary made her another cup of coffee, and said she must stay the night. Kim accepted gratefully. She said she'd be too frightened to go back to Jamal's flat that night.

At ten o'clock she telephoned Jamal. Mary couldn't hear the conversation but gathered from Kim that he was alone. He'd been frantically worried and had been out looking for her. He assured her that nothing had changed. She was to take no notice of those awful cousins of his. They'd always been difficult and weren't very bright – so she must forget all about it.

This cheered Kim up – always ready to see the best side of things – but Mary felt uneasy about the whole incident.

Next morning Kim said she'd slept well and went back to the hospital in a cheerful mood. She phoned in the evening to say she and Jamal had had a rapturous reunion, and all was well. Mary just hoped she was right.

The next few weeks she and Kim saw very little of each other, though Mary phoned Kim regularly to make sure there were no further visits from Jamal's cousins. She said that Jamal had assured her they wouldn't come again. Mary hoped he was right.

-20-
Mary visits Kim and they discuss books

It was an ordinary Friday when Kim invited Mary for supper. She'd returned to her own flat as soon as she came off duty because Al was coming to stay that night. They had a very happy evening, though Mary felt a little worried for her when Kim told her about her meeting with Jamal's parents.

'The weekend after our engagement party Jamal and I went up to Leeds to visit his parents. His mother was absolutely sweet and welcoming, but his father was hostile. He treated me with courtesy but made me absolutely aware that he didn't approve of the marriage. He said that he was sure I was a very nice person, but I wasn't a Muslim, and he was sure I wouldn't understand Jamal's way of life, and would take him away from his roots. I tried to assure him that I understood and respected Jamal's background, and that we'd discussed the difference in our upbringings very carefully before getting engaged. But then I made the mistake of saying that as Jamal was so westernised, I didn't think he was too worried about his Muslim background.'

'Oh dear,' said Mary. 'Not the most tactful thing to say!'

'No. I realised that as soon as I said it. It angered his father, though give him his due he remained courteous for the rest of the visit. We'd planned to stay for the weekend if invited, but no invitation was forthcoming, so we left earlier than we'd planned.'

'How was Jamal's mother?'

'Oh, she was lovely. She gave me a warm hug and told me I mustn't worry about her husband's attitude. But his father said that none of the family would be coming to the wedding, and he hoped Jamal would change his mind before it took place.'

'What did Jamal say to all this?'

'He insisted I was not to worry about his father's attitude. He said that this time, he wouldn't allow his father's prejudice to intervene.'

'What about the rest of the family? Did he tell him about the visit of those awful cousins?'

'I don't know, But he did say that, despite what his father had said, he knew some of his cousins would come as they were quite close. But he did admit there was another branch of the family that had members with extreme views – those I'd already met – but as he'd never liked them, and had never had much to do with them, they certainly wouldn't be invited to the wedding.

Kim told Mary she felt reassured, and that his father's hostility to the marriage had brought Jamal and her closer together.

As she was leaving, Kim told Mary that she and Jamal were looking forward to Sunday when Dan and Celia had invited them over to lunch - their first visit since Jamie's illness. They'd taken to Kim and Jamal, as had Jamie, and were keen to congratulate them on their impending marriage.

Looking back, Mary was able to recall every detail of that evening, though one crucial detail slipped her memory at the time. Right from childhood she and Kim had shared a love of reading, and often lent each other books they'd particularly enjoyed. Mary told Kim she'd recently read Sebastian Faulks' *Birdsong* and Kim asked whether she'd read his next book, *Charlotte Gray*. When Mary said she hadn't, Kim said, 'I don't think it's as good as *Birdsong* – less harrowing. But I think you'll enjoy it. I lent it to Al the last time he stayed, and he promised to bring it back this weekend. I'll pop home and collect it tomorrow morning, when Al goes to the mosque for his morning prayers, so I can bring it over on Sunday.'

'Al goes to the mosque?' asked Mary.

'Yes, whenever he stays. He goes off quite early in the morning. It's quite a distance – nearly ten miles.'

'I'm surprised.' I suppose I should have realised that, as a Muslim, he'd want to go to the mosque. Is he very devout?'

'Well, yes. Even when he's staying in Jamal's flat, he goes to his room to pray several times a day. He won't eat pork or bacon, and never drinks. You may remember, he stuck to orange juice at our party.'

'Yes, but I thought that was because he was driving.'

'No. He doesn't agree with alcohol.'

'But Jamal drinks?'

'Oh yes - and eats pork and bacon, and never prays!! I don't think I would ever have thought of marrying him if he'd been a fanatical Muslim – much as I love him.' She smiled and said, 'In fact, because I'm a Christian, he's taken an interest in Christianity. He's been reading a number of books about it, and even picks up my Bible from time to time to look at it.'

Mary felt pleased, knowing how much Kim's Christian faith meant to her. She'd been afraid Jamal might have tried to steer her away.

'Well, don't worry about the book, Kim. Another time will do.'

'No, it's no trouble. I've forgotten one of my files so it'll serve two purposes.'

As Mary got up to leave, she kissed Kim goodbye and said, 'See you Sunday. We'll be back from church by twelve.'

-21-
Kim goes missing

But the visit was not to be. Early on the Sunday morning, before they left for church, Jamal phoned Mary to say Kim had been called away. 'She's left a note saying she's had a call from a neighbour in Somerset saying her mother's had a severe stroke and been rushed to hospital. I'm so sorry about the lunch. We were looking forward to it.'

'Why don't you come on your own? We'd love to see you.'

'Thank you, but no. I think I'd better stay here until she phones. She doesn't seem to have taken her mobile phone with her. She must have left in an awful hurry because I found it on the floor in the hall.'

'Well, do keep me in touch,' said Mary, and Jamal promised he would.

It was the next day that the drama began to unfold - not that anyone realised that there was anything untoward

When Mary got to the office on the Monday, she telephoned Jamal to see if there was any news. He sounded very worried, and said he'd heard nothing from Kim. 'I suspect her mother must be very ill, and Kim's been at the hospital all night. But I don't know which hospital, and I haven't even got her mother's address.'

Mary said she couldn't help. She knew Kim's mother lived in Devon, but didn't have either her address or her new surname.' Jamal sounded a little surprised and said, 'I thought she'd have the same surname as Kim.'

'Oh no.' Mary explained. 'Her mother married again quite a few year's ago. But I haven't seen her since we were eighteen. And I don't know her new married name. But, Jamal, I'm sure Kim will get in touch as soon as she can.'

That assurance was to haunt Mary for a long time.

When David went to the hospital that morning he hadn't been long in his room when Jamal knocked on the door. He looked very worried. 'What's up?' David asked, and beckoned him to a chair.

'It's Kim. She was called away to her sick mother on Saturday, and I haven't heard from her since. She's left a note saying a neighbour had phoned to say her mother was seriously ill in hospital in Somerset, and she was rushing down to see her. She didn't leave an address or say where the hospital was – and I found her mobile phone on the floor, so I can't get in touch with her that way either.'

'Can't you contact her parents?' I asked.

'No. They're divorced. He's in America and her mother's remarried. I don't know her mother's new address. Kim's never talked much about her, though we did plan to go down and see her. I tried to find Kim's address book, but without success.'

'Can't you try Directory Enquiries? Her mother's address should be in that.'

'That's the problem,' said Jamal with a sigh. 'Mary knows her mother but she doesn't know her new surname.'

'Mary?' David asked, a little puzzled.

'Mary Gilburn. She's an old friend of Kim's. I thought she might know her mother's new name. Unfortunately she doesn't know her new address nor her married name. She married again, and lives somewhere in Devon.'

'Well, I'm sure Kim will get in touch as soon as she can. To be honest, I was wondering what had happened to her as she hadn't phoned to say she couldn't come in. Her mother must be very ill. But Kim's so sensitive, I'm sure she'll phone you as soon as she can get to the phone,' he said, 'but please let me know when you get any news.'

Jamal nodded, and went despondently back to his work.

For three days, there was no news of Kim and everyone began to get worried. Then on the Friday Jamal came to David's room looking absolutely shattered.

'Sit down man! Whatever's happened?'

He put his head in his hands, trying to suppress tears, and said, 'Kim's left me. She's called off the marriage.'

'I don't understand,' David said.

'I received a letter from Kim this morning. The post always comes early. She says her mother's illness has made her realise she can't go through with the marriage, and is going to stay on with her mother.'

'I don't believe it! Surely this is just a reaction to her mother's illness?'

'I hope you're right. But the letter seems so positive.'

David didn't know what to say. He was surprised. Kim had been on top of the world when he last spoke to her, and she and Jamal had seemed so happy at their engagement party. He realised that one never knows what goes on in a relationship, but felt something very serious must have happened to make her change her mind about the marriage.

'Can't you go and see her? You must talk to her about it. Something awful must have happened to her to make her change her mind so suddenly.'

'No, there's no address on the letter, so I still don't know where she is, or even where the hospital is. The postmark's too blurred to read.'

'Have you tried her mobile phone?'

'No. She left it behind.' 'I'm so sorry,' David blurted out,' you did tell me, but I didn't remember.'

He didn't know what to say or do to help, so made him a strong cup of coffee and asked if he wanted to go home. He declined, saying it would help him forget for a while if he carried on working.

After he left, David kept thinking about Kim. It was so unlike her to be insensitive in this way. She wasn't a cowardly person, and he would have expected her to confront Jamal directly rather than write a letter. It was out of character. He decided to telephone the admin department and see if Kim had phoned in there about her absence. The reply was negative. They'd all been wondering where she was. He surmised that her mother's illness, together with her decision not to marry Jamal, must be so traumatic she hadn't given any thought to work. He felt desperately sorry for both Kim and Jamal, and wondered if there was anything he could do to help.

-22-
Mary gets involved

David worried all day as did Mary whom Jamal had contacted early on. The whole thing seemed so out of character that he felt he really needed to talk to Kim if he could contact her. Half way through the afternoon he remembered what Jamal had said about Mary and decided to try and get in touch with her, and see if she had any ideas. He got Mary's address from Maud, the Hospice Appeal's secretary, and phoned her home. A lady with a warm voice answered the phone, and told him Mary was at work.

'Oh, I didn't realise she worked. Would you be able to give me her address?'

'Who is it?' she asked protectively.

'It's David Gardner, the hospital administrator. I know Mary through the hospice appeal.'

'Oh, yes, I know about you. You're Stuart Wilson's friend, aren't you? Well, Mary works at Lawrence's, the solicitors in Church Street. I'll give you her number if you like.'

'Thank you, yes. I need to speak to her urgently.'

He didn't know Mary worked in a solicitor's firm and presumed she was a secretary.

He phoned Mary, and could hear the surprise in her voice. He told her he wanted to speak with her about Kim, that Jamal had received a very upsetting letter from Kim, breaking off the engagement, and he wanted to see if she knew how to get in touch with Kim's mother.

'I know,' she said. 'Jamal's absolutely devastated.'

'You know he can't get in touch with her? I wondered whether you knew where her mother lived.'

'I'm afraid not. Her mother married again and I don't know her surname. '

Disappointed, David said, 'Can you think of any reason why she's done this? Jamal assured me they haven't had a quarrel or anything.'

'Well,' she said hesitantly, 'it may have been the visit of Jamal's awful cousins .... But, look, I can't get away from the office just now.' There was silence for a moment, then she said, 'Do you think you could come round to my home this evening so we can talk about it?'

David agreed, and then she added, 'Why not come and have supper with us. I'll phone Celia and tell her to expect you.'

Who's Celia, he asked himself, but refrained from asking. 'Well, thank you,' he said. 'I'd love to. Perhaps, between us, there's something we can do to help.'

Mary gave him her address, and he arranged to get there at seven. He didn't tell Jamal he was going to see Mary. It seemed best not to raise his hopes. But he spent quite a bit of time with him during the rest of the day. He begged David not to say anything to anyone. He couldn't bear people knowing Kim had left him. A Muslim hang-up, David thought, guessing how much Muslims hate losing face.

He felt really worried about Jamal being on his own when he got home, and told him that whether he liked it or not, he was going to ignore his request and tell either Alan Johnson, the oncologist, or Jane Masters, because he felt he needed to have someone with him. Jamal reluctantly agreed, and opted for Jane Masters. David telephoned her straight away and she said she would go over to see him that evening.

David left work early, and set out to find Mary's house. He took a bottle of wine with him, and wondered who it was that Mary had asked to organise a meal for them. Possibly the nanny, he thought.

It took him quite a while to find the house. It was down a narrow side road just outside the village. Had there not been a name board at the side of the road, he would have gone past it. The house was at the end of a long drive. It was quite a large Georgian house and somewhat reminiscent of the house of Samantha's parent's.

Mary opened the door and took him into a beautiful sitting room and introduced him to Celia and Dan. 'These are my son, Jamie's, grandparents,' she said.

He shook hands with Celia who said, 'We spoke on the phone. I'm so sorry to hear about Kim and Jamal. I thought they were a lovely couple and very well suited.'

'You know them then?'

'Oh yes, they've been here several times for lunch. Jamie's very fond of them.' And with that, a two year old rushed into the room and flung himself at his grandfather who was standing by the fire. 'Grandpa! Story! You promised.'

'Yes, young man, but first say hello to our guest, Mr Gardner.'

With that, Jamie turned and gave David a scrutinising look before walking over to him and solemnly holding out his hand, said, 'Hello, Mr Gardner.'

David took his hand, and, equally solemnly, said, 'Hello, Jamie.'

With that Jamie turned to his grandfather, took him by the hand and dragged him out of the room.

'They're great pals,' said Celia, 'and Jamie can twist Dan round his little finger. Dan will be gone quite a while. He's promised him two stories. So let's have a glass of sherry while we wait. After dinner, you and Mary can go up to her flat and see if there's anything you can do to help.'

'Won't you and Dan want to help too?' asked Mary.

'Yes, but perhaps later,' and with that Celia left the room and collected three glasses and a bottle of sherry.

It was a good half hour before Dan returned, and Mary asked him, 'Did Jamie twist your arm to read more than two stories?'

'Yes, I'm afraid he did. Not a problem, but …' he noticed David and said, 'I'm so sorry. When I'm with Jamie I get carried away. I forgot we had a guest.'

'Please don't worry. It's great to have such a close bond with your grandson. I'm afraid, if ever I have children, they won't have a grandfather to spoil them.'

Mary told them his father had recently died, and Celia and Dan shook their heads in sympathy, and they went in to dinner.

At the end of the meal, Celia shooed David and Mary up to Mary's flat and said she would bring up coffee. The flat was on the first floor, and Mary showed him into a very large well-furnished lounge. He couldn't help exclaiming, 'What a lovely room,' and Mary said,' Yes, I'm very lucky. I've been living here since Ben died.' She paused for a moment and then said, 'It's awful about Jamal and Kim. Does Jamal have no idea why Kim's broken off the engagement?'

David shook his head. 'No. He's emphatic that all was well between them. He said he's completely in the dark – and is absolutely shattered. I've arranged for Jane Masters to go over and sit with him this evening.'

'That's a very good idea,' said Mary.' 'It's awful to be alone when something as devastating as this happens,' and her eyes filled with tears.

Looking at her, David realised what an attractive woman she was. She was so quiet and unobtrusive that he'd never really noticed her until the engagement party.

'Did he think that awful visitation from his cousins had anything to do with it?'

'What visitation?' David asked, surprised. 'Jamal hasn't said anything to me about a visitation.'

Mary told him about Jamal's cousins who'd barged into his flat when Kim was there, and tried to persuade him to break off his engagement because she was not a Muslim. 'They said she would bring disgrace to the family. They even called her a whore, which Kim found deeply distressing. She said they were so aggressive she was afraid they would attack Jamal. She fled from the house and came to stay with me.'

David was shocked. He felt this could have been reason enough for Kim to want to break off the engagement.

Mary said Kim had been reassured by Jamal that there was no need to worry about his cousins, that they were just stupid ignorant boys. 'And she and Jamal seemed as happy as ever, despite the visitation. Kim never once said she thought of breaking off the engagement.'

'But perhaps her mother's illness made her re-evaluate the situation,' David suggested.

'Possibly. But I'd like to hear it from Kim herself. It seems so unlike her not to talk to Jamal directly. I can't bear the thought of her going through another heartbreak. 'What really worries me is that Kim hasn't got in touch. We've shared so many upsets over the years. She's not close to her mother, so I would have thought she would at least have told me if she was going to do something as drastic as breaking up with Jamal.'

They sat silent for a while, thinking. Then David said, 'It does seem very odd. As you say, they both seemed so happy at their engagement party and apart from anything else, she hasn't let admin know about her absence which is so unlike her. She's always been very conscientious.'

'I know. I just wish I knew where her mother lived. I know it's somewhere in Devon. Kim doesn't go and see her all that often. She finds her stepfather rather difficult – and her mother was never the easiest of women.'

A thought struck him. 'You've known Kim since childhood, and you know where she lived. Could there be people still living there who might know Kim's mother's address?'

'No, I very much doubt it. Kim's family moved away when we were about eighteen – it's a long time ago.'

Another thought struck him. 'We could try and find out which hospital her mother's in.'

'But how can we do that,' said Mary, 'if we don't know her name?'

'Oh goodness, I'm not thinking straight. You must think me very stupid.'

'Not at all,' said Mary with a smile, 'Everyone tells me you're a very good administrator, and the hospital couldn't do without you.'

David felt quite gratified by the remark, but said he didn't think he deserved the accolade. 'But what about you?' he asked. 'What do you do at Lawrence's?' He expected she would tell him she was a secretary, but instead said, 'I'm studying for my Articles. Things got interrupted when Ben died and I've only recently gone back.'

David didn't like to ask her about Ben, so instead asked where she'd studied, and was surprised to learn she'd been at Oxford at about the same time as he had. He told Mary he'd met his wife at Oxford and when he mentioned her name, she said she'd met her once or twice at the Historical Society. Life, thought David, is full of coincidences.

There didn't seem much more they could say or do about Kim. Celia came up with a tray of coffee, and they started chatting about all manner of things, and quickly discovered they had a lot of interests in common. But David didn't feel he should stay too long, so just before ten he got up to go. They agreed that if either of them thought of any way of finding Kim's mother, they would get in touch.

David said, 'I must just say farewell to your parents before I go. It was so kind of them to give me supper.'

'Oh, they're not my parents. They're Ben's parents.' It wasn't till later that it struck him that it was an odd way to refer to her in-laws

He went downstairs, said farewell to Celia and Dan, thanking them for their hospitality, and left. Although that was not the purpose of the evening, he'd enjoyed himself, and thought what a pleasant family Mary had. He still hadn't asked her about Ben, but felt that could wait for another time.

Another time! He pulled himself up short. What was he thinking about!

-23-
Aunt Judith and the search for Kim's mother

The next day was a Saturday and David was finishing his breakfast and reading the paper when he received an unexpected phone call from Mary. She said she'd been thinking about Kim half the night and had suddenly remembered Kim's Aunt Judith in London. She and Kim had often stayed there when they were children.

'That's wonderful,' he said. 'Have you got her telephone number?'

'No, that's the trouble I always knew her as Aunt Judith. I haven't got her number nor her address, and can't remember her surname – in fact, I'm not sure I ever knew it! But I think I can remember where she lives. I'm thinking of going up to London to try and find her.'

'Isn't that a bit of a wild goose chase?'

'No', replied Mary. 'I know it's just off Kensington High Street and the next door house has a blue plaque on it saying someone famous lived there – I can't remember who. But I'm sure I can find it.'

He thought she was a bit over optimistic, but when he said she had a good visual memory and was confident she could find it, he asked when she was thinking of going.

'This afternoon. Celia and Dan say they'll look after Jamie. There's a train at one fifteen which I thought I'd catch.'

'Would you like me to come with you?'

'Oh yes please. I was hoping you'd offer.'

David liked her directness. He had nothing planned, and said he'd pick her up at about a quarter to one.

They had a pleasant journey to London and found conversation easy. David revised his earlier opinion of Mary and realised she was an intelligent woman. But he still didn't know anything about her husband or how he'd died, and was puzzled about her relationship with Dan and Celia.

They arrived at Waterloo station, and took a taxi to Kensington High Street where they had decided they would start their search. It was a dreary day with a slight drizzle so they walked briskly, looking down all the side roads on either side of the street. David was beginning to feel extremely sceptical about finding the square, let alone the house, when Mary suddenly exclaimed, 'There's the square. I'm sure it's the right one,' and grabbed his hand and pulled him round the square, looking carefully at each house they passed. Then, at the far side of the square, she cried out, 'Look, there it is! That's the house. See the plaque!'

They knocked at the door of the adjacent house and it was opened by an elegant woman in her forties. Kim looked taken aback. 'How long have you lived here?' she blurted out.

The woman stared at Mary and David and looked angry.

'Oh, I'm so sorry,' said Mary, embarrassed. 'It's just that I'm looking for my aunt, and she used to live here.'

'Oh,' said the woman, softening a little. 'I don't think so. I bought this house from a couple of very elderly men who'd lived in this house for ever. I'm afraid you've got the wrong house.'

'I'm so sorry,' said Mary. 'I was sure it was next to a house with a blue plaque.

'Perhaps,' said the woman helpfully, 'it's the other side of the house with the plaque.'

'Good idea,' said David and thanked her for her help.

'Oh dear,' said Mary. 'What an idiot I must seem.'

'No you're not,' he assured her. 'Memory can play some funny tricks. Let's try the house on the other side.'

They walked along the road a little, and mounted the steps of the house two doors along. When they knocked at the door it was opened by a lady who peered at them through thick horn rimmed glasses. Mary didn't seem to recognise her.

'Yes,' she said pleasantly. 'What can I do for you?'

'Aunt Judith?' Mary sounded hesitant. Then, looking at the lady closely, exclaimed, 'Yes, it is Aunt Judith. You remember me? I'm Kim's friend. We used to come and stay with you when we were children.'

'Oh my goodness, yes! I recognise you now. It's my wretched eyesight. I can't focus very quickly. Do come in. I remember you well. She ushered them into the sitting room, and asked 'Where's Kim?'

Mary explained why they'd called, telling her that Kim had been summoned to her mother in hospital but hadn't left the address of the hospital or a telephone number, and that none of them knew Kim's mother's address, or even what her new surname was.

'That's why we've come to see you. We would have phoned first but I'm afraid I've lost your address,' said Mary apologetically.

'I'm amazed you found me,' said Aunt Judith. 'You must have a very good memory.'

'Not for surnames,' said Mary, then continued, 'Yesterday Jamal received a letter from Kim breaking off their engagement.'

'Broken the engagement! I don't believe it,' exclaimed Aunt Judith. 'I spoke to her only last week and she promised to bring Jamal up to see me as soon as they had a day off at the same time.'

'I know,' said David. 'That's why it all seems so strange. They were so happy at their engagement party a few weeks ago, and we all felt they were very well suited. And now she just seems to have disappeared.'

'When did she go off to see her mother?'

'Last Saturday,' said Mary. She and Jamal were coming to us for lunch, but Jamal phoned to say Kim had been called away in a hurry because her mother was very ill in hospital.'

'And she's not been in touch since?'

'No, only this letter calling off the engagement.'

'That's very strange. I gather she'd already moved in with Jamal,' and she smiled a little quizzically. 'I suppose that's something we've got to accept these days.'

'Oh, we're not together,' said Mary quickly, picking up the implication. 'It's just that David works with Kim, and we thought we'd join forces and see if there was anything we could do to help find her.'

A TORTUOUS PATH

David detected a slight lifting of the Aunt Judith's eyebrows as if she didn't quite believe Mary, but said, 'Well, the first thing we must do is phone Jack, Emma's husband.'

'Emma?' David asked.

'Oh. That's Kim's mother. Incidentally, I'm Aunt Judith, Judith Rippendale,' and she held out her hand to him.

'Oh dear, I'm so sorry,' said Mary. 'Where are my manners?'

'Well now, before we do anything, I'm going to make us all a cup of tea. You look frozen. I'm going to pop the fire on, and you just make yourselves comfortable. I won't be long.'

With that, she stood up, switched on an electric fire, which looked very like a real one, and left the room. David looked round the room and saw that it was elegantly and expensively furnished.

'I used to come here as a child with Kim,' said Mary reflectively. 'We loved this house. It was great for playing hide-and-seek. And Aunt Judith used to make us so welcome – she was so much warmer than Kim's own mother. That's why she moved in with her aunt when she came back from Africa.'

After a moment's pause, Mary added, 'I lost touch with Kim for several years, apart from Christmas cards, and we didn't meet up again till after Ben died,' said Mary.

David was about to ask her about Ben, when Aunt Judith came in with a tray laden with cups and saucers, a cake, and a plate of biscuits. She then went out again and came back with another tray with an elegant silver teapot, milk jug, tea strainer and sugar bowl. He was reminded of his visit to Samantha's family, and felt a lump come into his throat.

Aunt Judith poured and insisted they had tea before they did anything further.

When they'd finished, she said, 'Now to that phone call,' and she picked up the phone and dialled a number. After a few moments, she exclaimed, 'Emma! I thought you were in hospital. How are you?'

There was a pause, then Judith said, 'But we thought you were in hospital.'

She listened a moment, then, looking puzzled asked, 'You've never been in hospital?' There was a pause. 'But Kim got a message to say you were very ill, and she rushed down to see you last Saturday.' Another pause!

'Is Kim with you?'

Aunt Judith looked more and more puzzled, 'But you say you haven't seen Kim for months! I don't understand. I think you'd better to speak to David. Who's David?' said Aunt Judith somewhat impatiently, 'He's a colleague of Kim at the hospital. I think you'd better have a word with him. He's standing just beside me.'

With that, she passed the telephone to David. Kim's mother had obviously not taken in what Judith had said, and asked who he was. He told her he worked with Kim, and that she'd received a telephone call from a neighbour to say her mother had been rushed into hospital, seriously ill.

'Where on earth did Kim get that idea from?' said Kim's mother.

'Jamal told us Kim had a phone call.'

'Who's Jamal?' she asked.

David began to feel a little worried. 'Jamal? Why, he's Kim's fiancé.'

'Oh, him! They're not engaged, I hope. I think the whole idea is terrible – marrying a black man. I can't imagine what Kim's thinking about.'

For a moment, David thought the puzzle was solved – that Kim had been down to see her mother, and her mother had talked her out of the engagement. But he was quickly disabused of the idea when, in response to his request to speak to Kim, her mother said, 'Kim isn't here. I haven't seen her for months – ever since we argued about her black man.'

David wanted to shout 'Jamal's an ordinary human being! Not a 'black' man, but he thought better of it. The voice at the other end of the phone didn't sound too friendly.

'Well,' he said, feeling very sorry for Kim if that was her mother's attitude, 'she's just broken off her engagement.'

'Well, that's a relief!' said Emma. 'It would have been a most unsuitable marriage.'

'So she's really not with you?' David asked.

'No,' she said in an irritable voice, 'I said so, didn't I! I expect she's gone off by herself to some haunt or other. She doesn't confide in me ever. Perhaps when she does get in touch, you'll tell her that she might deign to telephone me sometime,' and with that she slammed down the phone.

David felt shocked. Her mother didn't seem to have taken in the fact that, if her daughter wasn't with her, that there was something fishy about the message she'd received from her mother's so-called neighbour.

They all sat looking at each other in silence for a few moments, trying to digest the fact that Kim's mother was not in hospital. David explained to Mary and Aunt Judith what Emma had said about Jamal, and they were both as shocked as he was. Aunt Judith said that Emma had always been a selfish woman. 'That's why Kim spent so much time with me during the holidays. And why, of course, she stayed here when her African romance came to an end.'

Mary said, 'I feel seriously worried. If Kim's not with her mother, and if Kim's mother's not been in hospital, where is she? Where did the message come from, and why?'

A TORTUOUS PATH

They discussed what they should do next. David felt the next step would be to go and see Jamal, and discover if they could elicit any more details from him - things he might have forgotten.

Aunt Judith said, in a very tight voice, 'I think you'll have to go to the police. It doesn't feel right to me. I think there's something seriously wrong.'

Mary and David agreed, and decided to return home straight away and see Jamal that evening. Mary telephoned Celia and Dan and told them what had emerged from their visit. They said they would look after Jamie, and they weren't to worry about the time they got back.

David phoned Waterloo station to find the time of the next train, and Aunt Judith called a taxi. When they opened the front door they saw it had started raining quite heavily. They left, promising to keep Aunt Judith in touch with any information that came to light. The taxi arrived, and Aunt Judith kissed them both warmly, and said she wished she'd met them in happier circumstances.

They got to Waterloo a quarter of an hour before the train was due. The rain and the wind which had increased during the afternoon left Mary shivering, and David put his arm round her and wrapped her close to try and warm her up. He realised it felt good!

They spent the whole journey discussing what they'd learnt from the phone call to Kim's mother. Nothing made any sense, except that both the note and the letter were obviously hoaxes. They couldn't get away from the frightening thought that Kim had been kidnapped. But why?

They kept returning to the visit of Jamal's cousins, and their demand that Jamal should get rid of his 'whore'. Kim told Mary it had been a terrifying visit and she'd felt very threatened. They couldn't get away from the awful possibility that Jamal's cousins had decided to take Kim away to threaten her into giving up Jamal.

They decided to go and see Jamal directly they got back and tell him that the note and the letter he'd received were hoaxes; that he should get in touch with the police immediately. Something was seriously wrong, and the sooner the police got involved the better.

On the train they phoned Jamal and asked if he'd had any news. David told him he was with Mary, and they were going to come and see him directly they got back. At this stage, David decided not to tell him about Kim's mother.

It was about 8 pm when they got back. It was still raining hard and was very slippery. Mary was wearing high heels and nearly fell over, so David had to grab her arm and keep her steady. They decided, in view of the weather, that they'd better have a quick bite to eat before going over to Jamal to break the news. There was a little cafe near the station where they got a bowl of soup and a sandwich, then David drove them to see Jamal.

Neither of them was looking forward to telling him what they'd learnt from Aunt Judith.

-24-
The police contacted

Jamal's flat was on the ground floor of a large Victorian house and he had the use of the only garage. He'd realised how fortunate he was, as he could access the garage from the house. As David and Mary drove up to the house, the rain that had obviously been falling all day glistened in the moonlight and it was obvious no one had been in or out of either the house or the garage for some time.

They rang the bell and Jamal opened the door, looking haggard. David could see Mary was shocked by his appearance because he heard her gasp before taking his hand and saying how sorry she was to hear his news.

Jamal ushered them into the sitting room. It was large and comfortable and one corner of the room by a small window had been set aside as a working area with desk and computer, and several bookcases. The rest of the furniture, sofa, armchairs and occasional tables were grouped round the large French windows which opened on to the garden with a vista of the park and a lake beyond.

'Can I get you something to drink – a coffee or something stronger?' Jamal asked.

They both shook their heads. 'No, thank you. We've been to London and stopped on our way back for a bite to eat and a cup of coffee.'

'Why are you here? Why are you together? Have you any news for me?' asked Jamal, looking agitated.

'I think you'd better sit down Jamal,' said David carefully. 'Mary and I have been to London to see Kim's Aunt Judith. We thought she would have Kim's mother's address. Her aunt phoned Kim's mother's number, expecting to speak to her husband. Instead, Kim's mother herself answered.'

'Then she's out of hospital - and Kim's with her,' said Jamal eagerly.

David shook his head. 'No, I'm afraid she's not. The news isn't good Jamal. Kim's mother has never been in hospital and she hasn't seen Kim for months.'

'Not in hospital …. But why? ….. I don't understand. It doesn't make sense.' As the implications began to sink in, he said, 'Oh my God! You don't think something's happened to Kim – that someone's trying to hurt us?'

'Jamal, it's very worrying. Obviously the message about her mother being in hospital was a hoax. But why? We think you will have to call the police and report her as a missing person. But before we do that, we need to know exactly what happened – when she got the telephone call, when she wrote the letter, in fact, why she wrote the letter.'

Jamal looked dazed. David continued, 'The first thing we need to do is to have a look at the message Kim left for you last Saturday morning.'

'I don't think I've still got it. It was just on a scrap of paper.' He thought for a minute. 'I think I threw it away, expecting Kim to phone when she arrived at the hospital.'

'Are you sure?' asked Mary. 'If you'd kept it, where would you have put it?' she persisted

'Oh. On my desk over there,' and he went across the room and searched through an untidy pile of papers. 'No. Nothing here. I'm sure I threw it away.'

'What about Kim's letter breaking off the engagement? Have you still got that?'

'Yes, I keep reading it again and again to try and understand.' Jamal was on the verge of tears, and Mary said gently, 'Jamal, do you think you would let us see it?'

'Of course. Why didn't I think of it before,' and with that he went to the bedroom and brought back the letter. He handed it to Mary. As she read it she drew in her breath sharply, but handed it to David without saying anything. Though he'd never received a letter from Kim, David knew immediately that it was not a letter Kim would have written. It said:

Dear Jamal

I am with my mother. She is very ill. I have been thinking a lot about marrying you. I think our marriage would be very dubious. We are not from the same religion or culture and I think happiness would not be ours. So I cannot marry you. I think my mother will get better and I will go and live with her. I will send back the marriage ring.

I am sorry but I think it is the best thing for both us. Please don't try to come to me. I hope you will find someone nice to marry.

Kim

David looked at Mary before saying anything. She shook her head slowly, and said, 'This isn't Kim's writing. She's got a very distinctive hand. I know it well. It's never changed over the years.'

'And it's a very odd sort of letter,' David joined in. 'Not the sort of letter Kim would write. It's not even good English. It's almost as though it's been written by a foreigner,

'What do you mean?' said Jamal anxiously. 'Do you think Kim didn't write it?'

'Just look at the handwriting, Jamal. Surely you don't recognise it?' said Mary.

'I don't think I've ever seen her handwriting. We've never had occasion to write to each other. We've always been able to meet up at the hospital.' He hesitated, 'Are you sure it's not from Kim?'

Then a thought struck him, 'If it's not from Kim, that would be wonderful. It would mean she hasn't broken off our engagement after all.'

Mary, who, David was beginning to realise, was very practical, said 'Well, just to make sure. Have you got any of Kim's MA notes here, so we can check whether it's her writing or not.'

'Of course. Why on earth didn't I think of it before? I'll go and get one of her files,' and he disappeared into one of the bedrooms where, he told them, Kim had her own desk and computer. He came back with a file labelled 'My MA notes' and handed it to Mary. One look at the writing confirmed their suspicion - the letter was not in Kim's handwriting.

David was gripped with a terrible cold feeling, and putting his arm round Jamal's shoulder said, 'This letter is definitely not from Kim. Just look at the writing and the wording.'

'Who on earth has written it, then? And why.' They could hear the panic rising in his voice as the possible implications of the letter began to sink in. 'Something's happened to her. She could be in danger, taken hostage. Oh God, where is she?' and he put his head in his hands and wept.

David took control. 'We must accept that there's nothing else *we* can do. We must call the police.'

'Yes, yes, of course,' said Jamal brokenly.

'And one of the things you're going to have to tell them about is the threatening visit of your cousins.'

Jamal looked shocked. 'How did you know about that? ..... Oh, of course, Kim came to stay with Mary didn't she. But that was a family matter – nothing to do with Kim's disappearance.'

Mary looked amazed. 'Are you sure, Jamal? It seems to me they were very threatening,' she said, looking intensely at him.

He shook his head, a bemused look on his face. 'I know they're difficult and extreme in their views, but I'm sure they wouldn't harm Kim.'

Again, Mary asked, 'Are you really sure?'

He pushed the thought away, but when Mary said he must tell the police about their visit when they came, he reluctantly agreed.

While this was going on, David went over to Jamal's desk and picked up the phone. The police didn't respond very positively to his call to begin with, saying they only took note of a missing person when they'd been gone for at least a week. David said that she'd now been gone for eight days, that they'd been told her mother was in hospital when she wasn't, and that they'd had a letter that was certainly a hoax. They reluctantly agreed to come out and see them, and said they would be with them within an hour.

Jamal made coffee while they waited and offered them a whisky, which Mary and David both declined. The police arrived just after eleven o'clock. There were two of them. They were very pleasant, but started by telling them that these cases were fairly commonplace, and that they would have to ask a whole lot of questions to try and get the full picture before they could do anything to help.

Jamal nodded, though a little reluctantly.

First, they probed quite deeply, trying to ascertain whether or not Jamal and Kim had had a serious quarrel. 'Most cases like this follow on from a domestic upset,' said the older policeman. This Jamal vehemently denied.

They asked about the note which said that Kim had gone to see her mother in hospital. Jamal said he'd thrown it away, and the policemen seemed quite concerned that Jamal hadn't kept it.

'It was only on a scrap of paper,' Jamal protested, and the police nodded - though David, who was observing them very intently, thought they were rather sceptical.

They then asked Jamal, 'When did you last see your wife?'

Oh, she's not my wife. We're just engaged. We're going to get married in the summer.'

'Well, when did you last see your fiancée? Does she live here?'

Jamal told them they were living together, and that he'd last seen her on the Friday morning when he'd gone off to the hospital. As far as he knew she'd followed him a couple of hours later. He didn't see her at the hospital that day at all, and as he was on call throughout the night, he hadn't returned home till the following day. He said he'd gone into town after changing - first to Sainsbury's, then to have a hair-cut, and got back about twelve to find Kim's note.

'And it said?' asked the policeman.

'That her mother's neighbour in Somerset had phoned to say her mother was seriously ill in hospital and that she was rushing down to see her.

'Didn't you find it strange that she hadn't telephoned you?'

'No, not at the time. We're not encouraged to take calls in the hospital.'

'Why didn't you telephone her? She must have had her mobile phone with her.'

'That's the point,' said Jamal. 'She' left her phone behind. I found it on the hall floor.'

'A pity. What about the letter breaking off your engagement. You say it's not written by your fiancée? Are you sure?'

Mary, exasperated, said to Jamal, 'Show them the letter and Kim's file with the notes in her handwriting.' The police, examined them, and agreed that they were not in the same hand.

They then questioned Jamal about possible friends Kim might have visited – 'a special friend, perhaps?'

'That's me,' said Mary. 'We go back to childhood. I think she would have told me if she planned to go off anywhere.'

'What about neighbours?'

'Oh, the flat upstairs is empty at the moment. They, Nigel and Penny, have gone to Australia for six months – and I never see the neighbours on either side. I don't know who lives there. The hedges are so high I can't see the houses from here.'

'Well,' said the older man, 'I think that's all we can do tonight. We just need a photograph of your fiancée and details of her car in case she's decided to drive somewhere.

Jamal went to the corner of the room, and brought back a photograph of Kim looking happy and very attractive.'

The police thanked Jamal, said they would circulate the photograph straight away. They promised to do everything they could to find her.

Jamal said anxiously, 'You will let me have the photograph back won't you.'

'Yes, of course. We'll make a copy and then you can have the original back.' With that, the police got up as if to leave, and Mary exclaimed.' But Jamal! You haven't told the police about your cousin's visit!'

The police, picking up immediately that there was information they hadn't been told, sat down again and asked Jamal to explain. Very reluctantly, he told them about his cousins' visit, without giving too many details. Mary immediately stepped in and told them that they had called Kim a whore and said Jamal must get rid of her.

The police took this very seriously, asking Jamal why he hadn't reported it. 'Threatening behaviour like this is very serious,' they said.' You should have told us.

'But they're family,' said Jamal, feebly. 'Very silly boys.'

'Well, you must give us their addresses, and tell me all you know about them.'

Jamal went over to his desk and rummaged around among some papers before coming back with a slip of paper. 'This is the last address I have for them. My other cousins might know if they've moved. I've given you their addresses as well. But I don't really know much about them. I've hardly seen them since they were children.'

'How old are they?'

Oh! I don't really know. About twenty I should think.'

'Hardly silly boys,' observed one of the policemen dryly.

With that, they got up and said, 'Well. We'll be in touch. It's a bad business. We'll do all we can to find your fiancée.'
'I think, Jamal,' said Mary after the police had left, 'you've got to face the fact that, now we know the letter wasn't written by Kim, it puts a whole new slant on her disappearance. I think the first thing you must do is contact your parents and find out more about those cousins of yours. I really think they may be the clue to Kim's disappearance.'

Jamal shook his head vigorously. 'I just don't believe they're involved. My family's not like that.'

'But Kim told me that when you both went up to see your parents, she didn't get a very warm welcome from your father. In fact, she told me he said he hoped you wouldn't go through with the wedding.'

Jamal looked embarrassed, but insisted that, though his father didn't approve of the marriage, he wasn't the sort of person to do anything about it.

By now, it was well past midnight, and Mary looked exhausted. It had been a long and emotional day. Though David didn't like leaving Jamal alone, he wanted to get Mary home as soon as possible so he asked Jamal whether he was working the next day. When he said no, David told him he would come over at noon and take him out to lunch.

With great effort, Jamal seemed to pull himself together, and thanked them for their support. 'How good it is to have such caring friends,' he said emotionally.

They left. David got Mary home just before one o'clock. He gave her a big hug and a kiss, and waited for her to get into the house before returning to the car. Though he was exhausted when he got home, it took him a long time to get to sleep.

Next morning when he woke, he felt so ill he thought at first he had 'flu. He took a couple of aspirins and went back to bed for a while, then dragged himself out of bed and dressed. But he didn't feel well enough to drive over to Jamal's house, nor did he think it fair to take over any bugs so phoned Jamal and said he wouldn't be able to come.

He said, 'Heavens, man! You sound terrible. Get yourself back to bed.' He assured David he would be OK, and promised to phone him if he felt a need to talk.

-25-
The police visit the hospital then interrogate Mary at her home

David still felt groggy on the Monday morning, though realised that whatever it was that had hit him the worst was over, so went in to work as usual. He hadn't been there long when he got a call from reception to say there were two policemen wanting to see him. He told the receptionist to send them up.

It was the same two who had come to Jamal's flat on the Saturday evening. They said it was just routine, but they needed to check on both Jamal and Kim's movements on the Friday and Saturday. David sent them off to the relevant wards, first phoning to warn the staff the police wanted to question them. By this time, news of Kim's absence had filtered round the hospital, and everyone guessed the reason for the police visit.

After well over an hour, the police returned to David's room. They looked grave, and said they needed to speak to Kim's friend, Mary, again. They wanted her address.

David explained that she worked. 'Would it wait till evening when she's home?' he asked.

'Well, yes,' they said a little reluctantly.

He gave them Mary's office and work numbers, and they left. About an hour later, Mary phoned to tell him that the police wanted to see her. She sounded a little worried, and he offered to be with her. She said they were coming at seven o'clock and David said he would grab a bite to eat and then drive over.

When he arrived he was met by Celia who said how anxious they were about the whole situation. 'I suppose they want to see Mary again because she seems to have been the last person to see Kim.'

'Yes, I suspect that's the reason.'

David went up the stairs to Mary's flat. She looked very worried and said, 'I can't think why they want to see me again. I think I told them all I know on Saturday evening.'

'I expect they want to find out if you have any other ideas,' said David, trying to reassure her. He'd hardly finished speaking when the doorbell rang, and a few minutes later, Celia ushered up the two policemen.

The older one looked at Mary and asked, 'Why didn't you tell us Kim was staying in her own flat on the Friday night? I believe you had dinner with her there?'

Mary looked a little bewildered. 'Well, yes.'

The policeman asked again, 'Why didn't you tell us?'

'Well, I'm not quite sure. We were all so upset about what was happening,' she paused, brows furrowed, then said miserably, 'I don't think I was thinking all that clearly.'

'You do realise,' said the older policeman pointing his finger at Mary in an accusing way, 'that you're probably the last person to have seen her before she disappeared?' It was clear that Mary hadn't taken this on board, and was upset by the harshness of the man's tone, but she said quickly, 'Oh I'm so sorry. I didn't think … didn't realise. Of course! She was staying at the flat for the weekend.' Mary looked appalled. 'I can't think why I didn't mention it. You must think me very stupid.'

The older policemen shook his head, and said, in a slightly gentler tone, 'No, these things happen. But perhaps you can tell me why she was staying at the flat. I thought she was living with Dr Khan.'

'Yes, she is … was! But they had an agreement that she would return to her own flat when Jamal had visitors. He only has two bedrooms you see.'

'But I thought you said they were living together. Surely there would be a spare bedroom in the flat for visitors?'

'Yes, of course. There are two bedrooms. But …this is a bit embarrassing,' said Mary with a slight flush, 'Jamal's a Muslim and although he's very westernised, he and Kim thought that neither his parents, nor his friend Al, who are all strict Muslims, would approve of them sleeping together before they were married. So they decided that, whenever any of them came to stay, Kim would return to her own flat.'

'So, who was staying?'

'Well,' she said, 'Al was.'

'That's strange,' said the policeman looking thoughtful. 'Why didn't Jamal mention it?'

Mary and David looked at each other. They didn't quite know what to make of the implications of this question.

'Well, Miss Gilburn, can you think of anything else that might help?'

Mary shook her head miserably, 'No I can't.'

'Well, if you do, will you contact us please.' The older policeman handed her a card, and they took their leave.

Mary was on the verge of tears. 'I just don't know. It gets more complicated by the minute. I'm just not thinking straight. I think I'll make us a cup of coffee.' With that she left the room, and David could hear her crying. He followed her into her kitchen and put his arms round her. 'I don't know what to say,'

She mopped her eyes and said, 'I must pull myself together.' She filled a kettle with water, put it on to boil, and found a couple of cups and saucers and put them on a tray. She then reached for a coffee pot, spooned in fresh coffee, filled a jug with milk, asked if he took sugar, poured the water into the percolator, and carried the tray into the sitting room. It was almost automatic, and he was amazed at so precise an action at a time of such anxiety.

When she'd poured the coffee, he asked her, 'Well, can you think of anything else? Was that really the reason Kim was back in her own flat?'

'Well, yes.' She thought for a moment. 'Well, partly. Kim doesn't really like Al so she likes to get away when he comes.'

'That's surprising. I thought Al was a charming fellow – fun to be with' said David, puzzled

'I know. He does seem charming. And he's a very old friend of Jamal – but Kim said there's something about him she doesn't like. She said she couldn't put her finger on it – but he makes her shiver.'

'But he was at their engagement party!'

'I know. Kim said that Al was Jamal's closest friend, and she couldn't hurt him by saying she didn't like him.'

'But what does Jamal think about Kim escaping back to her own flat when Al visits?'

'Well, I gather that both she and Jamal thought it best to keep Al in ignorance that they were living together.'

'Not easy to hide if someone's living there,' David said dryly.

'No, I suppose not,' agreed Mary. 'But perhaps she had her things hidden away.'

'I wonder why Jamal didn't mention Al's visit to the police?' David mused.

'I know. It's very strange. It's almost as if he's afraid to tell the police about any of his Muslim connections. You remember, he didn't tell the police about the threatening visit of his cousins. Kim was terrified. You'd have thought that Jamal would have wondered whether they were involved in Kim's disappearance. It seems as if he was trying to protect them.'

'Doubly strange when it's his fiancée who's missing! I think if it had been me, I would have wanted to explore every avenue – however unpalatable.'

'I agree,' said Mary. 'I think we should confront him about it.'

David said he would tackle him the next day. After discussing what the weather was doing, Mary put on the ten o'clock news and they sat companionably watching till the weather forecast came on. It wasn't too good. Storms were expected. David got up to go, and said, 'Try not to worry too much, Mary. There may be a very simple explanation to all this.' But he felt in his heart that there was not going to be a good outcome.

She took him down to the hall below where Dan and Celia emerged to find out what the police wanted. He said, 'I'll leave Mary to fill you in,' made his farewells, gave Mary a kiss, and went home, feeling very uneasy about the situation but also, to his surprise, with a warm feeling about the latter part of the evening.

The next day at the hospital, he saw Jamal as soon as he could between his rounds and invited him in for a quick coffee. He asked him why he hadn't told them that Al was staying that weekend.

'Oh, but he wasn't,' said Jamal quickly. 'He was going to come, but he didn't turn up. He said something had cropped up, and he had to go north, but that he would come the following weekend.' Then, looking a little puzzled, said, 'Why are you asking me this?'

David told him the police had been to see Mary.' They've discovered that Kim was staying in her own flat that weekend, and realised that Mary was probably the last person to see Kim before her disappearance.'

'But how do they know about Al?'

'Apparently, when they were checking up on Kim's movements, one of the nurses told the police that Kim was going back to her own flat that weekend because Al was coming to stay – and that Mary was going to have dinner with her.'

'It's impossible to keep anything to oneself,' said Jamal wryly. 'I just assumed, when I saw the note, that when Kim had the phone call, she'd popped back to the flat to collect a few things, left the note and dashed off.'

It seemed a reasonable conjecture, but sadly it didn't bring them any nearer to solving the mystery. Jamal went back to the wards and David carried on with his work.

-26-
Samantha invites David to London and finds Sir Ralph there

David had only seen Samantha once since his father's death and that had been a very unsatisfactory occasion. They'd been invited to a party at the home of her friends who lived in Surrey. David hadn't taken to them, feeling they were part of the 'idle rich' set who talked big but did little for society.

They'd been invited to stay the night but David was consigned to the lounge sofa. He consoled himself with the thought that he would drive Samantha back to her flat in London the next day where he could make love to her, but after breakfast, Samantha announced that she had to go and meet a client at the gallery. When David offered to take her there, she said it had all been arranged, and the client had expressly said he didn't want to see anyone else. So, with a chaste kiss, they parted – and David returned home despondent.

From then on, there had been the occasional phone call, but he sensed that the heady excitement of their earlier contact was rapidly evaporating. Kim's disappearance, the visit to Aunt Judith's, and the contact with the police put Samantha to the back of his mind.

So he was surprised when he received a phone call from Samantha immediately after the police visit to Mary, inviting him up to her flat the following day. She didn't say why, and he didn't ask, but he finished work early, and caught a train to London, arriving at Samantha's flat just after seven. She kissed him warmly, and then said she had a surprise for him. 'My father's come up to London unexpectedly. He's in the sitting room and wants to talk to you.'

He tried not to let Samantha know how unwelcome her news was, and did his best to look as though he was delighted to be meeting her father again. She took him into her sitting room, and Sir Ralph rose to greet him. 'Good to see you again,' he said. 'It's kind of you to come up and see me.'

David endeavoured to smile as he took in the implication of what Sir Ralph had just said. He'd been invited to London to see Sir Ralph, not Samantha! It was a hurtful thought, but he tried to put it aside as he felt intrigued at Sir Ralph's wish to see him.

Samantha left the room, saying she had to see to dinner, and Sir Ralph said, 'I was so sorry to hear about your father. Very sad for you and your sister. I imagine it's been difficult getting back to work again.'

'Yes,' David replied, 'but keeping busy is a help. You don't have time to sit and mope. And I must say I was amazed at how much work had piled up at the hospital while I was away, even though I thought I'd organised sufficient cover during my absence.'

'Yes,' said Sir Ralph. 'But it's difficult to replace the man at the top – even for a short time.'

David felt gratified that he had called him 'the man at the top' as he was really the number two in the hierarchy, but a little bit of vanity prevented him from correcting him.

David felt he should reciprocate by enquiring after his family, and added that he'd enjoyed his weekend with them all. 'Oh, they're all very well – but, like you, very busy.' Then he added, but he felt not very enthusiastically, 'You must come down and see us again sometime.'

Then he changed the subject and said, 'Samantha's been telling me about all the dramas at your hospital, but we must wait till we've eaten before we talk about it.'

David was amazed. He hadn't mentioned Kim's disappearance to Samantha and wondered how one earth Sir Ralph knew about it. Before he could ask, Samantha came in with a decanter of sherry, and poured a glass for each of them.

A TORTUOUS PATH

After they'd sipped their sherry, Samantha took them into her tiny dining room for dinner. It was an excellent meal, though David suspected it came mainly from the local delicatessen.

When they finished eating, Samantha ushered them back to the sitting room, saying she would bring in coffee when she'd cleared the table.

Sir Ralph and David sat down in Samantha's very comfortable chairs, but neither was relaxed. Sir Ralph had made it obvious that there was some serious business to discuss.

'I gather you've had a major drama at the hospital with the disappearance of Kim Anderson,' he said.

'Yes, that's true. It's all seriously worrying. But how did you know about it? I haven't spoken to Samantha about it, and the press haven't been informed yet, have they?'

'No, and we're going to withhold the information for a time – though we can't hold off for long as so many people at the hospital know Kim is missing.'

'Who's 'we'?' David asked.

Sir Ralph looked at David very carefully, then said, 'What I am about to say is confidential. Meeting you as I have, and hearing a lot about you from Samantha, I feel confident I can trust you not to share with anyone what I am about to ask you.'

David felt intrigued, and nodded assent.

'I have connections with the police. I can say no more than that. I know you have a lot of doctors at your hospital from all over the world, including many Muslim doctors.'

David said, rather angrily, 'You're not going to criticise them, I hope. The Health Service couldn't operate without them. Some of them are among our best doctors.'

'Oh yes, I'm sure,' said Sir Ralph. 'No, I have nothing against Muslim doctors, or indeed any foreign doctors. But I'm especially interested in one of them – Dr Jamal Khan. You may remember I asked you a few questions about him when you came down for the weekend?'

David nodded.

'And also about his friend Al Mercer?'

He nodded again.

'I understand Khan has recently got engaged to this missing nurse, Kim Anderson, and that they're living together?'

'Yes, they had an engagement party quite recently and Kim and Jamal seemed very happy. Jamal is absolutely distraught at her disappearance.'

'Was Al Mercer there?'

'Yes, he was the life and soul of the party.'

'Do you know what he does for a living?'

'Well, not exactly. I know he's a businessman and travels all over the world.'

'What's his business?'

'I really don't know. In fact, I don't know a lot about him. I've only met him a few times. But he seems very charming – and certainly very entertaining.'

'How does Dr Khan know him?'

David began to feel uneasy. These were probing questions. 'Well, I gather that he and Jamal were at university together. They became close friends, and I'm told that whenever Al comes to England he stays with Jamal.'

'Does he ever talk about politics?'

'Not that I know of.'

'Do you know where he lives in America – in fact, do you have an address for him?'

'Good heavens, no! I really hardly know him. Why on earth do you think I should have one?'

Sir Ralph nodded reflectively.

'May I ask why you're questioning me like this?' David asked.

'I'm afraid, David, that's something I can't tell you.'

'Oh,' he said bleakly. 'But if you know about Kim's disappearance, do you have any information about what might have happened to her?'

'Sadly, no. But we are very anxious for her safety, and that is why I'm questioning you about Dr Khan and Al Mercer.'

'But Jamal is devoted to Kim. He's absolutely distraught about her disappearance. I've never seen a man look so haggard and ill. In fact, I'm quite worried about him.'

'There's an old saying that appearances can be mistaken.'

'You're not implying that Jamal might be implicated in Kim's disappearance?'

Sir Ralph said nothing.

'You know, if you do, you're really barking up the wrong tree. I've got to know Jamal well during this last year, and though he's rather arrogant, he's a very good doctor, very sincere, very kind, and he's devoted to Kim.'

'Well, I hope you're right. But we would be really grateful if you could let us have any information you can glean about Al Mercer. It's really important, otherwise I wouldn't be asking you.'

'We?' David asked.

'Well, me, then! If you have any information, you can telephone me at this address. Only speak to me, and don't put anything in writing.'

David shook his head. 'All this is beyond me. It sounds a bit like some sort of spy story.'

'I know,' said Sir Ralph. 'I can understand your bewilderment. But please believe this is really important. You would be doing a service to the state if you were able to help us in any way. And I must repeat what I said at the outset. You must not discuss this with anyone!'

With that, as if on cue, Samantha returned with coffee. The conversation reverted to normal pleasantries. David didn't like the idea of prolonging the evening. The conversation with Sir Ralph had been too disturbing, and the fact that Samantha had used him was devastating. So, at about nine-thirty, he took his leave.

On the return journey the shock of Sir Ralph's request with all its implications left him feeling sick, but he could do nothing about it because the journey was very slow and there was no drinks trolley on the train.

His mind was in turmoil. He was angry at what he saw as Samantha's betrayal, and began to think she'd been using him all along. And he just didn't know what to make of Sir Ralph's interest in Jamal and Al. He realised he'd half indicated he was a policeman, but he somehow got the impression that that wasn't quite what his real role was in the affair. He kept thinking back to his visit to Sir Ralph's home and remembered how he'd been half expecting Sir Ralph to quiz him about his intentions towards Samantha, when all the time Sir Ralph had been wanting to find out about Jamal and Al!

He tried to analyse his relationship with Samantha. Several of his friends including Stuart and Kim had warned him 'to be careful.' He thought back to the time he'd been with Samantha in London, and remembered how they had, it seemed by chance, seen Al and Jamal at a distance. Was that coincidence – or was Samantha in on whatever was going on? He felt alternately angry and upset.

He asked himself what he was going to do about Samantha. Was this the parting of the ways? He couldn't bear the thought, but at the same time, he didn't like the idea of being a pawn in whatever game it was she and her father were playing. Then his mind flitted back to the dinner party at the Lambert's house. Again, he asked himself whether there too he'd been manoeuvred into taking Samantha out? He remembered Lady Lambert encouraging him to go and talk to Samantha, and had then asked him directly to look after Samantha. All very curious!

By the time he got home, his head was in a whirl and he drank a large glass of whisky, before tumbling into bed and falling into a deep sleep.

-27-
David muses on visit to Sir Ralph and Samantha

When he woke next morning David had a thundering headache and realised he was going to be very late at the hospital. He thought of phoning in and saying he was ill, but decided that would be foolish. He realised he needed to try and collect his thoughts and decide what he was going to do about Sir Ralph's request, and how it would affect his relationship with Jamal.

If Sir Ralph and others were interested in both Jamal and Al, there must be a reason. But what was it? What had they done or been suspected of doing? And then there was the disappearance of Kim. Was this connected? The questions kept going round and round and he could find no satisfactory answer.

He stumbled into his office at 11 o'clock and managed to keep his head down until just before lunch when Mick popped in as he often did. He exclaimed, 'David, what on earth's up? You look awful. Are you ill?'

He shook his head wearily. 'No, I'm OK. But I've got a big problem to sort out, and I don't quite know what to do about it.'

'Is it about Kim?' Mick asked immediately.

'No, I don't think so. And yet, maybe it is. I just don't know.'

'Have you had any lunch?'

He said 'No,' and realised he was hungry. He looked at Mick's sympathetic face, and said, 'I don't fancy going up to the dining room. Do you think you could bring something down for me?'

'Of course! Straight-away. What would you like?'

Having sorted out the menu, Mick departed – to return not long after with a tray of food and a glass of wine. 'To cheer you up,' said Mick pointing to the wine. 'Jamal was asking where you were.'

'Has he had any news of Kim?' he asked.

'No, and he wants to pop in and see you.'

'Try and shake him off, there's a good fellow. I don't want to see anyone at the moment.'

Mick gave him a surprised look, and departed.

David managed to get away from the hospital without seeing anyone, and spent the evening slumped in an armchair watching television – but he couldn't have told anyone what he'd watched – his mind was still in a whirl - his thoughts moving backwards and forwards from Samantha to Sir Ralph's request.

He kept asking himself whether he'd got it all wrong about Samantha – maybe she wasn't using him at all, and if he got in touch with her all would be as before. But he knew the relationship was over. He knew he should have felt deeply upset, but in fact, at that moment, anger was the prime emotion – anger that he'd been used.

He thought back to their love making, and realised it had all been a bit frenetic – very physical, very exciting, but lacking any tenderness or affection. And again, he felt used.

Then he thought about Jamal – a man he'd come to regard as a friend. He couldn't believe he'd done anything to warrant police interest. He was a very good doctor, very caring, and obviously deeply in love with Kim. Was Kim's disappearance connected with all this? It didn't make any sense. At the same time, he realised Sir Ralph's request had put doubts into his mind about him. Was he mistaken about him? Were there things about him they didn't know? And then he wondered how on earth he was going to relate to him with this suspicion hanging over him. He wondered whether he had the ability to act naturally with him, as though nothing had happened. He dreaded bumping into him in the hospital, and wondered how he was going to avoid an encounter.

Then his thoughts turned to Al Mercer whom he'd only met properly three times – at the hospital at that first charity meeting, at Kim's birthday party and then at their engagement party. He remembered how emphatic Al had been at that first meeting when he denied ever meeting David before, yet David had been absolutely sure it was Al he'd seen in London. He also remembered that Jamal had told them that Al had only just arrived in England from Israel. It was all very puzzling.

-28-
Second visit of police to Jamal

The next day he went to the hospital at his usual time, and Jamal popped in at about eleven. David steeled himself to act normally. 'Have you had any news of Kim?'

'No, nothing. The police haven't been back to me at all, and I can't get any information out of them when I've phoned the police station.' His miserable and haggard face stirred David to pity and he found it difficult to believe Jamal had done anything wrong

'I've got a problem,' said Jamal. 'There's supposed to be a meeting of the Appeal Committee tomorrow night, and I don't think I can go through with it.'

'Do you want to cancel it?'

'I'd like to, but there are some rather urgent matters outstanding – and it's a bit late in the day to contact everyone. I was wondering whether you'd consider taking over the meeting for me.'

David was taken aback but realised it would be sensible to carry on as before, so agreed.

'If you could come over to my flat this evening I could give you the paperwork and go through all the important things we need to discuss.'

David agreed, but declined his offer of supper. At this juncture he didn't feel happy at the idea of spending an evening with him, and hoped he would be able to get away as soon as the business was done.

David arrived at Jamal's flat just after six, and Jamal brought out the papers and letters that needed to be dealt with the next evening. He told David he ought to try and speak to Maud, the Appeal's secretary, before the meeting to warn her that he wouldn't be there.

They'd just about finished sorting out what was needed at the Committee meeting when the doorbell rang, and they found two policemen, not the same ones as on the previous occasion, standing on the doorstep. Jamal invited them in and asked eagerly, 'Have you news?'

They shook their heads, and it became immediately obvious that the helpful and friendly tone of the previous visits had markedly changed. David realised that one of the officers was more senior than either of the policemen the previous evening, and this time their questioning seemed to be hostile.

They first asked about Jamal's movements on the Friday and asked whether anyone could corroborate his statement. When he sharply replied 'of course,' they said, 'but you could easily have slipped home for a little while during that time – your flat is very near the hospital.'

'Not possible. I was working through the night.'

'Can you prove that?'

'Of course! Why should you doubt my word?'

The policemen said nothing, but looked carefully at Jamal.

David watched intently, feeling both anxious and confused. He wanted to say, 'But Kim was in her own flat. Why would he want to go home?'

As if to mirror his thoughts, the senior of the police asked, 'Then, did you go to Kim's flat?'

'I've told you,' said Jamal irritably, 'I was in the hospital all night.'

'What were you doing?'

Jamal then gave, somewhat reluctantly, a detailed account of his night's work, and the police seemed to be satisfied.

They then asked if he had a key to Kim's flat. He said 'no.'

'Isn't that rather odd, when you were living together?' said the younger policeman.

'No, not really. I don't think we'd got around to thinking about it. We haven't been together all that long and Kim hasn't had occasion to go back to her flat that often.'

'Why did she go back that weekend?'

'Well, her MA exam is coming up soon and she wanted to do some work.'

'Why couldn't she have done it here?'

'Because I was expecting a visitor and she thought it would be quieter in her own flat.'

'Who was the visitor?'

Jamal seemed a little reluctant to answer that, but said, 'My friend Al Mercer.'

'Why was he coming?'

'I told you. He didn't come after all.'

'Well, why was he going to come?'

'He always stays with me when he's in England.'

'Why does he come to England? What does he do?'

'He's a businessman.'

'That's not a very helpful reply,' barked the senior man. 'I thought you said you'd been friends for years.'

'I think you're putting words into my mouth,' said Jamal. 'I don't recall telling you anything about Al.'

'Well, is he an old friend?'

'Yes, I met him at university in the States.'

'So what's his business?'

'I really don't know,' said Jamal angrily. 'And what has all this to do with Kim? You come here, and you've nothing to tell me – and yet you're questioning me about things that are totally irrelevant.'

'Ok, OK! Then let's talk about something else. You say you haven't got a key to Kim's flat. Do you know where she kept it? I presume she had a spare key?'

Jamal shook his head. 'I really don't know. I wouldn't know where to look for it.'

'Then we must help you!' Both policemen got up from their seats and asked Jamal to show them the rest of the flat. David could see that Jamal was reluctant, but nodded to him to agree as he didn't think it would be a good idea to antagonise them.

The police proceeded to search the house – looking in drawers, cupboards, on hooks in the kitchen. David could see Jamal getting more and more angry, and wondered whether he would ask them if they had a search warrant. But he suspected Jamal was hoping they might turn up something. After about half an hour searching through the flat, they left, saying they would need to get into Kim's flat to see if she'd left any clues that would help them in their search for her. They warned Jamal they might have to break in, and Jamal nodded agreement.

When they left, Jamal begged David to stay, and he didn't have the heart to leave him. He poured them both a strong glass of whisky, and after they'd chewed over the police interrogation, he persuaded him, as it was getting late, to join him for some supper. He produced a typical English fry-up – bacon, eggs, mushrooms and baked beans – which confirmed to David that Jamal was not what one might call 'a practising Muslim.'

David left as soon as he could – once again his mind going round and round the whole mystifying situation.

He spent a miserable weekend. He'd nothing planned, and the weather was so unpleasant he didn't fancy his usual Saturday walk. He felt a great desire to confide in someone and discuss his conversation with Sir Ralph. He knew he'd been asked to keep the conversation confidential, but he convinced himself that he'd only tacitly agreed. He hadn't signed anything!

Like many others living alone, he found Saturdays the worst day of the week. After brooding about the police visit for most of the morning, he decided he would talk to his friend Stuart who'd seen him through all his bad times with Joanna. He telephoned to see if he could pop in and see him, but the phone was answered by Stuart's son, Adam, who said his parents were away on holiday, celebrating their Silver Wedding anniversary. This reminded him to check the invitation he'd received to their Silver Wedding party, and realised it was the following weekend. It gave him an excuse to get out of the house to go shopping to buy a gift for them.

He'd no idea what to get them, but saw a very beautiful photograph album, and knowing Stuart's son Adam was a keen photographer, was certain a lot of photographs would be taken at the party. He decided this would be an appropriate present.

Leaving the shop he noticed that the local cinema had a showing of *The English Patient*. He'd seen it before, but such was his depressed state, he decided it would pass the time to see it again. Afterwards, he thought ruefully that though he'd enjoyed seeing the film the second time round, it was not exactly the sort of film to lift his spirits!

Saturday disposed of he still had Sunday to get through. He usually tried to organise something – most often a game of golf in the morning, ending up in the local for a drink, and usually staying on for a pub lunch rather than cooking for himself. But the weather was still awful, with unseasonal thunder storms, so golf was out of the question.

Knowing that Stuart would not be there, he decided to stay at home – but then felt sorry for himself. He envied those who had a Christian faith and spent Sunday mornings in church. Thinking about it, he realised that quite a few of his friends were church goers – Christians he supposed he should call them – as well as a number of the people who had volunteered to help with the Hospice Appeal.

He passed much of the day reading the Sunday papers – and getting annoyed with them as he usually did. He watched some sport on the television, got himself supper, and then spent the evening in front of the television, not really taking on board what he was watching because he couldn't get out of his head the events of the past weeks – Kim's disappearance, the unsettling conversation with Sir Ralph, the end of his relationship with Samantha, and the visit of the police.

Trying to analyse the essence of a good relationship he thought about the couples he knew – his sister and James, very happy still after twenty years of marriage, Stuart and Susan about to celebrate their Silver Wedding Anniversary, Celia and Dan, whom he was beginning to get to know, who seemed devoted to each other and happy, despite the tragedy in their lives. Then he remembered Jane Masters and her vicar husband – again, they had what seemed a good relationship. It struck him that one of the things these couples all enjoyed was friendship, mutual interests and trust – something that had definitely been lacking in his relationship with both Joanna and Samantha. Unable to reach any sensible conclusions to his self-analysis, he went to bed.

-29-
David chairs Appeal Committee Meeting

The unsatisfactory meeting with the police followed by a weekend without seeing anyone left David feeling very depressed, and when Monday morning came he was more than a little reluctant to go to work. But he knew there was a pile of work waiting for him, and one of the first things he needed to do was speak to Maud, the Appeal's secretary.

It struck him as ironic that he, who had only joined the Appeal committee at the behest of the Chairman of the Health Authority to 'spy out the land', now found himself acting in the role of Chairman

He asked Maud to pop into his office at lunchtime. Maud was a mousy little woman, but greatly devoted to Jamal. When she came in, he told her that Jamal would not be able to be at the meeting that night as he had an important meeting to go to. Maud's face fell. 'Poor Dr Khan. He's had such a worry with that Kim disappearing without telling anyone. I never did think they were suited,' she said, almost venomously.

'Well, Maud, Dr Khan asked me to say nothing about Kim's disappearance at the meeting tonight. I know lots of people at the hospital already know, so I'm going to speak to Tracy Pilcher later on. But, as far as

I'm aware, no one outside the hospital knows yet, and it's best for Dr Khan if we don't talk about it,' David said in as soothing a voice as possible, though feeling very angry at her comments about Kim.

'Oh yes. We don't want to do anything to hurt Dr Khan. Would you like me to talk to Tracy?'

David accepted the offer gratefully, telling her it would be a tremendous help as he had a very busy day ahead of him.

Maud seemed pleased to be given such an 'important' assignment, and left the room with her head held high and a smile on her face. David reflected once again, how strange it was for older women to be so devoted to young men. But then, he asked himself, 'Who am I to be judgemental?'

The rest of the day passed quickly. He didn't relish the idea of spending the evening in a meeting, but realised he had no option.

Most of the Committee were assembled when he arrived at the Church Hall where Jane Master's husband was the vicar. As church halls go, it was quite comfortable and cheerful.

Maud and Tracy had set out a couple of tables and had already warned everyone that Jamal would not be there. David told them that Jamal had asked him to chair the meeting, 'But' he said, 'Jamal has given me all the relevant papers, and Maud has produced an Agenda, so we can proceed'.

Members of the Committee reported on their activities, and all seemed pleased with the amount of monies they were raising. They discussed charitable trusts which Mary had said she would work on. She had already approached a few who said they couldn't help till they were a bit further forward.

This brought them to thinking about where they would want to build the hospice when the money came in. David told them that the Health Authority was still reluctant to get involved with a building. Equally, he said, it would be good to be able to inform it of what was happening elsewhere in the country. Someone needed to take that on board and do some research. No one volunteered to start with, but then Mary said she would 'start the ball rolling'.

Margaret talked about an exciting project she and Alice were involved with. She said a well-known local artist, Gregory Miles, had agreed to help organise an Art Exhibition in the town. He said he would exhibit some of his own pictures, and get together a number of artists in the locality whom he knew.

Margaret said she'd managed to secure the use of the civic hall – and there would be no charge. Gregory Miles had negotiated the loan of art panels from the local art college, but transport had to be organised. 'This is just the beginning,' said Margaret. Then she listed all the things they needed to think about: invitations to the artists; how much commission to charge; arrangements for a Private View; list of guests to invite; posters to be designed and distributed; the media to be alerted; catering arrangements throughout the Exhibition; and a rota of stewards needed for the three days of the Show

David's head reeled as he listened. He hadn't known, 'til Margaret started talking, what putting on such an Exhibition would involve. He began to realise with a sinking heart, what an enormous amount of work was needed to raise the necessary funds for a hospice.

The whole meeting was positive, and David felt the committee was now beginning to work in unison. He hoped Jamal would be pleased when he reported back to him, and that it might cheer him up just a little.

One thing that became apparent during the meeting was that it would not be long before they would need an office and someone to man it. Martin Allardice offered to look into this – to see if anyone in the Borough knew of a spare room somewhere.

Tracey expressed her anxiety about collecting boxes – something Mary had raised at a previous meeting. 'We need to find someone to keep a record of where they are, and collect them in regularly. People tell me there's a lot of collecting box theft going on – people pinching them off pub and shop counters where they can't be tied down.'

Alice, who'd been signing up a number of Friends, said someone needed to take on responsibility for enlisting their help. No volunteers were forthcoming, and David asked Tracey to put it at the top of the next meeting's Agenda.

As Kim had not been able to attend the previous two meetings, people didn't comment on her absence, and David realised the news had not got round too far. A date for the next meeting was agreed and people started leaving. David signalled to Mary not to go as he desperately wanted to have a quiet talk with her. Despite Sir Ralph's injunction not to tell anyone about their conversation, he'd decided that he really needed someone to talk to. It seemed too big a burden to carry alone and he'd made no specific promise to Sir Ralph.

'David, Mary, are you coming across to the pub?' asked Martin.

'Not tonight. I've got lots of work waiting for me at home,' David lied.

'And what about you, Mary?'

'Sorry, I've got to get back to Jamie.' David was pleased she'd recognised his signal.

The caretaker came in, and David said to Mary, 'Let's go to the hotel down the road. It's got a nice bar and I need to talk to you.' They went out to their cars parked just outside when they were accosted by Mark. 'I need to talk to you privately,' he said. 'I see you're not joining the others.'

'What's it about?' David asked, guessing what he wanted to talk about.

'Kim Anderson,' he said.

David thought quickly. He knew that if he was reluctant, Mark would, as a journalist, start asking questions. So he told him that he and Mary were going to the hotel down the road, and invited him to join them.

The hotel was one which David had used on a number of occasions when he needed to entertain someone important. It was quite plush, but had a comfortable little bar which few people went into. When they'd settled themselves down with drinks, Mark said, 'Kim Anderson's disappearance. Several people have told me about it – but my paper has been embargoed from reporting it.' David nodded.

'Do you know why?'

'Not really. I've been told not to talk about it.'

'By whom?' asked Mary quickly.

'That I can't tell you, I'm afraid,' and gave her a warning glance.

'Can you tell us the story?' asked Mark.

'Well, am I right in thinking that, if you've been formally embargoed, you wouldn't publish it, even if you knew the facts?'

'Yes. No paper would dare to ignore an embargo like this.'

'Well, I'll give you an outline,' said David, and explained what had happened. 'When Jamal first got the note, he just thought Kim had gone off to be with her sick mother. But as time went on, and Kim didn't make contact, he began to get very anxious – especially as he didn't know the name of the hospital her mother was supposed to be.

'Difficult,' said Mark.

'But we all began to get worried as Kim hadn't contacted the hospital to explain why she was absent. Then Jamal received a letter, supposedly from Kim, breaking off the engagement. He was devastated.'

'I can imagine', said Mark again. 'Kim's a lovely woman.'

'We all thought it was so out of character that we wanted to get in touch with Kim and find out if she was alright. The problem was we didn't know which hospital Kim's mother was in. We didn't know her mother's surname (she'd married again) nor where she lived. We were at our wits end when Mary got involved. She was at school with Kim and used to spend time with Kim's aunt in London in the holidays. To cut a long story short, we managed to get in touch with the aunt and discovered that Kim's mother had never been in hospital.'

'Wow! Quite a story,' said Mark.

'But that's not all,' said David. 'We then discovered that the letter breaking off the engagement was a hoax. We persuaded Jamal to call in the police – and they are investigating.'

'Why on earth is the story embargoed,' said Mark. 'It would make front page news and would surely help in finding her.'

'I agree,' said Mary. 'Can't something be done about it?'

Mark and David both shook their heads. 'The law's the law,' said Mark.

He looked very grave. 'I don't like the feel of this. From what you tell me, I can't help thinking that something bad has happened to Kim. There's more to this story than just a disappearance. I suppose the police looked into the possibility of a row?'

'Yes. Jamal absolutely denies that they quarrelled. I believe him. He's devastated by her disappearance and is getting more and more worried that something awful has happened to her. And I must say Mary and I share his anxiety.

Mark nodded thoughtfully and got up to go. 'Thanks for putting me in the picture. As soon as the embargo lifts, I'll run the story. I'll need photographs of both Kim and Jamal.'

'The police already have a photograph of Kim.'

'Fine, I'll get it from them when we're allowed to print the story. Thanks for filling me in. I really feel sorry for Jamal. He's a nice fellow, very sincere. I like him,' and with that, he waved them goodbye.

David looked at the clock. It was now past eleven. He rose to his feet and said, 'I must talk to you Mary. It's too late now, but can I come and see you tomorrow?'

Mary looked a little puzzled, but said, 'Of course. Come to supper. I'll get Celia to organise something.'

'Thanks,' he said. 'I'm sorry to bother you, but it's important.'

'No trouble. It'll be good to see you.' She smiled, and he realised, for the first time that she smiled with her eyes, a warm caring smile.

They walked to their cars. As he kissed her goodbye, his spirits lifted a little. He realised that if he was going to confide in Mary about Sir Ralph, he would have to tell her a bit about Samantha. She was sure to ask him how he came to know Sir Ralph. What could he tell her about Samantha? He didn't want to look foolish, and tell her Samantha had conned him into going up to London. But equally, he wanted Mary to know that he was totally surprised by what had happened. His need to share his conversation with Sir Ralph with someone was so urgent that he felt he must put aside any anxieties. He'd thought about who to talk to. Normally, he would have gone to Stuart, but he was away for another week. He'd surprised himself when he'd decided he would make Mary his confidante.

-30-
David visits Mary for dinner and they discuss Sir Ralph and Ben

The next evening, he was welcomed warmly by Dan and Celia who, again, expressed sympathy about the difficulties over Kim's disappearance. After a meal which Celia provided, they retreated to Mary's flat.

David immediately launched into his story. 'Mary, I need to talk to someone about something that happened to me earlier this week. I shouldn't really be talking to anyone at all, but I really need to share with someone…..'

'Is it about Kim?' Mary asked quickly.

'Yes and no. Can I ask you to promise not to say anything to anyone about what I'm going to tell you?'

'Of course. Remember I'm a lawyer!'

'And I'm the last person who should be asking you to promise not to say anything, when I'm about to break my promise.'

'Could you get into trouble if you tell me whatever you want to tell me?'

'Possibly, But I don't think it will come to that.'

He then launched into an account of his conversation with Sir Ralph, telling Mary that he'd been invited up to London by his girlfriend Samantha, expecting a pleasant social evening, only to find that the invitation had really come from her father.

'What did he want to meet you for?'

He told her as much as he could remember about the conversation. 'It seems he – they – are trying to investigate Jamal and his friend Al for something. But he didn't tell me what.'

'So, what does Samantha's father do?' she asked. .

'That's the problem. I just don't know. When I asked him, he was evasive. He sort of hinted at the police, but I think it's rather more than that. He seemed to know a lot about the hospital and what was going on there. And he knew about Kim's disappearance – but as it's not got into the press yet, I don't know how he knew.'

'Could he have got the information from Samantha?'

'No. Samantha and I never talked about my work. And I've seen her only once since my father died – and that was at a party.' Mary looked a little surprised. 'Well,' he said, acknowledging the truth to himself, 'I think the relationship is at an end.'

'Oh, I'm so very sorry,' said Mary sympathetically. 'I won't ask about it – that is, unless you want to talk about it.'

'There's really not much to talk about. I think it's been cooling for some time. But I didn't really want to accept it. I don't think it would ever have worked. We come from very different backgrounds, and I think,' he said, realising it for the first time, 'Samantha's rather a shallow person.'

They sat quietly for a little while, then Mary said, 'This interest in Jamal and Al – what are they supposed to have done? Do you think it's connected to Kim's disappearance?'

'Possibly. But I can't think how. It's all quite mystifying. But I did sense that the police were rather hostile when they came to see Jamal the second time.

'I didn't know they'd been again.'

'Yes, they came and cross-questioned him about his relationship with Kim. They were definitely hostile. They wanted to know all about Al, and they didn't seem to understand why Jamal hadn't got a key to Kim's flat. They insisted on searching the flat for one.'

'Did they have a search warrant?'

'No. I think Jamal was tempted to ask them for one, but decided he'd better try and keep them sweet.'

'Did they find any spare keys?'

'No. So they say they'll have to break into Kim's flat.'

'I wonder they didn't think of it before!'

'So do I. I don't think any of us were thinking straight. We should have thought of it when we first knew the letter was a hoax. Incidentally, have you phoned Aunt Judith?'

'Yes,' said Mary. 'We've had several conversations. She's as worried as we are.'

They sat quietly for a while, then Mary, being practical, asked 'What are you going to do about Samantha's father's request for information? Are you going to give him any?'

'Well, short of asking Jamal directly for Al's address, I haven't any information to give.'

They discussed Jamal at length and both admitted they'd been worried about his relationship with Kim to begin with, but that, as they'd got to know him better, they liked him more and more, and saw him as a friend. They agreed their anxieties for Kim had been allayed, and that Jamal and Kim seemed to be a well-matched couple who were very happy and looking forward to their wedding in the summer. But, despite this, they both had to acknowledge that there were still things that concerned them. They had both been shocked to hear of the threatening visit of Jamal's cousins, and were conscious that Jamal, though he seemed totally westernised, was from a Muslim background.

They then discussed Al. Mary said she'd only met him twice – at the two parties at Kim's flat but hadn't had an opportunity to talk to him. David told her about the odd occasions he'd bumped into him when he was in London with Samantha, and then later at Kew.

When they'd exhausted conversation about Sir Ralph's request and Mary had urged him not to worry about it, David changed the subject and said, 'I really like Celia and Dan. They're so kind, and very interesting to talk to. You're lucky to have such lovely in-laws.'

'They're not really my in-laws,' said Mary quietly.

'But you said they were Jamie's grandparents?'

'Yes, they are. But Ben and I never got married.'

'Oh, I'm *so* sorry. I didn't mean to pry,' David said, embarrassed.

'No, you're not prying. Ben and I were going to get married, but he was killed in an accident the week before the wedding.' Mary spoke in a calm voice, but he could see it was a struggle.

'How terrible,' was all he could bring himself to say. He asked how it had happened and Mary told him, 'I met Ben at Oxford. For both of us it was love at first sight. We shared the same interests and spent all of our spare time together. Ben was doing a doctorate which meant he was at Oxford throughout my three years there.

We planned to get married after I'd completed my degree. I got a First, and was offered articles in a firm of solicitors in Oxford. We were planning that I would start directly we got back from our honeymoon. Ben already had a very nice flat in Oxford so housing was not a problem.

We were going to get married in September in Ben's local church with the reception afterwards at Ben's home.

Everything was organised and the wedding invitations sent out. Two weeks before the wedding Ben and I had planned to spend the weekend with Ben's parents to finalise arrangements. I'd gone down earlier by train, and Ben was motoring down from Oxford in time for dinner.

Seven o'clock came, then eight, then nine, and we began to get very worried. Then there was a knock at the front door. We rushed to greet Ben – but were met instead by two policemen with grave faces to tell us there'd been a serious accident on the motorway – that a lorry had run out of control and into Ben's car. They said they'd managed to get Ben out of the wreckage and rush him to hospital, but cautioned that he was seriously injured and we must expect the worst.

We rushed to the hospital and arrived just in time to see him before he died.'

David sucked in his breath, not knowing what to say, while Mary did her best not to cry. When she recovered her equilibrium, David said, 'How on earth did you cope?'

'Well, the next days were a blur. We had to arrange the funeral. That was difficult enough, but the wedding had to be cancelled and all the guests told of the changed circumstances. By this time the wedding presents and all the paraphernalia of a big wedding were beginning to arrive. Fortunately, Ben's sister–in-law, Felicity, who's very practical, came to stay and took over all the arrangements as neither Celia nor I had the strength to do anything.

'I can't imagine how you kept going,' said David.

'We had over a hundred relatives and friends at the funeral. There were many tributes to Ben and it was comforting to know how well-loved he'd been.'

'So what on earth did you do after the funeral?'

'My immediate future was quickly sorted out. I couldn't face going back to Oxford without Ben, and though some thought me foolish, I decided not to do my articles. The firm was very understanding and said they'd have me back if I changed my mind later.

'Ben's parents insisted I stayed with them. As you can imagine we were all traumatised. Dan became quiet and withdrawn, while Celia rushed around like a mad woman, doing all sorts of things to help her forget. I railed against God and couldn't understand how a loving God could allow such a cruel thing to happen. Our Vicar, Colin Masters and his wife Jane, whom you've met, were wonderfully supportive.'

'Yes, I can believe that. She seems a very caring person.'

'Yes, she is. She's been a great support to all of us.'

'So,' said David, still a little puzzled, 'tell me about Jamie.'

'Well, a few weeks after Ben died I realised I was pregnant. I told Celia and Dan straight away. They greeted the news happily, feeling, like me, that this was a way of holding on to Ben. They insisted I stay on at the Manor and live in the flat where we are now.

'That must have been a great relief for you! So how old is Jamie?'

'He's nearly three.'

'It's funny. Kim has never mentioned you.'

'Well, we hadn't seen each other for several years. I was away at Oxford and Kim was living in London with her Aunt Judith. She was going to come to the wedding – and she did come to the funeral, but there were so many people there I didn't get a chance to talk to her. It wasn't till just before Jamie was born that we got together again.

A few months after Jamie was born we decided to have him christened. We asked Kim to be one of the god-parents. The other was an old friend, Patrick, whom Kim and I knew as teenagers. Though we didn't articulate the feeling, we felt that the christening was the celebration we'd been denied when Ben died.

Soon after the christening Dan persuaded me to take up my career again. He found a firm of solicitors willing to take me on. We found a lovely nanny and I continue to live here in The Manor with Dan and Celia. They adore Jamie and are terribly kind to me, so it's all worked out very well. I enjoy working, and it's great having Kim nearby. She's been a wonderful support and helped me get out of myself by getting me involved with the hospice appeal.'

David was silent for a moment, trying to take in the awful time Mary had been through.

'I realise,' said Mary, 'how very fortunate I've been having such caring people as Dan and Celia to turn to. I don't know how I'd have coped without their help.'

David looked at her, and realised there was a sort of calm about her that he'd not noticed before. At the same time, it struck him that they shared the loss of a partner, though in very different circumstances. His loss was by betrayal – both by Joanna and now by Samantha – whereas Mary's was a loss beyond her control.

It made him think about what they were doing in trying to build a hospice. Here again, they were dealing with loss and bereavement – and he guessed that for both of them, loss was, in part, the motivation behind their involvement.

Mary said, 'But you've been through bereavement recently with the death of your father. I was so sorry to hear about that – and such a terrible illness. So awful to have to watch someone die in that way. I sometimes wonder which is the hardest – to watch someone die slowly, or have someone die without any warning.'

'I know. I've often wondered too. With my father I was grateful to have the opportunity to be with him, and say all the things I wanted to say before he died. The loss you had must have been far more difficult to cope with.'

They were both silent. It was a sort of companionable and soothing silence. Then Mary said she would make them a cup of coffee before they watched the ten o'clock news.

When he got up to go, Mary told him to try not to worry about Sir Ralph. 'If you don't know anything, there's nothing to tell him about. But I wouldn't say anything to Jamal. If there's a problem there, it will emerge. Meanwhile, the real worry is Kim. I get more and more anxious as the days go by. It's nearly a fortnight since she disappeared. I fear the worst.'

'So do I,' David admitted.

Mary took him down to the car. He kissed her goodbye and drove home, feeling much easier in his mind now he'd told Mary about the meeting with Sir Ralph.

The rest of the week passed quietly. Jamal had no further visits from the police, and there was no news of Kim. Mark phoned, asking if there were any developments - obviously keen to publish something, but news about Kim's disappearance was still embargoed. They agreed it would be very helpful, in the search for Kim, if the news of her disappearance could be made public, but they realised that Mark's hands were tied.

-31-
A Silver Wedding Party

Despite his anxiety about Ki, David's spirits were lifted by an invitation to Stuart and Susan's Silver Wedding celebration. He always looked forward to their social occasions. They were excellent hosts and had a circle of friends whom David had got to know well over the years.

When he arrived at the party it was in full swing. Everyone was assembled in the large drawing room where a fire with enormous logs glowed in the inglenook fireplace. The surrounds of the fireplace were of dark oak - beautifully carved with an intricate design of birds and foliage. Most of the beams of the low ceiling were also carved, and small latticed windows were dotted along either side of the room. The deep red velvet curtains, hanging by the widows, had been left open to show the gardens, both front and back, which were floodlit.

Susan, Stuart's wife, had told David that this end of the house was part of the original hall- house with a fire in the centre of the room. The smoke would have drifted up through an opening in the ceiling. The other rooms had been added over the centuries.

The room was furnished with antique furniture Susan had inherited from her father. There was an enormous carved chest, a beautiful mahogany table, some interesting carved chairs, and several ornate cabinets and bookcases against the wall. The oak floor was carpeted with richly patterned rugs in dark reds and blues. Altogether, it was a beautiful warm and welcoming room.

Greeted by both Stuart and Susan, David gave them his present which they opened immediately. They thanked him warmly, saying it would be just the thing for all their Silver Wedding mementos. This, reflected David, was typical of their kindness and sensitivity He'd found so often, when giving someone a present, that they put it aside with a 'thank you' and 'we'll open it later' – thus giving the donor the pleasure of seeing the present opened and appreciated.

It was a black tie occasion, and all the women were wearing expensive outfits, ranging from beautiful satin dresses, to the sequined trouser suits which were all the fashion. Despite the cold, a few even braved bare shoulders – though it made David shiver just looking at them.

He saw a group of people he knew standing near the fire and drifted over and joined them – the local doctor, Peter, and his wife, the hospital's consultant cardiologist, Andrew Johnson and his wife, and Jane Masters and her husband Colin.

Jane and Colin were full of their forthcoming trip to New Zealand to visit their daughter and grandchildren whom they hadn't seen for two years. They said they'd be away for a month, and everyone said, 'Wonderful,' realising how sad it was when children moved so far away from their parents.

They talked a little about the hospice appeal, but neither Jane nor David mentioned the disappearance of Kim. With the arrival of Mark from the local newspaper the conversation turned to the forthcoming Art Show. There was a considerable amount of artistic talent in the area, and they all felt the Show should be financially successful as well as enjoyable. They acknowledged that organising an Art Show required a considerable amount of effort, but felt that Margaret, who had taken on responsibility for it, was just the person to do it. At that moment, she and her husband Edward arrived and joined the little group. David knew that Susan was not over fond of Margaret, but Stuart liked Edward, her husband, so they were always included in their social gatherings. They all congratulated Margaret on what she was doing, and said they hoped it would be a great success.

Noticing Pamela Litchfield standing alone the other side of the room, David drifted over and joined her. 'Where's Martin?' he asked, for by this time, though he didn't like him, he didn't want to lose Pamela as a friend, and so had accepted the fact that they were a couple.

'He's not here,' said Pamela. 'We've split up – that is to say, we are no longer seeing each other.' She didn't look particularly sad as she said this, so he asked her what had happened.

'Well, I've come to the conclusion that he's not a particularly nice person. He's self-opinionated and pompous. I didn't realise it at first, but as I've got to know him better, I've realised he's not for me. In fact, I can understand why his wife left him.'

David couldn't help feeling glad, but said sympathetically, 'Well, I'm so very sorry. It must have been wretched for you. I know what it's like when a relationship comes to an end, but,' he added, 'I must say I'm glad. Knowing you as I do I don't think he would have made you very happy.' Nor, he thought to himself, would Samantha have made me happy.'

Noticing she hadn't got a drink, he took her arm and led her over to the corner where the waitresses had trays of glasses filled with wine and juices.

'There are a lot of people here you know, Pamela. Come and say hello.' They wandered over and re-joined the group he'd been talking to.

There was that happy buzz in the room which is always indicative of a successful party, but there were so many people there that it was some time before David noticed that Celia and Dan were among the guests. Though he'd already discovered that Celia and Dan were friends of Stuart, they'd never actually been at the same social gathering before. They were talking to Stuart, and he went over to greet them.

'How good to see you, David,' said Dan, holding out his hand.

'And you both,' he said, smiling.

'So you know each other?' said Stuart, with a slightly surprised look on his face.

'Yes,' said Celia, 'David's a friend of Mary, and we've met a number of times.'

'Is Mary coming to the party?' David asked.

'Oh yes, of course. But she's settling Jamie down first. The nanny's away and Mary's got a new babysitter. Though she's very nice, Jamie doesn't know her all that well. So Mary's coming on a bit later so she can settle them both down before leaving them alone.'

'That's good,' he said, more enthusiastically than he intended, and saw Stuart giving him a quizzical look.

Almost at that moment, Mary arrived wearing a peacock-blue, tight fitting, satin dress. She looked quite different – very elegant – and he realised it was her hair that was different. Usually shoulder length, this evening she had it coiled up. In the subdued light, it glistened a rich mahogany colour. Getting to know her as he had in recent weeks, he'd discovered she was both kind, sensitive, and very intelligent, but he hadn't thought of her before as particularly attractive. But as she walked in, he realised, for the first time, that she was an elegant and rather beautiful woman.

Without thinking, he greeted her with a kiss, and this caused Stuart's eyebrows to go up even further!

Stuart said, 'We're going to eat now, and I've asked our local madrigal group to sing grace for us.'

The grace was quite beautiful, and David felt pleased when Stuart told them the group was going to entertain them later in the evening.

They all tucked into the buffet which was set out on three separate tables so that no one had to wait too long to be served. He went to introduce Pamela to Mary but remembered they already knew each other as Pamela had been a school friend of Ben. It struck him what a small world it was – with so many people being inter-connected.

During the evening, David noticed Adam, Stuart's son, going round taking lots of informal snapshots. He felt pleased he'd chosen a photo album as a present. When he'd arrived at the party, Susan said to him, 'Do look at our wedding photographs. We've left them out for people to see. Sadly, we've all aged since then, but it's great to have a record of the day.'

David had a look at the album on the table, and realised what a very attractive couple they'd been. But watching them now, although he had to agree with Susan that they had aged a little, it was clear they'd both retained their good looks.

After supper, Adam got up and gave a heart-warming speech, telling them what wonderful caring parents they were – and sharing with them some of the more amusing things that had happened over the years. Then Peter, their doctor, got up and gave an equally warm speech, telling everyone about some of the community activities which both Stuart and Susan had been involved with over the years. He said it would be difficult to find better or more caring friends. Stuart responded, saying how important were long standing friends, and how fortunate they were to have so many of them there. Then he paid tribute to his wife, and said something which brought tears to many eyes, that Susan, as well as being the love of his life, was also his best friend.

Then a cake was brought in with twenty-five candles blazing – quite a feat thought David. The cake had been made by Adam's wife. Champagne was served, a toast given, and then Adam took some formal photographs, posing Stuart and Susan in front of the cake in the same way they'd stood cutting the cake at their wedding twenty-five years before.

Chairs were then magicked into the drawing room and everyone sat down. David found himself sitting next to Mary on one side and Pamela on the other, and enjoyed the sensation of having an attractive woman either side of him. He caught Stuart looking at him with a mischievous glance and winked at him.

Earlier, he'd noticed a harp standing in the corner of the room, and hoped it meant they were in for a harp as well as a madrigal recital. He loved baroque music and was not disappointed.

While the music played, he was conscious of Pamela sitting beside him and realised they shared the same situation - she with her broken relationship with Martin, and he with Samantha. He felt what a pity it was that there was no buzz between them. He'd always been very fond of her, and knew she would have made a very good partner, but that sort of buzz can't be manufactured. As she went to leave, he kissed her goodbye and said he hoped to see her again soon, and added, 'Do get in touch if you need to talk. Let's meet up for lunch sometime.'

As he was about to leave, Celia came over to him, and asked what he was doing the next day. When he replied that he'd nothing planned, she said, 'Why don't you come and join us for lunch.'

Delighted by the invitation, he said he'd love to accept. 'We always have a late lunch on a Sunday because our church service doesn't finish till about twelve-thirty,' she said. 'so we usually sit down about two o'clock. Come over about one o'clock, unless, that is, you'd like to come to church with us.'

'Oh no! No thank you,' he replied, feeling a little uncomfortable, 'Can I come over when you get back from church?'

'Of course,' said Celia, 'we'll look forward to seeing you.' He detected a slight look of disappointment on Celia's face.

As he left, he hugged Susan whom he was very fond of, and said what a splendid party it had been, and how happy he was that they had such a happy marriage. 'I'm very envious,' he told them.

'One day, it'll be your turn, I'm quite sure,' said Susan. 'It's just a question of finding the right person – someone who's a good friend as well as a lover.

Wise words, he thought. That was the conclusion he'd been coming to the previous weekend when he was so down in the dumps.

The next day was one of the most pleasant Sundays he'd spent in a long time. Celia had cooked a pheasant casserole. 'It's difficult to have a conventional Sunday lunch when we get back so late from church,' Celia explained. 'But with a casserole, I can prepare it beforehand,'

Jamie greeted David warmly, holding out his arms for a kiss. He asked him what he'd been doing all morning, and he said, 'We've been to church. Would you like to see what I did?' He proudly produced a printed picture of David and Goliath, which he'd coloured in very carefully in greens and reds.

'We have an excellent little Sunday school,' Celia explained. 'The lady who runs it is wonderful with children, and Jamie enjoys it. He stays with us for the first part of the service, then all the children go off to the church hall which is just at the side of the church. Then they all come back for a blessing at the Communion. It works very well.'

David nodded, wondering what it was that kept people faithful to the church.

They sat down to lunch, and stayed talking for a long time until Jamie got bored, and said he wanted to go and feed the ducks. The sun was shining, and a walk seemed very tempting.

'We've got ducks on the lake at the end of the garden,' said Mary. 'Would you like to come with us?' David agreed, but Celia and Dan declined, saying they'd rather stay and read the papers. Mary said to Jamie,

'It'll be very muddy after all that rain so you'd better put on your red boots.'

Boots safely on, Jamie displayed them proudly to David. 'Do you like my new boots? We got them yesterday.'

David examined them carefully and said, 'Well I think they're splendid.'

Mary smiled.

They set off for the lake. It was the first time David had seen the garden as it had been night time on his previous visits. The garden was large, more like parkland, with a lake way into the distance, and he realised what an unassuming couple Celia and Dan were – never giving any hint of their wealth or status in life.

Jamie skipped ahead excitedly - several pieces of bread clutched in his hand.

'He's very lucky to have such a lovely place to live,' David remarked, then felt he was, perhaps, being tactless.

'Yes, I thank God daily for Dan and Celia, and the chance to live here.'

Curious, he asked, 'Are your own parents still alive?'

'Oh yes. They live in the south. They're quite a bit older than Celia and Dan, and somewhat frailer. They're both retired so we see a lot of them. They come up and stay for a couple of days most months.'

'With you?' I asked.

'No. With Celia and Dan. They've become very good friends since Ben died, and Jamie loves seeing them. It's great because there's absolutely no jealousy between the grandparents. I rather fear,' said Mary wryly, 'that Jamie's a little spoilt.'

'But he's a delightful child,' David said quickly. 'So friendly and affectionate.'

'Not to everyone. He's taken to you in a big way, so that's lovely. But he can be very suspicious of new people.'

He felt gratified by Mary's remark. He'd had very little experience of small children with his sister's children growing up so far away in Scotland. But he also had to acknowledge that, underlying his gratification, was the thought that Jamie's approval boded well for the future – though at this stage he hadn't defined what that future might be.

The lake was much larger than he'd expected with ducks of various colours and sizes, as well as swans and moorhens. A number of them came swimming over as soon as they saw Jamie who got very excited and held out pieces of bread to them

The ducks fed, Jamie said, 'Mummy, can we play pooh sticks now?'

Pooh sticks! David's mind went whizzing back to his childhood when his father had taken him and his sister to a stately home where there were little bridges, and had introduced them to the game. Always a rather quiet man, on this occasion his father behaved like an excited school boy and became very competitive as they threw in twigs and watched them move slowly under the bridge to the other side.

'This takes me back,' he said. 'I used to play pooh sticks when we went on holiday to the Lake District. We all competed vigorously – my mother and sister as well as my father – and it was my mother who usually won!'

'Is your mother still alive?'

No,' he replied. 'She died before my father – in a hospice. She was a doctor too.'

''You were very fond of your father?' said Mary, a question in her voice.

'Yes, I was. I miss him a lot - though I didn't see him as often as I should have.'

Mary asked why he'd said that, and when he explained that it was because he lived so far away, Mary said, 'But that's not all, is it?'

Then he found himself telling her all about his feeling of loss, of sadness at the time wasted when he could have got to know him more, of the awfulness of his illness, and the courageous way he dealt with it. He realised that he'd bottled up these feelings ever since his father died, and hadn't been able to really share them with anyone apart from Kim.

'He sounds as though he was a very special man,' said Mary, squeezing his arm. 'You must never stop talking about him. I always found that helped when Ben died.' She gave him a warm smile, and they walked slowly back to the house Jamie dancing cheerfully in front of them.

Back in the house they were greeted by a blazing fire, tea and cakes. David made to leave after tea, knowing that that was the polite time to depart, but Celia said, 'Oh please. Don't go just yet. Jamie will be disappointed if you don't help bath him.'

He ended up staying the evening – helping first with Jamie's tea and then his bath, which, according to Mary, took longer than usual because Jamie saw him as a captive audience, and begged him to help him play with his ducks and tiny submarine.

Dressed in his pyjamas, Jamie then insisted David saw his bedroom, and introduced him to all his teddies, some fifteen of them, arrayed along the side of his bed.

Then Mary said, 'It's time to go to sleep now. Say goodnight to David.' With that, Jamie held up his face for a goodnight kiss. He felt overcome with emotion, remembering that the last time he'd kissed a small child was just after his father's death. Memories of his father came flooding back, and he felt near to tears. Mary looked puzzled. 'I'll explain later,' he said.

They spent the rest of the evening in Mary's flat upstairs. She produced a few sandwiches for supper, and while they were eating them, she asked him whether Jamie had upset him.

'Oh no!' he exclaimed. 'It was just that Jamie's hug made me think of my sister's children – and that led me to thinking about my father again. Silly, isn't it?'

'Of course not. It's these little things that often trigger memories. Seeing other toddlers with their dads, or Dan making some amusing remark can bring Ben to life again. But it's funny, you know,' she said musing, 'Now, after nearly three years, I often find it difficult to bring Ben's face to mind. I can still hear his voice, feel his presence, but I have to look at a photograph to see his actual face.' David nodded agreement.

They spent the rest of the evening watching a little television, and talking companionably, until ten when he thought he should be on his way. Mary escorted him down, and he popped his head round the door of Celia and Dan's drawing room and thanked them for a lovely day.

Mary walked with him to the car and he kissed her goodbye. As he drove off David realised they'd managed to avoid talking about Kim and Jamal. He felt more relaxed and content than he could remember in a long time, while Mary asked herself why, despite the anxiety about Kim, she'd enjoyed the day so muc

-32-
Jamal arrested

David returned to work on the Monday feeling refreshed after his weekend, but realised all the anxiety would come flooding back the minute he got to the hospital. It was now just over a month since Kim's disappearance. He'd watched Jamal getting more and more haggard. He would occasionally pop into David's office, but this happened less frequently.

Sir Ralph's request had, subtly, changed David's feelings about Jamal. He was angry with himself but couldn't help wondering whether Jamal really had done something wrong. He kept thinking about his relationship with Al and his evasiveness when he'd mentioned seeing Al in London and in the city by the mosque. Could there really be a problem? He liked to think not, but Sir Ralph had instilled that little worm of doubt which he couldn't rid his mind of altogether.

It was on the Tuesday morning when the bombshell struck. David arrived at his room in the hospital to find Mick standing outside, holding newspapers in his hand, waiting for him to arrive. He looked grief stricken. 'They've found Kim's car,' he said. 'It's in today's papers.'

David ushered Mick into the room and read the two reports – one in the local paper and the other in the *Mail*. The *Mail* had just a brief paragraph – 'Missing nurse's car found abandoned in the New Forest. Kim Anderson, a nurse at St Saviour's Hospital in Windsham, disappeared from home a month ago, ostensibly to visit her mother in hospital. She hasn't been heard of since.'

The local paper carried a much fuller report; with a copy of the photograph Jamal had given the police. Mark had clearly recalled all the information David and Mary had given him the week before - the note saying Kim's mother was in hospital when she wasn't, and the search for the address of Kim's mother, as well as the search for Kim herself. The report talked about Kim's work at the hospital where she was a much loved and respected nurse. It mentioned her engagement to Jamal, one of the hospital doctors, and said he was the person instrumental in starting an appeal for a hospice in the town. The paper urged locals to give the police any information which they thought might help in the search for Kim.

David felt a deep foreboding when he read the reports, but scarcely had time to digest the implications of the discovery of the car, when there was a knock at the door and two policemen entered.

He waved Mick away, and one of them said, 'As this is a hospital we thought you ought to know that this morning we have arrested one of your doctors – Dr Jamal Khan. He will not be coming to work today.'

David was stunned. 'Why on earth .... What's he supposed to have done?'

'I'm afraid we can't tell you that until he has either been charged or released.'

'Is it to do with the discovery of Nurse Anderson's car? I've just read about it in the paper.'

'Yes. It's connected. But that's all we can tell you.' With that, the two policemen turned and left the room.

It took David quite a while to digest the information and take on board that there were things he would have to do. The first thing, of course, was to inform the wards where Jamal was supposed to be working, that he wouldn't be coming in. Then he had to find cover for him – not easy as most of the doctors he might have contacted were already on duty, or had been on call all night. But after several phone calls, he found someone willing to step in. He told him that Jamal had been arrested, but suggested he kept the news to himself, although he realised the news would soon be round the hospital as people would have seen the police arrive.

David then called Mick back. He thought it was only fair to tell him what had happened, and knew he would be the soul of discretion. Mick was distressed when David told him Jamal had been arrested, and immediately realised that this was somehow connected with Kim's disappearance. 'I don't like it,' he said. 'I just feel so afraid something bad has happened to her.' He went away, nearly in tears.

David decided Mary should know straight away, but when he phoned her at her office, she told him she knew already. She said that when Jamal was asked if he wanted a solicitor present, he had immediately asked for Mary.

'I'm not yet qualified, and criminal cases are not going to be my field of work, so I told Jamal he would be better served by one of my colleagues, Julian, who specialises in criminal work. He already knows about Kim's disappearance as I've often talked about it but I've filled him in with a little of Jamal's background. I've told him we all think he's a good man, and would find it difficult to believe Jamal was involved in any criminal activity. Julian's not back yet, so I don't know anything more.'

'Have you heard Kim's car has been found?'

David heard her gasp. 'No.'

He told her the little he knew from the newspaper report.

There was a long silence. Then Mary said, 'That's very bad news. If Kim's car's been found, where's Kim? I have a sinking feeling Kim's been harmed – or even,' she added, near to tears, 'that she's dead.'

David agreed with her, but said, 'We mustn't give up hope yet.'

Mid-morning, Maureen, the sister on the ward where Jamal was working, came down to see David. The news had already got round the hospital that Kim's car had been found, that the police had been, and that Jamal had not come in. Maureen said that people were wondering whether Kim had been found. She was shocked when David told her that Jamal had been arrested. Maureen was one of Kim's friends and had been both at Kim's birthday party, and then at Jamal and Kim's engagement party. Like David, she had come to both like and respect Jamal, and been very happy for them both.

David said he would tell her when he knew anything more.

The news quickly raced round the hospital, which, being fairly small, was like a large family. Mick kept him in touch with people's reactions. Most expressed their disbelief that Jamal had done anything wrong, but a few muttered that they'd always thought there was something fishy about him. Others were neutral – especially those doctors who had found him arrogant. Jamal's arrest was the main topic of conversation throughout the day.

David had a large pile of work to get through, but found it hard to concentrate, not knowing what was going on. At about five o'clock, he had a phone call from Mary. She said she had news for him, but didn't want to talk over the phone. Could he call at her office, so that he could meet with Julian as well?

David went over straight away, pleased to be doing something, though he realised, from Mary's tone of voice, that the news was not good.

When he got to Mary's office he was introduced to Julian whom he hadn't met before. He was a middle aged man with, quite clearly, considerable experience of the law. He took them into his office and sat them down.

'I'm afraid the news isn't good. Jamal is still being kept at the police station.'

'What's he charged with?'

'He's not charged with anything yet. The police have forty-eight hours to decide whether or not to charge him. But I'm afraid it's very serious. He's being investigated for having bomb making equipment in his house.'

David was astounded. It was absolutely the last thing he would have imagined Jamal being involved with. 'But why, how ...?' words failed him.

'Apparently, the search was triggered by the discovery of Kim's car. There were traces of chemicals - hydrogen peroxide - in it.'

'But Kim couldn't possibly have been involved,' David exclaimed

'No, of course not. But the police believe Kim has been taken away against her will, and the abductor has used Kim's own car. They think the abductor had traces of chemicals on his clothes because traces of chemicals were found on the driver's seat. The discovery of Kim's car led to Jamal's flat being searched. There they found chemicals, and arrested him.'

'What does Jamal say about this?'

'He absolutely denies all knowledge of any chemicals. He asked the police questioning him where they'd been found,' said Julian.

'Did they tell him?'

'No. They wouldn't tell him anything – except, of course, that they'd found Kim's car.'

'He must be distraught at hearing that,' said Mary.

'Yes, he was in a terrible state. He didn't know the car had been found. He was arrested quite early, about six o'clock, and hadn't seen any newspapers. The news came as a terrible shock. I think it came home to him that Kim is either in great danger or even dead. I thought he was going to collapse completely.'

'What do you think's likely to be the charge?' David asked.

'Conspiracy to terrorism, I fear,' said Julian.

'But that's impossible. Jamal's no terrorist,' exclaimed Mary.

'No, I can't believe he is,' David said, though he couldn't help thinking about Sir Ralph's request for information about Al. 'What happens now?'

'I think,' said Julian, 'that in the circumstances, bail is almost certain to be refused.'

'Can we see him?'

'No. I'm afraid only his legal adviser can see him until he's charged or released.'

This was not something David knew, and felt dismayed that they wouldn't be able to question Jamal themselves. If there were chemicals in the flat, it was difficult to believe that he didn't know about them. And if he didn't know, how did they come to be there?

'What happens now?' he asked Julian.

'Well, as I said, he can be held at the police station for forty-eight hours while they question him. Then he either has to be charged or released. I rather fear he will be charged with conspiracy to commit an act of terrorism and will then be remanded in custody.'

'Will we be able to see him then?'

'Yes, a person is deemed innocent until proved guilty. So Jamal will be able to receive a limited number of visitors, and receive and write letters (though they will be vetted). But until the police have decided to charge him, only his solicitor, that is me, can see him.'

'Oh God, it's a nightmare. First Kim goes missing, now this!' Mary looked as though she was going to collapse.

'I don't think there's anything more that can be done at the moment,' said Julian. 'I think you'd best be getting home, Mary.'

She nodded, then turned to David and said, 'I can't bear it. Will you come back with me, please, so we can talk to Celia and Dan about it all? And we'll need to phone Aunt Judith – that is, if she hasn't phoned home already.'

David agreed readily – feeling both pleased that Mary had asked for his support, and glad not to have to go back to an empty house for the evening. Mary made a quick call to Celia, and then David followed her back to her home.

Celia greeted them with the news that, as Mary had suspected, Aunt Judith had phoned. Celia ushered them into the drawing room where, despite the fact it was June, a blazing fire was glowing in the hearth. Dan was sitting in an armchair by the fire with Jamie on his lap, reading him a story. When he saw them Jamie jumped up, ran to Mary and hugged her, saying 'Grandpa's reading me a Rupert story. He said I could stay up late till you came home.'

'Isn't that kind of grandpa,' said Mary.' Do you know, Rupert stories were my favourites when I was young.'

'And mine too,' thought David. 'What a cosy scene.'

Jamie jumped back onto Dan's lap and Dan finished reading the story. Meanwhile, Celia came in with two large glasses of sherry. 'You both need this after the day you've had,' she said. 'Sit down and make yourselves comfortable while I get the dinner.'

The story finished, Jamie moved across and snuggled down on Mary's lap. She asked him what he'd been doing all day, and he described the day from his visit to the nursery school with the nanny, a trip to the park, and the friend who'd come to tea. It struck David what a bright little boy he was – so articulate for a three year old - perhaps the result of living with three adults. But as he'd never spent much time with toddlers, other than on the brief visits to his sister and family, he realised he was not in a position to assess how bright he really was.

'I've built an enormous castle with my new bricks. Come and see, Mummy – and you too, Uncle David' he said.

'Don't bother Uncle David now. He's very tired.'

'Not at all,' he said, jumping to his feet. 'I'd love to see your castle.'

'Say goodnight to grandpa, Jamie, then we'll go and see your castle - and then you must go to bed,'

Taking Jamie's hand, Mary led them up to their flat where they inspected the castle, Jamie proudly explaining where the entrance was, where the soldiers stood, and how the portcullis worked. Mary said, 'It's bedtime now. Say goodnight to David.'

Jamie held out his arms for a goodnight kiss, and once again, David's heart lurched.

When he came down to the drawing room, Dan looked up from the newspaper he was reading, and said, 'This is a very bad business. I don't like the feel of it at all. But I think Mary should phone Aunt Judith directly she comes down. She sounds in a terrible state – though I don't suppose Mary's news will be of any comfort to her.'

Mary came down twenty minutes later and apologised, but said Jamie wanted her to read him another story as he hadn't seen much of her that day.

She said she thought it would be good if David was with her when she phoned Aunt Judith, so they went into Dan's study. Aunt Judith answered the phone immediately, and wanted to know if they had any further information about the discovery of Kim's car. Mary filled her in with all the information she had. Then she told her that Jamal had been arrested.

David could hear Aunt Judith's gasp of astonishment. She was shocked about Jamal's arrest, and told Mary that, though she'd never met Jamal, she couldn't believe that Kim's judgement could be so poor that she'd chosen to marry someone who was a terrorist.

She told Mary that Kim's mother had read the news that morning and, for the first time, seemed concerned about Kim's disappearance. She wanted to come up from Devon straightaway and go to Kim's flat, and had asked Aunt Judith to go with her. She put her off the idea, but told her she would be welcome to stay with her in London while the investigations were going on. This, apparently, she declined. But, said Aunt Judith, the arrest of Jamal puts a whole new slant on the situation. Perhaps it would help if she came up?

Mary asked David what he thought. He said they could do nothing until they knew whether or not Jamal was going to be charged – and in fact, whether the police had discovered any more information after finding Kim's car.

Mary then passed the telephone to David, saying he might be able to answer some of her questions more fully. He told Aunt Judith he agreed with what Mary had said, and felt that, however difficult, they would just have to sit back and wait. He promised her they would keep her fully informed of any developments – and agreed that the outlook was very grim.

After the call, Mary and David went back to the sitting room and told Celia and Dan about the conversation. 'One of the things I don't understand in all this,' said Celia, 'is how Kim's mother could be so uncaring. I would have gone mad if my son had gone missing like this.'

Kim looked at Celia and with a warm smile said, 'But Kim's parents were different. Her father was often abroad, and her mother was cold. I think in the holidays, Kim spent more time with my mother and me than with her own mother. She was a funny woman – never rude, but never interested in what we were doing.'

'But what about her father?' asked Dan.

'Oh, he was very nice – but we saw very little of him. I do remember him once taking us to London. We went to the Science Museum, then he took us out to supper, and on to the theatre to see *The Importance of being Ernest.* That was a lovely evening – we felt very grown-up – but I think that was probably the last time I saw him. He went off to America soon after the divorce.'

'Poor Kim,' said Celia. 'And now this!' She stood up, 'I think dinner's ready. Come and eat.'

After dinner Mary put on the alarm in Jamie's room, and they all sat round the fire and chewed over the situation. Uppermost in all their minds was the fact that they found it hard to believe Jamal was implicated in terrorism – and yet, how to explain the chemicals. The nearest they could get to an explanation was that Jamal's friend Al might be implicated. And if Al was involved, how could Jamal not be? But Jamal had told them that Al hadn't been there the weekend of Kim's disappearance – he'd postponed his visit at the last minute.

David told Dan of his meeting with Sir Ralph. There seemed no need to keep it a secret now that Jamal had been arrested. When Dan asked, he said he hadn't been able to get any information about Al's address or whereabouts, and Dan said that that was something the police would almost certainly try and get from Jamal.

They listened to the news at ten o'clock. It carried quite a lengthy report about Kim's disappearance, and the discovery of her car. They said that a man had been arrested in connection with her disappearance, but no name was given. There was a picture of the area in the New Forest where the car was found, and of police searching the undergrowth for clues. There was still a lot of mud around, so this was making the going difficult. The report left them silent for quite a while, as they considered the implications of the search.

David left soon after the news. Once again, he thought how lucky Mary was to have such caring people as Celia and Dan to live with, and then realised that, as a comparative stranger, he'd also been embraced by their warmth and kindness. It was a good feeling.

He got to the hospital next day to face a barrage of phone calls and visitors. But before the onslaught began, he phoned the police to see if they'd discovered anything during their search in the New Forest. The reply was negative.

Not long after, he had a distraught telephone call from Kim's mother. She'd decided she wanted to come down to Kim's flat. Could he get her the key? David explained that they hadn't been able to find a key, but said he would get in touch with the police, and then get back to her.

The police were, not surprisingly, unhelpful. They said the flat was part of a possible crime scene and they could not give anyone access.

Then Mark phoned and said he'd heard that Jamal had been arrested and wanted to come and see him before he printed anything else. David told him there was little new he could tell him, but that he'd be happy to see him if he wanted to come over. He said he would be with him in half an hour.

Then David had a call from the police. They wanted a list of all the overseas doctors in the hospital with a note of their religious affiliation. This worried him as it struck him as discrimination, and he told them so, but he finally agreed to give them a list of all the doctors irrespective of their race or creed. But he declined to provide them with a room in the hospital for interviews.

This was followed by a succession of members of staff calling to find out what was going on. He told them Jamal was still at the police station, and had not yet been charged with anything.

-33-
Sir Ralph asks David to visit him in London

He'd been half expecting to hear from Sir Ralph so was not surprised when he had a call from him asking him to come up to London that afternoon to see him at the Home Office. The request was polite but authoritative and David knew he couldn't refuse to go, but explained that it would be very difficult that day but could manage the following afternoon

The call brought back to him all his feelings of anger about Samantha's betrayal, but with everything that was going on, he tried hard to suppress these feelings, and got on with his work.

He hadn't long put down the phone when Mark arrived. David liked Mark. He thought him an interesting man with a great sense of humour and a belief in social justice and truth which he admired. David was very critical of the media, the press in particular, which he thought had far too much influence on politics and the public, and sometimes felt it was the media which governed the country, not parliament. But he felt Mark fell into a different category.

He had little more information to give than Mark had obtained from the police, but told him that Jamal's solicitor felt he was almost certain to be refused bail and charged.

'I suppose the discovery of chemicals in Jamal's flat is almost irrefutable evidence that Jamal is somehow involved,' said Mark. 'But the idea is mind-boggling. Jamal always seemed to be a man of principle with a care for humanity. Just look at his hospice project. How is it possible for a man wanting to provide specialist care for the dying to be involved in terrorism? It just doesn't make sense.'

'I agree. The solicitor tells us that Jamal vehemently denies all knowledge of the chemicals.'

'The trouble is that police jump to conclusions all too swiftly – especially if there's the possibility of a Muslim being involved. There's a lot of Islama-phobia around.'

'But how did the chemicals get there?'

'Doesn't he have a friend who stays with him from time to time?'

'Yes, Al. I've met him several times. I found him quite charming, though I must confess the authorities are interested in him.' Mark raised his eyebrows questioningly, but David didn't explain. 'Jamal says Al spends most of his time abroad and hasn't been around for some time. He was expected the weekend Kim disappeared, but cancelled at the last minute.'

'My God, the whole thing's a mystery. And then there's Kim. It doesn't look too good, her car being found. She's such a lovely woman. I've often wondered how she managed to
remain single for so long?'

'Mary tells me she had a tragedy in her life.'

'Mary?'

'Mary Gilburn.'

'How come? Is she a friend of Kim?

'Yes, she's Kim's oldest friend. They go back to childhood.'

'Then she must be very upset by what's happened. I like her. She's a very bright lass – but I believe she's had a tragedy in her life too.'

'Yes, her fiancé died in a car accident just before the wedding day,'

He couldn't avoid Mark's implicit question, so said, 'Kim's disappearance has brought us together quite a bit,' and then changed the subject. 'You realise, Mark, that this has implications for the hospice appeal. What do we do about it? Do we carry on regardless, or will we lose credibility if Jamal is charged?'

'I'm in a difficult situation. At the moment, most of the papers have only reported that Jamal has been detained for questioning. But the tabloids have already been speculating about his affiliations, and have been ferreting out facts about his life and relationships. It's more than my job's worth to remain completely unbiased and silent. I'll have to report the details and provide some analysis of the current terrorist situation. It's not going to be easy when I know and like the man.'

'Yes. Not easy!' David said sympathetically.

'In view of all the publicity and the fact that Jamal's a Muslim, people will point the finger at him and question his involvement with the appeal. I suggest we go low-key until we know what's going to happen to Jamal.'

David agreed.

'Well, I'd better be off. Let me know as soon as you hear any news. I'll keep plugging the 'missing nurse' angle in the paper though, if I'm honest, I don't have much hope Kim's still alive.'

'Nor me,' said David as he opened the door for Mark to leave.

The next afternoon he went up to London to see Sir Ralph. The size and furnishing of his office indicated that he had a very senior position at the Home Office and David regretted that he'd not done more homework to try and find out what was his area of responsibility.

He greeted David cordially and waved him to an armchair. 'Thank you for coming up. I know it must be a bit of an imposition, but I needed to talk to you a little more freely than when we last met. You've obviously been unable to find any information about Al?'

'No, except that he was going to stay with Jamal the weekend that Kim Anderson disappeared, and then cancelled at the last minute.'

'How do you know this?'

'Kim went back to her own flat as Al was coming to stay for the weekend.'

'Remind me. Why did she go back to her own flat, and how do we know she actually did?'

'Because her friend, Mary Gilburn spent the evening with her. Mary said Kim always went back to her flat when Al came to stay.'

'Do you know why that was?'

'Well, Mary said that there were two reasons. Kim didn't really like Al, and she also knew that Al, being a strict Muslim, wouldn't approve of her sharing a bedroom with Jamal.'

'That makes sense. But Jamal's a Muslim too?'

'Yes, but I suspect in name only. He doesn't behave like a Muslim – in fact, he seems totally westernised.'

'What about Al?'

'I've only met him a few times so I can't say from personal experience. But I gather Kim told Mary he was a very devout Muslim.'

'What do you think of Jamal? You've had quite a lot to do with him.'

'Well, I've always respected him as a doctor. He's very well thought of by the medical profession, although some of his colleagues don't like him very much because he's rather arrogant. He's very popular with the nurse which doesn't go down well! I was wary of him at first, but I've got to like him. He seems sincere and very caring, and, as you probably know, he started off this hospice project and has given a lot of his time to getting it under way.'

'Could it be a cover?'

'I suppose so. But if so, he's a very good actor!'

'And yet, the police have found bomb making chemicals in his flat! As a doctor, he'd know all about chemicals'

'Agreed. But Jamal denies all knowledge of the chemicals. He asked the police where they were found but the police wouldn't tell him.'

'Do **you** think Jamal is innocent?'

'I admit it's difficult with the evidence of the chemicals – but I still harbour the feeling that Jamal couldn't possibly be involved in terrorism.'

'Why,' insisted Sir Ralph, 'do you think that?

'Well, I suppose because I've never heard him make any remarks that would lead me to think he has terrorist sympathies. He's arrogant – but only about his medical expertise. He has a great sympathy for the problems of the Third World, but in any conversations we've had, he's always promulgated the idea of economic help – never any suggestion of terrorist activities.'

'But he's a Muslim,' said Sir Ralph.

'Yes,' said David, 'But why is it that everyone thinks all Muslims are terrorists?'

'I don't think they do,' said Sir Ralph quietly. 'But you must agree that many of the recent terrorist acts have been organised by Muslims. And, equally, you can't deny that bomb making equipment has been found in Dr Khan's flat. We can't be sentimental at this stage. It's national security we're on about.'

David had to agree.

'So, what about his friend, Al?'

'Well, as I told you before, I've only met him a few times, and he's always been very charming. But I must admit there are things about him that are odd. Jamal never likes to talk about him – almost seems secretive about his whereabouts. And,' he said, a picture flashing into his mind, 'I did once see him outside the new mosque in the city.'

'Tell me about it.'

'Well, there isn't much to tell. I was in a taxi on my way to the station when we got caught up in a traffic jam. The taxi stopped outside the mosque and I noticed two Asian men walking along with their arms round two young lads in a rather intimate fashion. One of the men was Al. It seemed, somehow, inappropriate.'

Sir Ralph nodded and said, almost under his breath, 'Just as I thought.' Then he asked, 'Are he and Jamal 'intimate'?'

'Goodness, no! Not in that way. Jamal's very much a ladies' man. Until he met Kim, he took out quite a few nurses at the hospital. He was very popular with them.'

'Did you speak to Al?'

'No. the taxi moved on.'

'Did you say anything to Dr Khan about seeing Al?'

'Well, yes. I did mention it to him, but he said it couldn't have been Al because he was abroad.'

'When was this?'

'It was in September. I was on my way to Scotland to see my father who was very ill.'

Sir Ralph nodded, as though this information was not unexpected. Then he said, 'Now tell me about Dr Khan and this missing nurse, Kim Anderson.'

'Kim's a senior nurse at the hospital – very much respected by all her colleagues. She and Dr Khan got engaged a few months ago. Although several of us were worried to begin with about a mixed marriage, we all felt they were well suited. They seemed devoted to each other, and were planning to marry in the summer. Kim's a very intelligent woman and I really don't think she'd have got involved with Dr Khan if she'd had the least suspicion he was involved with terrorism. And, as for Dr Khan, he's absolutely distraught about her disappearance.'

'People can be besotted by sex,' remarked Sir Ralph.

He made no reply, hoping Sir Ralph didn't think of him in that category.

'I expect, as you seem to know so much about what has been going on, that you've been told about Dr Khan's cousins.'

'Tell me.'

David told Sir Ralph what he knew of the cousin's visit.

'Yes. I do know this. The police are investigating. But I'm afraid that doesn't alter the fact that Dr Khan will be charged with conspiracy to terrorism.'

David nodded. 'Yes, I realise that's inevitable.'

'Well now,' said Sir Ralph, 'as you've been kind enough to come up to London to see me, I'll put you just a little in the picture. We've been watching Al Mercer for some months (his real name is Ali Mansour), and we know he's a friend of Dr Khan, and stays with him when he's in the south of England. We have evidence that Ali is a devout Muslim, and we're almost certain he's part of a terrorist network. We don't know yet how large it is, though we have identified some of the group. We feel Dr Khan must be implicated, though we have no evidence against him apart from the fact that Ali has been using his flat. I take on board what you've said about him, but unless some positive evidence turns up to lift suspicion from him, I think Dr Khan is almost certain to be convicted of terrorism.'

'So how do I come into all this?' David asked.

'We felt that, as you were connected with the hospital you might be able to glean some information for us about both Dr Khan and Ali Mansour. As you now realise, Samantha has also been involved in this surveillance. That's how she came to befriend you ...'

David couldn't hide his anger at this comment.

'Yes, I know,' said Sir Ralph soothingly. 'I understand how angry you must feel. But there are times when security and the needs of the state have to come first.'

David said dryly, 'Using people in this way is hardly the way a civilised country should behave.'

'There are times, I fear, when difficult means have to be used to get information. But it can't have hurt you too much, surely? You and Samantha had a good time together – but that's all. Samantha's not the marrying kind – in fact, she's a bit of a James Bond character. I don't think she'll ever settle.'

David couldn't respond to this remark without giving Sir Ralph the impression that he'd had rather different expectations from his relationship with Samantha, so nodded curtly and said, 'I'm afraid I do feel very angry to know I've been used in this underhand way.'

'We still need to 'use you' as you say,' said Sir Ralph, somewhat curtly. 'Before you leave, I must ask you to keep me informed of any information whatsoever that you get about Ali Mansour or Dr Khan – or indeed about the nurse, Miss Anderson. Though,' he added, 'I rather fear she may be dead.'

'Yes, I'm afraid that's what we are all beginning to think. It's a month since she disappeared, and now her car's been found it doesn't look good.'

Sir Ralph stood up and held out his hand. 'Thank you for coming up to see me. We do appreciate it. Please don't tell anyone about Al Mercer's real name. And please keep me in touch.'

With that, he pressed a bell on his desk and his secretary arrived and showed David out of the building.

-34-
Jamal in Prison

Mary found it difficult to settle down to work and any hope of studying was out of the question. Kim's disappearance was so unexpected it took her back to the unexpectedness of Ben's sudden death. She felt doubly sad that, just as Kim had found such happiness with Jamal – something she believed would never happen after Paul's betrayal – there was now the possibility that something awful had happened to her.

Looking back over the past month, she realised she wouldn't have coped without the support of Celia and Dan, and to her surprise, of David Gardner who she was getting to know and respect more and more. He was a real tower of strength. She'd scarcely known him before Kim and Jamal's engagement party when they'd sat next to each other. She'd found him a very engaging companion, and then when Kim disappeared came the unexpected phone call from him asking if she knew Kim's mother's address. From then on they seemed to share the whole burden of Kim's disappearance and Jamal's distress.

It was Dan who'd put the idea into her head of trying to find someone who might still be in touch with Kim's mother. He'd asked her whether she thought any of Kim's mother's old neighbours might know where she lived, and it was then that she'd remembered Aunt Judith.

It was a relief when David offered to come with her to London. She felt that the shock of discovering that Kim's mother hadn't even been in hospital, and that the note from Kim was a hoax, would have been unbearable to cope with on her own. As it was she was able to discuss the situation rationally and decide what to do next.

From that point on, it seemed the most natural thing in the world to share with David the slowly unravelling drama of Kim's disappearance and Jamal's arrest.

Mary had heard quite a bit about David before she met him. Dan and Celia's friend, Stuart. had talked about him, and said how lucky the hospital was to have such a good administrator. Kim had spoken warmly of him and said he was both a good boss and a good friend, and that he was very popular with the staff. Watching him at the meetings of the Appeal committee – not interfering but quietly taking everything in, and making the occasional sensible comment - made her realise why.

Mary couldn't help comparing him with Ben. They were totally different. Whereas Ben had been a flamboyant character, tall and very good looking with dark curly hair, and brown twinkly eyes, David was shorter and of a much sturdier build. He had mid brown hair, blue eyes and a kind face, and exuded a sense of quiet confidence which Mary had found very reassuring. In his black tie at Stuart and Susan's Silver Wedding party, she realised for the first time he was actually very good looking.

It occurred to her that, as well as spending a lot of time thinking about Kim's disappearance, she was also spending quite a bit of time thinking about David. This surprised her as she'd had no thoughts before of getting involved with anyone else. She realised they'd both had a deal of heartbreak in their lives – David with his divorce and his father's death, and now his break up with Samantha, while she'd lost Ben and now, possibly, her oldest friend.

Although Mary tried to put any thought of the relationship developing out of her mind she was aware that Jamie had taken to David in a big way, and often asked when 'Uncle David' was going to come again. She also knew that Celia and Dan liked David, and were gently encouraging the relationship when he visited. But with the situation of Kim and Jamal so uncertain, she knew now was not the time even to consider any new involvement.

Jamal, as they had expected, was charged with conspiracy to terrorism, and remanded in custody. It was clear from the beginning that there was no possibility he would be let out on bail with such a serious charge against him.

Julian went to visit him and told Mary that Jamal was absolutely adamant he knew nothing about the chemicals in his flat. Julian said he couldn't help believing him. He said Jamal wanted Mary to go with him the next time he visited, and they discussed what would be the best way forward.

A TORTUOUS PATH

'If we really think he's innocent,' Julian said, 'then we must try and establish how the chemicals came to be in his flat. We need to explore every possible explanation we can think of.'

''I can think of several possible explanations,' said Mary. She told Julian about the unfriendly reception Kim had received when they visited Jamal's parents in Leeds. 'Though his mother was quite friendly, his father had made no bones about not wanting Jamal to marry a non-Muslim. Then there was the threatening visit of Jamal's two cousins telling him to break off the engagement.'

Julian intervened, 'Jamal should have reported them to the police.'

'That's what I thought, but Jamal said they were harmless – and, of course, were family.'

'Any other ideas?' asked Julian

'Well, of course, there's Jamal's friend Al Mercer. Apparently he stays with Jamal whenever he comes to England. Kim doesn't like Al, and she thinks he doesn't like her. That's why she always goes back to the flat when he comes over.'

Mary suddenly realised she speaking in the present tense. She felt overwhelmed with anxiety and found it difficult not to cry.

'Did she say why she didn't like him?'

'No. She told me she had an uneasy feeling about him, but thought perhaps it was because he was a very strict Muslim. That's why she always moved out when he came to stay.'

'Do you know him?'

'I've met him several times but I can't say I know him. He always seems very pleasant – talks a lot about his trips overseas. But he mostly seems to address his remarks to Jamal –not to me,'

'Interesting,' commented Julian. 'The fact that Al is a strict Muslim is something we can explore with Jamal – what they used to discuss, and whether Al expressed any hostility towards the British,' said Julian. 'But first we need to ask Jamal whether Al had access to his flat.'

When they got to the prison on Friday Mary was shocked at Jamal's appearance. Not that he'd let himself go at all, but he'd lost an enormous amount of weight, and the skin of his face was stretched tightly across his bones. But he retained his dignity and courteously got up to shake hands, thanked Mary warmly for coming to see him, and asked how Jamie was.

Then he said, 'Mary, you must believe me. I'm not a terrorist. I know nothing about the chemicals found in my flat. I don't believe in terrorism in any shape or form.' Then he repeated, 'You must believe me.'

'I'd like to! But, Jamal, you can't get away from the fact that chemicals were found in your flat. How did they get there?'

'That's what's so terrible. I don't know! I've never seen any chemicals in the flat. I don't know where they were found, what they look like, or what sort of chemicals they could have been.'

'Have the police told you where they found them?' Mary asked.

Jamal shook his head.

'No,' Julian intervened. 'But they will have to soon under the right of disclosure of the evidence against you.'

'When will that be?' asked Jamal.

'Quite soon now,' said Julian.

'Jamal, you look ill. Are you being looked after properly?'

'Yes, I suppose so. The food comes regularly and is quite good. But ....' He hesitated.

'Are they treating you alright ... I mean, are you having any hassle?'

'Well, I can't say they're exactly friendly. In fact, the guards are quite hostile. I get called unpleasant names – Paki trash and the likes - and they seem to encourage some of the other inmates to bait me. But,' and he shook his head, 'none of this bothers me. All I can think about is wondering what's happened to Kim. I can't sleep for thinking about her, and fearing that something terrible has happened. If she's dead, I don't know that I can bear to go on.'

Mary could see he was on the verge of tears, and longed to put her arms round him, but she knew he would find it embarrassing. She'd observed in the past that she'd never seen any public physical display of affection between him and Kim, other than the occasional holding of hands.

Julian intervened, 'Jamal, if not you, who could have brought the chemicals into your flat? Could it be your friend Al Mercer?'

'Of course not. He's a very old friend. He wouldn't betray me by using my flat in that way.'

'Do you think he could be involved in terrorism?' Julian asked quickly.

'Of course not. I would have known if he had any terrorist inclinations.'

'Are you sure?' Julian persisted.

'Yes,' said Jamal, though Mary detected a slight hesitancy.

'What does he do for a living?' asked Julian.

'He's a businessman.'

'That's a bit vague. What sort of businessman?'

'I think it's some sort of financial business. I really don't know much about it.'

'So what do you talk about when he visits?'

'Oh, all sorts of things. I've known him for years. We were at university together. We talk about my work, our friends, our families .... life in general, the hospice appeal.'

'Do you discuss politics?'

'Well, not British politics. I don't think Al knows much about our political parties. He's lived in the USA much of his life. But we do talk about the third world – about poverty and injustice, and what the west should do about it.'

'Is he sympathetic to terrorism?'

'Absolutely not! We both believe that the way to help the third world is through education, economic improvement and equality.'

'That's your view. Are you sure it's his?'

Jamal nodded. 'Yes.' He looked worried, and then said, 'Why are you asking me these questions?'

Mary ignored his question and asked, 'When did you last see Al?'

'At our engagement party,' he replied. 'You were there.'

'Haven't you seen him since?'

'No, he was supposed to be coming the weekend Kim disappeared, but he phoned me at the hospital to say he wouldn't be coming after all.'

'Has Al got a key to your flat?'

'Yes, of course. Ever since we were at university, he's always had free access to my home.'

Julian and Mary exchanged glances.

'And you to his?' pursued Julian.

'Well, no. I don't think Al has a fixed home anywhere. He's always travelling round the world.'

That seemed rather a curious statement, but Julian didn't pursue it, so Mary decided to pursue the other line of enquiry she'd raised with him at his flat. 'Are you absolutely sure your father had nothing to do with Kim's disappearance?'

'Yes, absolutely,' said Jamal indignantly.

'And your cousins?'

Jamal shook his heads wearily. 'I can't answer for them. I hardly know them.'

'Jamal,' said Julian. 'If we are to prove you're innocent, we have to find evidence to support your claim.'

'But surely, under British justice, a man is considered innocent until proved guilty.'

'Yes,' said Julian. 'That's so. But the evidence against you is very strong. You must try and think of a way we can prove you had nothing to do with the chemicals – but it's going to be difficult. You must try and remember any little thing that might be relevant before we come next time.'

Jamal shook his head, a hopeless look on his face. But he rose to shake their hands and thanked them for coming. They promised they would return soon, but asked if there was anything he would like them to bring in next time they came. He gave them a little list – toiletries, the titles of several books (mainly medical), and pen and paper.

They said goodbye and promised to do their best to help.

As they left, Mary observed how dignified Jamal had been, and wondered how such a proud and educated man, as he almost certainly was, could bear to be in prison knowing he was innocent. She also knew how his heart must ache for news of Kim. It was now nearly five weeks since she'd disappeared, and there was absolutely no news of her other than the discovery of her abandoned car. She felt deeply sorry for him.

Discussing the visit on the way back to the office Julian and Mary agreed the situation looked very bleak. But both thought Jamal had been convincing, that he knew nothing about the chemicals. But how could they prove it? With the evidence of the chemicals in his flat, how could Jamal prove he knew nothing about them? If he was innocent, it was a mystery that needed, somehow, to be solved.

At the end of the day, David phoned to ask how they had got on so Mary invited him over for supper and said she would fill him in.

Celia, once again, gave them a meal. She had that wonderful ability to cater for extra people at the drop of a hat. When David arrived, he said, 'I fear I'm in danger of overdoing my welcome.'

Celia smiled and said, 'No, David, you're always welcome. But before you have a drink, Jamie wants you to go up and say goodnight.'

The four of them spent the evening turning over the little information Mary had gleaned from her visit to Jamal. The thing they couldn't get away from was the discovery of the chemicals in Jamal's flat.

Mary was upset when she discovered that David thought Jamal might be guilty because the evidence against him was so strong. She felt quite angry with him, and they argued until Dan stepped in and said they must just wait till more information was forthcoming.

-35-
A problem with the hospice accounts

The hospice project was the last thing on David's mind when he was reminded by Maud that the next appeal meeting was due. She wanted to know what to do – whether or not to send out the Minutes and Agenda. This jerked him into realising that they hadn't designated a Vice Chairman, and that for the last meeting Jamal had asked him to take over. With Jamal in prison he realised he was the obvious person to take on responsibility for doing something about the situation.

David told Maud he would give it some thought and get back to her in a day or two. He then decided to arrange a meeting in his office with some of the key people to discuss the situation. He invited Mark, Alec Wilson and Mary. He reluctantly included Henry Winchester, though he felt he was proving to be a lightweight as far as fund raising was concerned.

After discussion they all decided that in the circumstances it would be better to put the Appeal on hold. People in the community knew of Jamal's involvement and that he was awaiting trial on a charge of terrorism. Everyone felt it wouldn't do any good for the Appeal to be mentioned in public for the time being. They decided to send a letter to the committee members and to the two-hundred Friends who'd signed up, explaining that they would delay any further fund raising for the time being until they could sort out the gap left by Jamal's absence.

It was a wise decision because only the next day the police called on David and asked for information about the Appeal's accounts.

David, having joined the committee at the behest of the Chairman of the Health Authority had up to then taken little interest in the mechanics of the Appeal, and the request for information about the accounts pulled him up short. He told the police he didn't have any information to hand, but would get in touch with them as soon as he had.

Their request made David uneasy. He got in touch with Tracy Pilkington and asked her to come over and bring all the Appeal's accounts with her. He explained that he'd had a request from the police to see them. She seemed quite agitated and insisted she'd been keeping the accounts very carefully and they were all in order.

David told her he was sure they were and, to allay Tracey's anxiety, said that he thought it was just a routine police enquiry. In reality David felt it was a most unusual request and that it somehow related to Jamal's imprisonment.

Tracy said she would sort them out that night and bring them in the next day.

When she brought them along next morning the accounts were, as she'd said, in apple pie order. David suggested she left them with him for a while; that he would make copies for the police and then let her have them back.

He copied everything Tracy had brought – statements, account books, etc, but the paying in book presented a problem as there was no way he could photocopy it. He decided he would have to make a list of all the deposits in the book together with the dates.

When he'd photocopied everything he examined the bank statements carefully, surprised to see how little there was in the account considering all the fund raising activity that had been going on in recent months. He remembered Mary once commenting on how slowly the funds seemed to be growing, and decided he'd better get Tracy along so he could discuss it with her.

She looked apprehensive when she arrived but David told her there was nothing to worry about. He just wanted to know how she dealt with the monies that were raised. 'Well,' she said, 'I take the cash to the bank and pay it in with the paying-in slip. Al Mercer set it all up for me when we first started. If he's here, he does it for me.'

'Al again,' thought David. 'What's the name of the account?'

'Oh, it's called the New Hospice Appeal Account.'

David looked at the statements. They were headed 'Hospice Appeal Accounts. He looked at Tracy and said, 'These statements have a different name.'

Tracy looked at the accounts laid out on the desk before her. She looked flustered and admitted she'd never noticed they were different.

David asked whether it had ever occurred to her to wonder why the funds weren't growing much.

'Oh, I thought we were doing quite well,' she said indignantly.

'Did you ever think to compare the statements with what you were paying in?'

Beginning to realise that something was seriously wrong, she burst into tears. David decided the best thing would be to pursue the investigation on his own, so he sent her off with some soothing words, and the injunction not to say anything to anybody.

The encounter proved to him what he'd always suspected – that Tracy was not very bright. How, he wondered, had she come to be given the role of treasurer? If Al was implicated, had he realised how simple Tracy was and thought her the ideal person to dupe?

The implications of this discovery were so serious he realised he would have to take the papers home and look at them more carefully before handing them over to the police.

That evening, checking the statements against the paying in books, he discovered that neither the amount nor the dates Tracy had paid the cheques in coincided. There were regular payments into the Hospice Appeal Accounts a few days after Tracy paid in the money, but the amount didn't coincide with what had been paid in. In fact, they represented about a quarter of the money raised.

It was no wonder that the funds were not accumulating as fast as they should have and David realised they'd been very lax in leaving Tracy on her own to deal with the accounts. They'd all been negligent – and he felt particularly angry with himself.

He thought back to the first meeting in the hospital that he'd stumbled on nearly a year before at which Al Mercer had been present. Al had been so charming most of the time that David could understand how Tracy had accepted his financial suggestions without query.

And what of Jamal? Had Al made the suggestions in Jamal's hearing or had he taken Tracy aside separately? David knew he would have to ask her, but was not certain she would remember the details that far back.

If Jamal knew about it, that was a further nail in the coffin of his protestation of innocence. If he didn't, wasn't he negligent in not checking on the Appeals' finances? But then, so were they all.

He decided he couldn't keep this to himself. It was too serious. He knew the police would want to take away the accounts almost immediately so there was little time to decide what to do about the situation. He phoned Mark, Alec, Mary and Henry that evening, and asked them to meet him in his office at lunchtime the next day.

When they'd all assembled, he explained what he'd discovered and showed them the discrepancies between what had been paid in and the bank statements. All reluctantly agreed that there'd been a misappropriation of funds and decided that really there was nothing they could do other than hand the whole matter over to the police.

There were so many things they had to think about. How were they to tell the hard-working supporters that the funds they had raised had been misappropriated. Were they likely to get any back? What were the implications for Jamal? And could the Appeal continue?

They decided they would say nothing beyond what they'd agreed a couple of days before until they knew a little more. Mary said she would visit the prison and confront Jamal, but they suggested she shouldn't tell him to begin with about the police wanting to see the accounts. Just say that, with the end of the year nearly upon us, the accounts need to be audited so we need to know how they've been organised. That way, Jamal won't be frightened off, and you might get the truth from him.'

David realised he was tending more and more, to thinking Jamal was guilty, though Mary kept insisting that a man was presumed innocent until proved otherwise.

Soon after the group left the police came and took away the accounts.

As he had nothing planned for the weekend he decided, after thinking about it very carefully, to phone Mary and ask if she would like to come out to dinner with him on the Saturday. Celia answered the phone and said Mary was out with Jamie but would get her to phone when she returned. He spent the afternoon on edge, realising that though they'd spent several evenings together, they'd been mainly as a result of Kim's disappearance and Jamal's arrest. This would be the first time he'd invited her out on a date and he felt unaccountably nervous.

Mary phoned to say she'd be delighted. David said he'd pick her up at seven, but Mary insisted he came over before so he could see Jamie. 'He does love seeing you,' she said. David would have been pleased had he seen the blush when she realised what she'd said.

He decided to take Mary to a little pub in the country the other side of town. As they passed the local cinema, he pointed out that the film *Charlotte Grey* was showing for the next few weeks and asked if Mary had seen it. She said 'no', but that it was a film she wanted to see.

It was not until half-way through the meal that Mary suddenly said, 'Oh my God! I've just remembered something. *Charlotte Grey*! Kim said she'd just read it, and thought I would enjoy it. We were always lending each other books. She said she'd lent it to Al Mercer on his last visit and he'd promised to bring it back at the weekend. She said she'd pop back to the flat in the morning and collect the book while Al was at the mosque, and would bring it over when she and Jamal came to lunch on Sunday.'

'But what's that got to do with Kim's disappearance?' said David, noticing Mary's agitated look.

'Well, don't you see! I tried to persuade Kim not to bother, but she said she needed to get some notes from the flat so it would kill two birds with one stone.'

'I still don't understand,' persisted David.

'Well, if the book is there it means Al must have visited after all.'

'But Jamal says Al cancelled his visit.'

'Yes, I know. But I keep thinking that Al is somehow involved with Kim's disappearance. What if he did go back to the flat after all and didn't tell Jamal? What if he went there while Jamal was at work and planted all the chemicals without letting Jamal know?'

David had to concede that Mary had a point, though he couldn't believe that Jamal could have been unaware there were chemicals in the flat. He also conceded it would be a good idea to get police permission to search the flat and see if the book was there – but secretly felt it would be a waste of time.

He'd hoped that, just for once, they'd be able to spend time together without talking about Kim and Jamal. After they'd agreed they would get in touch with the police on Monday, they managed to spend the rest of the evening in easy conversation. Mary told David about her happy childhood, and the interesting year she'd spent with the water project in Pakistan before going up to Oxford, 'I loved it there and was tempted to forego Oxford and stay on – but realised that would be foolish. But I do hope to go back sometime.'

David asked whether she'd been put off by the poverty and primitive living conditions. 'No. I could have been, But the people were so friendly and so appreciative of what we were doing, one tended to see them rather than their background. It may seem silly, but I felt embraced by their warmth.'

It was such a revealing remark that David smiled. Mary continued, 'The people seemed so full of joy despite their poverty. They had a great sense of humour – and I loved their bright colourful costumes. As I said, I'd like to go back there sometime – but it will have to wait till Jamie grows up,' she added, smiling.

'They were Muslims of course?' asked David.

'Oh yes. But not at all like the stereotype picture we have of Muslims over here. They were, on the whole, a gentle people.'

'Is that what made you warm to Jamal?'

'No. I was wary of him to start with. He was very different to the people I met in Pakistan – more self-confident and arrogant – and of course, more educated. And I confess I was anxious about his Muslim background. Many of them seem to have a more militant attitude over here. I suppose it's because of a need to establish their identity. But,' she added reflectively,' I've warmed to him as I've got to know him. And I don't think Kim would have fallen in love with him if he hadn't been a good man.'

'But,' said David, 'you told me about Kim's boyfriend in Africa who let her down so badly. Could her judgement not have been as good as you think?'

Mary thought for a while then said, 'No. I think Kim learnt her lesson with Paul. For a long time I didn't think she would trust any man again. That's why I'm sure she was very careful before committing herself to Jamal.'

David discovered during the evening that Mary had a great sense of humour and regaled him with Jamie's comments. She also told him about some of Ben's escapades while at Oxford. 'It's only recently I've been able to talk about Ben,' she said. 'I suppose my life is beginning to fall into place a little now I've started to work and study again.'

'Did you always want to be a lawyer,' David wanted to know.

'Yes, since I was in the sixth form. That's what got me into Oxford I think.'

'What attracted you about the law?'

'Justice,' said Mary firmly. 'So many people suffer because they can't get access to a lawyer.'

'But,' argued David, 'justice is only available to those who can afford it.'

'That's not true. People without means can have access to a lawyer.'

'But that's changing.'

'Yes, I know. But we're fighting against the change.'

'Does it ever worry you that lawyers are paid so much more than, say, teachers who are often as well qualified but only earn half the amount a lawyer does.'

'Yes, I agree, I think society needs to wake up to the inequalities of pay.'

'Are you a feminist? 'asked David, quite amused by her vehemence.'

'No, Definitely not,' said Mary firmly. 'I think the feminists have done themselves a lot of harm. I've always felt that equality is something that should evolve rather than be imposed.'

'An interesting view,' said David. 'I wonder how many women would agree with you?'

'Well, what do you think David?'

'I confess I tend to agree with you. When it comes to choosing between a man and a woman equally well qualified, one almost always chooses the man. That's because, if you employ a woman and she then has a child, you have to go through all the paraphernalia of employing someone else for a short time – with all the attendant problems of training and explaining. Yes, I do agree with you.'

With that, David noticed the barman looking as though he was trying to close down so reluctantly said, 'We ought to be going.'

'Would you like to come over to church tomorrow? We're having a Bring and Share lunch afterwards at the Rectory. Jane Masters won't be there as they're in New Zealand, but our young curate will be taking the service and he's very nice.'

'No thanks,' said David hastily. 'It's not my sort of scene.' Then, seeing the disappointment on Mary's face, he kicked himself for being so clumsy.

'I'm sorry, I didn't mean to be rude. It's just that I've never been a churchgoer.'

'That's OK,' said Mary. 'I've been a churchgoer all my life, and so was Ben and all his family. It all depends on how you've been brought up doesn't it,' and with that she smiled and took his arm as they went to the car

It had been a lovely evening and he was sad he'd turned down the invitation for the next day. But he couldn't withdraw his refusal now, and also realised it would be hypocritical if he'd accepted the invitation under false pretences.

They drove back quietly, and he kissed her goodnight at the door - for the first time wishing it had been more than a perfunctory embrace.

He spent a rather miserable Sunday, knowing he could have been enjoying the company of Mary, Jamie, Celia and Dan. He determined that, if a similar invitation came his way, he would accept it and be prepared to tolerate the church service. After all, he told himself, 'I enjoy church music, I like old church buildings, and I know Mary worships in a beautiful Grade 1 listed church.'

For Mary, David's rejection of her invitation left her feeling sad. It made her wonder whether there was any chance of the relationship going further if he was so hostile to church going and Christianity.

-36-
Mary visits Jamal in prison

After her dinner with David, Mary felt rather flat. But the service the next morning and the Bring and Share lunch afterwards revived her spirits and made her realise how much her Christian faith and her fellow Christians had supported her after Ben's death. She felt sad David didn't share her faith.

After the service the congregation went across to the home of one of the churchwardens for lunch. There they found a table ladened with food. There was such an abundance, it seemed there would be far too much for the everyone to eat, but it had all disappeared by the time they left.

They felt the absence of their vicar, Colin and his wife Jane who were visiting their son in New Zealand but the young curate, Andrew, in charge during their absence, did a sterling job speaking to everyone and making a special point of spending time with the children.

Once they got to the house Mary didn't see Jamie at all. He was swept up by Jane Master's thirteen-year-old grand-daughter, Susie, and her friend Ellen, who kept Jamie amused all afternoon. Mary found it interesting to see how the teenage girls were enjoying looking after the toddlers, and thought it was probably related to their emerging maturity.

Although it was a pleasant occasion, the thought of Kim's disappearance and all the events that followed, were never far from her mind - Jamal's imprisonment, the chemicals found in his flat, the discovery that the hospice appeal's accounts had been tampered with, and now the possibility that the book Kim lent to Ali might give a clue to Kim's whereabouts.

After Jamie went to bed, Mary discussed it all with Dan. She realised she and Julian would have to visit Jamal again in the next day or two, and asked Dan, who had been a barrister, for advice as to the best way of questioning Jamal to get at the truth. He suggested various strategies which would help them establish, to their own satisfaction, Jamal's guilt or innocence. Mary still wanted to believe him but had to admit that things looked very black.

-37-
The search of Jamal's flat for the novel, *Charlotte Grey*

On Monday, Mary told Julian about Kim's plan to go back to Jamal's flat to collect the book she had lent Al. Julian agreed it could be significant, and made arrangements with the police to have access to Jamal's flat that evening.

Mary asked David to go with her. As they entered the empty flat, Mary felt the absence of Jamal and Kim. They began the search with no idea what the book looked like – hardback or paperback – and as the flat was littered with books, they realised it was going to be a long job.

They looked in all the obvious places first –tables, desks, shelves in the kitchen, and bedside tables – but to no avail. Then they started on the many bookcases throughout the flat – some in each room. Julian took on the bedroom and Mary tackled the floor to ceiling bookcase in the sitting room, standing on a chair to reach the top shelves. It was a laborious task, trying to read the vertical spines. She hadn't taken on board before that some spines read from top to bottom and some from bottom to top. By the time she'd tackled three shelves, her neck began to ache with moving her head from left to right to read the titles. But then, to her amazement, she saw, on the fourth shelf down, sitting a little proud from the others, *Charlotte Grey* with a little piece of paper sticking out from the top. She cried out to Julian who came running from the bedrooms.

'Don't touch it,' he cried out. 'There may be finger prints.' He told the policeman who had accompanied them to the flat, and was sitting in the kitchen reading the paper, to ring the station and ask for forensics to come and check the book. He was a little reluctant at first, but Julian pointed out that they'd found what was probably an important piece of evidence.

Forensics arrived and took the book down carefully from the shelf.

'What's on the piece of paper,' asked Mary eagerly.

The forensic expert looked at it, and said, 'It just says "Enjoy. Kim".'

Mary and Julian looked at each other. 'It's just what we suspected. Al is definitely involved.'

They made arrangements to visit Jamal in prison the following day. When they arrived, he looked more haggard than ever, and though he remained spruce in his appearance, he seemed to have lost his zest for life. The first thing he asked was whether there was any news of Kim, and it was distressing to have to tell him there was none.

Seeing him looking so forlorn made Mary wonder about his parents, so she asked him if they'd visited him. He shook his head. 'You two are the only people I've seen since I've been here,' he said bitterly. I don't think my parents could face seeing me in prison. It's bad enough for them losing face without having to come to a prison.'

'Do they write?'

'Yes, I've had several letters from them, and some sweetmeats. But no visits.'

'What about the rest of your family?'

'I've only heard from my cousin, Kasim. He tells me the family are angry with me because the police have arrested those two cousins who came to visit me and threatened Kim.'

'That's a good thing,' said Mary. 'They are real thugs and deserve punishment. And they may well be responsible for Kim's disappearance.'

Jamal shook his head. 'I don't think so. As I said before they are just silly boys.'

Julian and Mary looked at each other and raised their eyes in amazement.

'Well, Jamal,' said Mary, 'let's move on. There are one or two questions we need to ask you. 'I'm sure you don't really want to think about the Hospice Appeal at the moment, but there are certain things we need to sort out while you are in prison. The first is the accounts. Do you know how they are organised?'

'Well, no. I left that to Tracey. She's the Treasurer. She used to produce a statement at each meeting saying how much we'd raised.'

'What about outgoings?'

'None, as far as I'm aware. I don't think anyone has claimed any expenses for their fund raising activities. I presume they would have deducted their expenses before paying over what they'd raised.'

Mary nodded. 'Do you know which bank Tracey was using?'

He thought for a moment, then said, 'No. But I think it may have been Barclays. I left all that to Al to organise with Tracey. He's a business man and knows much more about money than I do.'

'Did you not get involved at all?' asked Julian.

Jamal shook his head ruefully. 'No, I must admit I didn't. There didn't seem to be any need.' He saw Julian and Mary looking at each other, and asked anxiously, 'Why? Is there a problem?'

Julian answered carefully, 'There may be. We don't know yet. But some of the money seems to have gone missing.'

Jamal looked shocked. 'But how?'

'That's what the police are investigating.'

'But how? Why? I don't understand.'

Mary told him that this was just one of the things they needed to ask him about because it all seemed so complicated – with Kim's disappearance, and now this discovery of chemicals in Jamal's flat.

'Jamal, I'm afraid we must ask you again about the chemicals in your flat,' said Julian.

'Go ahead,' Jamal said wearily. 'But as I told you, I know nothing about any chemicals. I don't even know where they were found.'

'In your garage,' Mary intervened.

Jamal looked slightly relieved. 'Well that explains something. I only go into my garage to take the car in and out. The garage is still full of junk from the previous tenants, and I've been too busy to get around to sorting it out,'

'Well, that's one explanation,' said Julian dryly. 'But the police tell us the six cartons of chemicals, wire and bits of metal were clearly visible. Surely you would have seen them?'

Jamal shook his head.

'But you say you go in and out of your garage every time you take out the car. How could you have missed them?'

Jamal shook his head wearily. 'I don't know. I've never seen anything like that in the garage.'

'Do you know what was in the cartons?'

'No. But I presume it must be hydrochloride, otherwise the police wouldn't have been concerned.'

'How do you know that?' Julian's voice was hostile.

Jamal looked at Julian, almost with contempt. 'Everyone knows that. You only have to read the newspapers to know that hydrochloride is used in bomb making.'

'Who said anything about bombs?'

'I'm not a fool,' said Jamal angrily. 'If I'm here on a charge of conspiracy to terrorism, it must be because they suspect me of trying to make a bomb.'

Julian nodded. 'Fair enough. Well then, how did hydrochloride come to be in your garage?'

'I have no idea?'

'If you didn't put it there, who did?'

'I don't know.'

'Has Al Mercer got a key to your flat?'

'I told you before that he has. Why are you asking me that again?'

'Just answer the question, please, Dr Khan,' said Julian sternly. He and Mary had agreed that they would have to question Jamal in a vigorous and almost hostile fashion if they were to get at the truth. 'If we are to help you, we must ascertain all the facts.'

'Well, yes, I understand,' said Jamal apologetically. 'Al's always had a key to my flat. I told you, he's a very old friend – we shared a flat together at university in the States. He always stays with me when he's in this part of England. His movements are so erratic that I never know exactly when he's going to arrive, so he has a key and lets himself in.'

'So he could have put the chemicals in the garage.'

'No!'

'It would have been quite easy for you and Al Mercer to have planned to use the chemicals found in your flat?'

'Of course not.'

'Why are you so sure? He's a Muslim like yourself.'

'That doesn't mean to say he's a terrorist,' said Jamal angrily. 'Why do you people always suspect Muslims of terrorism?'

'You people! Is that how you think about the British?'

'Of course not! But there's a terrible hostility towards Muslims at the moment, you must agree.'

'Not surprising is it?' said Julian looking straight at Jamal.

'Are you absolutely certain your friend Al could not have been responsible for the chemicals?' Mary asked, remembering what David had told her about Sir Ralph's questioning.

'Of course not. I've known him for years. He's never had terrorist leanings.'

'What does he do for a living?'

'He's a businessman.'

'What's his business?'

'I'm not quite sure. He travels all over the world.'

'Yet you say you know him well.'

Julian's remark struck home, and Jamal began to look a little uncertain, but said nothing. 'So he could have been involved with a terrorist group without you knowing.'

Jamal shook his head wearily.

'What do you talk about when you are together?' asked Julian, and when Jamal didn't reply, he said, 'Do you discuss politics?'

'Of course! I would think most intelligent people discuss politics – but not in the sense you are trying to ask me. We talk about poverty in the third world and how it can be relieved, about good government, about inequality. But not,' he said emphatically, 'terrorism.'

'Do you think you really know Al?'

'What do you mean?'

'Are you sure you know what his real interests are? You don't seem to know much about his business.'

Jamal began to look agitated.

'What does Al come to England for?'

Jamal shook his head.

'How often does he come over?' asked Mary.

'About every two months – at least, that's how often he stays with me.'

'When did he last come?'

Jamal shook his head. 'I can't remember. Probably in May... Yes! Definitely May. He came to our engagement party.' And with that remark, she could see Jamal was on the verge of tears.

Julian persisted. 'Have you seen him since?'

Jamal shook his head. 'No. He was supposed to be coming the weekend Kim disappeared – that's why Kim went back to her own flat. But he cancelled at the last minute.'

'When did he cancel?'

'Well, he phoned me at the hospital in the early evening. I told him I wouldn't be there as I was working all night, but I would see him in the morning. He said that if I wasn't going to be there, he would stay with other friends.'

Julian and Mary exchanged glances, the same thought occurring to both of them. Mary said, 'So it was only *after* you said you'd be away all night that Al cancelled?'

Jamal nodded.

'Could Al have gone to the flat while you were at the hospital?'

Jamal saw where their questioning was going, and looked very upset. 'Well, I suppose he could have. But he didn't leave a note or anything to say he'd been there.'

They didn't think they'd get any further with that particular line of questioning so thought it was time to turn to the evidence of the Sebastian Faulk book.

'What do you know about your friend Al's reading habits?

Jamal looked puzzled. 'What do you mean? What's it got to do with all this?'

'Did you know Kim lent Al books?'

'No. I don't think I did. But I know they're both great readers.'

Mary couldn't help noticing that Jamal was speaking about Kim in the present tense. She could see he was longing for an explanation, and didn't see any reason for prevaricating, so told him about Kim's conversation with her about *Charlotte Grey*; that Kim had said she would go back to the flat to collect it the day she disappeared, and how they'd found the book back in his flat.

Jamal looked shocked as he realised the implications of what Mary had said.

'You see,' said Julian. 'If you are indeed innocent, as you say you are, someone else must have planted those chemicals. And it seems to us that, if it's not you, it might be Al.'

A TORTUOUS PATH

Jamal shook his head wearily.' I see where you're coming from. But I don't believe Al is involved in terrorism.. Al's probably my closest friend. Surely I'd have known.' He thought for a moment, and then added, 'someone must have planted the chemicals – but how on earth are you going to prove anything. It looks like I haven't a hope of proving my innocence'

He looked absolutely shattered. 'I would never have imagined, a few weeks ago, that my life could be turned upside down like this with everything I value being taken away – Kim, my work, my reputation, my freedom. It's a nightmare.'

Mary longed to comfort him but knew she couldn't. Julian said that he thought they'd talked enough for one day – and that there were certain avenues they needed to explore before they came back to see him again.

When they left the prison, Mary couldn't get Jamal's sad face out of her mind. He was one of the most handsome men she'd ever met, with his dark wavy hair, fine features, penetrating brown eyes and warm and engaging smile. Kim had told her that when he first came to the hospital, all the nurses were after him.

On first meeting him she'd thought him arrogant and a bit distant, but as she'd got to know him, she realised he was sensitive and considerate as well as very intelligent. That Jamie liked him was a plus point for Mary when she tried to assess him.

Now, looking at his careworn face she couldn't believe that he was guilty of terrorist activities despite all the evidence to the contrary. She couldn't begin to imagine what he must be feeling. For her, when Ben died, the anguish was terrible, but at least she knew what had happened to him, and knew, too, that however inconceivable it seemed at the time, she would ultimately have to get on with her life. But Kim's disappearance was a different matter altogether. Where was she? Was she still alive? Who had taken her? Had she been hurt? If she was dead, had she been raped or brutally murdered? She felt that this not knowing must be agonising and would have driven many people over the top with despair. She felt only admiration for Jamal – that he managed to remain courteous and sane under all their questioning.

-38-
The Symposium

A few days after he and Mary had dinner together, David had a phone call from Stuart suggesting they meet in a pub for a drink. He wanted to hear more about the events of the last weeks – the discovery of Kim's car and Jamal's arrest. Knowing he could trust Stuart absolutely, David told him all he knew including the problem of the missing appeal funds and Sir Ralph's interest in Jamal and Al Mercer.

'You knew all about that, didn't you,' he said, almost accusingly.

'Yes. I did,' said Stuart, a little wryly. 'I know Sir Ralph through my government contacts. He asked whether I knew anyone who might have contacts with a Dr Jamal Khan who worked in my local hospital. Obviously, I thought of you, and gave him your name. He told me his wife was a relative of the Chairman and would make contact with you through him. That's all I know – except that you told me about the dinner party invitation. Knowing what a devious person Sir Ralph is, I became very worried when you got involved with Samantha. I did try to warn you, but I fear you were rather smitten!'

David nodded – a little shamefacedly. 'Yes, it doesn't seem I'm all that good at judging women!'

'Not to worry. One day, the right person will come along – unless she has already?' he asked slyly.

David refused to rise to the bait. 'Let's change the subject,' he said.

'Well, tell me about Jamal and Kim.'

He told him all he knew, and how upset they all were - especially Kim's friend, Mary who'd known her since childhood

'Do you think Jamal had anything to do with Kim's disappearance?'

'No. Of that I'm absolutely certain. He's devastated, and Mary tells me he looks more gaunt and wasted each time they go to the prison to see him. But I don't think his family approves. He had an unpleasant visit one evening from two of his cousins when Kim was at his flat. They called her a whore, and told Jamal to get rid of her. Kim was terrified.

'I'm not surprised. What did Kim do?'

'Well, she left the flat immediately and went to stay with Mary. But the whole incident seemed to blow over pretty quickly. Jamal told Kim that his cousins were stupid, ignorant young men, and she was not to worry about them.'

'Did they tell the police?'

'Not till much later.'

'So they could be involved with Kim's disappearance.'

'Yes, I think it's a strong possibility.'

Then Stuart asked, 'Do you think Jamal's guilty?'

'I've very ambivalent feelings about him. In many ways, Jamal seems such a caring person I can't believe he's involved in terrorism. On the other hand, there are a number of small events which I can't quite explain away. And then there's Sir Ralph's suspicion that Jamal's involved with a terrorist group.

'He's a Muslim isn't he?

'Yes, but from all accounts, he's not very devout. Kim told Mary he never goes to the mosque, and does all the things Muslims are not supposed to do

'But now Jamal's been arrested do you think he's guilty?'

'As I said I feel ambivalent. Jamal's such a caring person. But I can't help wondering whether Jamal's relationship with Kim is a cover?'

'What an awful thought,' exclaimed Stuart. 'Well, I suppose we'll find the truth eventually.

David wearily agreed.

'Why I wanted to see you today,' said Stuart, 'was to ask whether you'd like to come with me to a Symposium in London. It's all about terrorism and the effects of different religious beliefs on our society. It's being organised jointly by a group of Christian, Muslim and Jewish clerics who are worried about the appalling terrorist activities that are happening here and overseas, the growing Islamophobia in this country, and the Jihadi movement. The Symposium aims to emphasise the commonality of all three religions, despite their differences.'

'Sounds interesting,'

'Well, it's next Saturday. I'm going up to London the night before, and staying with my sister. You know her, of course. If you'd like to come with me, I'm sure she'd be happy to have you stay.'

Knowing all the questions that lay ahead with Jamal's trial, David thought it would be helpful, so agreed to accompany Stuart the following Friday.

When they arrived at the Symposium David was overwhelmed by the number of clerics present – Christians with their clerical collars and coloured shirts, bearded Imans in long black garbs, rabbis identifiable by their dark suits and skull caps, and a sprinkling of Sikhs and Hindus. Among them David was relieved to see a number of laymen in lounge suits.

The chairman of the proceedings was a civil servant who explained that the object of the gathering was to discuss the increasing threat of terrorism, and consider ways to stop the threat escalating. He said a member of the government would put it in the context of world affairs and explain why the threat of terrorism was real, while a speaker from the Met would outline what was happening in society today. Then a Muslim Imam would talk about Jihad and its implications for world peace. This would be followed by a Christian and a Jewish speaker who would outline their basic beliefs and try to demonstrate the similarities as well as the differences between the three religions.

They would then be asked to get into small groups to discuss how terrorism was affecting society's attitudes. He hoped the discussions would be positive and they would consider possible ways in which they might develop a cohesive sense of British identity, and combat prejudice on the one hand, and distorted ideas on the other.

Stuart murmured to David, 'Sounds as though it's going be an interesting day.'

'Yes. His comment about the terrorist threat being real is rather close to home, isn't it?'

David felt this even more when the speaker from the Met insisted that terrorism was a real threat, not an imagined one, and that the authorities were constantly on the alert. Questioned from the floor, he said it was not possible to give any details, but the authorities were aware of small cells of terrorists throughout the country; that members of these cells were integrating themselves into society, appearing as ordinary citizens carrying on conventional ways of life. A common factor was that many terrorists were people who had been displaced, and were living away from the land of their birth. Osama Bin Laden was a case in point. Many of them were sophisticated, highly educated, and computer literate. Everyone should be on their guard, and report any suspicious circumstances.

The talk made David think about his own ambivalent attitude to Jamal and realised that all the things the speaker was saying could be applied to him. He was sophisticated, highly educated and computer literate. The only thing that didn't apply was that he hadn't been displaced but had been born and bred in Britain.

David felt even more uneasy when the speaker talked about militant Imams grooming young men into believing that they would go to paradise if they became suicide bombers. He remembered the time he'd seen Al outside the mosque walking along with his arms round two young men.

The speaker pointed out that suicide bombing was a cheap and effective way of creating terror and death. It was almost impossible to pick out a would-be suicide bomber in a crowd – so many people these days carried rucksacks – and it was only by patient investigation and surveillance that they could be found. That was where the public came in.

The next speaker was an Islamic scholar from Oxford who emphasised that Islam was basically a peaceful religion, and that Jihad was an aberration. It was in essence a political movement, and fundamentalism was a form of nationalism in religious disguise. Its adherents promoted the idea that the west was aggressive, and that Islam was under attack. But, he said, terrorists were not really motivated by Islam. Their aim was to get rid of the American presence in Pakistan and Afghanistan, and in the Arabian peninsula. Groups like Al-Quaeda were intent on world domination.

The only real hope for the future, as far as Britain was concerned, was for a more focused education of young people about tolerance and the British way of life. They urgently needed to work to try and persuade disenchanted young Muslims of their British identity. Equally, they needed to foster a greater tolerance of people from different ethnic groups, and, perhaps most important of all, they needed to try and stop people living in segregated communities.

Over a brief interlude for coffee Stuart said, 'Well, I must say they're giving us food for thought. I do agree about people not living in segregated communities. Your hospital's a case in point. You have a great variety of ethnic doctors and nurses yet they all seem to work happily together – almost as a family. It's when people cut themselves off into little community groups that troubles arise.'

'But that doesn't apply to Jamal does it?'

'No. I suppose not. Does what we've just heard affect your thoughts about him?'

'I just don't know. I like the fellow – but there are so many little things that make me doubt.'

'Difficult,' said Stuart sympathetically, but could say no more as they were summoned back for the next speaker.

The next speaker was an academic, working on comparative religions. He gave an interesting exposition of the various faiths. David had never read the Koran nor known much about Muhammad and hadn't realised that as a young man, Muhammad had come under the influence of Christian and Jewish teaching. Then, in about 610 AD, he'd had a vision which made him believe he was a messenger of God and from then on believed the Jews had corrupted the Scriptures, and that Christians, by worshipping Jesus as the Son of God, had disobeyed God's injunction to worship God alone. Muhammad believed it was his mission in life to bring back people to the true path.

'Wow!' thought David. 'No wonder Islam is seen as a militant religion.'

David knew a little more about Judaism - that the Jews acknowledged that Jesus was a great prophet steeped in Judaic beliefs and customs, but did not believe he was the Messiah. What he hadn't fully realised was that the Jewish Torah was more or less the same as the Old Testament.

During the ploughman's lunch which followed, it was obvious the talks had captured people's imagination and there was a lively buzz of conversation. But it was not long before they were all sent off to different groups.

David saw that the groups had been carefully composed. In his group were two rabbis - one born and brought up in England, the other, from Russia; two Imams - Malik from England and Zaid from Pakistan; a Baptist minister, Simon, from Bradford, who'd always worked in down-town urban areas, a Sikh and a Hindu priest; and an Anglican clergyman, Bob, who'd been in Arab countries for most of his ministry. Then there were three laymen – Isaac, a young Jewish academic, Sulieman, a primary school teacher, and David. Looking round, he had a sort of feeling of deja vue because Suleiman's face seemed familiar, but couldn't think how or where he'd met him.

When the discussion began, it was clear that the Baptist minister, and the Iman from Pakistan, were going to dominate the proceedings. They started by discussing, their similarities and agreed that the basic tenet of all three religions was a strong moral and caring code. Jews were told to be gracious and merciful, Muslims were told to act with justice, fair dealing, and kindness to orphans and widows, while Christians were enjoined to feed the poor, the hungry and the destitute and to love their neighbours as themselves. But there the consensus ended.

Simon weighed in on the barbarity of Islamic punishments – of a religion which allowed the stoning to death of adulterers, of public executions, lashings and mutilations of criminals. 'No wonder civilised people hate Islam.'

'But what about your Old Testament and the vengeful God who allowed thousands to be killed when the Jews wanted to go back to the promised land?' said Zaid

'Surely,' said Bob, 'what is needed is compassion and tolerance.'

The rabbi from England agreed.

David said very little – telling people he was here just to observe.

They asked Isaac and Suleiman how they found life in Great Britain.

Isaac replied first, saying, 'I've never experienced any intolerance. I don't feel different. My family keeps all the Jewish festivals, but it doesn't really affect our way of life.'

'What about you, Suleiman,' asked Bob. 'Are you happy here?'

Suleiman shook his head violently. 'I've been called 'paki scum' a number of times, and my wife gets spat on when she goes out wearing the bourka. Your so-called western tolerance! It's a figment of your imaginations!'

'That doesn't happen where I live,' said Isaac.

'Normal where I live,' said Suleiman fiercely. 'But Jews are as bad as the rest!'

Then Zahid muscled in and said the west was corrupted by immoral secularism – by its sexual immorality, pornography, gambling, intoxication, and homosexuality. At the mention of homosexuality, David saw Simon nodding in agreement. Zahid went on to say that many Muslims feel threatened.

'Hey, hey, let's leave it there!' said Bob. 'What we've been asked to do is discuss whether there's any way forward. Have any of you been involved in local action to help alleviate the threat of terrorism?'

'Well, yes,' said Malik, the elderly Iman. 'We've been trying to get Muslim and Christian youths together in clubs. And, before Friday prayers, we take aside the young men and try to get them to think about tolerance and care for our fellow human beings.'

They all agreed that this was a good idea and a possible way forward. They also thought it would be helpful if the 'clergy' from all three religions met regularly and worked together with disadvantaged groups and organised some community projects. Most agreed on the need for vigilance and the duty laid on all of them to report any suspicious activities. They also agreed they needed to speak out in their places of work and worship.

The discussion was lively and interesting, and David felt that, on the whole, their group comprised tolerant and caring people. But he suspected that they were not perhaps representative of their communities as a whole. And the outburst from Suleiman left him feeling uneasy.

They were soon called back to a plenary discussion with one person in each group reporting back. They were all thanked for coming and were told they would be receiving a report based on the notes made by each group

Stuart and David travelled back in a sombre mood. They talked about their discussion groups and found they'd had similar experiences. David told Stuart about Suleiman's outburst, and his feeling that he'd seen Sulieman, before, but just couldn't think where. They discussed Jamal's imprisonment, and wondered whether what they'd heard had any relevance to his guilt or innocence. David felt a shiver go through him when he thought about what the man from the Met had said about educated Muslims integrating themselves into western society. Was this what Jamal and Ali had been doing?

-39-
Mary and David's pub lunch

A few days after the Symposium and Mary's visit to Jamal in prison, David invited Mary to lunch. He picked her up from her office. It was a bright sunny day, and the countryside looked beautiful, with the leafless trees standing stark against the blue sky. But there was a real nip in the air. As they walked into the pub which was full of Christmas lights, he realised with a jolt that it was nearly Christmas which he hadn't given much thought to other than knowing he'd be joining his sister and her family whom he hadn't seen since their father's funeral.

They found a table by the window and, glancing across the room, they saw two members of the hospice appeal committee, Alice Mountjoy and Alec Williams, sitting cosily at a table in the opposite corner of the pub, holding hands. It gave David a bit of a shock, as he knew they hadn't met before the appeal committee was formed. Another potential marriage break-up, he thought sadly. Mary had seen them too, and said, 'Oh dear. How sad. I've seen them together before.'

They seemed oblivious to the people around them, and Mary and David, almost by instinct, tried to make themselves invisible by sitting with their backs to them.

Mary told David about all the questions she and Julian had put to Jamal saying that Julian had been fairly fierce with him, but Jamal had said nothing that gave her any feeling that he was guilty of terrorism.

'But the chemicals in the garage?'

'Well, it seems to me there's a distinct possibility that it was Al Mercer who planted them. Jamal obviously didn't like the idea – Al being such an old friend. But both Julian and I felt that Jamal didn't really know Al. He didn't know what his business was, why he came to England, or where he went to when he was abroad. And he couldn't give us an address to contact Al as he said he was always travelling around.'

'But he must have known about the chemicals if they were in his garage.'

'Well, he told us he'd asked where the police had found them, and they wouldn't tell him. When Julian said they were in the garage, he seemed surprised – but said the garage was full of rubbish from the previous tenants and he'd never got round to sorting it out!'

'But how could they have got there?'

'Well, Julian and I are wondering whether Al planted them in the garage the night before Kim disappeared. As you know, Kim went back to her own flat that weekend because Al was coming to stay. But Jamal said

Al hadn't come after all. However, when we questioned Jamal further it emerged that Al had phoned Jamal at the hospital. When he learnt Jamal was to be away all night, he'd said he wouldn't stay after all, but would go to friends. Is it possible that Al, knowing Jamal was going to be away, went to Jamal's flat and left the chemicals there? He had a key.'

It seemed a possible explanation, but David wondered how it could be proved.

He then told Mary about the Symposium and that it had left them feeling more than a little apprehensive. 'They seem to think there are little terrorist cells all over the country waiting to be activated. And what really troubles me is that they told us that many of these terrorists are educated, sophisticated people who insinuate themselves into local communities as ordinary, everyday, citizens. I ask myself - could that be what Jamal and Ali have done?'

'Al, for sure,' said Mary. 'But I don't think Jamal falls into that category.'

'I very much hope you're right,' he said. 'but unless someone can find who planted that bomb-making equipment, there isn't a hope of acquittal.'

With that, the food they'd ordered arrived, and they talked of other things. Looking at the decorations, she asked what he was doing for Christmas. He told her he was going up to Scotland to stay with his sister.

'Oh,' she said, 'of course. Dan and Celia were going to invite you to spend Christmas with us if you were on your own. But, of course,' she repeated, 'you'll be wanting to spend this first Christmas without your father, with your own family.'

David couldn't help feeling disappointed as was Mary, but she said brightly, 'Well, you'll have to come over when you get back. Will you be staying there for the New Year?'

'I don't know yet. It depends what my sister has in mind.'

'Tell me about her,' she said.

He described the family – his sister and her work, her husband and their four children. 'You'd like them.' Mary was so easy to talk to that he found himself telling her how they'd all reacted to his father's death, and about his own feelings when he died.

While they were talking, they noticed Alice and Alec leaving the pub. Although David suspected they'd seen them, they slipped out without acknowledging their presence. He and Mary left soon after, and David drove her back to her office before returning to the hospital.

It was a couple of days later when Stan Pointer, a senior police inspector, called on David. He said, 'I take it that, now Jamal Khan is in prison, you are in charge of the hospice appeal?'

'Well, yes and no. I'm not formally in charge, but it seems it has fallen to my lot to look after things while we decide what to do.'

'As I thought. Well, I want to bring you up to date with what we know about the Appeal's money. You know, of course, that some of the money in the Hospice Appeal Account (£598,000) was transferred to another account called the *New Appeal Account*. It was the statements of the *Hospice Appeal Account* that were being sent to your Treasurer, Tracy Pilkington, while the name of the account holder of the *New Appeal Account* was Andrew Minton (notice the initials!) with an address in Watford. But we've been to the address and the house is occupied by tenants who have only been there three weeks. Andrew Minton's tenancy agreement came to an end on the 13th October - a week before the disappearance of Kim Anderson and not long before we found the chemicals in Dr Khan's flat'

'And the money?'

All the money from New Appeal Account accounts, £598,000 in all, was transferred to a Swiss Account. This is something we are now investigating.'

'Can the money be recovered?'

'Too early to say. It will depend on further investigation, and the decision of the courts. I will keep you informed of progress.'

'Will you be able to keep this confidential for the moment? If the news got out before the money is recovered, it would put an end to the hospice project.'

'Yes. It doesn't need to become public yet. But don't pin your hopes on recovering the money.'

David thanked him, not that he felt there was much to be thankful for. It was a huge amount of money to go astray and he felt they had all been negligent. He knew they couldn't blame Tracey – though it was her incompetence that had allowed this to happen. They should have supported her and been more attentive to what was going on. David was angry with himself as well as with his fellow committee members.

He decided, once again, that he needed to call together what he now thought of as the inner circle – Mark, Alec, Mary and Henry. They were appalled to discover how much money had been siphoned off, but all agreed to keep it to themselves for the moment. However, they asked David to go and see Jamal and try to discover whether he had any inkling of what had happened.

When he got to the prison he was shocked by Jamal's appearance. Mary had told him he wasn't looking too good, but David hadn't expected to see him looking so thin and gaunt.

David told him about the missing Appeal money, and could see he was genuinely horrified, but when David told him that the police suspected that Al Mercer was involved, Jamal shook his head and said, 'Not possible!'

David decided to be blunt. 'Look Jamal. You don't seem to know all that much about your friend's affairs. And it seems to me that you've always been a bit reticent about Al when I've spoken to you about him. I've met him on several occasions, and when I mentioned it to you, you denied he'd been in England, and said it must have been someone else. But I have no doubts it was Al on each occasion I saw him. What's been going on, Jamal? We need to know.'

Jamal had a closed expression on his face, and shook his head as though he wasn't prepared to answer.

'Jamal. You say you know nothing about the chemicals in your flat. The police, and several others, think Al may be implicated. You deny all knowledge – but things look very black for you. If you don't tell us all you know, what hope have we of proving your innocence?'

Jamal was silent for quite a long time, then said, 'All I know is that Al was in financial difficulties and was dodging creditors. He didn't trust anyone and made me swear not to tell anyone he was in England.'

'But he came to the meetings at the hospital and to Kim's parties!' David exclaimed, puzzled.

'Well, yes. But by then, he'd paid off his creditors so he didn't need to hide.'

This seemed a rather feeble explanation, but it was all David could get out of him. As Christmas was just a week ahead, David said he would come and visit when he got back from Scotland.

He'd done no Christmas shopping and found himself braving the crowds on the Saturday before Christmas. As well as his sister and family, he wanted to get presents for Mary and Jamie as well as Celia and Dan as he'd enjoyed so much hospitality from them. Jamie was easy, and so were Dan and Celia, but Mary was difficult. He wanted to get her something special – but at the same time, didn't want to get anything that was too meaningful. He realised he was becoming very fond of her but after his experiences with Joanna and Samantha, he needed to go very slowly, In the end, he purchased a beautiful but inexpensive turquoise necklace which matched the dress she'd been wearing at Stuart's Silver Wedding party.

Mary asked when he was going up to Scotland, and when he told her he was travelling after work on the 23rd, she invited him round for dinner on the 21st. He decided to take his presents round with him, and to his surprise they presented him with gifts as well. He felt very touched. His were a gesture of thanks, but he felt theirs were a measure of affection.

Jamie, who was allowed to stay up for a while, was very excited. He insisted David went and inspected the tree, and then showed him the stocking Mary had made for him – a very large canvas foot with a red ribbon round the top. He told him all about Father Christmas and how he was going to leave out a glass of whisky and a mince pie for him, as he was sure to be cold after travelling round with the reindeers in the sky. His little face was lit up with excitement, and David wanted to give him a great hug.

When David went to leave, Celia kissed him warmly goodbye, and Mary said, 'I hope Christmas won't be too difficult for you all. I'll be thinking of you.' Then she gave him a hug, and waved him off.

-40-
David's Christmas visit to Scotland

David took several things to read on the train but spent most of the time thinking about Mary. He had to acknowledge that he was becoming increasingly fond of her – but not in the way he'd felt about Samantha - or indeed Joanna.

Once again, he tried to analyse his failed relationships. He asked himself if his expectations were too high. Was he looking for something that didn't really exist? If that initial spark, that sexual frisson, was not there, did it mean that love was missing? Was that spark an essential ingredient of a good and stable relationship, or could one be built without it? What in fact was love within a relationship? Was it sexual attraction or just friendship and trust? Could one exist without the other?

He'd scarcely noticed Mary to begin with. It wasn't until their paths crossed when Kim disappeared, that he'd really got to know her. In the last few months, they'd shared all the problems surrounding Kim's disappearance and Jamal's arrest, and as each problem emerged, he'd turned to Mary for her opinion and advice. Then he thought about Mary's own chequered life – and little Jamie who'd wormed his way into his heart.

He read a little, dozed a little, and after some five hours arrived in Edinburgh where he had to change trains. Edinburgh was not David's favourite station with its confusing levels and a roadway that seemed to divide it in two. As the time between trains was usually limited he was always scared he wouldn't find the right platform in time.

When he got to Perth just before midnight, James was waiting for him at the barrier. The drive to their village took nearly an hour, but Alison had stayed up and greeted him with a tray of food and drink. She said the children had gone to bed – but Steven had obviously heard the car driving in and came rushing down to greet him. He'd grown in the three months since he'd last seen him. He gave David a big hug, which made him feel very emotional as he thought of his father, and how close he and Steven had been.

Alison said, 'I've put you in Dad's flat. I thought you'd like that - but if you'd rather not, there's a bed made up in the spare room.

A TORTUOUS PATH

It gave David a jolt when he thought about being in his father's flat. But after thinking about it for a moment, realised he would like the feeling that he was, in some sort of way, close to him, so said 'yes.'.

Although they all felt their father' absence, it was difficult to be sad at Christmas when there are children around. Christmas Eve was spent in preparation. James had to work in the morning, and Alison did some shopping, while David and the children spent time wrapping presents and adding more decorations to the house. Various friends popped in and out during the day, and David felt strangely happy.

Little Jack, who was as excited as Jamie had been earlier in the week, was persuaded to go to bed only after he'd placed a mince pie and whisky in the hearth ready for Father Christmas. Susie went to bed a little later, equally excited, but David suspected that at age eight, she was not quite sure whether Father Christmas really existed!

They had a late supper, and then Alison, Jenny and David went to the Midnight service at their local church while James stayed at home to look after the other children. The Christmas Midnight service was the only service, other than weddings and funerals, that David ever attended. It was a tradition going back to childhood. He loved the service – the church beautifully decorated and candlelit, the familiar carols, and the sense of excitement and mystery. This year was no exception, and as he sat enjoying the service he thought about Mary for whom a service like this, though special, would be part of her regular worship. What was he missing, he asked himself.

The two younger children woke very early Christmas morning and, from his father's flat he could hear their happy voices as he lay in bed. He'd gone straight to sleep the night before. It had been a very long day. But now, the sun shining into the flat, he had time to think about their father and all that he'd meant to them. The flat was much as he'd left it, with all his books in the many bookshelves, and his desk with its lap-top still as it was. He realised that Alison had not been able to bring herself to sort it out yet. Only the clothes were missing.

As in all families, Christmas Day followed its usual pattern - preparing food, opening presents, having champagne, smoked salmon and tit bits at midday. Getting on for 3 o'clock, they sat down to their Christmas dinner, which took until the light faded. Then it was time for games which they all joined in. It was a hilarious and noisy time, and David felt how lucky they were to be able to enjoy a family Christmas. He was mindful of all those without families, and his thoughts turned to Jamal languishing in prison, not knowing where Kim was, or what had happened to her. He thought of Mary and Jamie, and Celia and Dan, and asked Alison if he could use the phone to ring some friends to wish them a happy Christmas.

Mary answered. She seemed delighted he'd rung. She asked him what they were doing. He told her about their day, and asked she had been doing. She said her parents were with them, and Celia and Dan's son and family, and they'd all had a lovely time, especially Jamie who'd had a wonderful day with his cousins. She said she'd popped in to see Jamal the day before, and had taken him some goodies, but that he seemed very low.

They chatted for a while, then she said, 'I must go. Jamie's calling. It's lovely to hear you.'

'I'll call you when I get back,' he said, 'Give my love to Jamie and Dan and Celia,

When he returned to the sitting room, Alison gave him an enquiring look.

'Mary – the friend of Kim who disappeared?'

'Yes,' said Alison, 'you've mentioned her several times. Tell us more.'

'Well, she's a lawyer. She's a widow – a very young widow – or rather – oh dear, it's all rather complicated. She was engaged to be married, and a week before the wedding her fiancé was killed in a road accident (not his fault). Instead of a wedding, there was a funeral. I just can't imagine what she must have gone through.'

Alison and James both looked shocked.

'So she went back to work?'

'No. A week or two after Ben's death she discovered she was pregnant.'

'Oh, how awful,' exclaimed Alison.

'No, I don't think it was. She says it was a way of somehow holding on to Ben.'

Alison nodded. 'Yes, I can understand that. What did she have – a boy or girl?'

'A little boy. His name is Jamie. He's nearly three – an absolutely delightful child. I'm very fond of him,' he added – and then realised he'd given himself away.

He could see that Alison and James were wondering about his relationship with Mary – but tactfully refrained from asking. Instead, Alison said, 'How does she cope with a child and a job?'

'Well, that's the lovely thing. Her future in-laws, Dan and Celia live in a large house in the country. There's a separate flat in the house, and when Ben died they asked Mary if she'd like to live there. They persuaded her to go back to work when Jamie was a year old. She has a nanny, and Dan and Celia spend a lot of time helping to look after him.'

'How wonderful for Mary after such a tragedy,' said Alison, then asked, 'How did you first meet her?'

David embarked on a lengthy explanation about the Hospice Appeal, Kim's disappearance, Jamal's arrest, and the attempts he and Mary had made to get in touch with Kim's mother. James wanted to know how Jamal came to be accused of terrorism, so he told him all about the chemicals, the police suspicions, the conversations with Sir Ralph, and the growing suspicion that his friend Al was involved.

'Didn't your father meet Jamal?' asked James. 'I seem to remember he spoke quite warmly about him – said he was a very caring and thoughtful man.'

'Yes,' David replied. 'They took to each other and were planning to have lunch together when Dad next came down to visit.'

The mention of his father put a little cloud on the evening, and it wasn't long after that they all went to bed.

Boxing Day was bright and sunny, so they all went for a long walk stopping off at the pub for a drink and a snack before returning home for more games. David had realised before that Alison's children were insatiable as far as games were concerned. This year, the favourite was *Risk,* a board game that involved conquering the world with armies of tiny soldiers. It was quite a complex game as far as strategy was concerned, and David enjoyed it to begin with but, like *Monopoly*, it went on for hours as armies wrestled with each other for possession of continents. By the end of the holiday, David did all he could to avoid playing. James, who had a week off, saved the day by buying *Colditz* which the children decided was as much fun, and didn't take quite so much time to finish.

David felt very happy being with the family. He and Alison were able to talk about their father without feeling too upset, and they made some decisions about what to do with his possessions. James and Alison had considered letting the flat, but decided to keep it for themselves and their friends, and David whenever he wanted to visit.

One evening they went to an amateur production of *Jack and the Beanstalk*. It was hilarious and they all enjoyed it – especially the children. Jenny, who was sixteen the week before Christmas, pretended to be superior about pantomimes but eventually deigned to go along and quite obviously enjoyed it though wouldn't admit it for fear of losing face

They visited several friends of Alison and James whom David had got to know over the years. It was a very happy week, and when the time came for him to return south he felt sad to leave, but excited at the thought seeing Mary and Jamie again. Mary had phoned after Christmas to find out when he was returning home as she said Celia was giving a party for Dan's sixtieth birthday on the Saturday after Christmas and hoped he would be back in time to be there. When he told her he would, she said, 'That's great! Dan will be pleased. And you'll be able to meet my parents as they're staying on for the party. And Celia said, if you can come you must stay the night so you won't have to worry about drinking.'

When he told Alison about the invitation, it led to one or two quiet conversations about Mary. He confided his uncertainties about what was important in a relationship, and she said firmly, and without hesitation, 'Friendship and trust. As time goes by, sex is only of secondary importance for many couples. All my friends agree. Your Mary sounds lovely. You must bring her up to meet us.'

David hadn't thought that far ahead, nor actually thought of Mary as 'his Mary', but the idea appealed to him, though he was hesitant in his response. 'She may not want to come. We're not exactly a couple.'

'No, but it sounds as though you should be. From what you tell me, I think she must like you a lot. Why don't you ask her to marry you?'

The idea both attracted and scared him. 'I don't know about that,' he said.

'Go for it,' were Alison's last words to him as he boarded the train at Perth.

-41-
Dan's 60th birthday party

David caught a very early train in order to be back in time for Dan's party. He just had time to buy Dan a birthday present at the bookshop at King's Cross Station, choosing a copy of the new biography of Charles Darwin.

Ignoring the post that had accumulated over Christmas, David dressed rather more carefully than usual, packed a few overnight clothes as well as casual clothes for the next day, and set off at about seven o'clock.

Mary opened the door but before she could greet him properly Jamie came rushing down the corridor and gave him a big hug. David felt emotional at this show of affection. 'It's grandpa's birthday. And I'm staying up for it,' he said excitedly. 'You've got to come and see grandpa and say happy birthday.'

'Hey,' said Mary smiling, giving David a quick conventional kiss on either cheek, 'Let Uncle David get in first. We've got to show him where he's sleeping tonight. You go first and show him the way.'

Jamie took his hand and led him up the main staircase and along a corridor to a beautifully furnished bedroom.

'This is your room,' said Jamie proudly. 'And my grandma and grandpa are sleeping with us in our flat.'

'He's so excited about the party,' explained Mary. 'Come down as soon as you're ready.'

David followed her down fairly quickly, carrying the present for Dan, who was in the drawing room talking in a very relaxed fashion to a good-looking young man with red hair. Dan jumped up when he saw him and said, 'It's good to see you David. I'm so glad you're back in time – not that sixty is exactly a birthday to celebrate,' he added wryly.

'Oh, I don't know. Sixty's a fine age to be – with good experiences to build on, and years ahead to do what you want with your life! So, happy birthday! I hope you'll enjoy this. It's been well reviewed.'

Dan unwrapped it straight away 'David,' he said with a beaming smile. 'You couldn't have chosen anything better. I've wanted to get hold of a copy of this ever since I read the reviews. Thank you so much. And now,' he added, turning to the young man he'd been talking to so intimately a few moments before, 'I mustn't forget my manners! This is Patrick, a very old friend of Mary. And this is David – I was telling you about him earlier. He's a very respected administrator at our local hospital.'

They shook hands – but without any warmth on David's part. Dan's introductory comment - 'a very old friend of Mary' – worried him. Patrick obviously knew Dan well judging by the intimate way they were talking when he came into the room.

When Dan added, 'Patrick's staying too, so it's going to be a very happy family gathering,' David felt his heart sinking even further.

David tried not to glare at Patrick, but his insides were churning. He thought he'd been invited because he was a special friend of Mary – and now, here was someone at the party who'd known Mary for a long time and seemed to be quite at home. He felt confused and upset.

He didn't have time to think further before Celia came in with an elderly couple, 'These are Mary's parents, Sybil and Henry,' she said. They seemed much older than Dan and Celia, and quieter and more retiring. But they were welcoming, and said Mary had told them a lot about him, and that it was good to meet up at last.

That reassured David a little until they went on to say how good it was to see Patrick here. They'd known him for such a long time.

Other guests began to arrive – among them were some he knew - Stuart and Susan, Margaret and her husband Edward, Peter, his doctor, and his wife, and Jane and Colin Masters, just back from their three-month trip to New Zealand. Then Anthony (Dan and Celia's son) and his wife, Felicity, arrived with their two children – much to Jamie's delight. The children gave Jamie a hug, and whisked him straight off to the playroom. Mary said Jamie had spent a wonderful time at Christmas with his cousins who'd made a great fuss of him as the baby of the family

Then Pam Litchfield arrived, and David realised that Dan and Celia had invited some of Mary's friends to the party so she didn't feel left out.

It was a very relaxed evening with about thirty people there. Celia had brought in caterers so she could enjoy the party without anxieties about the food.

David couldn't help glowering in Patrick's direction, and Celia must, to his chagrin, have noticed because she came up to him and put her hand through his arm. 'It's so good to have you here – and Mary's old friends. She's known Patrick since she was sixteen and they were all together at Oxford. He was a good friend of Ben, and when Ben died Patrick gave us a lot of support. But he and Mary have never been an item.' She gave his arm an encouraging squeeze, and waved him over to Jane and Colin Masters who were walking towards them.

Both embarrassed and reassured by Celia's remark, David realised it had propelled him into realising how very important Mary was becoming to him.

But, for the moment, his attention turned to Jane. 'Did you have a good time in New Zealand?' he asked.

'Wonderful. But there's always the problem of parting. It's good to be back – but it's sad to know it will be at least a year before we see our daughter and her family again.'

David nodded – realising the wrench it must be to have one's loved ones living so far away. For him, Scotland had seemed like another planet but at least he'd been able to get up to see his parents within a few hours. He felt sorry for those families whose children emigrate, some of whom they never see again. He realised he'd been fortunate in having his family comparatively nearby.

Jane said, 'I was devastated to hear the news of Jamal's arrest. Our neighbours told me as soon as we got back. They knew I was involved with the hospice appeal. I just can't believe he's involved in terrorism.'

'I know. It's difficult to believe. But the police have found chemicals in his garage.'

'Yes, that's what my neighbours said. But I can't believe they were put there with any intent.'

'Sadly, there was bomb making equipment with the chemicals.'

'But you say Jamal denies putting them there.'

'Yes. Emphatically. And Mary believes him. She's been to see him several times, and her boss is acting as his lawyer. But the incontrovertible fact is that chemicals and bomb making equipment were found in his garage. If Jamal didn't put them there, who did? That's the difficult question.'

'Could anyone else have put them there? Didn't Jamal have a friend who often stayed with him?'

'Yes, Al. The police are investigating that. We discovered just before Christmas that Al may have been there the night before Kim disappeared, and it's just possible he was responsible for the chemicals. But that doesn't put Jamal in the clear. They were, after all, found in his garage.'

'There must be some mistake,' said Jane firmly. 'I know Jamal well, and I'm absolutely sure he would never get involved in terrorist activities. How could a man who wants hospice care for the dying want to blow people up? It's right out of the question.'

'But he is a Muslim,' David murmured.

'You're not saying, I hope, that all Muslims are terrorists!' said Jane, looking quite angry.

'No, of course not. But one has to accept that in all the recent terrorist activities Muslim's have been involved.'

'But that's just the point. Jamal was deeply concerned about the image the public and the press have of Muslims. And, more important, he was very worried about the young Muslims who were getting involved in terrorist activities. You know, of course, that he's a founder member of a group trying to wean young Muslims away from the influence of the militant elements in the Muslim community? I forget what it's called.'

'No,' said David, surprised. 'I didn't know that. He's never spoken to me about it.'

'That's not surprising. I know he kept it very much to himself. He hated acknowledging that there was a terrorist element among the Muslims in England.'

'When did he tell you all this?' he asked, curious that Jane seemed to know much more about Jamal than he did.

'Well, if you remember, you sent me over to see him the night he got the letter from Kim saying she was leaving him.'

David nodded.

'As you can imagine, all he talked about to start with was Kim and why she'd left him. I suggested gently that it might be because Kim, being a very committed Christian, was having second thoughts about marrying a Muslim. This he denied emphatically. He said they'd sorted all that out before they entered into a serious relationship. He told me he felt very sympathetic to the Christian religion and the teachings of Jesus – though the resurrection baffled him. This led us on to talking about the relationship between Muslims and Christians – and it was then that he told me of his anxieties about young Muslims being drawn into terrorism, and that he and a few friends had set up an organisation to try and combat it.'

'I wonder why he's said nothing about it to me or to his lawyers?'

'Perhaps he's worried it might incriminate him – working with a group of Muslims.

'Perhaps,' he agreed.'

'But, you know,' said Jane, 'I really don't believe that Islam is an important part of Jamal's life. I think his Muslim upbringing is something he acknowledges when he's with family and friends, but is not significant otherwise.'

'Why do you say that?'

'Well, he's been along to our church with Kim on several occasions. He wouldn't have done that if he'd been a strict Muslim would he?'

David had to agree.

That comment reminded him of his refusal to accept Mary's invitation to the church and the Bring and Share Lunch, and he felt foolish thinking how much more difficult it must have been for a Muslim

Then they were joined by Stuart, and Colin asked how the hospice appeal was progressing. David told them about the embezzled appeal funds. They were shocked and asked all sorts of questions. David admitted to feeling guilt that they hadn't kept their eyes on the accounts. 'But we are keeping quiet about it for the moment. We don't want to damage the possibility of ever getting a hospice for the town.'

David then told them about his growing suspicion that it was Al who'd planted the chemicals in Jamal's flat. He explained how they'd proved that Al was there around the time Kim disappeared when he could have dumped the chemicals. He wasn't going to mention Sir Ralph's involvement in the situation, but Stuart asked, 'Did Sir Ralph get in touch with you again?'

The remark confirmed David's belief that he'd been set up to find information about Al right from the beginning of his involvement with the hospice appeal. It made him realise how complex and devious were the workings of the secret service.

Before they could talk any further, Anthony, Dan's son, asked them to raise their glasses to Dan on his sixtieth birthday. Dan stood there beaming, his family, including Mary and Jamie, surrounding him with a love and affection that was almost palpable. What a lovely man, David thought, and what a lovely wife, and he realised how good it would be to be part of that family.

His jealousy of Patrick had been abated by Celia's timely comment, and he thought he would go over and talk to him. He and Pamela were chatting happily in the corner, and he felt hesitant about joining them, but Patrick waved him over. 'What a lovely party. And how nice to get to know Mary's friends. Pamela's been telling me how you and she have known each other for years – rather like Mary and me. There's something special about old friends – I suppose it's because you can just be yourself.'

David agreed. 'And you knew Ben of course?'

'Yes, a very special person. We were all devastated by his death – it took a lot of coming to terms with. I think Dan and Celia, as well as Mary, have borne up very well. And of course, little Jamie has helped – though Mary was very anxious when she first discovered she was pregnant.'

'You were there?' David asked

'Yes, I spent quite a lot of time with them. They seemed to need someone from outside the family who knew Ben well. But it was a terrible time. Ben's brother and sister-in-law were wonderful. In fact, it's a great family. I love them all dearly.'

At that moment, Mary came over and took David by the arm and asked him to come and talk to her parents. Much older than Celia and Dan they had clearly come from a less affluent background. But from what she said it seemed that, in her quiet way, Mary's mother, Sybil, was as much involved in local activities as were Celia and Dan. She worked two days a week as a volunteer in the local hospice, and helped with a children's charity on another day. David wondered whether this was why Mary had agreed to come on the hospice committee. Her father, Henry, who seemed less approachable, had been a Rotarian and now retired, belonged to *Probus* and played golf twice a week. Both of them were active members of their local parish church.

It struck him that wherever he turned in this new social circle he seemed to be getting involved with people who were active Christians. What, he wondered again, was he missing?

Mary's father asked David about his work in the hospital. He'd been a local government architect involved with the building of the town's new local hospital. They soon got into an animated discussion about hospital buildings and the most effective way they could be maintained.

Mary's mother talked about Kim, and said she'd known her from the age of eight. 'Such a terrible thing, her disappearance,' she said. 'She was a beautiful child, with those bright auburn curls – and she had a lovely personality. She put Mary in the shade – but she was never stuck up about it. But, of course,' she added. 'you knew her quite well too. She's a colleague, isn't she – or rather, was?'

David nodded. Then she started asking him about himself so he told her a little about Joanna and the divorce. She murmured, 'How sad,' but then changed the subject.

As the evening wore on David realised Patrick and Pamela were still sitting in the corner of the room engaged in animated conversation. It struck him how very good it would be if the two got together.

Most of the guests left around midnight, Stuart and Susan taking Pamela home. The rest of them – Anthony and family, Mary's parents, Patrick, and David were all staying. Dan picked up Jamie who'd fallen asleep on one of the sofas in the drawing room and carried him up the stairs. After thanking Dan and Celia for a lovely evening David kissed them all goodnight and went up to bed

Though the bed was comfortable, David couldn't get to sleep. The events of the evening and the various conversations whirled round in his head. He thought about the conversation he'd had with Jane when she told him about Jamal's anxieties about young Muslims being drawn into terrorism, and that he and a few friends had set up an organisation to try and combat it. This made him think about the Symposium when the elderly Iman, Malik, had told them about his organisation which was trying to get Muslim and Christian youth together. He realised it sounded similar to the onee Jamal was involved with.

Then David tried to analyse his hostile response to Patrick before Celia had so tactfully told him they were not an item. He realised he didn't want anyone else to have Mary. Did that mean he wanted to marry her? The thought frightened him. After his disastrous relationships with Joanna and Samantha, was he capable of embarking on marriage again? And would Mary have him if he asked her? All these thoughts flooded his mind and it wasn't until after four o'clock that he fell asleep. He was the last to come down to breakfast. Only Celia was there looking after Jamie – the rest had left for church except for Patrick, who, said Celia with a twinkle in her eye, had popped over to see Pamela.

David apologised for his lateness, but Celia assured him not to worry. 'You've had a hectic time with that long train journey down from Scotland. It's so good you were able to come. Mary was really pleased when you said you'd be back in time.'

'Well, I certainly wouldn't have wanted to miss the party. It was such a splendid evening. I hope Dan enjoyed it.'

'He loved every minute of it,' said Celia with a smile. 'The only thing that saddened him was the absence of Ben. You would have liked him, I know.'

'You must all miss him dreadfully,' he ventured.

'Yes, but life has to go on – especially Mary's. She's far too young to remain alone for the rest of her life. We keep trying to assure her that we wouldn't feel hurt if she married again. We know she loved Ben deeply, and we know she loves all of us and, whatever happens, will remain part of our family. But we hope she marries again.'

With that she looked directly at him. 'I'm not trying to interfere, but I know Mary cares for you, and I think you care for her. I just wanted you to know that if you did decide to come together, you would have our blessing.'

Then she kissed the top of his head and, picking up Jamie, left the room.

David sat bemused. This was the second time he'd been encouraged to propose to Mary. Curiously, he didn't feel in any way he was being pushed – merely that people saw something good in the relationship that augured well for the future.

He'd been invited to stay for lunch so decided to go for a walk while the family were at church. He put on his winter coat and boots and, stopping first at the kitchen to tell Celia, set out towards the lake and into the woods beyond. When he got back the family had returned – full of the service and the sermon which all declared to have been very moving.

It was a noisy and lively family lunch with the children keeping them all amused with their antics. After lunch, Mary's parents, Sybil and Henry, as well as Anthony and family, had to leave as they all had long distances to go. Just before leaving, Henry pressed his hand and said, 'It's been good meeting you. Do get Mary to bring you down to see us,' and Sybil kissed him and said, 'Yes. Do. We'd love to see you.'

After they'd all left David made a move to leave but was pressed to stay on. He hesitated. 'I've only just got home and I didn't have time to unpack let alone look at the post and the ansa phone messages before coming to the party – and I go back to work tomorrow.'

'Oh, do stay on for a little while,' begged Celia. 'The house will seem so empty now everyone else has left. Why don't you have a walk and go after tea? That will give you the evening to unpack and sort yourself out. It's lovely and sunny out there – sad to waste the chance to enjoy the countryside. We'll look after Jamie.'

He was easily persuaded. He and Mary wrapped up warm and set off the same way he'd gone in the morning. They were unusually silent. He took her hand, and she laced her fingers through his. When they got to the woods, he took her in his arms and kissed her – not the fraternal kiss of the last few months, but a sweet and lingering kiss that set his pulses raging.

'I've been wanting to do that for a long time,' he said.

'Me too,' replied Mary.

The next hour was the happiest he'd spent in a long time. They found an old seat in the woods and sat down. David put his arms round her, and she nestled her head on his shoulder. David felt content and relaxed. This was not the overwhelming physical desire he'd felt for Samantha but something much gentler.

They talked – about Ben, about Jamie, about Joanna and Samantha. They talked about families and work. Mary said she'd take him down to see her parent's soon and show him where she'd been brought up. David told her that Susan wanted him to take her up to Scotland. They talked about work, about Dan and Celia and how lovely they were. In fact they talked about everything under the sun – but neither of them mentioned the word *love* or *marriage*.

It began to get dark and they made their way back to the house. Jamie was looking out of the window, waiting for them, Celia standing just behind. David felt she must have seen they were walking hand in hand because she gave him a conspiratorial little smile when they got back.

He left soon after tea, and when he got home, he spent the evening trying, once again, to analyse his feelings. It had been wonderful holding Mary in his arms, and he realised that he loved her – but not with the passion he'd felt for Samantha and Joanna. Was that, he asked himself, a good enough basis for marriage? She was intelligent, interesting to talk to, though rather serious much of the time. She was a wonderful mother. She was caring and sensitive. She'd come through a terrible tragedy with what, it seemed to him, was great courage. And she was very attractive in a quiet way, with a smile that lit up her face and made people feel special. He wondered how it was, at those early meetings, that he'd scarcely noticed her. He came to the conclusion that she was one of those people who sit quietly in the background, observing what is going on, before making any contribution to the discussion. He remembered how stunning she'd looked at Stuart and Susan's Sliver Wedding party, and realised she was a person who was not particularly interested in her appearance. Though he'd never seen her angry he suspected she could be quite fierce if crossed

As he thought about Mary and the weekend, it struck him that this was the first time they'd been together without once mentioning Kim or Jamal. The weekend had been a sort of milestone in their relationship – putting it onto a completely new basis. He knew he was holding back a little, but he was so frightened of making a mess of another relationship, that he wanted to be sure before committing himself. He was also a little anxious about Mary's religious belief, and wondered how far that might impinge on their relationship.

He felt amused rather than pressurised by the discreet encouragement he was receiving from all sides – but at the same time realised what a generous person Celia was, in, as it were, letting Ben go and encouraging Mary into a new relationship. He remembered with pleasure the way Celia and Dan's son and daughter-in-law had been so welcoming, as well as Mary's parents, and felt confident that if he and Mary were to get together, they would be embraced in a wonderfully warm and loving family.

-42-
Kim found

Though he loved his job, David never enjoyed going back to the hospital after a holiday because work usually piled up in his absence. This time, most of it had been dealt with. Jim, his new deputy, was a keen mountaineer, and was happy to cover for David at Christmas and in the summer so he could be away at Easter time to go to India for a month's climbing in the Himalayas.

A TORTUOUS PATH

One of the first people to greet David on his return was Mick Ellison. They exchanged accounts of how they had spent Christmas, and then David told Mick about Dan's sixtieth birthday party. Mick immediate response was to say, 'Mary's a lovely lady – just like Kim in many ways. She'd make you a good wife,'

This was the second time Mick had shown his match-making tendencies. David knew he was just speaking out of concern for his welfare so laughed and said, 'I'm not sure Mary would have me!'

Mick looked at David quizzically, and then told him he'd been to visit Jamal just before Christmas and had taken him a few goodies. David was both surprised and impressed, and felt a little ashamed that he hadn't been to see Jamal before he left for Scotland. Mick said how shocked he was with Jamal's appearance – how thin and gaunt he was.

'I just don't believe he's guilty of terrorism,' Mick declared. 'He works so hard, and he's so caring of the patients, and he's passionate about getting a hospice for the dying. How could he be involved in planning a terrorist attack to murder people? It just doesn't make sense.'

'I agree ….. to a certain extent,' said David hesitating. 'But we can't get away from the evidence of the bomb making equipment in his garage.'

'I know. That's what makes it so difficult. But I can't help wondering if that friend of his, Al, has anything to do with it. I never trusted him, you know. He always seemed friendly, but there was something about him I never liked.'

'That's interesting. That's exactly what Kim said.'

At the mention of Kim, Mick's face fell and he looked as if he was about to burst into tears. 'I keep thinking about her. She was such a lovely person – so kind, always looking out for other people. I have the awful feeling that she's dead. It's such a long time since she disappeared.'

Mick's words were prophetic. That evening there was a report on the News that a young woman's body had been found in the New Forest. David's heart sank when he heard it, as that was where Kim's car had been found.

The next morning the police arrived at the hospital. They said they'd found the body of a young woman who matched the description of Kim. They'd been in touch with Kim's mother, but she was so traumatised by the news that she refused to go and identify the body. As her employer they asked if David would go.

David's heart sank – both at the thought that it might be Kim, and at the thought of seeing her in what would, after all this time, be a terrible state. But he felt he had no option, and agreed.

The police said they would fly him down in the police helicopter that afternoon, as there was no point in bringing the body up if it wasn't Kim.

David wanted to talk to someone about it as he felt, like Kim's mother, traumatised at the thought, but he knew he shouldn't speak to anyone at the hospital until it was confirmed that it was Kim. Equally he didn't want to talk to Mary knowing it would upset her too much. The only two people he felt he might talk to were Stuart and Dan but in the end decided to go it alone.

The police collected him at two o'clock, and they flew to the mortuary at Southampton where the body had been taken. He knew in his heart that it was going to be Kim.

It was the worst thing he'd ever had to do. One look at the body lying on the table was enough. He nodded his head at the man in charge, touched Kim gently on the forehead, and left the room feeling sick at heart.

The inspector who'd accompanied him into the mortuary put his hand sympathetically on David's shoulder and said, 'Thank you. That was a very difficult and painful thing to have to do. You knew her well?'

David nodded and said, 'She was one of my senior nurses and a great friend,'

'So sad,' said the inspector. 'Why don't we go and have a cup of coffee somewhere quiet and you can then ask me anything you want to know.'

They went to a little side room and within a few minutes a tray of coffee arrived.

'Where was she found?' was David's first question.

'In a little clearing in the middle of the forest.'

'Who found her?'

'Well, it's rather a long story – bizarre in fact. There was a car crash in which a sixteen year old boy was involved. He was taken to hospital and though his injuries weren't serious, he was in a terrible state and kept crying and screaming that it was a judgement on him. This went on for some time, and eventually a hospital psychiatrist was called to see him. In the course of several sessions the psychiatrist gradually prized out of the boy that he'd been involved in the robbery of a jeweller's shop in Lyndhurst.'

'I remember. It was quite a dramatic robbery and they never found the thieves.'

'That's right. Well, the psychiatrist hadn't heard about robbery, but he probed further and discovered that a report had indeed hit the headlines a few months before and realised the police needed to be called in.

The police eventually persuaded the boy to tell them about the burglary but he absolutely refused to tell them where the silver was hidden or the name of his accomplice. He said he didn't dare - his friend would kill him if he told them his name.

Unable to do anything as there was no evidence, the police left.

'But what's all this got to do with Kim?'

'Well, despite the fact that he hadn't been arrested, the boy continued to have nightmares and agonised screaming fits. These were so severe the hospital didn't feel it could discharge him and sent him to a special psychiatric unit.

After some weeks, the psychiatrist eventually discovered the reason for the boy's distress. He told her he'd been digging a hole to put the stolen silver in when he saw a woman's face staring up at him from the bottom of the hole.

He said he was terrified and wanted to tell the police but his friend said that if they did, they would be accused of murder. He made him promise never to tell anyone. The boy said he'd been haunted by the dead woman's face every night since.

The police were called back, and after very careful handling, the boy finally agreed to show them where they'd buried the silver provided they gave him police protection. He still refused to give them the name of his accomplice.

Accompanied by staff from the psychiatric unit, the boy took them to the place deep in the forest where they'd hidden the silver. The hole was already well covered over with brambles and ivy, but when they dug down the police found both the silver and the body of a woman.'

'Kim,' said David putting his hands over his face to hide his tears.

'Yes, your friend Kim. It might be a slight consolation for you know that when the body was exhumed, they found she was fully clothed, and had been laid out carefully, with arms crossed and covered with a dark green blanket. There was no sign of sexual assault, and the cause of death was a single stab wound to the heart.'

David agreed it was a comfort to know she hadn't been sexually assaulted, and realised it might be a help for Jamal when he had to come to terms with Kim's death.

Flying back, David was in a state of shock. He knew it would be a long time before he would forget the beautiful face of Kim in such a state. The story of her discovery was so bizarre and shocking that he felt completely lost.

He needed to talk to someone and sort out both his feelings and how he would break the news to everyone. He begged the police to withhold the details until the next day so that he could prepare people for the shock. The police, to his relief, agreed.

He went home and telephoned Dan and told him the news. 'I don't quite know how to break it to Mary,' he said. 'I know she'll be terribly upset. And then there's Jamal - which will be even more difficult.'

Dan was immediately understanding. 'My dear boy, you've had a terrible ordeal. Why don't you come straight round. You don't want to be on your own. Have supper with us. Celia and I will break it to Mary gently that you've got bad news, and you can tell her the details.'

David was glad of the chance to be with people. He'd been dreading the thought of spending the evening at home alone after the trauma of the day. Apart from wanting to comfort Mary, the thought of having the chance to discuss with Dan the implications for Jamal gave him some relief.

He thought about the curious way shock takes over the mind so that it doesn't function normally. All sorts of thoughts and questions came flooding into his mind as he travelled to see Dan, not least who had killed her, and what was the motive for murdering a person who was so loved and admired by all her colleagues and friends.

He knew he would have to go and see Jamal and tell him the news – that is, unless the prison authorities had already done so. He realised it might give him just a shred of comfort to know that Kim hadn't been sexually assaulted – and that her death, with just the one stab wound to the heart, would have been swift. But he wanted to know, before he saw him, what Jamal would be allowed to do. Would he be able to go to the inquest? Would he be allowed out to attend her funeral? What effect would it have on Kim's colleagues at the hospital? Did Aunt Judith know? What would happen to Kim's flat? Had she made a will?

Celia opened the door when he arrived and gave him a hug. 'I'm so very sorry. I know you were very fond of Kim as a colleague and friend – and you must have had the most awful day. Come and sit down in the warm and I'll get you a drink.'

Dan was in the drawing room and jumped up to greet him. 'What a sad business. It's what we all feared – but that doesn't make it any easier. Mary's very upset as you can imagine. She's putting Jamie to bed at the moment.'

David told Dan all he knew and discussed with him how they should tell Jamal. He knew he would have to be the one who told him, but didn't fancy going alone – nor did he think it wise for Mary to go as he felt sure she would break down. Dan said, 'Why don't you ask Jane Masters to go with you? She knows Jamal, and I think Mary told me Jane spent the evening with Jamal the night he got the letter from Kim saying she was leaving him. She's such a warm and sympathetic person, as well as being a counsellor. She'd be the ideal person to go.'

David nodded. 'That's a good idea.' They went over the whole sad affair, and wondered who on earth would have had a motive for killing a woman who was so kind and so much loved.

Mary came down and David gave her a hug – all memory of the previous day having flown completely from his mind. She'd obviously been crying. 'Oh David, it's so awful. I can't believe it. She didn't deserve it. What monster can have done it?' and she burst into tears again.

It was Dan who took her into his arms and comforted her while David looked on helplessly.

Celia called them in to supper and they spent the whole time talking about Kim's murder. 'We must phone Aunt Judith,' said Mary. 'I expect she knows already if Kim's mother knows, but I think she'd like to hear from us.'

After they'd finished supper, they phoned Aunt Judith. As they suspected, she'd heard the news and was planning to go down the next day to see Kim's mother. She sounded very upset, but admitted it was news she'd been afraid of hearing ever since Kim disappeared.

David then phoned Jane Masters to see if she would come with him to the prison to see Jamal. She agreed straight away, and David said he would get in touch with the prison first thing next morning.

He didn't sleep much that night, He kept thinking about his visit to Jamal. How would he break the news that Kim had been murdered. Telling someone their loved one had died was bad enough, but telling them they had been murdered had all the elements of nightmare.

The next day Julian made the arrangements with the prison for Jane and David to visit Jamal. As it was not to be till the afternoon, he knew the hospital staff would have to be told before the news was made public.

David decided to send a memo to each ward sister, and to each department, telling them briefly that Kim's body had been found and that she had died of a single stab wound. He thought it was important to tell them that she hadn't been sexually assaulted. He said she'd been one of the most respected and loved members of the hospital family and that she would be deeply missed. He finished by saying that, in due course, there would be a Memorial Service for her.

He got no work done at all that morning as his office was besieged by both the press and the staff who wanted to know more. Mick was one of the first visitors – in tears, as were so many.

In the afternoon he and Jane set off for the prison with heavy hearts. Jamal's face lit up when he saw them, but quickly looked alarmed when he saw their faces and realised they were the bearers of bad news. He listened to them without comment, turned his head away, and sat in total silence, not moving a muscle.

David couldn't recall too much of that visit – he felt so terribly sad for Jamal. Jane was wonderful and eventually helped Jamal to cry – tears he'd been bottling up ever since Kim had disappeared. She held him close as one would a child and he sobbed on her shoulder.

David left the prison overwhelmed with sadness, realising there was nothing they could do or say to ease Jamal's grief. But before leaving they asked to see the prison governor and begged him to ensure that Jamal received sympathetic treatment in the days ahead. He agreed.

The next few weeks were a complete blur. Kim's death seemed to have enveloped them all in a black cloud which they couldn't shake off.

The press had a field day and the hospital was besieged by reporters trying to find out more about Kim.

David tried to keep them out of the hospital but failed. The press focused on the amazing coincidence of the thieves digging a hole to hide the silver in the very place Kim's body had been buried. They speculated on the odds of such a thing ever happening again. One paper explored the possibility that the boys had been involved in Kim's murder, but the dates of Kim's disappearance and the robbery didn't tie up.

There were long articles about Kim and her relationship with Jamal and they made much of the fact that he was now in prison on a charge of terrorism. They wrote about Kim's popularity as a nurse and as a person.

They also speculated on the whereabouts of the boy's accomplice. The police had very quickly identified who he was and where he lived but he had disappeared from sight and there was a big police hunt out for him. They discussed the odds of burying the proceeds of a robbery with the finding of a dead body.

Mary and David met up from time to time, but it was as though the closeness of the weekend of Dan's party had never happened. They couldn't put aside the fact that one of their friends had been murdered. It was something none of them had ever imagined happening to someone they knew – and it set them all thinking about their own mortality.

-43-
Kim's funeral

As the cause of her death was very clear-cut, the police allowed Kim's body to be released and her funeral to take place. Kim's mother agreed that Kim should be buried in the small village church where she'd worshipped for the last few years. Jane's husband, Colin was to take the funeral service in the morning, to be attended just by relatives and close friends, as the church was so small. Then in the afternoon there would be a Memorial Service in the big town church.

Kim's father, Charles, flew over from America and stayed in a local hotel. David spent the evening before the funeral with him, knowing he would be completely alone otherwise. David liked him. He was an interesting man who was clearly very fond of Kim even though they hadn't seen much of each other during the last few years. But, he said, they'd kept closely in touch with letters and long telephone calls.

A TORTUOUS PATH

He was deeply upset by the murder of his daughter, but David was impressed by the fact that, though he expressed the hope that her murderer would be found soon, he didn't call for vengeance. David had always been sickened when newspapers gloried in reporting the horrific expressions of vengeance made by bereaved relatives, and the call for the death penalty to be re-introduced.

He wanted to know about Jamal, and said he would like to visit him in prison before he returned to America. He obviously knew quite a lot about him from Kim's letters, and said he thought there must be some huge mistake about the chemicals found in his flat. He just couldn't imagine Kim getting involved with a terrorist. David promised to try and arrange a visit before he went back to America.

It was a small group that arrived at Kim's local church for the funeral. Everyone waited in silence – that incredible hush that descends on a church waiting for the coffin to arrive. Jamal and his guard slipped into the front seat in the church and David was pleased to see the handcuffs had been removed. Jane followed him in and sat on Jamal's other side.

The funeral was very moving, with a beautiful tribute given by Colin, who, as Kim's vicar, knew her well.

After the service, Kim's body was interred in the corner of the churchyard - tranquil, beautiful and unspoilt – a fitting resting place, thought David. Jamal stood at the graveside, tears running down his face. He threw a single red rose into the grave, and then walked away with his guard without speaking to anyone.

Jamal had at first declined the offer to go to the Memorial Service, but then changed his mind. Jane persuaded the prison authorities to let him and the guard go back to the vicarage for lunch before the service in the afternoon. The rest of them - Aunt Judith, Kim's mother and her husband, Mary's parents who had known Kim as a child, and Kim's father - were all invited back to Dan and Celia's house for lunch.

There wasn't a great deal of time before the Memorial Service that afternoon. Any embarrassment with both Kim's parents being there was alleviated by the presence of Mary's parents and Aunt Judith who had, of course, known them both before the divorce.

David had helped with the planning of the Memorial Service by asking several friends of Kim to give a tribute - her nursing friend, Maureen; Eric, one of the junior doctors; Andrew Johnson, the oncologist whom Kim had worked with; and Jane. They all agreed. Mary felt she was too close to Kim and wouldn't be able to carry it through without crying. Mick shyly asked if he could pay tribute. David was surprised at his courage, but said, of course. He knew he would also have to give a tribute though he realised he wouldn't find it easy to control his emotions.

When they got to the church it was packed. David had done his best to find cover for those colleagues of Kim at the hospital who had particularly wanted to go to the Memorial Service, and it seemed half the hospital's staff was there. Jamal with his guard and Jane, slipped in at the back at the last minute, as he didn't want to be seen.

David sat with Kim's family and Mary and her parents in the front and held Mary's hand tightly throughout the service. Dan and Celia, not wanting to intrude, sat in the body of the church

In as much as a Memorial Service can be said to be lovely, Kim's was. There were her favourite hymns and readings, and the tributes were moving. Nobody left the service without realising what a special person she was, and there were many in tears during the service – David's included.

He managed to speak to Jamal for a few minutes before he was whisked back to prison, promising to visit him in the near future and do all he could to help with his defence.

They all went back to Dan and Celia's house for tea where the atmosphere was a little more relaxed now the funeral service was over. It was always a surprise to David to find how helpful and cathartic funeral services could be by providing some sort of closure – though he realised the real grieving was yet to come.

Kim's mother and step-father left soon after tea as they had to get back to Devon. Though Aunt Judith was invited to stay on, she had to get back to London as she had a meeting to attend the next day. She promised to keep in touch, and Mary and David said they would go up to London to visit her.

David thought about Aunt Judith. He realised that in life one meets people with whom one has an instant rapport, and Aunt Judith was one of these. He drove her to the station, and just before she got on the train, she said, 'You and Mary would make a good couple.'

He laughed and kissed her goodbye, saying, 'Well, yes, it has occurred to me!'

When he got back he found Mary's parents and Kim's father were still there. Dan and Celia had invited them all to stay. He could see that Dan and Kim's father had a lot in common and were enjoying an earnest conversation. He joined them. They were talking about Jamal and his relationship with Kim. Dan said he'd met them together once or twice, and felt they were very well suited.

Kim's father asked David what he thought of Jamal and wanted to know about the terrorist charge He told him that Jamal was a fine and dedicated doctor but the evidence against him was very difficult to disprove. David told Kim's father that he had now come to believe that somehow Jamal was a victim, and that his flat had been used without him knowing.

Kim's father asked 'What about that friend of his? Kim told me he stayed there from time to time. But I don't think she liked him.'

'No. She didn't. That's why she went back to her own flat when Al visited.'

'Is Al a strict Muslim? I gather Jamal isn't.'

'Yes, I believe so.'

'Could he be the one who planted the chemicals?'

'That's something I'm beginning to believe. But Jamal is a loyal friend and is not happy with the thought.'

'I look forward to meeting him. I'd really like to know what it was that brought him and Kim together. I'd like to think they would have been happy.'

David said, 'I think they would have been very happy. Tomorrow, I'll try and organise a visit for you to see Jamal before you go back to the States.'

Then Mary broke up the conversation by asking David to go up and see Jamie. Although it was getting on for nine o'clock, Jamie was still wide-awake. He'd spent the whole day with the nanny who'd stayed on to keep him out of the way. But now he wanted time with his mother, and had refused to go to sleep before she came and read to him. ''When he heard you were here, he insisted you came up to see him.'

So they went up together to the flat and sat on Jamie's bed and talked to him before reading one of his favourite stories – Beatrix Potter's *The Tale of Benjamin Bunny.*

They went downstairs, and David decided it was time to leave. He took Mary in his arms and said, 'When this is all behind us, we'll have time to think about where we're going. But not just yet! It's all been so traumatic I don't think any of us can think straight at the moment.'

Mary nodded agreement. He kissed her gently and left – the long and emotional day at an end.

-44-
Kim's father visits Jamal in prison

One of the first things David did when he got to the hospital the next morning was to arrange with the prison for Kim's father, to visit Jamal. It had to be an early visit as Charles was flying back to America the next day. He asked David to go with him and David agreed - arranging to collect him and give him lunch before driving him there.

David asked Charles why he wanted to see Jamal.

'I want to meet the man who was to be my son-in-law. I feel it's one way to keep Kim's memory fresh,' and with that he wiped tears from his eyes.

When they got there, Jamal rose to greet them, looking even more gaunt than the previous time David had seen him.

'I've brought Kim's father to see you. He wanted to meet you before he went back to America.'

Jamal looked a little wary, but Charles put him at ease straight away. 'Jamal, I'm so very sorry - for you, for me, and for all Kim's friends. What can I say? What can anyone say? We've all lost someone very special. I loved Kim dearly – as I know you did - though I hadn't seen her for quite a time. But she told me all about you. I needed to come and see you.'

Jamal's face brightened a little, and he nodded as he held out his hand to shake Charles's. 'I can't believe it's happened,' he said simply. 'Who would want to murder such a sweet and kind person? I don't think she had an enemy in the world.'

'I agree,' said Charles. 'She had such a sunny temperament, and was always so kind and considerate to people. It doesn't make sense. I just hope and pray they find who did it, and bring him to justice.'

'You know we were planning to marry in the summer?'

'Yes. Did you know I was planning to come over for the wedding?'

'No. Kim hadn't told me that.'

'Well, I'd planned to come over a little before so I could get to know you. Mind you, I almost felt I did know you. Her letters were always full of what you were doing and about your hopes for the future. In her last letter, written the day before she disappeared, she told me about your plans for the wedding, and what you intended to do together in the future.'

'The day before she died!' exclaimed Jamal. 'We were so happy then.'

'I know,' said Charles quietly, touching Jamal gently on the shoulder.

'I keep asking myself why someone would want to kill her. I go over it again and again, and just can't think of any reason. Everyone loved her. I keep thinking it must have been someone who wanted to hurt me by hurting Kim.'

'Well, I'm sure that's what the police are investigating.'

'You do know how she died?'

'Yes, of course. And that's something you must try and be thankful for. Her death would have been swift – and she wasn't assaulted in any way – which must surely give you just a little comfort – I know it does me.'

Jamal nodded, unable to say anything.

'But I think you may be right in thinking that the person who killed her wanted to harm you. It might explain why those chemicals were planted in your flat.'

Jamal nodded

'Can you think of anyone who could do this to you? What about that friend of yours, Al?' I hadn't told Charles about Al's real name as Sir Ralph had asked me not to mention it for the time being.

Jamal shook his head. 'I've known him for years. I don't believe he would do that to me.'

'Kim didn't like him, you know?'

'No I didn't. Did she tell you that?'

'Yes, on several occasions. It was the one thing she seemed unhappy about.'

'She never told me!'

'No, I think she was protecting you. She didn't want to spoil your long standing friendship with Al.'

Jamal was very quiet for quite a few minutes. Sitting as far out of sight as possible, I reflected how like Kim that was – always thinking of other people.

'Tell me,' said Charles. 'Do you know when your trial will be?'

'No. I gather from my lawyers that they are investigating a whole terrorist plot. This means I'm going to be here for a very long time.'

'Bail?' asked Charles.

'No, my lawyer say there's not a chance. It's such a serious charge.'

Charles looked very distressed when he heard this, and asked Jamal how he was going to pass the time.

'Well, up to now, I've not been able to do anything – thinking and wondering about Kim. But now I know the worst I must try and pull myself together and do something - studying, anything to pass the time. It's all so soul destroying in here.'

'It must be. Have you thought what you might study?'

'Probably oncology and palliative care. That's what I was getting interested in before all this happened. Kim would have liked that.'

'Yes, she would. Is there anything I can do to help – send you books or something?'

Jamal brightened for a moment. 'Well, it would be good to know what's going on in the States with palliative care – and in fact, if the hospice movement has got going there yet.'

'Good. That's something I really can do to help. It's good to know you're beginning to think a little positively. I know it's not easy.'

'Well, I keep trying to think what Kim would have wanted me to do. We often discussed religion. I always remember once, when we were discussing hospice care and bereavement counselling, Kim told me a story about King David in her Bible. You know the story?'

They both shook their heads.

'Well, King David had done something very wrong and not long after, his son became very ill. King David thought God was trying to punish him and kept asking for forgiveness, begging God to save his son. He lay in sackcloth and ashes, refusing to eat or do anything. But the boy died. To the surprise of all his servants, King David immediately accepted the situation, got up, washed, dressed himself in clean clothes, had a meal, and went back to work. He even managed to praise God.'

Charles and David looked at each other, aghast. 'What a story! You don't believe God is punishing you by letting Kim be killed?'

'No, of course not. It was just that when the boy died, David accepted the inevitable, and started to build his life again. That's what Kim tried to help her patients do, and that's what I must do, even though I know it's going to be very difficult.'

'You quote the Bible,' said Charles, surprise in his voice. 'I thought you were a Muslim.'

'Yes, I am - by birth. But over the years, I've had a close look at all the major religions.'

'And what conclusions have you come to?' asked Charles.

'Well, that all the major religions are seeking a path to God.'

'That's interesting. I think I would agree with you. But you know Kim was very committed to her belief.'

'Yes, of course. And I respected that. I even went along with her to her church on a number of occasions. That's where I met Jane,' he added, turning to David.

'Jane?' enquired Charles.

'Jane Masters, She's the wife of Kim's vicar. Jamal and I got to know her through the hospice appeal.'

'How's the appeal going? Kim told me all about it.'

'I don't really know. I haven't been able raise any interest. David will know more than I do.'

'I must come another time and tell you what's happening,' said David, 'but not now. I think we'll have to go soon. The guard is looking at us.'

'Well, Jamal,' said Charles, standing up. 'It's been good to meet you. I think Kim chose well. I would have enjoyed having you as my son-in-law. I'll keep in touch. And when you get out of prison – as I'm sure you will – you must come over to the States and visit me.'

Jamal's eyes filled with tears as he shook Charles' hand. He couldn't say anything, but nodded his thanks.

On their drive back to the hotel, Charles said he was impressed with Jamal and couldn't believe he was involved in terrorism. He said that if there was anything he could do David must let him know. He asked about the legal process, saying he had been out of the country for a long time and had forgotten the details. David explained that legal costs were involved in the employment of a solicitor and a barrister, and Charles asked him to let him know if there were any financial difficulties in that direction.

Then he said, 'I didn't come over when Kim went missing. At first, I thought she'd just gone walkabout. Then, when it seemed more serious, I didn't think I could do anything positive to help by coming. But Judith, my former wife's sister, kept me up to date with what was going on' Then he added, 'I gather you and Mary did a lot to help in tracking down my former wife. I've always liked Mary. I've known her since she was a child – but of course I was away a lot, so I didn't see much of her. She's grown into a very lovely woman – both as a person and in looks.'

Then he gave David a penetrating look, and asked, 'Are you married?'

'Divorced,' he replied briefly.

'I thought so. So what about Mary?'

'Not you too,' David laughed. 'People keep trying to get us together.'

'And you. What do you think?'

'Maybe.'

'I'm in a second marriage you know. And extremely happy! I recommend it.'

Then he said, 'I know you've always been a good friend to Kim. She often mentioned you in her letters. Thank you for all you've done to try and find her.' With that, he held out his hand and said goodbye, promising to keep in touch.

As David watched him go into the hotel, he thought what a very special person he was, and understood from whom Kim had inherited her warm and generous personality. He felt overwhelmed with sadness at her loss; for Jamal incarcerated in prison for no one knew how long; for Charles grieving the loss of his only daughter; for Mary grieving for her friend; and for the whole messy world they lived in.

For Mary the weeks after finding out what had happened to Kim passed in a blur. The funeral had been helpful, but she hadn't realised how much a part of her life Kim had been. The thought that someone who was both a contemporary and a friend should have been murdered in such a brutal fashion was almost more than she could bear.

Dan and Celia did their best to comfort her, but Kim's death re-awakened all the misery and sadness that followed Ben's death. The happiness of the day following Dan's birthday party, when she'd begun to feel she and David might have a future together, evaporated – and she almost felt she didn't want to see him, she was in such a state of emotional turmoil.

David, Jane, and Kim's father, had all visited Jamal, and Mary knew she would have to summon up courage to go and see him herself. David had told her about his visit, giving her a fairly detailed report. She was surprised when she learnt that Jamal had told Charles he'd sometimes been to church with Kim. David said he felt that was a pointer in the direction of Jamal's innocence - that he wasn't a fanatical Muslim - but he didn't see how it could be used as evidence.

Before arranging to visit Jamal, Mary was so apprehensive she telephoned Jane. As a bereavement counsellor, she felt she was the best person to give her advice as to how to approach him. Jane said 'Just be yourself. Let him talk about Kim if he wants to, and tell him how much you valued your friendship with her. You've been through a terrible loss yourself, so try and think what helped you.'

Armed with this advice, Mary visited Jamal the next day. When she arrived, he held out his hands and clasped hers tightly. 'Thank you for coming,' he said. 'I knew you would.'

Mary nodded, near to tears. Jamal said, 'You've known Kim even longer than I have. She always talked about you and your childhood friendship. She said you were her best friend. You must feel her death as much as I do.'

'Well, she's always been a part of my life – apart from the time I was at Oxford when we lost touch for a while. I could never have imagined our friendship ending in this horrific way.' She couldn't help it, but the tears flowed and so did Jamal's. They held hands and said nothing for what seemed like an age, and then spent the next hour talking about Kim - her warm nature, her popularity and kindness, the cruelty of her murder. They talked about the way she'd died, and agreed that, though horrific it could have been much worse. They explored what might have been the motive and touched very briefly on whether her death had any connection with Jamal's arrest and suspected connection with terrorism.

Mary found herself feeling closer to Jamal than ever before, and when she left felt able to give him the hug she'd been afraid of giving on earlier visits.

She knew from experience that people have to go through various stages of grieving. For her, the first stage had been Kim's funeral, and the next the visit to Jamal. David tried to persuade her that knowing what had happened to Kim had lifted the heavy weight of anxiety they had carried for so many months, and they should now try to get on with their lives again.

'I'm not suggesting we should stop mourning but there's nothing we can do now to help her, and life has to go on.'

Mary tried to agree, but found it very difficult because there was still the weight of anxiety about Jamal's imprisonment and impending trial. She was convinced he was innocent, and it was a great relief to her when she realised David now shared her view. For quite a time it had seemed that he thought Jamal was guilty, and she'd felt irrationally angry with him.

Though Kim's death had made her want to distance herself from David for the immediate future, she didn't want to shut him out of her life completely. He'd become too important for that. She just wanted space for herself. But of course, their common interest in both Jamal's situation and the Appeal meant they continued to meet quite often. It was difficult for her to explain to David the intensity of her sadness for Jamal. She realised she'd become obsessed with thinking about his situation.

-45-
The Appeal Resumed

Charles' question about the hospice appeal had made David realise he'd given no thought whatsoever to the Appeal since before Christmas. But Kim's funeral, widely reported in the press, and Kim's association with Jamal, brought the general public's attention back to the appeal, and he received a number of phone calls asking what was happening. He decided he must take some action, and first phoned the police to see if there were any developments in tracing the missing money. The reply was in the negative.

He then called a meeting of the little group he'd convened before – Mark, Henry Winchester, Mary and Alec – to discuss the way forward. They met in a local pub after work. David told them about the many enquiries he'd receive and felt they couldn't hold back any longer the news that the money had been stolen. They all agreed, and fixed a date for a meeting. They contacted Jane to see if their church hall was available, and David said he would speak to Maud the next morning and get her to write to all the supporters who had signed up as Friends.

They decided that David should be absolutely honest and tell them about the money, and would ask whether, in the circumstances, they wanted to continue with the appeal.

Next morning, after drafting a letter, he called Maud into his office and asked her to circulate it to the Friends. On asking how many they'd got, she said there were two-hundred-and-twenty. David was surprised and realised that a lot of quiet work had been going on behind the scenes.

They fixed the meeting for two weeks ahead, and come the evening, they found about a hundred and fifty people sitting expectantly in the hall. They'd decided that the little group David had called together beforehand – Mark, Henry, Alex and Mary - should sit with him on the platform to give the meeting some semblance of formality. Maud, as secretary, also joined them, but Tracy was conspicuously absent.

After welcoming everyone, David said that they faced a very upsetting and difficult situation. As they all knew from the papers, Jamal in prison awaiting trial, but now they had learnt that most of the money they had raised had been stolen from the appeal's account. He said the police were on the trail, but didn't have much hope of recovering it, and that they would all have to decide whether or not to continue with the appeal.

There was a combined gasp in the hall followed by many questions, the first one being 'how much was in the account?'

When he told them £593,000, there was a gasp. People stood up to express their amazement that they had raised so much already, while others expressed anger. Very soon came the question David had been dreading, 'How come no one was aware of what was happening to the money?'

That was a difficult question to answer and he'd decided beforehand that the best response was 'mea culpa.' But that didn't satisfy people. Some said, 'And what about Dr Khan? He started it all. And now he's in prison. Has he taken it?'

David tried to assure them that Jamal was not the culprit, but not everyone accepted that. There was a lot of anger around, and he let it run on for a bit, believing it was not a good idea to stifle discussion. After about ten minutes, he called the discussion to an end.

'What we have to do now,' he said, 'is to make a definite decision about what to do. There are two options. Option one is to forget about the appeal, and if the money turns up later, to make a decision then as to what to do with it. The other option is to continue with the appeal and start fund raising again.

'It's a difficult decision. I know how demoralising this situation is, and how hard it would be to start again. It's up to this meeting to decide what we do. So that everyone has a chance to express an opinion, I suggest we get into small groups to discuss it. I think that should take about twenty minutes. Then, at the end of twenty minutes, I would like each group to take a vote, and report back.'

Having agreed this strategy beforehand, the little sub-committee sprang into action and helped arrange the assembled Friends into groups.

There were twelve groups round the hall, and the five members of the sub-committee took on two groups each to listen to the discussion and get the feel of the meeting. The discussions were very lively, sometimes heated, but always very considered.

After twenty minutes David called the meeting to order and asked for reports back. All but one of the groups, to their great surprise, voted to start again.

They'd decided what they would do if the vote went that way, so David now asked the meeting to elect an interim committee He'd hoped to avoid it but it seemed inevitable in the circumstances that he would be asked to take the chair. Someone proposed that all the members of the little group which had convened the meeting should be elected en bloc, and that this group should have the authority to co-opt people as it thought fit.

This proposal, though it went against all his personal inclinations, was eminently sensible and they all agreed to serve - if that was the decision of the meeting. Put to the vote it was agreed with a huge majority. Those voting against were mainly those who thought they should give up the idea of continuing the appeal.

At the end of the meeting, a number of people came up to David and said they realised what a difficult time it must have been. Others said how delighted they were with the decision and that they must now pull together and make up for lost time and lost money. A few asked about Jamal, but seemed wary about probing too much.

The next day David decided he should speak individually to each of the former committee members to ask if they wanted to continue to serve. He'd already been told by Tracey that she didn't want to be involved any longer because she felt the problem had been her fault. David tried to reassure her that she'd been used, but in his heart, he couldn't help but agree with her.

When he asked Maud to come and see him, she too said she didn't want to continue. She didn't give a reason but he suspected it was because Jamal was no longer involved. He'd been aware right from the beginning that it was Jamal's charms that had made her volunteer. He asked her if she would continue acting as secretary till their first meeting when they would find someone else. She agreed.

Of the others, Margaret, Alice, Jane and Mick all agreed to stay on. Henry Winchester, full of bluster, said that, much as he would like to stand down, he felt he couldn't resign, as it would let them all down. David smiled to himself because, as far as he could see, he had done very little in his role as chairman of fund raising to raise any money.

This meant that, including Kim and Jamal, they had now lost five members of the committee - Tracy and Maud, as well as Martin Allardice. When David telephoned him to tell him about the outcome of the Friends' meeting, he told him brusquely that he was now far too busy to be involved any more. David suspected this was because he and Pamela had split up. He wasn't sorry to lose him as a person, though realised he might have been useful as a Borough Councillor.

All this meant they had a depleted committee, and they needed to recruit a few more members. He knew of several people who were interested in the hospice movement, and felt that now was a good time to try and approach them.

One of the people he really wanted to bring back into the fold was Betty Andrews, the hospital's catering supervisor. She'd been very hurt by

Alec's crude put down at their first meeting, and he totally sympathised with her. His father's illness had prevented him from trying to persuade her to stay, and by the time he got back from Scotland, it seemed the moment had passed. However, he realised they'd lost a really useful member of the team. As someone from a decidedly working class background, he knew she wouldn't have the contacts to raise money from the well-to-do, but they needed to tap all the social groups in the community whether it be for small or large amounts of money. He knew Betty's involvement with a large circle of friends and numerous union acquaintances, and with her enthusiasm, was ideally placed to make people aware of what they were about. So David began a 'charm offensive' and after two or three talks, she agreed to re-join the committee.

It seemed that now was the time to try and build bridges with the group in his village, led by Stuart and Peter, who'd wanted to set up a hospice-at-home organisation. They both had the ear of the Health Authority, and had a considerable amount of experience with medical and political matters. David felt that if he could persuade them of the value of having both in-patient beds and a home care service, they might be able to join forces.

So, a few days after meeting with the Friends, David invited them both out to lunch and put the proposal before them. He'd studied all the information Jamal had produced about the growing hospice movement and was able to feel moderately confident when they started discussing his proposal. They both expressed deep anxiety about costs, but agreed to go away and think about it. A few days later, they came back and said they would join the committee.

Now that Martin Allardice had resigned from the committee, David persuaded Pam Litchfield to join the committee.

David arranged to hold a meeting of what he now thought of as a management committee in the home of Margaret. He felt he'd made progress, and was hopeful they might be able to move the appeal forward again. He couldn't help smiling wryly at how tortuously he'd been drawn into heading up the appeal, and felt determined to hand over the reins as soon as possible.

Margaret had coffee and biscuits ready for them on arrival, and seated them round her large dining table which David was glad of because it seemed more business-like. Before the meeting, he'd telephoned Alec to tell him he'd managed to bring Betty back into the fold, and warned him to be on his best behaviour, and be especially nice to her. Alec agreed – ruefully apologetic about his tactless comments before.

When Betty arrived Mary noticed Jane going straight up to her and saying how absolutely delighted she was she was coming back on the committee – that they needed people like her to keep them on their toes. Betty beamed, and Mary felt the first hurdle was crossed.

The only real stranger to the group was Dr Peter Langton. Most people already knew Pamela Litchfield, and quite a few knew Stuart Wilson. Mary noticed that Alec and Alice were sitting on opposite sides of the table, and wondered whether the liaison that she and David had observed before Christmas was still continuing. Seeing how they passed glances across the table, she assumed it was.

Once the introductions were over, David opened the meeting with a brief tribute to Kim and said he thought they would all like to spend a minute in silence and remember her. Several tears flowed.

Then he said that the first thing they had to do was to find a Chairman and a Secretary. He said he'd only taken on the role of chairman as a temporary measure because he'd found himself at the centre of all the police enquiries, and felt he was obliged to try and sort out the mess. But the role of Chairman was not one he sought and he would be more than happy to hand over to someone else straight away.

It was obvious this was wishful thinking on David's part, because everyone insisted that he was the best person for the job. After some discussion, David agreed to stay on for the time being.

He then turned to the role of secretary. He told them that Maud had resigned, and that although he'd asked her to come to the meeting she'd declined and had passed over to him all the papers in her care.

There was a big silence as David looked round the table, and everyone lowered their eyes. Jane said she'd already offered to produce a newsletter and felt she couldn't take on any more though felt the role of secretary shouldn't be too onerous at this stage as the main job would be to acknowledge donations. She suggested that, perhaps, someone could take on the role on a temporary basis while they looked outside for a permanent secretary. 'We have two-hundred Friends, many of them retired and wanting to do volunteer work, so it shouldn't be too difficult to find someone,' she said.

At this, Margaret offered to step in for the time being, saying she would do her best to find someone competent as soon as possible. 'After years of secretarial work before I got married, I vowed I would never do any again,' she said ruefully.

They all appreciated her offer.

Stuart offered to take on the role of treasurer and get the books and proper processes set up – and then they might find someone else to continue.

With these basic roles sorted David said, 'In the light of all that's happened – Kim, Jamal's imprisonment, the stolen money – we're in a 'make or break' situation. The next few months will be critical. We need to progress very quickly both with the fund raising and with the negotiations with the Health Authority. Our first priority is the latter.'

They considered the problem with the Health Authority at length, and eventually agreed to go back to them with a joint proposal. They agreed the team would be led by David, Stuart, and Peter, and at the last moment they decided to include Mark who, they felt, with his knowledge of the media, would be a useful addition to the group.

The discussion then turned to fundraising David reminded them of what they'd all committed themselves to before the catastrophe

Mary said she would continue working with charitable trusts, but wouldn't be able to make much progress until they knew whether the Health Authority was prepared to help.

Betty, her enthusiasm restored, said they ought to have both a Street Collection and a House-to-House Collection because they would bring the Appeal to the notice of the public quicker than anything. Mary could see Mark smiling to himself – aware that Betty was overlooking the importance of the media. But he said nothing.

Betty said she would be happy to organise them. She spent some time explaining the superiority of collecting boxes over envelopes – pointing out that with envelopes one had to call twice whereas with a collecting box, if someone was out, that was too bad. She argued that collecting boxes might be expensive to begin with, but they could be used over and over again, so in the long run they were the cheapest option.

Alec nodded agreement, and offered to source the best value boxes.

'We'll also need labels with the name of the appeal on it – and an address,' said Betty.

This brought Mark into the conversation. He said that if they were going to go ahead quickly, they would need a corporate image that could be easily recognised. He said his paper had a designer on the staff, and he would get him to produce some designs. Alec and Alice agreed to join Mark in a small committee to come up with something to put before the next committee meeting. 'We need something both simple and representative,' said Mark, 'something that people will easily recognise.'

Betty, once again enthusiastic and full of ideas, said they would also need to get things to sell with the Appeal's name and logo on them – pens, pencils, tea towels, cards, tea-shirts etc.

Henry Winchester demurred. 'Where's the money coming from?' he asked gloomily.

'Well, we've still got quite a bit left. We can't expect to raise money without spending some beforehand,' said David briskly.

They all agreed. Mary noticed that Henry sat back and said little more throughout the meeting. She really felt, despite all he'd said about himself at earlier meetings, that he was going to be a dead loss.

Alec turned to Betty and said, 'I'll try and outsource some reasonably priced goods to sell, and then perhaps you could come to my office, and we could decide which would be the best things to market.'

Betty beamed at him, and David felt the breach had been healed.

Betty's enthusiasm seemed to generate ideas all round. Pamela, new to the Committee, said that she'd been amazed to discover at the Public Meeting how many Friends the Appeal already had. 'With so many Friends, we have the basis for some very successful fund raising – but only if we organise them properly. Friends in isolation won't be very effective. What we need to do is organise the Friends into local groups – each with a chairman - so that each group can organise events locally. Then we can have a whole network of fund raising groups.

They all thought this was a good idea, but someone asked 'what about large-scale fund raising events?'

'Oh, they can go on alongside the local group events. We need both,' said Pamela firmly.

'Who's going to set up this organisation?' asked David.

Pamela said she'd be happy to take on responsibility for local groups, but that for big events, they would need to set up one-off committees just for each event. 'With all those volunteers, it should be easy to recruit people for special events.'

When Mary asked her whether she'd really have time to do this with her full-time job, Pamela startled everyone by saying she would only be working part-time in the future.

They all found this quite surprising and wondered what had triggered her decision to go part-time. Mary made a mental note to get in touch later and ask her.

'We'll need a database for our volunteers so we know who can offer what,' said Stuart. 'I think I know someone who might organise it for us. I'll try and find out by the next committee meeting.'

'But we haven't got our own computer,' said David. 'Maud has been using the one at the hospital.'

'That's not a problem,' said Mark. 'There are several old ones at the paper – all in working order - though not absolutely up to date.'

'So where are you going to put it?' asked Henry grumpily.

They all looked at each other. It hadn't occurred to any one that they might need an office if the appeal was really to get under way. Alec said it was just possible he could release a small room at his office – but it would be very small.

Then Mick Ellison turned to David and said, 'There's that empty cabin at the back of the hospital. Do you think that might be made available?'

'Good suggestion,' said David. 'I'll see what can be done,' and beamed at Mick.

What a thoughtful man Mick is, Mary reflected. He never contributes much to discussion but whatever he says is always carefully thought out and to the point. She'd often heard Kim and David saying that he was a very valuable member of the staff and realised that, however humble his position in the hospital hierarchy, he was one of those people to whom others turn for support and consolation.

The meeting seemed to be drawing to a close when Margaret said, 'I think we should re-launch the Appeal with a major event – something that catches the public eye.'

All agreed this was a good idea. A large fete was ruled out because the weather was inappropriate. An Antiques Road Show was suggested, but some thought it was a bit early to embark on until they were more widely known.

Then Margaret said, 'What about a Ball? My husband has business contacts with Lord Marston, who owns Storrington Park. He might be able to persuade him to let us have a Ball there.'

'Great idea,' said Alec and Mark in unison.

Margaret, looking excited, said, 'We could target the main business people in the area and the local gentry - and make it the sort of prestigious occasion, which people wouldn't want to miss. We could charge £100 for tickets. Mark could promote it in the media and it would help us with our entry into the wealthy ection of our community'.

As Margaret outlined her ideas, everyone became enthusiastic. Mark said that as soon as they'd secured the venue, he could start promoting it in the local rag. Pamela thought this was where the groups could be harnessed– one group to provide the food, another to organise a tombola, a third to secure significant raffle prize, and so on.

Alice told them her brother had his own band. It was very successful and she thought she could persuade him to bring it along and not charge too much.

'Before you all get carried away,' said David, looking at his watch. 'Are we all agreed this is a good idea?'

They all nodded. 'Then, as it's getting late, I suggest that, as soon as Margaret knows whether or not we can have Storrington Park, we set up a small committee to meet and plan the whole event.'

When he'd secured the assent of everyone present – except for Henry Winchester who muttered that not many people would be willing to pay that much for a ball - he called the meeting to an end, setting a date for the next committee meeting a month ahead. 'This will give us all time to sort ourselves out. '

Margaret then stood up and said with a big smile on her face, 'As we've got off to a really good start, I think we should have a little celebration.' She called her husband who produced champagne. Conversation became general, and someone asked for news of Jamal. David and Mary filled them in. Everyone wanted to know whether they thought Jamal was guilty, and Jane and Mary both stated their belief that he was the innocent victim of a frame-up.

'What evidence do you have?' asked Stuart. 'I found him quite a difficult character.'

'So did I to begin with – but when you get to know him, he's charming.'

'That doesn't make him innocent.'

'I know. But he absolutely denies any knowledge of the chemicals in his flat.'

'But that's easily said if conviction is facing you.'

'I know. But there are all sorts of pointers to his innocence. He kept asking us where the chemicals were found, and when he was told it was in the garage, he said that he'd never had time to clear out the stuff left behind by the previous tenants.'

'But you can't get away from the fact that he's a Muslim,' intervened Margaret. 'And most of the terrorist atrocities are done by Muslims.'

'Isn't that a bit prejudiced?' said Stuart mildly.

'No. I'm not prejudiced. But whenever a suicide bombing is mentioned in the news, there's always a Muslim implicated.'

Mark agreed. 'I'm afraid Margaret's right. And there's no doubt that Jihad is an Islamic concept. I don't think any of us should underestimate the terrorist threat that exists. Not much is made of it in the media – largely I think to allay public unease. But believe me, it's there.'

Then David joined in and told them about the Symposium he'd attended and the dire warnings of the man from the Met. 'But I don't think it's all gloom,' he said. 'In the discussions we had with the Jewish, Islamic and Christian clerics there seemed to be considerable consensus about the need to focus on the young and help them break down religious barriers. It seemed that quite a lot of work was being done in that direction.'

'Yes,' agreed Jane eagerly. 'And that's what Jamal was involved in before he was arrested.' She then told everyone about the young Muslim's group Jamal was involved with.

People expressed surprise, wondering why Jamal hadn't talked about it. Jane said it was because he thought the young people would be frightened off if it became too well known.

'I believe there's hope for the future if society can get the Church and the Muslim hierarchy working together,' said David. 'It's the fanatical Muslims we have to fear.'

Mary said quietly, 'I know Jamal isn't a fanatical Muslim. When he and Kim started going out together I cross-questioned Kim about Jamal's Muslim background as I was worried for her. Kim told me he never went to the mosque and seemed to ignore most of the Muslim taboos. She said he behaves just like a conventional westerner and always got very distressed when there were reports of Islamic violence and terrorism.'

'I can vouch for that,' intervened David. 'I was with him on the day of the nine-eleven attack in New York. He was appalled by the atrocity, and angry about what it would do to Islamic relations with the world. I agree with Jane and Mary. I think he's the victim of a frame-up.'

Mary smiled warmly at David for this confirmation that he now believed Jamal to be innocent, and as he was sitting beside her, took his hand and squeezed it.

Jane joined in 'I've seen quite a bit of Jamal since Kim disappeared. We've had long conversations about life and religion, and I can assure you he's not a terrorist. He's interested in world religions, and he's been to our church with Kim on a number of occasions. I don't think he would have done that if he'd been fanatical. And he seems to be cut off from his family. He hardly ever sees them – and they've not been to see him since he's been in prison.'

They all went quiet. Mary felt they had almost convinced everyone of Jamal's innocence, and when Betty suggested it would be nice to send him a card with their good wishes on it, everyone agreed

It was nearly eleven o'clock when the gathering dispersed. They felt they'd put the appeal on track again, and would soon be making progress. David squeezed Mary's hand as they left and said he would get in touch in a day or two.

-46-
Weekend with Aunt Judith

Although it was the last thing David had wanted, he realised before the meeting that it was inevitable he'd be asked to take on the Chairmanship. He knew that if he did, he would have to commit a lot of his spare time to it. He resolved, before the meeting, that if asked, he would agree to take on the role for one year, which would give everyone time to find a replacement.

The one thing that made him feel more confident about the situation was the calibre of the reconstituted committee. They were all competent and committed people – with the exception of Henry Winchester. But even he, with his contacts in the locality, David felt could be useful. The addition of Stephen and Peter was a huge bonus, and David knew that now they had agreed to combine forces they would give him every support.

He felt the Appeal was now on a firm footing. The group seemed to have 'gelled' which was such an important factor in successful group endeavours – and if all the promises made by the members of the group were fulfilled, there was a good chance they would soon start moving the Appeal forward in a significant way.

This thought was reinforced by the news David received from the police a few days later. The missing money was now in a Swiss bank account and they apparently felt a little more hopeful about tracking down the owner and getting the money back. But they warned David that it could take a very long time before the money was actually recovered.

A day or two after the meeting he received a long letter from Kim's father, Charles, thanking him for his support during his stay in England. He said:

My dear David,

It was for me a very sad return to England, knowing the terrible way my beloved daughter had been taken from us all. Somehow, while I was away in America, the enormity of what had happened didn't really hit me, and it was only as the plane approached England that it really came home to me that I would never see Kim again.

I don't know how I would have coped with the following few days without your company and support. I can't really express how very grateful I am. The fact that you were a close friend of Kim and loved and valued her, enabled me to talk about her and cope with all the emotions of the funeral.

I have a suspicion you had a hand in organising the Memorial Service, and I would like to say what a help it has been, remembering all the wonderful things people had to say about Kim. Thank you for sending me copies of all the tributes. I will treasure them always.

It was good of you to organise the visit to Jamal. I liked him, and can't believe he's guilty of terrorism. I don't think Kim would have got involved with anyone who didn't share her compassionate view of humanity

I was shocked to see the prison. Not the right place for a man of Jamal's medical background and knowledge. I can imagine how devastated Kim would have been had she been alive to see it.

As he was to be my son-in-law, I should very much like to help him. Having been away from England for so long, I am not well acquainted with the workings of the English legal system – but I wonder whether we could get him out? I would be willing to stand bail for him. It would be a way of honouring Kim's memory. I would be really obliged if you could let me know the procedure. I'm sure it's quite different to the way the States go about bail procedures.

I am willing to offer a substantial sum, as I feel confident Jamal wouldn't let me down.

Now, my friend, I thank you again for all your support during this harrowing time. Please know that if ever you come to the States, our home is always open to you.

Yours ever Charles Anderson

What a generous man, thought David as he read the letter and contrasted Charles' attitude with that of Kim's mother who had been remarkably calm throughout the day of the funeral, and had even made a derogatory remark about Kim's involvement with a Muslim.

When David and Mary next visited the prison they showed Jamal the letter from Charles. That he had won the confidence of Kim's father seemed to cheer him up a little. He agreed to apply for bail as Charles had hoped, but Mary warned him that in view of the seriousness of the charge, it was unlikely to be granted.

'I realise that!' said Jamal. 'Since I've been allowed to have my laptop in prison I've been accessing the internet to find out how English law actually works. I just had no idea before about its complexities and procedures. I suppose that applies to everyone. It's been quite a learning curve!'

David nodded sympathetically. 'The time must pass very slowly for you.'

'Yes, but I've managed to discipline myself into getting on with some medical reading – something I didn't have a great deal of time for when I was working,' he said ruefully. 'I must confess the prison authorities are being quite helpful in getting books for me.'

'It's such a waste of your medical expertise having you shut up like this in prison,' David said angrily. 'All those patients in hospital you could be caring for. I'm having the devil of a job trying to find replacements for you. I just wish we could find out how on earth those chemicals came to be in your garage.'

'Indeed,' said Jamal with a closed expression on his face. 'And who murdered Kim?'

Jamal, as always, looked clean and trim, but he'd lost a huge amount of weight and looked gaunt and aged. Mary was clearly deeply troubled by his appearance, and David could see she was nearly in tears. When they left, she gave him a big hug, and Jamal seemed to cling to her for a moment as though finding comfort in her embrace.

Despite feeling sorry for Jamal, David hated to admit it but felt almost jealous of him. The happiness he'd felt about his relationship with Mary after Dan's birthday party was now just a memory. Though he and Mary had been in each other's company several times since Kim's funeral he felt she was distancing herself from him. They'd had no physical contact other than a brief kiss on the cheeks. In some ways, he realised that the shock of Kim's murder had left them all bewildered with a feeling that the equilibrium of their lives had been shattered. David knew he had to leave Mary space in which to come to terms with all that had happened. He also realised that this tragedy had happened at a very delicate stage in their relationship. He hadn't asked her to marry him – nor in fact had either of them mentioned the word 'love', but he'd almost come to the decision to ask her to marry him, when Kim's body was found. Since the discovery, and the funeral, Mary's attitude towards him had subtly changed. He understood why and just hoped that, as she came to terms with all that had happened, she would come back to him.

Seeing her give Jamal such a warm and spontaneous hug made him feel jealous, but he steeled himself not to say anything as he drove her back to her office.

A letter from Aunt Judith a couple of days after their visit to Jamal, seemed to bring the situation to a crunch point. She wrote thanking David for all the funeral arrangements, saying how much they'd helped in the awful circumstances of Kim's death. She said how much she would like to see them both again, and wondered if they would care to come up to London and visit her.

'It would be lovely to see you both again and talk about Kim and keep her memory fresh. I still haven't really come to terms with her death. It's too horrible to think about. I know it might not be all that exciting visiting an old lady, but I wonder if I could tempt you to come for a weekend. I could get some concert or theatre tickets and make it a special weekend for you both. You've been through so much with all the anxiety about Kim's disappearance and Jamal's imprisonment that I thought a weekend away might be a help.

I am writing to Mary as well.

My love and thanks to you. Do let me know if you'd like to come.

Yours affectionately

'Aunt' Judith

David was pondering how to answer it and what Mary's response might be when he had a phone call from Celia, saying they hadn't seen him since Kim's funeral and wondered whether he'd like to come for lunch on Sunday – 'after church of course'.

David accepted – while wondering why it was Celia and not Mary who had given the invitation. It was soon obvious why. After lunch Celia said, 'I gather Judith has invited you both to London for a weekend. Dan and I think it would be a great idea – get you away from all the sadness here. Dan and I would look after Jamie if you'd like to go.'

David wasn't sure whether Celia was just being kind or whether she'd picked up the strain in their relationship. Whatever it was, he and Mary almost simultaneously, thanked her and said it would be lovely.

'Good. That's settled then. Why don't you telephone Judith now and fix a date. That would give her time to get some theatre tickets for you.'

David felt that they were being propelled into a decision, but they went to the phone and rang Aunt Judith. She was delighted and asked what they would like to see. As neither of them had been in London for a long time, they said they would leave it to her. She said she'd get back to them in a day or two and arrange a date.

Somehow, this broke the ice a little. But when they went for a walk after lunch, Mary said Jamie was to come too. David felt she was protecting herself from too intimate an encounter.

A day or two later Aunt Judith phoned Mary to say she'd booked tickets a fortnight hence to see *Billy Elliot* and would they like to come up to London on the Friday evening.

David collected Mary after work on the Friday. This was the first time she'd left Jamie overnight and felt very emotional about it despite Celia and Dan's reassurance that all would be well. Jamie, who'd spent so much time with his grandparents, didn't seem in the least bit concerned.

They went by train rather than driving in London. On the journey they chatted about everything under the sun – except their relationship. They avoided talking about Jamal and Kim, although Mary told David how much her law studies had been interrupted by the recent events, and that she now had to get down to serious study. Discovering a shared interest in art they resolved to go to the National Gallery over the weekend. Mary told David she enjoyed painting herself, though had very little time to do any.

They arrived at Aunt Judith's in time for a late dinner. She greeted them warmly and David realised how much she appreciated their coming. When they'd first met, she'd seemed so confident that it hadn't struck him that she might be lonely, but over dinner, she told them how much she enjoyed having people to stay – 'especially at weekends which are the times most people living alone feel loneliest'.

The next morning after a leisurely breakfast, Aunt Judith asked what they would like to do. They suggested a visit to the National Gallery.

'Great idea,' said Aunt Judith, 'I'll call a taxi for you.'

'But you must come too,' said Mary. 'It's you we've really come to see.'

They persuaded her to come with them and discovered she was knowledgeable about art. She led them to the galleries of the Renaissance painters and told them her favourite painting was Leonardo's *Virgin of the*

Rocks. They spent some time quietly looking at this picture with the beautiful serene faces of the two women.

'Reminds me of Kim,' said Mary quietly to herself.

Aunt Judith heard, and squeezed Mary's arm.

After visiting all the Renaissance galleries, they had a snack in the gallery's restaurant before returning to Aunt Judith's house for tea. It was then that they talked about Kim. They knew this was something Aunt Judith needed to do. She was very sad she'd never met Jamal, and wanted to know what they thought about him. They assured her that he was a good man and were sure he'd somehow been framed. Then she talked about Kim's parents. She was scathing about Kim's mother and said she was one of the most self-centred people she knew, but her father was a very caring man and Kim had adored him. She was devastated when he went off to America and at one time had planned to join him when her nurse training was finished, but the arrival of Jamal on the scene had put paid to the idea.

David told her about Charles' offer to stand bail for Jamal, and about their suspicions that Jamal's friend, Al was implicated. They explained that there were a lot of pointers to Jamal's innocence, but they were all too insubstantial to stand up in court.

As they talked about her they were all near to tears. However, after what Aunt Judith called 'high tea', they cheered up and set off to see *Billy Elliot* which Aunt Judith had already seen and enjoyed. She said it was just the sort of show to help them forget the traumas of the past weeks.

Returning in a more relaxed frame of mind they discussed over a nightcap what they would do the next day. 'I'd very much like to go to Westminster Abbey but that's not really your cup of tea, is it David?'

A little taken aback, David quickly collected his thoughts and said, 'No, but I'd be very happy to go.'

'Me too,' said Aunt Judith.

Aunt Judith ordered a taxi for the next morning so they didn't have to worry about buses and the underground.

It was the first time in many years that David had been to a communion service, and he felt a little isolated as he watched everyone going up to the communion rail to receive the bread and the wine, but the music was wonderful, and he was amazed to think the small choristers could read such complicated music and produce such beautiful sounds.

They took Aunt Judith out to lunch, and then walked in St James Park before returning to her house for tea.

Both David and Mary felt more relaxed after the two days with Aunt Judith. They had enjoyed her company. She kept abreast of contemporary issues and made many thoughtful comments about contemporary life and politics which they found challenging. On the journey home David tried to raise the subject of their relationship, but she put her hand on his arm and said, 'David, not now. Give me time.' He took her hand and kissed her palm, and said, 'Ok. Not now. But it's hard.'

'I know,' she said sympathetically, 'But it's all been hard. I can't really think straight just yet.'

And with that they changed the subject

-47-
The neighbours return

It was a few days after the visit to London that things began to take a new and encouraging turn. David had a phone call from a total stranger who asked to come and see him. He said it was in connection with Jamal. Intrigued, David agreed that he should come with his wife to the hospital at the end of the day. They introduced themselves as Penny and Nigel Jones, and said they lived in the flat above Jamal. They'd just returned from a four-month trip to India and heard the news about Kim's murder and Jamal's arrest. 'We just don't know what to do. As Jamal worked here at the hospital we thought we'd come and talk to you first.'

David looked puzzled.

'Well, we think it all happened the night we went to India. But we want to check the date before we do anything about it.'

'Well, that's easy enough. I can do that right away.' David opened his desk diary and said, 'the 16th of October.'

They looked at each other, nodding. 'As we thought,' said Nigel. 'That's the very night we left. We had just a couple of hours sleep and got up at 3 o'clock. It was still dark. We heard a car arriving and thought it a bit strange in the middle of the night so went to the window to see who it was. We recognised Jamal's friend Al, whom we'd met once or twice when he was staying with Jamal. He had the garage door open and he and another man were unloading some things from the boot of their car. They looked like big round canisters. They must have been heavy as both men were lifting them. It seemed strange to be doing that in the middle of the night, but as it was Al and he obviously had a key to the garage, we thought perhaps he'd just arrived back from a late flight.

We thought no more about it till we got back to England at the weekend and learnt about Jamal being arrested and Kim's murder. We felt we ought to go to the police, but wanted to find out the facts first.'

How David stopped himself from leaping up and hugging them, he didn't know. For this seemed to him to be the bit of evidence needed to get Jamal out of prison. Jamal had a very strong alibi for that time. He was on duty all night at the hospital with a number of witnesses to confirm it. If the chemicals were delivered while Jamal was working, it seemed to David to be confirmation of his denial of all knowledge about them. He realised that, standing on its own, it wouldn't be enough to prove his innocence, but together with the discovery of the return of Kim's book to the flat by Ali, there could no longer be any doubt that Ali was at the flat the morning Kim disappeared. It also seemed to him that this was possible evidence of the link between Kim's disappearance and the chemicals in the garage – something he'd begun to suspect when Mary told them about the return of the book.

Not wanting to jeopardise this very significant piece of evidence he thought he should speak to Mary and Julian before encouraging them to go to the police. He phoned their office and found Julian was still there. He agreed to see Nigel and Penny straight away.

David went with them to Julian's office where Julian and Mary were waiting for them. Mary was very excited about the information, but Julian urged caution saying that the Crown Prosecution Service might take the view that the fact that Ali was using Jamal's garage might indicate that Jamal had given him permission to do so. As it appeared that Ali had a key to the garage and to the house, that could weaken Jamal's claim to be ignorant of what was going on.

Julian said that the first thing they must do was to confront Jamal with this new piece of evidence and assess his reactions.

Nigel, Penny and David left the office feeling more than a little deflated by Julian's cautious attitude, and David realised that, once more, they were in for a period of waiting.

He had dinner with Mary the next evening in her own flat, which he felt was progress. Hitherto, all his meals with Mary had been taken along with Celia and Dan. Jamie was already in bed when he arrived but demanded a story and a goodnight kiss before David joined Mary for supper. She proved to be a very good cook, and it wasn't till after they had eaten that she told David about her visit with Julian to see Jamal.

Jamal had apparently taken the news very badly. He couldn't believe his long standing friendship with Al had been betrayed in this way, and, to begin with, tried to think of explanations, even trying to convince himself that the reason for the chemicals being in his garage had been misinterpreted – that they were not intended for bomb making but for something quite innocent. Apparently Julian quickly disabused him of this idea. Jamal was so distraught by the revelation of Al's involvement with the chemicals that he asked Mary and Julian to leave. He said he just couldn't cope with the information at the moment and needed time to think and come to terms with it.

Mary said they'd agreed with Jamal to delay going to the Crown Prosecution Service with the information for a day or two, particularly as they'd not yet processed the application for bail.

David wasn't surprised by Jamal's reaction. If he was innocent, then discovering that he'd been betrayed by his best friend was very hard to take in and accept. David remembered how he'd felt when he discovered Joanna had been betraying him with her counsellor.

There were a lot of puzzling things about Jamal's relationship with Al which he felt needed clearing up before proceeding further. He agreed with Mary that he would try and visit Jamal in the next day or two. As things were developing he felt the time had come when he could divulge what Sir Ralph had told him, that Al's real name was Ali Mansour

David decided not to overstay his visit that evening. It was the first time he and Mary had been together in her flat since the discovery of Kim's body, and he didn't want to jeopardise their relationship in any way. He left at ten after kissing her briefly.

Two days later he visited Jamal in the prison. David decided there was no point in beating about the bush, so he told Jamal straight away that he'd come to quiz him about Al.

'But that's what the police have been doing endlessly,' said Jamal looking despairing.

'Well, yes. I'm not surprised. But I need to ask you. There've always been things that puzzled me about your relationship with Al, and if we're to help you, I need some straight answers.'

Jamal nodded.

'Let's get the facts sorted out first. When and where did you meet Al?'

'I met him at university.'

'How did you come to meet him? You were studying different subjects.'

'We met at the political club.'

'You were both interested in politics?'

'Yes. But only theoretically. Neither of us wanted to enter politics.'

'Are you sure about Al?'

'Oh yes. He was much more interested in international affairs.'

'Was he active in that direction?'

'Not as far as I know.'

'I believe you shared a flat in your last years of study?'

'Yes. The person I'd been sharing with had completed his study and his room was vacant. Al happened to mention he was looking for somewhere to live and I invited him to share with me.'

'You were good friends.'

'Yes. I trusted him …' At this point Jamal looked near tears.

'He's a Muslim like you?'

Jamal nodded

'From what Kim told Mary, he's a staunch believer.'

'Yes.'

'Then how come he has a name like Mercer?'

'Well, his real name is Ali Mansour. But he changed it to Mercer because he said he was tired of being labelled a Muslim fanatic all the time.'

'Did you believe him?'

'I did at the time ..... but now, it makes me wonder,' said Jamal thoughtfully.

'What does Al do for a living?'

'He's a businessman.'

'That's a bit vague. What's his business?'

'I really don't know. He was travelling all the time, but we never discussed what he was actually doing.'

'How come he stayed with you in England?'

'Well, it seemed quite natural. We'd lived together for a couple of years – very amicably. It seemed quite normal for me to welcome him to my home in England when he was here.'

'Did he have a key?'

'Yes. We both had such erratic hours it seemed the best thing to do.'

'Jamal, you've always been a bit cagey about Al's visits to England. I've seen him once or twice in London and you've denied it was Al, and insisted he was still in the States.'

Jamal nodded his head. 'I know. It's because Al asked me not to tell anyone he was in England. He said he had business complications and some people were out to get him. When I looked anxious about it he said there was nothing to worry about – but a lady was involved which made it more complicated. I asked no more.'

'Did he always stay with you when he was in England?'

No. He often stayed in London with friends.'

'Did you know them?'

'Not really,' said Jamal. 'I only met them a few times.'

'Was one of those times when you met in The Tandoori restaurant in London?' he asked, watching Jamal's face carefully. You were with a group of Asians – and you all seemed to know each other well.'

Jamal looked puzzled. 'How did you know that?'

'I was meeting a friend there and arrived early. I saw you all sitting in the corner, having a heated argument.

The expression on Jamal's face was difficult to read.

'What were you all talking about? You didn't seem too happy.'

Jamal shook his head slowly. 'No. I remember. I wasn't happy. They were all slagging off the British. I didn't think that was fair, and said so. I left soon after.'

Remembering Sir Ralph's words, a thought struck him. 'Do you remember who was there – any of their names?'

Jamal shook his head slowly. 'No. I don't think so.'

'Try and remember,' David urged. 'It could be important.'

Realising the implications of what David had just said Jamal tried to recall their names. After a few moments, he said, 'Well, I remember a few of the first names – but I don't think I ever knew their surnames. There was Kabir, Faisal, Malik, Hakim ….. ' He thought for a minute, then said 'and of course, Suleiman, Ali's business partner.'

David drew in his breath. Suleiman was a name he'd heard before. He made a mental note to try and recall where later.

'Did you meet up with them often?'

'No. As I said, I only met them a few times. Al was one of those people who kept his friends in compartments. There are people like that – they haven't got the confidence to bring their friends together. I accepted that this characteristic was part of Al's lack of confidence.'

'Yet when I've met him he's always seemed to be the life and soul of the party.'

'Yes, I know. But that's because none of you were close friends.'

A pattern was beginning to emerge in David's mind about Al – a secretive man, ready to use his friends as and when needed.

At this point he was tempted to tell Jamal about the suspicions of Samantha's father, and how he'd been unwittingly drawn into the enquiries, but he thought better of it – realising it might compromise Jamal's defence, so he turned to the subject of Kim. David knew this would be a difficult matter for him to discuss

'How did he take your engagement to Kim?'

'We never discussed it, but he seemed to accept it. You remember, he came to our engagement party.'

David thought carefully before he asked the next question. 'Before Charles mentioned it, did you know what Kim thought of him?'

Jamal's face clouded over and he shook his head. 'Why do you ask that?'

'Can you answer the question please?'

'Well, I think she was OK with him. She never said anything against him.'

'Do you know why she kept her flat?'

'Well, she thought it would be good to go back there to study.'

'Would it surprise you to know that Kim went back there when Al visited you because she didn't trust him?'

Jamal looked startled. 'She never said anything to me about Al. How do you know that?'

'She told Mary.'

Jamal shook his head, trying to take in this new piece of information.

'Now I need to ask some questions about Al and the hospice appeal. How come you involved him when he was out of the country so much?'

Jamal thought carefully before answering. 'Well, he was staying with me once and we talked about hospices and the need to raise money to set one up in the town. Al said he thought that a great idea and would be willing to help with the finances and put the Appeal on a good footing. He put in a thousand pounds of his own money as a starter.'

'And now the money has gone missing,' David said dryly.

'Are you suggesting it was Al who stole the money?'

'It's something the police have been giving thought to.'

Jamal shook his head despairingly.

'My whole world seems to be falling apart. First Kim, then arrest, and now these suspicions about my supposed best friend. I don't think I can bear it.'

'I'm afraid there's something else you might have to accept?'

'What's that,' asked Jamal anxiously.

'Well, we know Al went back to the flat the day Kim went missing, and we know Kim planned to go back to your flat ....'

'No! No! No!' cried Jamal. 'Not that as well,' and burst into tears.

David wished at that point he had Mary or Jane with him. They would have known what to do. David felt somewhat embarrassed and tried awkwardly to pat him soothingly on the shoulder but Jamal brushed him aside. 'I think you must go.' he said. 'I can't take any more at the moment.'

David accepted his dismissal, realising he would have felt the same in such circumstances.

He phoned Mary to tell her about his visit and she told him to come over and have supper. This pleased him as he felt it indicated their relationship was beginning to make progress again.

As he drove over, something kept nagging him, and he suddenly remembered where he'd heard the name Suleiman. It was the name of the young teacher in their discussion group at the Symposium. He'd started by joining in the discussion in a reasonable way but had become aggressive when talking about how he and his wife had been treated when they first came to Britain. He obviously had little love for the British. After thinking about it, David realised that Suleiman must be a very common Muslim name but he thought he would give Sir Ralph the names Jamal had remembered just in case there was a connection.

He tried to put his visit to Jamal out of his mind – the visit had been too upsetting. He turned again to thinking about his relationship with Mary, and how different it was to his ardent pursuit of Joanna and his passionate relationship with Samantha. Was this true love, he asked himself again? Was this the sort of love that was the foundation of the secure and long lasting relationships that he'd seen in Dan and Celia, Stuart and Susan, and

Jane and Colin? He really began to feel that he wanted to get his life on an even keel. As he drove towards Mary's home he thought about Jamie and realised he very much wanted to be a father.

So he was very pleased when Mary asked him if he would like to bath Jamie while she cooked supper. Now nearly three, he was a very bright child and asked David all sorts of questions about the hospital, and told him about his weekend with his grandparents.

'I haven't seen your house,' he said. 'Can I come and see it?' The question startled David. He 'd never thought to invite them but he quickly recovered and said, 'Yes, of course. When your mummy has time to bring you over.'

'I haven't got a daddy you know,' he said confidentially, 'I've got two grandpas and two grandmas, but I'd like to have a daddy,' and David was sure he was looking hopefully in his direction.

'Well, perhaps one day you'll have a daddy,' he said rather conspiratorially.

'I hope so.' Then he changed the subject and said, 'Will you read me a story. Mummy's reading me a story about a very naughty boy. But I'm not naughty. I just like it 'cos he does all sorts of naughty things.'

David lifted him out of the bath and dried him, and thought, this is what it would be like to be a father. He took him along to the kitchen where Jamie kissed Mary goodnight and said, 'Uncle David's going to read me a story so you don't need to come.' He flung his arms round her neck then took David's hand and led him to his little bedroom.

He produced a book David had never heard of, *Where the Wild Things are,* and realised he'd missed out on so much over the years.

After he'd read to him, he tucked him in and joined Mary in the kitchen. She placed a gin and tonic in his hand and said, 'You deserve it.'

'Not really,' he insisted. 'I love it. He's such an engaging little boy.' Then he went on to say something he hadn't intended to say yet, 'I wish he were mine.'

David could feel Mary tense, so changed the subject and asked what she was cooking.

He told her about his conversation with Jamal, and they both agreed his explanations were consistent with his protestations of innocence. 'All we can do now is wait for the Crown Prosecution Service to react, and for the bail application to be heard,' said Mary. 'But I have a horrible feeling that Jamal will have to go to trial. And even that is going to be problematic.'

'Let's forget about Jamal and relax. There's a good film on tonight which we could watch if you'd like to.'

David agreed readily, and after supper they sat cosily on the sofa, and Mary accepted it when he put his arm round her. As the film neared the end, he was wondering how far this intimacy would go when there was a scream from the bedroom and Jamie came in crying. 'He's had a bad dream,' she said, cradling him. I'm afraid I'll have to go and cradle him until he gets to sleep again. Perhaps you can let yourself out.'

His hopes crushed, he kissed the top of Jamie's head and Mary's cheek, and went regretfully home.

But before he went to bed, he dropped a brief note to Sir Ralph giving him all the names that Jamal had remembered.

-48-
Jamie invites himself to David's house

After he left, Mary lay on Jamie's bed cradling him to sleep, thinking about the evening she'd just spent with David. It had been so easy and pleasant, despite the situation with Jamal and Al which had brought him over.

She reflected on the contrast between their ordinary everyday lives and the drama that was unfolding around them - Kim's disappearance and murder, the threat of terrorism, Jamal's imprisonment, the embezzlement of the hospice appeal money, and now Al's probable implication. But she knew that for those involved in the situation 'life had to go on'- something she was all too familiar with after Ben's death.

Kim's death had upset her deeply and she found it profoundly difficult to come to terms with. The thought that Kim was no longer alive was bad enough, but to accept that it had been such a terrible end was almost more than she could bear. It reduced her own confidence. If, she asked herself, something so horrific could happen to Kim whose life in many ways mirrored her own, what was there to stop her becoming a victim herself? It was very disturbing, and made her feel desolate and insecure. She thought about Jamal so unjustly imprisoned, and then had to consider whether her belief in his innocence was influenced by his charm and good looks. The fact that the neighbours had witnessed Al bringing in the chemicals was reassuring, but at the same time Mary knew it didn't let Jamal off the hook.

When Jamie finally fell asleep Mary crept back to her own bed but found she couldn't sleep. She started thinking about David, and wondering where their relationship was going. She knew he wanted it to go further – the remark he'd let slip earlier in the evening led her to believe he had marriage in mind. But was she ready to marry again, and if so, was David the right person? She'd come to like and value his company very much – but it wasn't quite the same as the feeling she'd had for Ben when it had been love at first sight, and where she couldn't bear to be away from him.

But she had to admit, David occupied her thoughts a lot these days, and a great bonus was the fact that Jamie liked him. Moreover, she knew that Celia and Dan were fond of him. Celia had hinted several times that she thought David was right for her. She realised how generous that was. If she and David did get together it would mean that someone would be taking the place of their beloved son.

Still unable to sleep Mary felt she should pray about it for guidance. But this brought back the recollection of David's lack of belief. That had never been a problem with Ben. They were both Christians when they met, as were their families. But she knew David didn't believe, and until Kim's funeral and their visit to Westminster Abbey she'd never known him enter a church or express any interest in Christianity. She'd always believed that the ideal marriage partner was a fellow Christian, and wondered whether she would be denying her faith if she let her heart rule and married David? It brought her up sharply when she realised she'd actually used the word 'married'. She realised she was very fond of David but wondered whether what she felt was love.

She began going over the times she'd spent with David. She thought about his failed relationships with Joanna and Samantha which he'd been absolutely honest about, and asked herself whether the fact that her relationship with Ben had also ended, though for a rather different reason, was a good basis for a second marriage.

These thoughts whirled round and round till the small hours when she finally fell asleep with nothing resolved.

At breakfast next morning, Jamie suddenly said, 'I want to go to Uncle David's house.'

Mary, surprised, asked him why.

'Cos I like Uncle David and I want to see his house.'

'Well, we can't just go. We'll have to wait till he invites us.'

'He said we could go when you had time,' Jamie persisted.

Mary felt put on a spot and told Jamie to finish his breakfast as it was getting late.

Somehow, she'd never thought about where David lived or even what his house was like. Now she realised that Jamie's request had pushed her into making a few decisions. She knew that if they visited David's home, it would move the relationship on.

The crunch came the following week when Celia invited David for Sunday lunch. When they went for a walk in the afternoon, Jamie who'd been running ahead, suddenly stopped, looked at David and said, 'When can we come to your house?'

David turned to Mary with a questioning look. Feeling cornered, she said, 'Yes, we'd love to come. I've often wondered what your home's like.'

'Well, it's nothing special. Not like your home. But it's comfortable, and I've got a nice garden. Why don't you come over next Saturday? I'm not a very good cook, but I'll cook lunch, and then I can show Jamie my model railway in the afternoon – and my tortoise.'

Mary, much to Jamie's delight, said, 'That would be nice – but if we come, let's make a pact that we don't talk about Jamal and all his problems.'

'Agreed,' said David.

Jamie grabbed David's arm. 'What's your tortoise called?'

'Henry,' said David.

'So it's a daddy tortoise,' said Jamie reflectively.

'Well, yes, I suppose he is.'

'What does he eat?'

'Oh. Lettuce and all sorts of things.'

Amazed by this revelation, Mary asked, 'How on earth can you look after a tortoise when you're away so much?'

'Not a problem. Stuart and Susan – you know them – take him in when I go away.'

-49-

Mary and Jamie visit David's home

Jamie was so excited at the thought of the tortoise and the railway that it was all he could talk about the following week. 'We're going to Uncle David's house on Saturday and he's going to show me his tortoise and his railway,' he proudly told Dan and Celia.

Mary felt strangely excited about the visit. Up to now their social contacts had always been on her territory and not on David's. She didn't know what to expect as David had never talked about his house.

On the Saturday, Jamie was up even earlier than usual, ready dressed in his best clothes. He even managed to get his jumper on the right way round. Directly they'd had breakfast he said, 'Can we go now?'

'Not yet, Jamie. We must give Uncle David time to cook lunch.'

He was quiet for a little while then started pestering her to 'go now'. Giving up the battle, she took him to the local park so he could play on the swings and roundabouts. But this didn't placate him for long and by a quarter to twelve, Mary could hold out no longer. She bundled Jamie into the car and set off for David's village, a ten-mile drive through beautiful countryside.

David's house was just off the village square, a modest but pleasing nineteen-eighties house with a good sized front garden.

David heard them coming and welcomed them at the door – sporting a bright red plastic apron covered with white rabbits. Jamie threw himself into David's arms and gave him a big kiss. Mary's greeting was more sober.

'Can I see Henry now,' said Jamie eagerly. Giving Mary a wry look, he took Jamie's hand and led him through the kitchen door into the garden. There, in the middle of the lawn, sat Henry peacefully nibbling a lettuce leaf.

'Can I hold him?' Jamie asked eagerly.

'Well, just for a moment. But he's heavy and he doesn't like to be held for long. Why don't you sit on the grass and I'll put him on your lap.'

Jamie sat down and a smile of pure joy came over his face as the tortoise put his head out and started looking round

Mary and David looked at each other and smiled - sharing the pleasure of Jamie's happiness.

After a few minutes, David said, 'I think Henry would like to go back to his house now. Come and see where he lives.' He picked up the tortoise and, with Jamie walking beside him, placed Henry in the large wire run at the side of the lawn. 'Now Jamie, you sit and watch him while I go and get your mummy a drink.'

With that he took Mary's arm and led her indoors. 'Welcome to my home'' he said, then took her in his arms and kissed her – a kiss to which she responded so warmly that she surprised herself.

It was not long before Jamie came running into the house. 'Now can I see your house?'

David laughed and said, 'OK. Let's do a tour.'

It wasn't quite the modest house David had said. It had three bedrooms, a very large sitting room, a study and a large kitchen which was already laid up for lunch with a bunch of red tulips in the middle.

Except for the study, the house, though tidy and clean, seemed very bare. David apologised for it saying, 'There's nothing of Joanna's here. She took virtually everything with her – even the curtains. I had to start again.'

But David had put his mark on the study. It was full of books, papers and photographs. There were two big desks – a computer on one and a pile of papers on the other. On the bookcase, which went from floor to ceiling, stood wedding photographs of his parents, his sister and husband, and a number of pictures of their three children. There were photos of hospital and village events, and one of David dressed up as a nanny in a village pram race. It made Jamie laugh when Mary pointed it out to him. On the wall were two large watercolours of the Lake District which David said was his favourite place for a holiday.

While Mary was looking at his collection of books, Jamie said, 'I like your house, Uncle David. Can I come and stay here?'

David, looking at Mary, said carefully, 'We'll have to see,' and taking Jamie's hand, led him through to the sitting room where Mary saw that

David had placed a number of children's books on the coffee table. There was *Dr Seuss's ABC,* the *Very Hungry Caterpillar, Charlie and the Chocolate Factory, Winnie the Pooh,* several Beatrix Potter books, and a large book full of pictures of everyday objects. Some of the books were old, with David's name written in them in a childish hand, but it was obvious David had been out and bought some new ones especially for their visit. Mary felt touched.

It wasn't long before David called them in for lunch. Though he'd insisted he wasn't a very good cook, he had in fact prepared a delicious meal which Mary noticed he served on a Beatrix Potter plate for Jamie and guessed he'd been out and bought that as well.

After lunch David sent Jamie off on a quest for a box of toys which he said he'd hidden somewhere downstairs, Mary looked at him quizzically. It wasn't long before Jamie came back triumphant, carrying a box which contained a selection of old and brand new toys including a red plastic train set.

'David, you're so naughty. I know you've bought them specially for Jamie.'

He laughed. 'Why not. Jamie's very special and I really love him.' Then, looking carefully at Mary, he said, 'And you know I love you too. I want us to be together.'

'Is that a proposal?' said Mary, not quite sure how she would respond if it was.

'Well, yes. I suppose it is.'

Mary was quiet for a moment then said, 'David, we both love being with you. But I need time to think about it. I think I'm still hung up about Kim, and all that's happened these last few months.'

She smiled at David and he said, trying to hide his disappointment, 'I do understand. I can wait,' then said quickly, 'Let's go for a walk,' I'd like to show you round the village. We can take Jamie to the playground.' With that, he pulled Mary to her feet, and went into the hall to find their coats.

Holding Jamie's hand on one side, David put his arm round Mary the other, and they set off for a tour of the village. It was one of the prettiest villages in the area and Mary felt she could happily live here. She realised she was beginning to give serious thought to the idea of settling down with David. His abrupt and indirect proposal had startled her, and she was grateful to him for not pursuing it.

It struck her that, among David's many virtues, was one of sensitivity – something she much valued in people. She wondered what the downsides of his character were. To date she hadn't encountered any.

As they were walking round the medieval church they bumped into Stuart and Susan with their two small grandchildren. Stuart greeted them - a knowing twinkle in his eye as David still had his arm round Mary. 'What are you doing here?' he asked.

'Well.' Mary responded quickly, 'Jamie invited himself to lunch with David. So here we are!'

'What do you think of our church?'

'Oh, it's beautiful. But I've been here before – to a wedding'

'Of course. I remember,' said Susan. 'It was Roseanne's wedding wasn't it. She's your mother-in-law's god-daughter isn't she?'

'Ben's mother,' Mary murmured.

'Oh I'm so sorry. Clumsy of me. But I always think of her as your mother-in-law.'

'So do I,' said Mary. 'She and Dan have been absolutely wonderful to me.'

As they talked they noticed the three children eying each other carefully before running off round the church.

'What are you going to do now?' asked Susan. 'Would you all like to come back for a cup of tea? We've got a swing and a climbing frame in the garden.'

Mary looked at David wondering whether he'd be disappointed if they accepted the invitation, but if he was, he didn't say. 'Great,' he said. 'It's obvious the youngsters are enjoying being together. We were off to the playground anyway.'

'Good. That's settled.' said Susan. 'I'll go and put the kettle on.'

They followed Susan slowly – the children dancing round excitedly. Mary hadn't been back to Stuart and Susan's house since their Silver wedding party. This time, they were able to see the garden – beautifully designed and maintained.

They watched the children on the swing and climbing frame until it got dark and then went in for tea. Though David and Mary had managed to avoid mentioning Jamal's name all day, Stuart raised the topic immediately they sat down.

'Well David, what's this new development? You said you'd fill me in next week, but as you're here you might as well tell me now. I'm sure Mary knows all about it already.'

'Well,' said David, 'There's now evidence that it was Jamal's friend Al who put the chemicals in his garage.' He then told Stuart about what Jamal's neighbours had seen the night they went away on holiday. 'Of course, it doesn't entirely exonerate Jamal. The prosecution may say that Jamal gave permission for the chemicals to be stored in his garage, but I've been to see Jamal and told him what his neighbours witnessed, and he strenuously denies knowing anything about it.'

'And you said he was very upset when he realised that Al might be implicated,' added Mary.

'What's Al like?' asked Stuart.

'Well, I haven't seen him all that often, but I've always found him very amiable. He's a good story teller – full of laughs. Though,' David added reflectively, 'he's always been a bit cagey when asked about his business.'

'He's a Muslim isn't he?' asked Stuart.

'Yes – and I gather a fairly devout one. I think his delivering chemical in the middle of the night is very sinister. But whether this has anything to do with Kim's disappearance I don't know.'

'I never liked him,' Mary said fiercely. 'He knew I was Kim's best friend but he never bothered to speak to me. If I'm honest, he gave me the creeps – though I couldn't tell you why.'

Stuart looked thoughtful. 'It gets more and more complicated doesn't it. As you say David, the crunch question will be whether or not Jamal gave Al permission to put the chemicals in his garage. It's going to be almost impossible to decide. Jamal will need a very good lawyer if he's to get off.'

'I agree,' said David.

At that moment Susan called them in for tea and they changed the subject.

When Mary said it was time to get Jamie to bed, David asked whether she would like to go back to his house first. She said no – glad of the opportunity not to discuss his proposal any further.

Celia was on the phone in the hall when they got back. Putting her hand on the receiver, she asked how the day had gone, and Mary said, 'I'll come down for a chat when I've got Jamie to bed – unless you're doing something.'

'No, just a quiet evening in,' she replied.

Jamie was worn out after his exciting day, and went straight to bed. As Mary kissed him goodnight, he said to her, 'I do like Uncle David. I hope we can go again.' She ruffled his hair and said, 'I'm sure we will.'

When she went down, Dan was nowhere to be seen. 'He's in his study – some work to do,' said Celia vaguely. Mary knew he was being tactful.

While Dan was the person Mary turned to whenever she had any practical problems to deal with, it was Celia she would talk to about emotional problems. It sometimes surprised her when she thought about it. Celia was a formidable looking woman and many people felt scared of her. She was tall and angular, wore glasses, and often had a forbidding expression on her face. But she was in fact the kindest and most caring woman one could imagine. Mary had got on well with her from the first time they met.

She told Celia about the day and about David's proposal, and tried to explain how confused she felt.

'How does David feel about it?'

'I don't really know. He isn't pressing me for an answer – and seems to understand that I need time. The trouble is, I don't really know why I'm hesitating. He's kind, he's warm, he's intelligent and, very important, he loves Jamie and Jamie loves him. But he's not Ben. I don't think I would ever have the same relationship with him that I had with Ben.'

Celia put her arms round her. 'I know,' she said. 'You and Ben had something very special. But no two relationships are alike, and I think that what you have with David would be a very good basis for a happy marriage.'

'But the spark isn't there!'

'I know – but that spark wears off in many marriages.'

Mary wanted to, but didn't ask whether the spark between her and Dan had worn off.

'If David isn't pressing you for an answer, I think you should both go on getting to know each other better. After all, you haven't known him that long – at least, not really known him. Give it time. One thing, though, that you might do is take him along to see your parents. They did invite him when they were here at Dan's party, didn't they? It might be helpful to see him in your home environment.'

'Bless you!' Mary gave Celia a warm hug. 'That's good advice. 'I'll phone Mum to see when they're free, and then suggest it to David. Now I must go up and do some studying. The exams are getting all too close, and I've done very little since Kim's disappearance.' With that, she kissed Celia goodnight and went up to her flat.

David spent the next Sunday with Mary and the family. It was becoming a habit. Anthony, Felicity and children were there as well, and after lunch Anthony and David offered to do the washing up as the dishwasher had broken down.

It was the first time they'd had a real conversation and as Anthony was a lawyer the conversation turned inevitably to Jamal. David brought him up to date with the neighbours' revelation, and though Anthony agreed that it was a pointer in Jamal's favour, he felt that the evidence was circumstantial and Jamal's hopes of getting off were tenuous.

After they were nearing the end of what seemed a marathon effort, Anthony suddenly said, 'And when are you two going to get together properly?'

David looked a little surprised, and asked what he meant.

'Well, you and Mary, of course. You're obviously very well suited.'

He didn't know quite what to say, so said, rather lamely, 'Well, I'm working at it.'

Seeing David was somewhat embarrassed by the question, Anthony said, 'Great! I'm sorry if I was intruding. It's just that we all want Mary to be happy.'

'So do I, but it's up to Mary.'

'And Jamie of course - but he's obviously very fond of you.' And with that, he took David's arm and led them back to the sitting room.

-50-
David visits Mary's parents

For the next fortnight David was away at a conference in Manchester and when he got back Mary phoned him and invited him to go with her to her mother's sixtieth birthday party.

'It won't be a big party. Just us and a few friends. We'd have to stay the night as it's too far to go there and back in one day.'

David accepted the invitation with enthusiasm, hoping that, despite Mary's depression about the death of Kim, it was a good sign for the future.

They set off early on the Saturday morning. During the week he'd been out and purchased a car seat for Jamie and a birthday present for Mary's mother. The former was easy, but David found it difficult to buy a present for someone he didn't know very well and in the end, bought a silk scarf and hoped she would like it.

When David arrived to collect them, Mary came out with the luggage and said, 'I must just get Jamie's car seat from my car.'

'Don't worry.' I said. 'I've got one for him in my car.'

Mary gave him a quizzical look. 'You're not trying to bribe me are you?' she said laughing.

'Of course not,' he replied with a twinkle. 'Just planning ahead!'

For the second time they'd agreed not to talk about Jamal over the weekend but their plans were thwarted. On the radio that morning there was a report of another terrorist attack in Pakistan – a suicide bomber had blown up a car in a crowded market place, and a large number of people had been killed. Apart from the horror of the attack they also felt that a terrorist act like this would not enhance Jamal's chances of getting off. It slightly dampened their mood.

However, Jamie's happy chatter at the back helped to dispel the gloom, and as they neared Mary's parents' house Jamie pointed out excitedly, 'There's Granny and Grandpa's house.'

David felt that the weekend would be a make or break in their relationship. He'd met Mary's parents at Dan's party but didn't know much about them. Mary had told him they'd lived in the same house ever since they were married.

'Didn't your father ever want to design his own house?' David asked, knowing he was an architect.

'No. They've always been perfectly happy here – both with the house and with their life-style. It's never occurred to them to think of moving. It's got two double bedrooms and a small box-room so it just wasn't big enough for Jamie and me to live there when Ben died. That's why I was so grateful when Celia and Dan offered me a home. It was a real God-send.'

David wondered what Mary thought when she first saw Ben's beautiful country mansion!

When they arrived, Mary's parents stood at the door waiting to welcome them. After kissing Mary and hugging Jamie, they turned to David smiling and said, 'It's so good to see you. We've really been looking forward to your visit.'

'Thank you. It's good to come. I think birthday wishes are in order,' he said with a smile.

'Yes,' said Mary's mother. 'But I'm not sure reaching sixty is something to celebrate!'

'Well, you don't look it,' David said sincerely,

'I agree,' said Mary's father. 'Sybil doesn't look a year over forty! I'm a lucky man.'

'Get along with you,' she said smiling. 'Come on in. You must be dying for a cup of coffee.'

'Grandpa, I want to see the ark,' said Jamie tugging at his grandfather's arm.

'Ok young man, But you must just wait until I've taken David's case upstairs and given him a drink.'

'Uncle David,' corrected Jamie primly.

'Oh! Uncle David then!' he responded with a smile in David's direction.

He showed David into a tiny bedroom, apologising that there wasn't much room 'to swing a cat. 'But I think you'll find the bed comfortable.'

After they'd eaten a substantial lunch Henry said, 'I think, David, it's time we took this young man to the park and let the women get ready for the party.'

David saw Mary giving him a little secret smile and he realised he would have no opportunity to say 'no'.

It was a sunny afternoon and Jamie skipped happily in front of them. As they walked along, Henry pointed out some interesting eighteenth century houses which he said had survived the bombing. David asked him about the War and Henry said he'd been a teenager at the time but could remember vividly the bombing and devastation. He told him about the public and domestic air raid shelters, the guns and barrage balloons, the shortage of food and clothing, the camaraderie, and the fact that so many households lacked adult males because they had all been called up.

'I don't think people today have any idea how very difficult it must have been for women during the war – and even after, when food was still short and rationing continued,' he said. 'How things have changed. We have wonderful medical care, free education, high standards of living, and plenty of food. I don't think people realise how fortunate they are.'

David agreed.

Henry asked about David's work at the hospital and wanted to know what changes they were making in the organisation. David had a feeling of *deja vue*, remembering his encounter with Samantha's father when he thought he was about to be questioned about his intentions. How wrong he'd been. With Henry, David felt there was no doubt he was being probed, albeit very tactfully, to find out what sort of person he was.

They talked about Kim's tragic death and Jamal's imprisonment. He wanted to know whether David thought him innocent. When he said 'yes', Henry said he was glad. 'I can't imagine Kim getting involved with someone who was not intrinsically a good person. Sybil and I feel Kim's death keenly, you know. As a child she was often in the house – almost like a second daughter – vivacious and yet very caring. I really feel for Mary. They were close. I hope you're able to comfort her,' he added with a smile.

'I do my best,' David replied. 'Kim was my friend too. She was greatly respected at the hospital and always ready to listen to people's problems.'

'There's an old saying 'the good die young', he said 'and I sometimes think the good Lord likes to take back to Himself those he especially loves.'

Henry suddenly startled David by saying, 'You're not a believer are you?'

'Well, no. It's somehow never been something I've felt called to. I think, perhaps, you could call me an agnostic – someone who's still searching.'

The answer seemed to satisfy Henry and he turned to Jamie, who was happily coming down the slide, 'It's time to go back to Mummy and Grandma.'

Just before they got back, Henry said,' I know it's early days, but if you and Mary do get together I hope you won't let the tragedy of Kim's murder intrude too much on your relationship. You must, in time, put it behind you.'

David thanked him for his understanding.

When they returned to the house it had a festive air with balloons and a large banner saying 'Happy 60th Birthday'. The dining table was laid with food – hidden by a large damask tablecloth.

Sybil's brother and his wife had already arrived. He was the spit image of Sybil and seemed as warm and cheerful as she was. The other guests arrived soon after and the house quickly seemed full.

Among the guests was Mary's cousin, Jonathan, who started asking David questions about Kim whom he'd known quite well. 'I always liked her, you know. I'm sure that doctor must be guilty.'

'We don't think so,' said David. 'I think Jamal's probably innocent but it's going to be difficult to prove,' and he told them what the neighbours had seen on the night they went on holiday.

'Well, it's been a very strange story, hasn't it? When the boy who robbed the jewellers confessed about the body the press had a real field day didn't they! The boy was apparently traumatised by his discovery.'

'No wonder,' murmured one of the guests.

'Yes, agreed. But they haven't caught the other boy. He's still at large.'

'The police still_haven't been able to get the boy to reveal his name. '

'Apparently he was terrified of the other boy. That's why he won't tell the police.'

'That's the problem. There's a lot of bullying among these gangs with older boys terrorising the younger,' said Henry.

'What a very strange thing,' said Jonathan, not wanting to let go of the story. 'If the boy hadn't been in a car accident and ended up in hospital we might never have known where Kim's body was.'

'And we still don't know how she got there.'

David, watching Mary while this conversation was going on, saw that she was getting increasingly upset. He managed to change the subject quickly by asking Jonathan what he did for a living and the subject of Kim's death was dropped.

David was aware that the guests at the party were eager to find out what Mary's 'new boyfriend' was like and felt he was under scrutiny. But he realised it was because they were all very fond of Mary and deeply concerned about her happiness. One or two mentioned the tragedy in Mary's life – and then felt embarrassed they'd mentioned Ben's name in front of him, but David was at pains to indicate that he knew all about the sad time she'd been through and was deeply sympathetic to her loss. He also made a point of letting them know how fond he was of Jamie.

Mary allowed Jamie to stay up for the party. He looked angelic with his fair wavy hair and angelic features, and everyone said that Sybil and Henry were lucky to have such a gorgeous grandson.

Henry produced champagne for the toast and made a little speech, saying what a wonderful wife and mother Sybil was. 'She doesn't look sixty, does she? In fact, if I hadn't seen her birth certificate, I wouldn't have believed it.' With that, he kissed her hand, and gave her a warm smile.

Halfway through supper, Sybil's goddaughter, Henrietta, arrived with her boyfriend. When Mary introduced her to David, she looked him up and down with an appraising eye, and then said with a twinkle, 'Yes, I think you'll do.'

Her mother was shocked and apologised saying, 'You just can't keep these young people under control these days.' They all laughed.

As soon as Henrietta and Roger had eaten their fill, they turned their attention to Jamie. 'I love kids,' said Henrietta. 'I want lots when I get married.'

David looked in Roger's direction to see his response, but Roger busied himself studiously in conversation with Henry.

Jamie somehow managed to keep going until 10 o'clock when he fell asleep on the sofa, and Mary carried him up to bed.

When all the guests had left Henry poured a nightcap for them while they discussed the party and agreed it had been a lovely evening.

Sybil turned to David and said with a smile, 'Now they've met you the family will know who I'm talking about,'

They were sitting chatting quietly when the telephone rang. Henry took the call. It was their neighbour, Beverly, with a crisis on her hands. Her eight-year old daughter had been taken ill; the doctor had just visited and said she must go straight to hospital. He'd arranged for an ambulance to collect her and it would be arriving any minute. Beverly said she wanted to go to the hospital with her little girl, but couldn't leave the other two children alone. Could Sybil help?

'Tell her I'll come in straight away,' said Sybil, getting up, and beginning to collect some things together.

'No! Sit down mother. It's your birthday.'

'We'll both go,' said Sybil firmly

Henry agreed. 'Yes, both go and then you can decide what to do. We'll look after Jamie.'

Then he turned to David and said, 'Her husband's in Afghanistan at present and her mother died a couple of years ago, so we keep an eye on her. She's quite young, and has three small children to look after on her own. It's not easy.'

At that moment they heard the ambulance arriving, and Mary and Sybil got up and left.

'What if the child's in hospital for a long time?'

'I can see the two children moving in here!' said Henry, with a resigned look on his face. 'Not that I'm not fond of the children – they're good kids, but it makes life complicated.

An hour later, Sybil returned and told them, 'Beverly's phoned. Melanie's on a drip. The doctors suspect meningitis, but won't know till after the lumber-puncture's been analysed. I'm going to go and sleep next door. Mary offered, but she doesn't know the children as well as I do, so it's best I go.'

Henry nodded agreement, but said, 'What a sad ending to your Birthday.'

'Oh, but it's been lovely! I've really enjoyed it – and I'm so glad you were able to come, David, 'she said, turning to him with a smile. 'As long as Melanie gets better, it will just have added a bit of drama to the evening.'

With that she went upstairs to get together some night things and toiletries. Then David walked her round to the neighbour's house, and brought Mary back.

He woke quite early to the sound of Jamie's chatter, and when he'd showered and dressed, came downstairs to find Mary getting breakfast ready, and no sign of Henry.

'Where's your father?' he asked. 'Has he gone next door?'

'Oh no,' said Mary. He's gone to church. 'He's had to take the service this morning, so he had to leave early. It's a family service.'

'I didn't realise he was a clergyman,' said David, puzzled.

'Oh no! He's not ordained. He's a Reader.'

'What's that?' David asked, having never heard the term before.

'A Reader's someone who's done a special training for three years so he can help in the work of the parish. He can take all the non-Eucharistic services like morning prayer, evensong, and funerals, but he can't baptise anyone, or administer communion because they're sacramental services.'

On the few occasions he'd been to a church service, it had never occurred to David to think about the different roles of the people involved in the service and realised how ignorant he was about church affairs.

Sybil came back soon after ten with the two children who were obviously quite at home in the house. Within minutes, Peter, who was six, was playing happily with Jamie, while Rupert tucked himself in a corner of the sitting room with his play station.

It was an anxious morning. Every time the phone rang, they thought it might be Beverly from the hospital.

Sybil and Mary got on with preparations for lunch as they needed to leave soon after.

Henry returned about noon, and told them they'd had an interesting visiting preacher at the service that morning. 'He's a Member of Parliament and a Christian. He represents a multi -faith constituency. He told us about the work that was going on in his constituency through co-operation between leaders of the various ethnic and religious groups, Muslim, Hindu,

Sikh and Catholic. He said he believes it is only by working together across the ethnic and religious divide that terrorism can be suppressed.'

It made David think of the Symposium he'd attended in London, and told Henry a little bit about it.

Lunch just after one o'clock was a traditional Sunday roast. During the meal Jamie had a tantrum because he wouldn't eat his main course and wanted only pudding. Henry tried to insist he ate some of his dinner first, but Jamie wasn't having it. It was the first time David had seen him in a bad mood – and had forgotten what childhood tantrums were like. It took him back to when his sister's children were young.

Just as they were leaving, the phone rang. It was Beverly from the hospital saying that it was not meningitis, and that her daughter was much better. Henry immediately offered to go and fetch her when she was ready, while Sybil said she would hang on to the children.

All this was arranged as though it was the obvious thing to do, and David thought how lucky Beverly was to have such caring neighbours.

Musing on the weekend later, David thought that if Mary eventually agreed to marry him, he would be happy to have Sybil and Henry as his in-laws. He'd disliked Joanna's parents intensely, and thought he would have been overawed by Samantha's parents if that relationship had developed,

Then he remembered his amusement when one of his friends announced he was going to meet his girlfriend's parents before proposing because he needed to find out what his girlfriend would be like when she grew older! And now, if Mary did agree to marry him, here he was doing the same thing.

-51-
Offer of land for a hospice

A few days after the visit to Mary's parents. David received a phone call from Martin Allardice asking him to meet him at the Council offices. As David hadn't seen him since his withdrawal from the appeal committee, he thought he was going to get more complaints about the hospital, and almost decided not to go. Then he thought better of it, and felt quite guilty when he learnt what Martin wanted to talk about.

Martin told him that the Council had been considering what to do with a derelict acre of land at the edge of town and they'd been persuaded to offer it to the Hospice Committee. 'It'll need quite a bit of work clearing the land, but all the amenities are there because there's a small but expensive little development at the side of it. It's peaceful, and overlooks a lovely area of farmland.

'It's a very generous idea,' David said doubtfully. 'But it's way out of town, and there's no bus service there.'

'I know, but I think, with a little pressure from the Council, the bus company could be persuaded to extend one of its routes.'

David knew that one of the main problems the appeal would have to face was the acquisition of land, and couldn't believe it was about to be solved. He asked Martin why it wasn't going to be used for housing development.

'Well, there's a covenant on the land which says it can only be used for amenities for the town.'

'How on earth, Martin, did you persuade the Council to consider using the land for a hospice?'

'It's not really my doing. I'm merely the go-between. It's all thanks to the new Mayor. His first wife died in a hospice. And now tragedy's struck again. His young niece is dying in a children's hospice in Devon. He'd already decided to make the hospice appeal his charity for his year of office, and when the question of this derelict piece of land was raised, he suggested it could be used for the hospice.'

'And has the Council agreed?

'Yes, in principal. But I was asked to sound you out first, before it came to the Council as a formal proposal.

David felt somewhat surprised at the Council being so generous, and wondered whether there was some hidden agenda. But an offer like that was not to be sneezed at. He felt relieved at the thought that one major hurdle might have been overcome, but remained doubtful about the location of the site.

'Discuss it with your committee,' said Martin. 'We'll need to know before the next Council meeting in a month's time. I don't want the Council's generosity to go off the boil because of delays.'

'Ok,' said David feebly. 'And thank you for your efforts on our behalf.'

'I should add,' said Martin, 'that's it's all strictly confidential at the moment. You'll have to ask your committee not to tell anyone about it until it comes back to the Council, and a formal decision is made.

'Not easy. As you know, we've got Mark on our committee.'

'Yes, but his paper has to accept embargos when necessary.'

David nodded. 'OK. Well, thanks again. I'll be in touch.'

He summoned a special meeting of the committee to discuss the offer. There was great enthusiasm to begin with, though as the discussion proceeded, everyone realised there would be a number of serious hurdles to overcome – the main one being the location and lack of public transport.

'Can we trust the bus company to respond to pressure from the Council and extend the route?' asked Alec

'Provided we can get the public behind it as well, I think the answer is yes,' said Mark.

After lengthy discussion, they all agreed to accept the offer, and David was deputed to report back to Martin. Mark promised to keep the matter out of the newspaper until the Council had made a formal decision.

At the next Council meeting, the proposal to give the land for a hospice was accepted.

This put the Appeal on a whole new footing with a hospice for the town now firmly on the agenda. Mark blazoned the news across both the local newspaper and the freebie paper, which he also edited. He put in a photograph of each member of the committee, with a little explanation of the area of fund raising they had committed themselves to.

Offers of help began to come in from all directions. Alice reported that the newspaper article had prompted several organisations to invite her to come and speak to them about the hospice. Pamela said that several of the Friends had offered to set up local groups, and she was going out to visit them. Someone with a beautiful garden had contacted Margaret and said she would organise a Garden Safari in May or June when gardens would be their best. Betty said that several pubs had phoned her and offered to have collecting boxes on their counters, while one publican said he would organise a Pub League Darts Competition for the appeal.

When Margaret phoned David to say that Lord Marston had agreed to let them hold the Ball at Storrington Park, he called a meeting for all those interested in helping organise it. To his surprise, everyone on the committee turned up.

Margaret, more animated than they'd ever seen her, told them that the owners of Storrington Park were so delighted with the idea of a Ball that they said they could have the venue free of charge. She'd already enrolled an assistant – Betty. It would have been difficult to find two people from more contrasting backgrounds, but they'd obviously gelled, and had started planning the event.

David started the meeting by finding a date and then handed over the Chair to Margaret, saying she was obviously more experienced at this sort of thing than he was.

Margaret beamed. 'Well, if the Ball's to be really successful, there's lots of things to think about.' She listed them one by one: catering, crockery and cutlery, a bar; a licence; tickets, music, a raffle, a tombola or bottle stall, and most important of all, wide publicity.

By the end of the evening, it seemed everything was under control. Alice's brother had a band and she was sure he wouldn't charge; Pamela knew of caterers; Alec offered to organise the bar and get the licence; Mark agreed to take on publicity and contact all the businesses in the area; and

Margaret said she would get her husband to help her contact their wealthier friends and acquaintances. Alec was sure one of his colleagues in the printing business would organise the tickets, and Betty said one of her friends had had just set up a new business and she was sure she would lend all the cutlery and china gratis as it would be such good publicity.

David, amazed it had all been sorted out so quickly, said 'I realise I haven't promised anything,'

'Nor me,' Mary murmured

'But I'll do whatever I'm told to.'

'That's a risky promise,' said Mark, laughing.

'I know,' said David. 'But I haven't any expertise in this sort of thing.'

'But you've got lots of contacts,' said Margaret firmly. 'You can, for example, invite the Chairman of the Health Authority. You know him well,'

Mary saw David wince, and realised it made him think about the way he'd been inveigled into the relationship with Samantha. But he said bravely, 'I'll try, but I can't promise anything.'

Moving on reluctantly from discussing the Ball, Alec said that now things were on the move, they needed to set up a marketing group. He also raised the question of having a charity shop in the not too distant future.

Mary then raised the subject of charitable trusts. She said these would be the most significant part of their funding, but firm plans were needed before trusts would consider an application. Now they had the offer of land, they should start thinking about what sort of building they wanted, so they set up a small sub-committee to discuss this further.

When he thought about the meeting later, David realised that everyone present had made significant contributions to the discussions except for Jane who, unlike her usual enthusiastic self, had been quiet throughout. He made a mental note to contact her later to see if all was well.

As they left the meeting Pamela buttonholed Mary and David and invited them to dinner the following Saturday.

-52-
Dinner with Pamela and Patrick

It was the first time he'd been to Pamela's home. and also the first time, he realised, that he and Mary had been invited anywhere as a couple. 'Was this progress,' he asked himself.

'Come on in,' said Pamela, kissing them both, while Patrick greeted Mary with an affectionate hug before pouring them a drink. He seemed very much at home. Then she said, 'We've asked you here specially tonight as we want you to be the first to know. Patrick and I are getting married.'

A TORTUOUS PATH

Mary and David were astonished at the speed of their romance, knowing that Patrick and Pamela had met only a few months before at Dan's sixtieth birthday party. David couldn't help thinking about how slowly his relationship with Mary was developing, but he gave them both a hug and said, 'That's wonderful.'

Patrick told them they were planning to marry at the end of the following month.

'Wow! You're not wasting any time!' said Mary.

'No,' said Pamela. 'But we want a family and I'm getting on a bit. So we thought we'd get married straight away.'

'You're not moving away are you?' asked David, thinking of all she'd committed herself to doing for the hospice.

'No. We're going to live in the area. Patrick's already got a job teaching locally, and we're going to live in my flat until we can sell both our flats and buy a house.'

'That's wonderful,' said Mary enthusiastically. 'It'll be great having you around, Patrick. Now, tell us about the wedding.'

'It's going to be a church wedding just after Easter. Jane's husband, Colin, is going to marry us. And we want you two to be involved. Mary, I'd love it if you would be my Matron of Honour.'

Mary looked startled. 'Aren't I a bit old?'

'Of course you're not. It's me that's getting on a bit! I'm not planning a conventional white wedding with an elaborate white dress and masses of bridesmaids. But I do want a church wedding, and I do want some support, and I'd love it if you'd agree.'

'Well, of course,' said Mary. 'I'd love to. It'd be a great honour!' and they all smiled at the pun.

'And,' said Patrick turning to David, 'I don't know many people locally, and as you're such a good friend of Mary, I wondered if you would be one of my ushers?'

David felt he should accept for Mary's sake, so said, 'I'd be delighted.'

'Well, that's all settled then. Time for dinner,' said Pamela.

Looking round the flat as they sat down at the table they saw Patrick's things scattered round the room and realised he'd already moved in. 'Patrick's a very good cook,' said Pamela, 'so he's prepared the main course.'

The dinner was excellent and they all drank a fair bit of wine. Conversation flowed. They discussed the coincidence of their friendships - that Mary and David had both known Pamela but through different routes; and that Mary and Patrick's friendship went back to their teenage days. Patrick told them about his new teaching job at the local comprehensive school and expressed his suspicion that teaching there would be rather different from teaching in the grammar school where he'd been for the last ten years. David agreed, thinking about the rather mixed reputation of the local comprehensive school.

'I saw your grammar school when we went to Mary's mother's sixtieth birthday. Henry pointed it out to me when we took Jamie to the park. Quite an impressive place!'

'Yes, from the outside. But not quite so impressive inside! The school I'm going to is much better equipped!'

They talked about the hospice appeal and the unexpected offer of land which they agreed was extremely generous, and very unusual for a Council to behave in this way. Talk of the hospice led them to talk about Jamal.

'Pamela's told me all about Dr Khan and his sad story. I gather most of you think he's innocent?' said Patrick.

'Yes. But the problem is, it's going to be difficult to prove. All the evidence is circumstantial.'

'When's the trial?'

'We've just heard. It's a month after Easter. David and I are going to see him next week to tell him the good news about the land - to try and cheer him up a bit. My boss has obtained the services of a very good barrister which, incidentally, Kim's father is paying for.'

The thought of Jamal's impending trial altered the atmosphere a little, and as it was getting on for midnight, Mary decided it was time to leave. On the way home they were both silent – chewing over the surprise news they'd just received.

-53-
Mothering Sunday

The talk of an Easter wedding reminded David it was time to phone his sister to arrange his annual Easter visit to Scotland.

Alison had been the only person he'd really talked to about his relationship with Mary, and when he phoned her she said, 'Don't you think, now you've visited her parents, that the time is ripe for you to invite Mary and Jamie here?'

He thought about it – and agreed, 'But I'm not at all sure what her response will be.'

To his delight, Mary agreed. They arranged to go to Perth by train. 'Too far for you to drive,' said Alison. 'No need to bring much for Jamie. I've still got a lot of the children's things in the attic. There's the old pushchair, a car seat and lots of toys. I haven't had the heart to throw them out - although,' she hastened to add, 'I'm not planning to have any more children!'

David found it difficult to suppress his excitement and when he next went to Mary's house for Sunday lunch he shared a conspiratorial hug with Celia in the kitchen.

Over lunch, Mary and Celia were discussing the next Sunday's service at the church. 'It's Mothering Sunday,' said Celia. 'I gather the Vicar's organised several trays of primulas for the service. Mr Andrews is getting them at a discount from the local nursery.'

'That's good,' murmured Mary.

'Tell me about Mothering Sunday,' said David. 'Is it just to do with mothers?'

Dan said the service went back a long way. He explained that, as with so many festivals, the early Christian church had taken over a Roman festival which was held in honour of the mother goddess Cybele. From early times it was celebrated on the fourth Sunday in Lent to honour the Virgin Mary and 'mother church.'

He then went on to explain that over the years the emphasis had been more and more on mothers. In earlier centuries, domestic servants were given the day off to visit their mothers, and that was probably how the term Mothering Sunday had come about.

'What about Simmel cakes?' David asked. 'I heard Celia talking about baking one.'

'Well, they're cakes baked specially for Mothering Sunday. They're supposed to be covered with eleven marzipan balls representing the eleven apostles who remained faithful to Jesus when he was arrested in the garden of Gethsemane.'

'Interesting,' he said.

'Why don't you come along with us next Sunday and see what it's all about. It's usually a packed service with lots of children there. Jamie will love it.'

'We'll see,' said David, giving Dan a grin, knowing they were gently trying to draw him in.

By Sunday he decided not to be churlish and agreed to go to church with Mary and the family. As Dan had predicted, the church was packed with many families and young children. David was relieved to find it was not a communion service, and felt able to relax. After the first hymn, the children were taken off to a side chapel and Jamie went happily along with them.

Although David knew the vicar, Colin, he'd only heard him preach at Kim's funeral but was impressed with his Mothering Sunday sermon. He talked about the way Biblical teaching impinged on present day life. He discussed the role of mothers, but also included fathers and grandparents, and emphasised the importance of a child's early life and upbringing. He said many people became Christians because they'd been taught about Jesus on their mother's knee.

Two thirds of the way through the service, when the children had re-joined their parents, Colin invited them to the altar to collect flowers for their mothers. David watched Jamie toddle up with the other children, with Dan walking discreetly behind not wishing to curb his independence but anxious about him carrying his pot of primulas down the steps. David felt quite emotional as he saw Jamie walking very carefully back from the altar, concentrating on every step, holding the pot proudly in both hands, his face wreathed in smiles. He handed the primulas to Mary, and David could see she felt equally emotional as she gave Jamie a hug and a kiss.

Then an older child came up to Celia, and handed her a pot of primulas. 'My mum said to give it to you 'cos you do so much for the church.'

'Why, that's lovely,' said Celia, with tears in her eyes. 'Thank you so much, Karen. That's really kind. I'll take great care of them,' and she turned to the other side of the aisle with a thank you smile to the girl's mother.

After the service everyone stayed behind for coffee. There were quite a few people whom David knew and he was made very welcome. Colin came up to him and said, 'Well, David, it's good to see you here. I know it's not your sort of thing, but I hope we can tempt you to come again.'

'Maybe,' he said. 'But where's Jane? She's not here, is she?'

'I'm afraid she's not well, so stayed at home.'

'Nothing serious I hope?'

'Well, we're waiting on test results. It's an anxious time. But everyone's praying for her.'

Colin looked so worried that David didn't like to ask more, but said, 'I'm so sorry. I hope the results are good. Do give her my love and tell her I'll be thinking of her.'

Colin squeezed his hand, said 'Thank you. She'll be glad I've seen you,' and moved away to talk to one of his parishioners who was standing just behind him, eager for a word.

David made a mental note to go and visit Jane as soon as he got back from Scotland.

-54-
Mary and Jamie go to Scotland

Jamie woke early on the morning they were to set off for Scotland. Mary was almost as excited as he was. She'd never been to Scotland, and was looking forward to meeting David's sister and family. She knew they meant a lot to him and felt a little apprehensive, realising the visit could be a make or break time for her relationship with David,

Mick had volunteered to take them to the main line station, nearly two hours away. 'You don't want all the hassle of public transport when you have young Jamie in tow,' he said.

Mary admired Mick. She liked the easy camaraderie between him and David, though David was in essence his boss. As she'd got to know David, she began to realise how much people liked and respected him

It was difficult to contain Jamie's excitement. It was the first time he'd been on a train, and to go on holiday with Uncle David was an added bonus.

Knowing it would be a long journey to Scotland, David had booked first class seats. Mary felt this was an unnecessary extravagance but David said he felt this was a special occasion, and wanted to treat them. Mary had an assortment of toys and books for Jamie to play with on the journey, but Jamie had also insisted on bringing his large teddy. When she'd tried to dissuade him, David took Jamie's side and said it wouldn't be a problem. 'Of course, he can take Big Ted,' so she had to give in.

It was the Thursday before Easter. The train was crowded and Mary felt grateful to David for treating them to a first class compartment which they had to themselves. Jamie kept rushing back and forth from the window to the corridor, excited by everything that was going on. But when a train went hurtling past in the opposite direction, he flung himself into Mary's lap crying that a monster had just gone past! It took a little while to calm him down.

David insisted they had lunch on the train – another exciting experience for Jamie. He kept standing up in his seat and looking round the restaurant car, making slightly embarrassing comments about the lady in a sari at the next table. Then he spied a Jewish rabbi and commented on his 'funny' hat. Fortunately, they seemed to like children because they both acknowledged Jamie's comments with an understanding smile.

When they got back to their seats both Jamie and David fell asleep. Mary sat watching them and felt a sense of deep contentment. She realised that when David proposed again, as she knew he would, her answer would be yes.

They reached Edinburgh in the late afternoon where they changed trains, and had a further hour's journey to their destination. David's brother-in-law, James, was waiting for them. He greeted David with a hug, shook hands with Mary, and then solemnly bent down to shake Jamie's hand – much to Jamie's amusement.

Mary had imagined David's family lived in a town, but as they drove from the station in the half-light she could see it was little more than a very large village, surrounded by trees and hills. Their home was only ten minutes from the station - a Victorian house with a modern annexe on the side. David's sister, Alison was waiting at the door to greet them. 'I've so been looking forward to meeting you,' she said warmly, kissing Mary on both cheeks, 'And this must be Jamie,' she said, bending down to say 'hello.' Jamie looked up shyly and murmured 'yes', and buried his head in Mary's skirt.

Then David, giving her a big hug, kissed her, and said,' It's great to see you, sis. It seems such a long time since Christmas.' Before Alison could say anything, a little girl pushed her aside and jumped up into David's arms and kissed him warmly. 'This,'' said David turning to Mary, 'is Susan, my very special girl. Say hello to Mary and Jamie, Susan'. She gave them a speculative look, and then said shyly, 'Hello,' but before waiting for a reply, tugged David away, saying, 'You're in granddad's room. I'll show you.'

Smiling, Alison turned to Mary and said. 'You must be exhausted after your journey. I suggest I take you up to your room so you can sort yourself out and freshen up before dinner.'

James took her case, and Alison, taking Jamie's hand, said, 'I thought Jamie would be happier being with you in a strange house, but there's a spare room next door if you'd prefer.'

'No. You're right. I'll keep Jamie with me.'

She showed them into a large and very comfortable room with two beds, a large mahogany wardrobe and dressing table, a desk, two armchairs, and a washbasin in the corner. 'I hope you have everything you need. The bathroom's down the corridor – not en-suite I'm afraid. These Victorian houses weren't built for that. Would you like me to bring you a cup of tea for you while you unpack?' Mary declined, saying they'd had a drink on the train.

'Well, I'll leave you to it,' she said. 'Shout if there's anything you need. I'll just be downstairs in the kitchen getting the children's tea ready.'

Mary looked out of the window, and though it was nearly dark she could see the outline of hills beyond the garden. She had the feeling that this was going to be a very happy visit, and breathed a sigh of contentment. While she unpacked, Jamie jumped on both beds, and placing Big Ted on the bed nearest the window said,' This is my bed.' Then, discovering the toys which Alison had thoughtfully put in a large box in the corner, he started exploring the contents. By the time Mary was ready to go downstairs, the floor was littered with toys. 'Home from home,' she thought ruefully.

When Mary went down, Alison said, 'Tea or a drink? Dinner won't be that long, but I thought we'd feed the children first.'

'Then tea,' she said, and followed Alison into a spacious farmhouse kitchen where she'd set out the children's tea.

Little Jack, who was almost the same age as Jamie, was sitting solemnly at the table. 'Say hello to Jamie,' said Alison. Jack obeyed – albeit very shyly. He had blonde hair, and a very sweet face. He seemed quite a bit taller than Jamie. Then Susan came bouncing in. She was a sturdy little girl with dark hair and a fringe. She was wearing glasses and had an ugly brace over her teeth. 'We hope she'll soon be rid of that,' said Alison pointing to the brace. 'But she's done very well with it.'

The three children eyed each other suspiciously. 'They'll soon break the ice,' said Alison confidently.

They all, Jamie included, tucked into the lovely spread Alison had prepared, and when they'd finished, she said, 'Now, Susan, take Jamie and show him the playroom. Half an hour, then it's bath time.'

Mary held her breath, wondering whether Jamie would go with them, but to her delight, he got down from the table, accepted Susan's proffered hand, and went off with them.

'Well, that's a good start,' said Alison. 'Let's go and join the men and have a drink.'

Mary took to Alison straight away. She was warm and friendly, and there was no mistaking she was David's sister either in manner or physique. Her husband, James, was tall and very good-looking. He had a confident air, but a pleasant manner and she felt at home almost immediately.

After half an hour Alison and Mary bundled all three children into the bath. Then there was a small problem. Both Jamie and Susan wanted Uncle David to read them a bedtime story, so they compromised and put all three children in Jamie's bed and summoned David to read to them.

Much to her relief, story time over, Jamie settled down and fell asleep quickly. It had been a long day for him.

At dinner Mary met the two older children – Jenny, a beautiful poised girl of sixteen who was about to take her GCSEs and had been revising when they arrived. Steven, at thirteen, was more taciturn. It was obvious his voice was just breaking and he had that rather sullen look that one often sees in boys of that age. David said later that he had changed, even since Christmas, as he used to be much more open and friendly.

They had an excellent dinner. The evening was spent catching up with news, and planning what they would do during their visit.

They spent quite a time talking about schools and the many problems teachers face these days. Alison was a primary school head, and they spent quite a time talking about schools and the many problems teachers face these days. Mary said she was glad she was in the legal profession and not in education.

Then Alison talked about her own children and said that Susan was not the easiest of them. She was exuberant, but ever since her grandfather died, she was prone to fly into terrible rages. 'It was a traumatic time for all of us, and I think children take a very long time to assimilate what's happened. They don't have the vocabulary to express their hurt. I've seen it with some of my pupils.'

James, who was a lawyer, wanted to be brought up to date with Jamal's situation. They discussed Jamal's forthcoming trial, and tried to evaluate the strength of his plea of innocence. Like David and Mary, James felt dubious about the chance of a not guilty verdict – mainly because he saw no way of proving that Jamal had not given Al permission to put the chemicals in his garage.

David said, 'It's the last thing I ever expected to be involved with. Here we are, living comparatively conventional lives, when we're suddenly involved with both a murder and the activities of a terrorist gang.'

James reminded them of the ordinary primary school teacher who turned out to be the leader of a terrorist gang. They all agreed that it must have been a terrible a shock for his colleagues at the school to discover they'd been working alongside a terrorist. 'And,' said Alison, 'it must have been traumatic for you all, especially for Jamal (if he is indeed innocent) to discover his best friend had been deceiving him and was involved in terrorism.'

'And,' added David, 'may even be implicated in his fiancé's murder. A horrendous thought!'

'It doesn't bear thinking about,' said Alison with a shudder.

Then David said, rather bitterly, 'It seems to me we can so easily be deceived. Samantha never gave me the slightest indication that she was involved in counter espionage. She managed to keep that quiet right up to the end of our relationship. And I didn't think I was a gullible sort of person.'

'No. It's awful the way you were used,' said Alison sympathetically – at the same time, looking at Mary to see if she was bothered about David's reference to Samantha.

Mary said, 'Well, I suppose if national safety is at stake, these secretive methods have to be used. Look at nine/eleven.

Everyone nodded.

'Well, all I know is that Dad was very impressed with Jamal,' said Alison. 'He only met him the once but he often talked about him, and was looking forward to meeting him again.'

They went to bed early as both Mary and David were exhausted. After a warm bath, Mary fell asleep instantly and woke next morning with brilliant sunshine pouring into the room and Jamie sitting quietly in the corner playing with his toys. Alison, hearing her moving around, brought up a cup of tea.

After a leisurely breakfast James said he would take them on a tour of the area. Alison elected to stay at home as she wanted to go to the Good Friday meditation in the church. Jenny said she needed to do more revision and Steven, after thinking about it at length, decided he would go and visit a friend. So, David and Mary, James and the three younger children set off on an expedition, agreeing to meet back at home for a late sandwich lunch.

Glimpses from the car and from the bedroom window gave Mary only a taste of the beautiful area David's sister lived in. The town comprised just one main street with Georgian buildings on either side. There were clothes shops displaying tartans, craft shops with windows full of quality goods, all designed, said James, to attract the wealthier tourists who were the main visitors to the town. The grocer's shop on the corner was tastefully set out with a mouth-watering display of Scottish malts, salmon and pheasants, and an assortment of unusual pickles and preserves, while the art shop window displayed paintings of mountains and lochs.

It seemed that the main street was all there was on one side, with hills rising behind, while the other side of the street abutted on to a little square with a war memorial and some small very old cottages, one or two of which advertised themselves as tearooms.

At the end of the square were iron gates through which they could see what looked like a ruined abbey. The gates were open and they discovered that the ruins were deceptive – for while one end was roofless and typical of a mediaeval ruin, the other half was roofed over and proved to be the parish church. There was a service going on so they walked round the ruins – the children playing hide and seek round the columns that still remained. The abbey abutted on to a large expanse of grass stretching down to a fast flowing river. The area was full of trees with long bare trunks reaching up to the sky.

They wandered down to the river and saw, to the left, the bridge they'd crossed over the previous night. It had five arches, and James told them it had been built by General Wade in the 1700s, when he'd built a network of military roads to suppress the Jacobite rebellion. The whole area was enchanting, and Mary took a lot of photographs with her new digital camera.

When they got back very late to the house, Alison had prepared a light lunch, and they spent the rest of the afternoon relaxing. Steven inveigled them into playing a game Mary hadn't heard of before, *Risk*, which was about world conquest. As Jamie was happy playing with Susan and Jack, and Alison was busy preparing dinner, they couldn't find any excuses to say no! Mary soon realised it was a game that involved tactical skill as well as good luck when throwing the dice, and before the hour was out, much to her relief, her army of tiny soldiers had been totally wiped out. But she was amused to see that the game brought out all the competitive instincts of the three males left battling for victory.

Alison, seeing her leaving the table said, 'You're lucky to be free. *Risk* is a game that can go on for hours. I always do my best to be busy when they suggest I play. *Rummicubs* is my mark. It's fun – and it takes less than twenty minutes to finish a round. I often play it with Susan – and Steven sometimes deigns to join us if he's got nothing better to do.'

Mary smiled, amused by Alison's confession.

'You wait,' she said, 'till Jamie's a little older! Now, I suggest you go and put your feet up and relax with a book. I've got some work I must do this afternoon, but after that, I'm free for the weekend.'

Though Mary had been there for less than a day, she already felt relaxed, and suspected it was because they were getting right away from the trauma of the last eight months.

They had an early evening meal so that all the children could join them. Conversation was lively. Being an only child, Mary hadn't come across the cut and thrust of discussion in a family with teenage children. It was interesting to hear the way the two bright teenagers interacted with their parents and discussed serious contemporary issues.

After they'd put the smaller children to bed, they all sat down to watch the television film, made in 1999, of the life of Jesus. Mary had seen it before but had forgotten how accurate it was – based largely on the Gospel of Luke.

The film prompted a lot of discussion about Christianity. Alison was obviously a committed Christian and much involved in her local church. So too was Jenny. Mary suspected that James was a little more ambivalent, though he said he often went along with Alison to the parish church. David admitted that he'd run away from Christianity at the age of eleven, and had never bothered since. 'Not,' he said, 'that I have any quarrel with Christianity. I'm quite happy to believe in the existence of a God, and I can accept all the Christian tenets, but I find the idea of Jesus being the Son of God, and rising from the dead, less easy to accept.'

They argued about this for quite a time. 'So what exactly do you believe?' David eventually asked.

Alison and Mary looked at each other and thought for a minute while they tried to organise their response.

'Well,' Alison said at last. 'I can't imagine my life without faith. I suppose, if you want me to define it, I could recite the creed – I believe in one God, the Father Almighty, Creator of Heaven and Earth…And Jesus Christ, his only Son, our Lord, who was conceived of the Holy Spirit and the Virgin Mary,'

'Suffered under Pontius Pilot,' Mary joined in, 'was crucified, dead and buried. On the third day he rose again from the dead, he ascended into heaven, and he will come again in glory to judge the living and the dead.'

So you believe in an afterlife?' David asked, and they replied in unison, 'Yes.'

'And is that what motivates you?'

'No, of course not,' said Alison. 'I think we're all flawed people, and that Jesus died on the cross to save us. But I believe that, through the Holy Spirit, God releases love and compassion for our fellow men. I think God's there for us all the time, changing and renewing us.'

'And,' Mary added, 'I think it means that we are called to be loving people, caring for our neighbours, being forgiving even when we don't want to forgive.'

'But Christians are among the most contentious of people,' said David.

'Yes, of course,' said Alison. 'But Christians acknowledge that they are sinful people – we say it in the Confession every week. If we ask forgiveness, and acknowledge that Christ died for us on the Cross, God forgives us – and I believe empowers us into loving our fellow men, and into social action.'

Mary said, quietly, 'I don't know how I would have coped when Ben died had I not believed in a loving God. There were times when I felt abandoned by God, but then someone told me the footsteps in the sand story,'

'Oh, I know the story,' said Alison. 'It's about a man in deep trouble who felt abandoned by God because, when he was in a barren place, he saw only one set of footsteps in the sand, and believed he was walking alone. But God said, 'My child. I was with you all the time. When there was only one set of footsteps, it was because I was carrying you.'

'I like that,' murmured David.

They went on arguing about Christianity till the early hours, discussing why God allowed suffering, the notion of free will, why God needed Christ's sacrifice on the cross, what it meant to live a Christian life. David expressed his belief that, if there was a God, and He was a loving God, then surely he must love everyone, not just Christians. He felt that all religions, however different, must be an expression of a search for God.

Alison and Mary had to agree, but both said that they believed Christianity was the highest expression of God's revelation to man.

The discussion really taxed them to articulate what they deeply believed, but it wasn't easy. During the course of their discussions David revealed that he'd started reading the New Testament. He said he wanted to try and find where Mary was coming from.

They woke quite late on Saturday morning. Mary felt surprised Jamie hadn't woken her, but when she got up, she found the three younger children in the sitting room, wrapped in blankets, watching children's television.

After a leisurely breakfast Alison announced that they were going to take them all to visit Glamis Castle. As there were nine of them, they had to take two cars. Mary joined Alison with the three younger children, while James took David, Steven and Jenny.

On the drive they passed through beautiful countryside – small lochs, hills in the distance, and woods with deer roaming freely. Mary felt this was an area she could happily live in - though when she said this Alison pointed out that it was a very cold place in winter with lots of rain and snow, and was no-where near as warm in summer as it was in the south. 'But,' she said, 'I wouldn't like to live anywhere else. It would be difficult to find a more beautiful part of the country. And,' she added, 'you should see it in the autumn when all the trees turn to red and gold. You must come up again then. The colours are absolutely glorious.'

It was one of those perfect spring days, and when they got to the castle, they found the daffodils on either side of the mile long avenue beginning to open. Alison was delighted, but was quite surprised when Mary told her they'd had daffodils in bloom for several weeks. The six hundred year old castle, former home of the Queen Mother, was an impressive sight with its solid red brick walls and its red rounded turrets. James proved to be very knowledgeable about its history, and kept Jenny and Steven, as well as David and Mary, enthralled. But the three younger children quickly tired of the house and Alison took them into the gardens where there was a special children's play area. Afterwards they had a lunch in the restaurant.

It was the news on Saturday evening that brought them back sharply to Jamal. The police had raided a house in Leicester in the early hours of the morning and arrested three terrorist suspects - all Muslims. The arrest mirrored the discovery of bomb making equipment in Jamal's garage. This time, bomb-making equipment had been found in the cellar of the house. Though no names were given, their immediate thought was that Al might be one of the arrested men.

They spent the rest of the evening wondering what implication this news might have for Jamal's trial, which was to take place four weeks after they got back. For the next two days they listened avidly to the news – half hoping to see Al's name among the detainees. But when eventually the men were named, Al was not among them. James said he thought Jamal's fate would depend on the jury. He might get off with a liberal minded jury, but not if many of them were hostile to immigrants. He thought it would be touch and go for Jamal. Mary agreed.

The next day, Easter Sunday, they all set off to the parish church, David included, much to Mary's delight. As with all Easter Day services, it was joyful, and the church resounded to the acclamation, 'Hallelujah, Christ is risen! He is risen indeed.' The preacher challenged them to take care of the marginalized in society – and spoke especially about the homeless and the immigrants who were often not welcomed in their midst. It seemed quite pertinent to their current worry about Jamal and the increasingly hostile attitude to the Muslim population in the UK.

The congregation was warm and welcoming. Quite a few people knew David and wanted to know how he was getting on in the south. When Mary was introduced, she felt that knowing looks were being exchanged about David's 'girl-friend' – especially when they saw she had Jamie in tow. She found it quite amusing.

After the service, there was an Easter egg hunt for the children in the abbey ruins at the side of the church. Jamie went off with Susan, coming back later clutching four tiny Easter eggs with a delighted smile on his face.

Alison had been up very early that morning preparing a special Easter lunch – turkey and all the trimmings. Mary helped by laying the table and 'clearing the decks', so that all the cooking utensils were washed up as they went along. They tucked in to a delicious meal, and after they'd finished, the children disappeared while David and James did the washing up.

James told David he and Stephen were going to see the osprey which had just arrived in Scotland for the twenty-first successive year. Each year it made a nest high up in the trees on the far side of the nearby loch and could be seen from the nearby bird centre that had a television screen which showed the osprey sitting on the nest. David said he would like to go along with them.

When the men left, Alison and Mary settled themselves comfortably in front of a blazing log fire in the sitting room. Though the day was bright and sunny, it was still quite cold, and the fire was welcoming. Mary felt an instant rapport with Alison and they fell into easy conversation.

'David tells me you had a very sad time with Ben dying just before your wedding day. I just can't begin to imagine what you must have gone through. And then to discover you were pregnant!'

'Yes. It was a terrible time. But Jamie's arrival was an enormous blessing. It transformed all our lives – Celia and Dan's as well as mine.'

'Tell me about Celia and Dan. They sound lovely.'

'Yes. They're very special people. I've been very blessed.'

'David likes them a lot.'

'Yes, I know. And they like him. In fact, I rather suspect they've been trying to get us together for some time,' she said, smiling.

'And are they going to be successful?' Alison asked with a questioning look.

'I rather suspect they will be,' Mary said with a grin. 'I expect David's been talking to you.'

Alison nodded. 'He's had a hard time – what with Joanna, then Dad dying, then Samantha. Dad's death was particularly hard for him. He was so busy with his work he didn't get up to see him as often as he would have liked, and then when Dad died so unexpectedly he took it really hard.'

'Yes. I realised that. It was just after your father died that I first got to know David.'

'Was that through the hospice appeal?'

'Yes.'

'I expect you know we've all had experience of hospices because both our parents died in our local hospice.'

Mary nodded.

'Did David tell you that James has just been asked to be a trustee of the hospice?'

'No. He didn't. But that's such a worthwhile thing to do.'

'So how did you become involved with the hospice appeal?'

'It was through Kim whom I've known since we were children. She introduced me to Jamal, and he persuaded me to join the committee. I didn't think I could offer much, but Dan persuaded me to say yes.'

'And so you met David!'

'Yes, but it was quite a long time before I had any conversation with him. I don't think we really noticed each other until we found ourselves sitting next to each other at Kim's birthday party.'

'So we have the hospice appeal to thank for bringing you here,' she said smiling. Then she asked, 'What about your parents? Are they still alive?' then added ruefully, 'Oh, I'm so sorry. It sounds as though I'm giving you the first degree!'

'Don't worry! I don't mind. It's good to talk. Yes. My parents are still alive. They're rather older than Dan and Celia. They're still living in the house where I grew up. They live a long way away from me, and it wouldn't have been possible for me to live with them. But Dan and Celia have a very big house with a separate flat and they were very keen for me to live with them because it was their grandchild I was carrying. But they are also very generous. They invite my parents to come and stay several times during the year so we can all be together. I think I've been very lucky – despite Ben's death.'

'But you've also had all the horror of your friend, Kim's murder as well! It must be horrendous knowing someone close to you has been murdered.'

'Terrible,' said Mary, shuddering at the memory. 'You read in the papers about these things happening, but you never imagine it's going to happen to someone close to you. In fact, these, last six months have been horrific – with the discovery of Kim's body (I was the last to see her), then Jamal's arrest, and the disappearance of the hospice appeal money. It's really left me in a sort of state of numbness. And of course, in the midst of all this I've been getting to know David. But I haven't really been able to think straight about our relationship. David's been wonderfully supportive, but I think he must have felt baffled by my behaviour at times.'

Alison nodded. 'But David's also been very upset by all that's happened. He was very fond of Kim. I know at one time he quite fancied her! You've both been through such a hard time, both suffered loss. But perhaps now is the time to move on?'

'I agree. But until we know about the outcome of Jamal's trial, I don't think either of us can really settle down to a normal life.'

'What about your studies? I think David said you have final exams later in the year.'

'Yes, all being well, I should be articled by the end of the summer.'

'Well, good luck. It can't be easy trying to study, work, and look after Jamie.'

'I really can't complain. In many ways I'm very lucky. Celia and Dan are always on hand – and keen to look after Jamie if I can't be there. But now, what about you? Tell me about your school.'

After they'd chewed over education, Alison said, 'Now, to get back to you and David. James and I wondered whether you'd like to borrow one of our cars tomorrow and go off exploring on your own. We could point you in the direction of some really beautiful countryside and an excellent hotel for lunch.'

'It's a lovely idea. But what about Jamie? He had a real tantrum when David took me off without him one evening.'

'But then he didn't have the other children to play with.'

'Well, I must admit, he seems very happy and settled here.'

'Yes. My kids love having him here – even Stephen, though he's much older. They all think he's a poppet! I really don't think you need to worry about leaving him. In fact, I suspect he wouldn't really notice you'd left!'

'Ok. You win! If David agrees, it would be lovely.

David was all for the scheme, so they set off next morning in Alison's car with details of where to go, and what to see. Mary felt a little trepidation as they said goodbye to Jamie, but as Alison had predicted, he seemed more than happy to wave them goodbye and go off with Susan and Jack.

Mary smiled to herself as they drove off, knowing full well that Alison had engineered this day for her and David to be alone. It was a bright sunny day with a clear blue sky, flecked with tiny white clouds. James had mapped out a route which took them through a couple of small but interesting towns before reaching open countryside. They drove through beautiful scenery, passing wide rivers, fast flowing streams, little lochs, and distant hills shading from purple to a misty grey. The trees were just beginning to wake from their winter sleep, and the branches were tipped with shimmering shades of green and yellow leaves. They saw turreted castles hidden among the trees, waterfalls, highland cattle, deer, and rabbits scuttling across the road in front of them. Birds sat in the middle of the road, ignoring their on-coming car till the very last moment, and red squirrels scampered in the trees. They drove for miles alongside a loch, with hills on the far side stretching into the distance, and Mary forced David to make frequent stops so she could take photographs with her new camera.

Eventually they arrived at a small hotel nestling at the side of the loch. They were expected. James hadn't told them, but had booked them in, asking the hoteliers to make a fuss of them. They had a leisurely pre-lunch drink in a small sitting room overlooking the loch, and then were called into a panelled dining room with portraits of men in highland dress, and shields and highland weapons, and musical instruments ranging along the wall. There was only space for four tables in the room, and the other three were occupied by Scotsmen – several of whom were wearing kilts.

'How would you like to wear a kilt?' Mary asked David, teasingly. 'I think you'd look splendid in one. Shall I buy you one for your birthday?'

'Don't you dare,' said David laughing. 'I'd feel ridiculous.'

It was a fixed menu, but they were served with what one can only be described as a gourmet meal with some excellent wine. Coffee was served in the sitting room where a log fire blazed in the large fireplace. No one else joined them, so they sat back to enjoy the coffee and delicious sweetmeats which the manager brought in for them.

'I could stay here forever,' said Mary, feeling happy and relaxed.

'How about coming here for our honeymoon?' said David with a twinkle in his eye.

'But you haven't proposed to me – and I haven't said yes,' she protested, laughing.

'Well then,' said David, getting down on his knees, 'Mary Gilburn, will you marry me?'

She looked at David with his lovely warm smile, his sensitivity, his impression of strength and reliability, and realised she loved him – not in the way she'd loved Ben, that was a one off, but she knew she loved David in a different way, and that she could be happy with him. So she said, simply, 'Yes.'

David rose from his knees and took her in his arms and kissed her. But, aware that people might come in at any moment, they decided to go for a walk down to the loch, and when they were out of sight of the hotel and other people, they embraced properly. It was the perfect setting for romance – the water on the loch lapping gently along the shore line, the tall trees, still bare, casting shadows over the water, the hills on the other side of the loch fading into the distance, the little plops of sound as the fish leapt to the surface of the water, while large birds of prey wheeled overhead.

'Yes. We must come back here for our honeymoon,' she said, and felt his arms hug her close as he agreed.

On the drive back, they discussed their future. They decided to tell just their respective families and, in the interest of sensitivity, not say anything to anyone else till after Patrick and Pamela's wedding and Jamal's trial.

'The first thing we must do when we get back is talk to Jamie. I know he's only little, but I think he's old enough to understand,' David said.

She agreed, but said, 'I don't see it as a problem. Jamie loves you.'

'I know. But Jamie's happiness is paramount,' said David.

When they got back, Alison and James were there to greet them, and guessed from their faces what had happened. 'I think you engineered it for us,' said Mary.

'Of course,' said Alison, trying to be modest. 'We just wanted to give you a little shove!'

'Where's Jamie,' Mary asked, 'Has he been OK.'

'Fine, He's been as happy as a sand boy,' replied Alison.

At that moment, the children came rushing in and Jamie flew into David's arms, ignoring his mother altogether. He started telling him excitedly all they had been doing that day – including building 'an enormous' castle in the garden. 'Come and see,' he said, tugging at David's arm.

David obediently went off, and when they returned, he said to Jamie, 'How would you like to have a daddy?'

Jamie looked speculatively at David and said, 'Well. I'd like to have a daddy if it's you.'

'Well, Jamie, I'd like to be your daddy. Do you think Mummy would like that?'

Then, turning to Mary, Jamie said, 'Uncle David says he can be my daddy if you say yes.'

Mary felt very emotional as she gave Jamie a big hug and kiss, and said, 'I'd love David to be your daddy. Give me a hug.'

Jamie jumped into her arms and gave her a kiss, then turned and gave David a big hug. Mary was not the only one who was trying to hold back tears.

'This calls for a celebration,' said James, trying to bring them down to earth. They'd obviously been prepared for this news because he brought in a bottle of champagne and glasses which he had waiting in the kitchen.

'Are you going to have a white wedding?' asked Jenny.

'It will certainly be a church wedding. I'm not too sure about wearing a long white dress.'

'But you'll want bridesmaids won't you?' said Jenny persistently.

'Of course,' Mary replied. 'I hadn't thought about that.' Then, seeing Jenny's hopeful face she said, 'Do you think you and Susan would like to be bridesmaids?'

The expression of delight on Jenny's face confirmed that she'd read her expression aright.

They spent the rest of the evening talking about their future. They thought they couldn't get married till Mary's exams were finished.

'The children go back to school in August. If you could have it in late July,' said Alison, always practical. 'We could come down the week before and combine a holiday with your wedding.'

'Great idea,' said David.

When they told Alison and James they wanted to spend their honeymoon in the hotel they'd just been to, Alison immediately said they'd look after Jamie while they were away.

The evening passed too quickly. Mary felt she'd been embraced with warmth by David's whole family, especially by Alison. She realised that since Kim's death, although she had a number of good friends and acquaintances, she hadn't felt close to anyone in the way she did with Kim. She thought Alison was going to fill that gap, and looked forward to the future when they would meet again. She put out of her mind the thought of the trial which lay ahead.

-55-
Mary and David's engagement

Mick met them at the station and drove them home. They'd decided to tell him about their engagement as they knew they could trust him to keep it to himself until they made it public. Mick said he was very happy for them - that he'd thought for some time they were right for each other, 'not like the doubts I had about Kim and Jamal to begin with,' he couldn't help adding.

When they got back to the house and before they could tell Celia and Dan their news, Jamie leapt into Dan's arms and said, 'Uncle David's going to be my daddy.'

Celia hugged David saying she'd hoped they would get together as she thought they were so well suited while Dan said it was the best thing that could happen to Mary, and was delighted for Jamie as well, as he'd observed how fond he was of David.

Celia had dinner ready and insisted that Mick stayed for supper. Before they sat down Dan opened a bottle of champagne and toasted their future.

They wanted to hear about the holiday, their plans, and how Jamie had got on with David's nephews and nieces. Jamie, who'd slept on the train, stayed up for dinner and chattered away about all the things they'd done, about David's family, and especially about Susan whom he'd taken a great shine to.

Mary told them they'd phoned her parents to tell them about their engagement. They'd decided to keep the news to just the family, Aunt Judith and Stuart and Susan, until after Patrick and Pamela's wedding. 'As the wedding's only a fortnight off, we don't want to take away attention from their day,' Mary explained. Celia and Dan agreed.

'Well, as soon as you announce your engagement we must have a party to celebrate,' said Dan.

David noticed Mary shudder and knew she was thinking back to the last engagement party they'd attended – Kim and Jamal's.

When he left with Mick soon after ten, David had the happy thought that he wouldn't have many more months of returning to an empty house.

He returned to work the next morning to be faced with a mountain of work and was glad there were only two days before the weekend break.

They decided that Mary would visit Jamal and tell him the news of their engagement. They knew it would be hard for him after Kim's murder, but felt they owed it to him to tell him the news themselves, rather than have it filter through to him on the grapevine.

Julian accompanied Mary as Jamal's trial was imminent. She said Jamal was very (she used the word 'gracious') when she told him the news, and he wished them every happiness.

Julian discussed with Jamal the arrest of the terrorist group in Leicester – all Muslims. He told Jamal that the police suspected it was the terrorist group Ali had contact with. 'I'm afraid,' Julian warned, 'that it's not going to help your trial. If the jury are in any way prejudiced, they will associate all Muslims, and of course you, with terrorism.'

Jamal was very angry at the suggestion but accepted it could be prejudicial, and just hoped the barrister who was to defend him would be able to disabuse the jury of the thought. He told Mary how grateful he was to Kim's father for procuring him such a high profile barrister.

David made a point of spending the next Sunday lunch time in the pub so that he could tell Stuart his news. Stuart had been a supportive friend throughout his troubles and when he heard about the engagement said how happy he was for both him and Mary, and said he thought they were ideally suited. He insisted David went back with him for lunch so he could tell Susan as well

'I think you've found the right person at last. She's a lovely girl – has come through a very difficult time with great courage. I think she'll make you very happy.' With this endorsement, and Susan's evident delight, David felt happy.

He explained they were not telling people until after the trial and the wedding of Patrick and Pamela.

Stuart asked what he was doing about an engagement ring and when David admitted he hadn't really thought about it, Stuart said if he planned to buy one, he could recommend him to a friend of his who had a jeweller's shop just behind Trafalgar Square.

When they telephoned Aunt Judith to tell her their news, she promptly invited them to come up and visit her. 'I feel you're family,' she said. 'We've shared so much during these last months, it's heartening that there's such a happy event to celebrate.' David agreed and felt, in some curious way, that Aunt Judith was a sort of replacement for the parents he'd lost. He'd grown very fond of her.

They went to London the following weekend, and Aunt Judith wanted to hear about Jamal's situation. She said she'd followed it as closely as she could in the newspapers – but knew she'd missed a lot of the finer details. 'I can't help wondering what Kim would have made of all this. In fact, would the bomb making equipment have been found if Kim hadn't disappeared? Perhaps the one good thing that's come out of all the horror is that the discovery of the equipment meant the bombs weren't used.

This was something that hadn't occurred to either David or Mary before and they both went very quiet

A TORTUOUS PATH

The next day they went along to the jewellers recommended by Stuart. It was an old family firm, and Stuart had been brought up with one of the partners. They had a great time looking at rings – and Mary finally chose an oval ring with a sapphire in the middle surrounded by diamonds. They also purchased their wedding rings – two identical gold bands. 'You'll have to keep them safe, David,' said Mary. 'I'm the world's worst at losing things.'

They decided they would announce their engagement at the hospice ball, now just a month ahead.

The following week was very busy. First, they had an appeal committee meeting to discuss the arrangements for the Ball. Everyone was there except Jane who sent her apologies. The members of the committee had all done what they promised. Alec produced the Ball tickets - quite large and very impressive - on white card with gilt edges, and the newly designed logo at the top. The RSVP was to Margaret.

Mark handed David a bunch of tickets which he said he must try and sell –added that he must do his best to sell some to Sir James Lambert, the Chairman of the Health Authority, and his wealthy friends.

This was something David didn't look forward to on two counts. First, because Sir James hadn't been in favour of any commitment by the Health Authority to a hospice, and he didn't know how he would feel now that the Council had offered them a piece of land to build on. And secondly, because, since his split with Samantha who was his wife's niece, he'd felt very uneasy in his presence and had done his best to avoid any conversations that touched on the personal.

But he knew he couldn't let the side down and must do something about it, so after the next meeting of the Authority at which Sir James was present, he broached the subject of the Ball.

To his surprise Sir James was very agreeable. He said how glad he was that the Council was prepared to give them the land, and although the position of the Health Authority was the same, in that it could not finance a hospice in total, he felt that it might be able to help in some measure with the running costs. This was encouraging news. He said he would be delighted to come to the Ball, and would get his wife to do some canvassing among their friends to see if they could get up a party.

Then he amazed David. He said, 'David, I feel I owe you an apology,'

David looked surprised.

'I fear I quite inadvertently led you into a very difficult and hurtful situation when I invited you to dinner. Neither my wife nor I had any idea what we were letting you in for when we encouraged you and Samantha to spend time together. We had no idea that Samantha and her father were involved in the secret service. I still don't know what their roles are – but what I do know is that you were caught up as a sort of pawn, and I am very sorry.'

David at first didn't know how to respond to this very gracious apology. Then he pulled himself together and said, 'Well, thank you. I must confess it was all very hurtful. But one has to move on. It's been quite a learning curve for me,' he added.

'And am I right in thinking that you and Mary Gilburn are, what I think the young call, 'an item'?

Surprised, he said, 'Well, yes. We've just got engaged. But how did you know?'

Sir James smiled, 'Well, I didn't know you were actually engaged. But Celia and Dan are old friends of mine! And then there's hospital gossip. It's difficult to keep much secret in a closed community like a hospital.'

David couldn't help but laugh

Sir James went on to ask about Jamal and his current situation. David told him about the confirmation of Al's involvement with the chemicals, and that they were now waiting to hear whether that would be enough to get Jamal released.

It was curious the effect Sir James' apology had on David. He felt he'd been used, and found it comforting to know that Sir James had been as caught up in the situation as he was.

Pamela and Patrick's wedding was a few days later. As one of the ushers David had to arrive early at the church. His fellow usher was a colleague from the school where Patrick had been teaching.

Celia and Dan had Jamie in tow, looking very grown up in a miniature sailor suit. They arrived with Mary's parents, who'd known Patrick since he and Mary were in their teens.

Patrick arrived with his best man, and Pamela and Mary arrived soon after. Pamela looked radiant, in a three-quarter length satin dress in what seemed to David to be a rather sweet but old fashioned style. Her shoulders were covered – something, Mary told him, Colin always insisted on. Mary herself looked beautiful in a long grey-green dress which suited her dark hair and complexion. Both Mary and Pamela wore circlets of flowers in their hair.

As Patrick and Pamela had planned, the reception was a fairly small affair, held in a local hotel which had an attractive reception room looking over a lake. There were about fifty guests. Neither Pamela nor Patrick had large families. In fact, it seemed to David that Mary's parents, and Celia and Dan, were the nearest to a family that Patrick had.

David was glad to see Jane there, but felt very concerned by her appearance. She looked thin and white, and he noticed she made a point of sitting down whenever she could.

It was a very enjoyable reception with amusing speeches. Mary and David both felt happy for Pamela. David had known her for years and was very fond of her, but though he'd taken her out from time to time, he'd quickly abandoned her when Joanna came on the scene. After the reception they waved the couple off, feeling they were well suited, and had made a good choice. Mary hoped that their wish for parenthood would soon be fulfilled.

-56-
Jamal's trial

Soon after the wedding, Jamal's trial began. Both Mary and David were to be called as witnesses. There was, inevitably, a great deal of interest among the hospital staff about the trial, and a few of Jamal's colleagues arranged leave in order to be present. Some had genuine sympathy with Jamal, but there were those who, for one reason or another were less sympathetic.

The indictment was straightforward - conspiracy to terrorism. The prosecution said that in the course of investigating the disappearance of Dr Jamal Khan's fiancée, Miss Kim Anderson, the police had discovered chemicals and bomb making equipment in Dr Khan's garage.

The police witness described how they had made several visits to Jamal's flat. They visited the first time to take down details of Miss Anderson's disappearance. On the second occasion they went to ask about the visit of Dr Khan's friend, Al Mercer (alias Ali Mansour) to the flat the night before Kim's disappearance. Throughout the trial, Al Mercer was referred to by his real Muslim name. On being questioned, the police reported that Dr Khan said that though Ali had planned to visit that weekend, on learning that Dr Khan was working on the Friday evening, he'd cancelled his visit.

The police witness said that, after the discovery of Miss Anderson's abandoned car with traces of chemicals in it, they made a subsequent search of Jamal's flat and discovered chemicals and bomb making equipment in his garage.

At this point Mary had to go in the witness box because she was the last person to see Kim before her disappearance. The prosecution asked Mary to explain why Kim had gone back to her own flat, and Mary told the court that she had returned there because Kim did not like Al who was coming to stay with Jamal that weekend. The prosecution elicited the fact that Ali Mansour, despite Jamal's denial, had, in fact, gone to Jamal's flat that night because he had left a book on a shelf in the flat which he'd promised Kim he would return that weekend.

The prosecution wanted to bring in details of Kim's murder, but Jamal's barrister said it was not relevant, and the judge ruled it as inadmissible.

Jamal was then called into the witness box. The prosecution established that Jamal had been born in Pakistan, had come to England when he was eight, and he and his family had obtained British citizenship. He had then gone to America at the age of sixteen to stay with relatives when his parents' business collapsed, and had remained there to finish his education. After he'd qualified as a doctor in America, he had returned to England and was now working as a hospital consultant.

Jamal was asked whether, considering his various residencies and the fact that he was a Muslim, he felt more affinity with his Muslim roots and Pakistan than with the UK. This he vehemently denied.

The prosecution then started probing into Jamal's Muslim roots, asking whether he'd been brought up as a Muslim. Attempts by Jamal's barrister to say this was not relevant were overruled. The judge said Jamal must answer the question. He affirmed that he'd been brought up in the Islamic faith. The prosecutor then suggested that his Muslim upbringing must have coloured his attitude to life and society in general. Jamal protested that he thought religion was a private matter, and that no one should be judged because of his or her religious affiliation. He challenged the prosecution by saying that he'd always believed that Great Britain was a country that prided itself on tolerance and equality. 'No one,' he said, 'should be condemned because of his religion.'

'But surely,' said the prosecution, 'you feel very angry about the abuse and attacks that many Muslims are currently suffering. Doesn't it make you want to do something about it?'

'Of course,' agreed Jamal. 'But not through violence and terrorism.'

'So how would you propose to tackle it?'

'By protest, publicity, and education, and by trying to get the young away from the influence of militant mullahs.'

The prosecutor raised his hands in a dismissive gesture, and turned to the bomb-making equipment found in the garage. Jamal vehemently denied all knowledge, and said that he knew the garage was full of detritus from the previous tenants, but that he had never had the time or inclination to sort it all out. The prosecution made a good case for not believing that he didn't know what was in his own garage. But Jamal's barrister humorously asked how many people knew the contents of their garages. He said if it was his garage, he would not be able to say what was there, other than that it was very untidy, and a dumping place for a whole variety of 'detritus'. This produced nods of agreement and laughter in the court.

A TORTUOUS PATH

The prosecution then moved on to Jamal's relationship with Ali. Jamal admitted that he had a long standing friendship with Al which the prosecution immediately seized on, saying that after all these years, he must have known much more about Ali than he revealed. Jamal pointed out that many people keep their personal lives private. But that Jamal seemed unable to produce any information about Ali's work, acquaintances or address did not go down well with the prosecution nor, it seemed, with the jury, who looked sceptical.

Jamal's barrister endorsed Jamal's comment about people's desire for privacy. He said that it often happens that people know very little about their friends' real lives, or what goes on behind closed doors. This produced a few nods of agreement in the courtroom.

Jamal's statement that he was working at the hospital throughout the night previous to Kim's disappearance was accepted by the prosecution without comment, as several people were prepared to give alibis.

It was the next witnesses, Penny and Nigel Jones, Jamal's neighbours, whose evidence produced a gasp in the court. They said that they'd seen Ali Mansour and another man at about three o'clock in the middle of the night before Kim's disappearance, unlocking Jamal's garage, unloading heavy objects from their car, and putting them in the garage. Nigel (and Penny in particular) were very distressed about having to give evidence for the prosecution because they'd expected to be called for the defence, but they were assured that they would be called again.

The prosecution made great play of the fact that, if Ali had a key to Jamal's garage, Jamal must have given him permission to place the chemicals there – and must therefore have been complicit in the terrorist plot.

This was the nub of the prosecution's case, and Jamal's barrister knew it was going to be very difficult to refute.

When it came to the turn of the defence, Jamal was called immediately. He denied all knowledge of the bomb making equipment in his garage, He said he was scarcely aware of what was in his garage as he just opened the garage door, got into his car and drove off – often in a hurry to get to work - and he certainly never had time to look around. Similarly, when he got home at night, he just opened the garage door, parked his car, and entered his flat through the door inside the garage

Asked whether he was aware of all the stuff at the back of the garage, he said it had been left behind by the previous tenants and he'd never got round to looking at it.

Questioned about the night before Kim disappeared, he said he'd received a phone-call at the hospital from Al at about five o'clock in the afternoon. When he told Al that he was working that night, Al decided he would go and stay with other friends.

The prosecution asked whether he thought that strange, but Jamal said that it often happened, as arrangements with Al were always flexible

Questioned about his relationship with Al he said he'd been a long-standing friend. He'd shared a flat with him in America, and had continued the contact when he came to England.

Asked by the defence what he felt when he discovered Ali was associated with a group of terrorists, Jamal said he was horrified and felt betrayed by someone he'd hitherto trusted.

Why, he was asked, had Al changed his name from Ali Mansour to Al Mercer? Jamal explained that Al had found his Muslim name an impediment in his business dealings, and had decided to adopt a more American style of name.

The prosecution made great play of this, saying it was surely a mask for his terrorist activities.

Jamal's barrister then started asking questions about his relationship with Kim. He tried to elicit the sympathy of the jury by telling them of Kim's murder and the extreme grief suffered by Jamal. He was at pains to say that not only was Kim a white person, she was also a Christian. He tried to demonstrate that, had Jamal been a fanatical Muslim, he would never have contemplated marrying a white girl, let alone a Christian.

The prosecution tried to dismiss this by saying the engagement was merely a cover-up, but Jamal emphatically denied this, saying a date for the wedding had been set, that they'd planned a civil wedding with a blessing in a church afterwards. Throughout this part of the questioning, Jamal nearly broke down in tears.

Character witnesses were then brought in. The first was Jane Masters who'd struggled to court despite being desperately ill. She'd promised that she would get to the court if it was the last thing she did. They didn't know then how prophetic her words were.

Jane explained that she'd known Jamal for quite a long time. They'd worked together at the hospital, and he'd persuaded her to help with the charity he'd set up to build a hospice for the town. She said she also saw him from time to time on Sundays when he accompanied Kim to church. She told the court about the evening she'd spent with Jamal the day Kim disappeared. She said that, in order to divert his anxiety a little, she'd persuaded him to tell her about the other charity he was involved with – a charity that was trying to get alongside young Muslims who felt marginalized by society, and were being brain-washed by militant imams. She told the court that he was appalled by terrorism, and felt it threatened the whole structure of society.

The defence barrister questioned Jamal at length about this organisation. Jamal explained that a lot of disenchanted Muslim youths were being groomed by radical imams to believe that terrorism was a way to paradise. These imams were making great play of the fact that so many Muslim youths were being stopped and searched in contrast to white youths who were left alone. They also said that the detention of potential terrorists indefinitely without charge was an affront to Islam. The imams were grooming young Muslims to believe that the only way to stop this so called persecution and uphold Islam and Muslim identity was terrorism.

Jamal explained that his organisation worked by trying to bring together Muslim youth and white youth in social and domestic settings. Muslim youths were consciously paired with white youths, and were encouraged to visit each other's homes.

Jamal said the base line was that, in the pursuit of terrorism, imagination was suppressed. His charity was hoping to make young Muslims aware of the suffering and hurt caused by terrorism. The next step was to try and involve them in active help and reparation, and then to encourage them to develop a pride in their British citizenship.

The prosecution suggested the charity was merely a front for him to help in the radicalisation of young Muslims - otherwise why had he not made public his involvement with this charity.

Jamal, trying to suppress anger, said that giving too much publicity to the charity would have been counter-productive, and would have engendered suspicion in the minds of the very youths they were trying to rescue.

The prosecution sneeringly said that there was little evidence that the charity was being successful. Jamal replied that the charity was at an early stage, and his arrest and imprisonment had inevitably delayed progress.

David was then called to answer questions about Jamal's work at the hospital, and his involvement with the hospice appeal. He told the court that it was Jamal who was the inspiration behind the appeal. Asked about Ali, he explained that he had seemed a very minor player in the charity, although it now appeared he might have been responsible for embezzling the funds.

The judge ruled this remark as inadmissible.

Nigel and Penny were then called back and questioned about seeing Ali and another man depositing the chemicals. Asked how they were sure it was Ali, they said they had met him socially on a couple of occasions, and so thought no more about it – though they admitted they thought it was a strange hour to be depositing goods at Jamal's home. They explained that, as they were leaving for a three-month visit to New Zealand that same night, they thought no more about it.

The judge took a long time summing up, and ended by saying to the jury that the key thing they had to decide was whether they believed that Dr Khan's garage was used without his knowledge. If they thought that Dr Khan, by giving his friend, Ali Mansour, a key to his flat and garage, did so in the knowledge that Ali would use the premises for bomb making, then they must find him guilty. If, on the other hand, they believed Dr Khan's claim that he knew nothing about the bomb making equipment and Ali's terrorist activities, then the jury must find him not guilty.

David felt that, though he was convinced that Jamal was innocent, the judge's summing up of the evidence was as fair as it could be, with a slight leaning towards a not guilty verdict.

The jury went out, and they waited for hours for its return. By five o'clock, they had not returned. The jury foreman was summoned by the judge, and he said they had been unable to reach a verdict.

The judge then adjourned the court, and the jury were sent off to a hotel for the night.

The court resumed next morning, and the jury went off. The foreman was called back three times, and the third time, he said there was absolutely no possibility of the jury reaching a decision – that it was divided in half.

The judge had no option but to dismiss the jury as a hung jury and refer the case to a further trial.

Though it was a relief to them all that Jamal hadn't been found guilty, they all felt desperately sorry for him. He would now have to return to prison for a further period to await a second trial. Jamal's barrister tried to get him bail, but once again was refused.

-57-
The Charity Ball

The appeal committee met just a week after the trial, and the mood was sombre. Before they got down to business, they discussed the trial. By this time all the committee members were convinced that Jamal was innocent. They felt sorry for him, knowing that he had a further period in prison awaiting a second trial whose outcome was uncertain.

A further cause for gloom was the absence of Jane. David told the committee he'd had a call from her husband who'd told him that she had cancer. It had spread throughout her body and she was not expected to live. Colin said Jane had asked him to send her love to all the committee and say how sad she was not to be going to the ball. He said she'd collected a number of tombola prizes before she became too ill, and insisted he bring them over whatever happened to her. Colin said that it was in situations like this that one realised a hospice was so greatly needed. But, he added, Jane was receiving excellent care from the local GP surgery and the ancillary services.

A TORTUOUS PATH

They were all near to tears when David finished relaying the message. Jane was loved by everyone.

David tried to divert attention from the sadness they all felt by bringing the meeting to order. The only topic on the agenda was the Ball. The first task was to discover how many tickets they'd managed to sell, and they were delighted to discover they'd sold all two hundred. They congratulated themselves on an amazing, achievement - considering this was their first major event.

Alec attributed the success to the venue, Mark's excellent publicity in the local rag, the publicity surrounding Jamal's trial, and his association with the hospice appeal.

They agreed that the venue was key. Storrington Park had never been open to the public. Many of them had passed it daily on their way to work. From the road, one got intriguing glimpses of the house through the trees. An early Georgian mansion, it was set high up on the hill, and was mentioned in some of the local guidebooks.

Though Margaret and her husband had played a part in persuading the owner to let them use the house for the ball, it was thanks to Alec that Lord Marston had finally agreed. Alec had installed computer and photocopying equipment in the house, and had discovered that he and Lord Marston shared an interest in aeronautics. In the course of conversation he learnt that Lord Marston had recently lost his father in less than happy circumstances in a private hospital. When he told Alec how angry he was that his father's pain had never been brought under control, Alec told him about the philosophy of the hospice movement and that he was involved with a group trying to raise money for a hospice in the town. Lord Marston said that Margaret and her husband had already mentioned the hospice appeal to him, and the proposed ball. He said he'd been thinking about making the house available, and that now, hearing more from Alec, he was happy to offer his house as a venue

With nearly all the tickets sold, they realised that, at £100 a ticket and with no costs for either the venue or the band, they were at the outset guaranteed a substantial amount from the evening. Added to that was the tombola and the raffle.

'And the Auction,' announced Margaret triumphantly. 'I've managed to obtain the gift of a new car worth over £15,000,

They all exclaimed in amazement and asked Margaret who was the donor.

'That I can't tell you,' said Margaret. 'The donor wants to remain anonymous. All I can tell you is that his mother recently died in a hospice, and before she died, she instructed her husband to donate her car to our appeal.'

Though David realised they must respect the donor's wish for anonymity, he felt they must write and thank him for the generosity of his late mother. Margaret said she would convey a letter of thanks to him.

Someone asked Margaret, 'Why an auction?'

'That was the donor's suggestion. But he said if it didn't meet its reserve at the auction, we should sell it privately.'

They spent time sorting out the finer details of the event, deciding they would have a welcoming party at the entrance to the ballroom, comprising David, Mary, Margaret and her husband, together with Lord Marston and his wife - if they were willing.

Pamela, back from her honeymoon, said she had a group of ladies from a nearby village, lined up to deal with the catering. Alec said he'd arranged with Lady Marston for a group of them to visit Storrington House the following week so they would know their way round, and see what facilities were available.

Margaret, Pamela, Mick, Betty and David together with the two village ladies visited the house late on the following Wednesday afternoon. It was interesting to see it close up for the first time. It had an early Georgian facade with fantastic views over the countryside. The interior was like a mini stately home. Mary could see that Betty, in particular, was overawed by both the surroundings and by Lady Marston, an elegant woman in her mid-sixties, who greeted them warmly. She was accompanied by Bert, whom she introduced as her handyman. Margaret, having made sure beforehand that they were all aware she already knew Lady Marston, introduced the party, explaining their respective roles at the ball.

Lady Marston took them round the house, showing them first the ballroom, and then the dining room. She said she and her husband would hire tables and chairs for the event, but warned them that the kitchen was a considerable distance from the dining room, but that there were large trolleys for conveying food from one to the other. She asked about china and cutlery, explaining that their Spode china was too valuable to use on such an occasion. She looked relieved when Pamela explained that one of the Friends of the appeal had a china hire business, and would be providing all the china, glasses and cutlery.

She then took them back to the columned hall, with its wide curving staircase, and showed them the cloakroom and toilets. Pamela said she would find someone to be responsible for these. Lady Marston suggested that the hall, being large, would be a good place for both the bar and the tombola. Mick, who was completely un-phased by the environment, said, 'A good idea to have the tombola near the bar – a shrewd suggestion, Lady Marston!'

She smiled warmly at Mick then said, 'Now, you're not to worry about clearing up at the end of evening. I suggest you leave everything just as it is, and come back in the morning to clear up. You'll all be very tired after your efforts.'

They thanked her for the suggestion, which they were to appreciate very much on the day itself.

The recce completed, they departed with grateful thanks for making her beautiful home available. David felt exhausted by the thought of all they would have to do. Though he'd attended a number of large charity functions over the years, he'd never realised how much work went on behind the scenes. He'd found it interesting to see the way different members of the group responded to both Lady Marston and the house where she lived. It struck him that, whatever people said, class divisions in society were still very much in evidence.

The next day he visited Jane. When Colin had phoned to tell David how ill she was he said she would love to see him if he had time to pop in. But she'd insisted she would quite understand if he was too busy. This self-effacement was so typical of Jane's consideration for others that David felt choked.

Jane was still at home. Though she was in bed, she was sitting up. As he kissed her he felt tears welling up, she looked so ill. But she welcomed him warmly and said, 'Don't cry David. We've all got to die sometime. I've had a blessed life, and if the Good Lord wants to take me home now, so be it. All I hope is that my family in New Zealand arrive before I die.'

Then the tears flowed and Jane clasped his hand saying, 'You've been a good friend, David. I hope you'll be happy.'

When he was able to talk, he told her that he and Mary had got engaged while they were in Scotland.

'Wonderful! I've been hoping that you and Mary would get together. I've always felt you were made for each other. Mary's such a warm and caring girl. She's had a very hard time – but I'm sure you will make each other happy. Have you told Jamie yet?'

He nodded.

'And what does he say about having you there all the time?'

'Well, he seems thrilled at the idea. He's been telling everyone he's going to have a daddy. We've always got on very well and I'm very fond of him. He asked me the other day when he can start calling me daddy. I felt very emotional as you can imagine. It's all very wonderful. More than I deserve.'

'Don't be silly, David. You've had a hard time as well. You deserve some happiness. Now, tell me about the plans for the ball.'

He told her about the visit to Storrington Park, and the offer of a brand new car to be auctioned. She seemed delighted. Then they talked about

Jamal's trial. He told her he thought it had been very courageous of her to go to the trial when she was so ill.

'I was determined to go – even if they had to take me in a wheel chair. Jamal is a man of integrity and doesn't deserve what's happened to him. I just hope and pray for a miracle – that something will be found to prove his innocence.'

They agreed this was going to be difficult.

Jane returned to her own predicament. 'David, when I die, I would like you to do something for me. I know the parish will take care of Colin, but I would be happier if I knew he had friends outside the parish who would look after him.'

David promised he would keep in touch with him.

Then she pointed to a large box in the corner, and asked him to take it with him as it contained prizes for the tombola.

By this time she was looking exhausted, so David kissed her goodbye. It was to be the last time he saw her.

Her funeral was the week before the ball. Colin was too upset to take it himself, so he got an old friend of the family to conduct the service. The church was crowded, and the service was billed as 'a celebration of a life.' Jane got her wish and her family arrived from New Zealand just a couple of days before she died. At the funeral there were tributes from her son and New Zealand son-in-law, as well as from an old friend of the family, and a colleague from the counselling service. The wake afterwards was ironically held in the same hotel they'd been in a few weeks earlier for the wedding of Patrick and Pamela. It was also in the same church where Kim's funeral had taken place, and many of those present couldn't help thinking back to that sad occasion.

But, as they all knew, life has to go on. It wasn't easy to throw off their sadness, but they had the Ball to prepare for a week later. David tried to soften the grief by saying they must make it a great success in memory of Jane and Kim as well.

The day of the Ball dawned bright and sunny, and they all trooped across to Storrington Hall in the morning to prepare for the evening's festivities. Mary and David acted as dogs-bodies, doing whatever was asked. As it was May, they realised people would be arriving in the daylight and so would be able to enjoy the beautiful view before entering the house.

They spent a quiet afternoon, playing with Jamie. Mary's parents arrived in time for tea. They were staying for the weekend to look after Jamie as both Celia and Dan were going to the ball. It was the first time David had seen them since their engagement. Mary's mother gave him a big hug and said how pleased she was to hear their news. Mary's father, rather more formal, shook him by the hand and said he hoped they would be very happy. They wanted to know all about their wedding plans, and about Jamie's reactions. 'Though I can see,' said Mary's mother, 'that Jamie is very fond of you, so that's a good omen.

Mary and David left early to be ready to help receive the guests. Mary looked stunning in a full-length kingfisher-blue dress with her hair up in an elegant coiff. She was wearing the engagement ring for the first time and David looked forward to telling their friends that Mary had agreed to marry him. He knew that quite a few had been wondering whether they were ever going to get together, and knew they would be happy for them.

Betty and Pamela were there already setting up the tombola. They were very excited about the quantity and quality of the prizes that people had donated, and were looking forward to a very profitable evening.

Mick and Stuart had also arrived early to set up the bar. Though Alec had promised to be there too, there was no sign of him. As they'd decided to give everyone a glass of wine as they arrived, Mick and Stuart were busy opening bottles.

Mick looked his usual dapper self with a yellow carnation in his buttonhole and David felt a deep surge of affection for him. He'd been such a true friend throughout his time at the hospital

Henry Winchester had declined to come or to help, and David wondered why he'd bothered to join the committee in the first place. Mark and his wife, and Dr Peter and his wife, were among the first to arrive. They'd undertaken to circulate and promote the hospice appeal. The only people not to appear early were Alec and his wife, and Alice and her husband.

Lord and Lady Marston, Margaret and her husband, and Mary and David stood waiting in the beautiful columned entrance hall to receive the guests. David tried to suppress the feeling of anxiety he had about the evening. They'd planned everything carefully, but it was a big undertaking and they'd taken a lot of money from people for the tickets. His anxiety must have shown, because Lady Marston squeezed his arm and said, 'Don't worry, Mr Gardner. It's going to be a splendid evening. You've done all you could to make it a success.'

As the guests started arriving they could see them through the doorway exclaiming both at the view and at the shining new car that was sitting outside with its label 'FOR AUCTION'. They were equally admiring of the beautiful hallway, and said as much to Lord and Lady Marston.

It was obvious the ladies had taken great care with their attire. There's something about beautiful long dresses which give an air to an occasion and many had spent a great deal of money on their outfits. Most had eschewed the current fashion for wearing evening trousers, and David felt the evening was akin to the sort of costume dramas seen on television. He began to feel confident the ball was going to be a success.

Alec arrived late, after the line-up, looking very cross, but full of apologies for not being there earlier. He said his wife, Margery, had been delayed. David hadn't met her before and was surprised to find she was not the glamorous wife he'd imagined Alec to be married to. She was rather dowdy despite wearing an elaborate and very expensive looking dress, and like Alec, looked exceedingly bad tempered. David suspected they'd had a row. He began to understand why Alec had been attracted to Alice.

Alec promised to come back and help as soon as he'd settled Margery somewhere. Mick told him not to worry, that they were managing quite well. Patrick, overhearing the conversation said he would help with the bar, as Pamela didn't really need his help.

She and Betty were already doing a brisk trade on the tombola. At £5 a ticket, David had been afraid they wouldn't have many takers, but the quality of the prizes was so good that people's gambling instincts were activated, and they brought ticket after ticket in the hopes of winning one of the big prizes. Towards the end of the evening one of the guests went round the ballroom showing everyone the 'bargain' pair of black socks he'd won on the tombola. 'Cheap at the price,' he said with great jocularity. He'd spent £70 on the tombola trying to win a prize, and the socks were all he'd come up with! The photographer from *Our County Today* magazine, whom Mark had lined up for the evening, captured him trying on the socks and it duly appeared along with many other photographs of the Ball in the next edition.

Mary and David had no other duties other than to circulate. They spent a wonderful evening telling friends their news, receiving their good wishes and dancing together for the first time They both felt on a high, and their only anxiety was the non-arrival of Alice. Their anxiety was allayed when she appeared just before supper, until they discovered that she was on her own and was looking a little distraught. When Mary asked her she insisted she was OK, and that her husband was not well. When they suggested she joined them shook her head and she said she would go and help at the bar. This alarmed them a little, as they'd seen Alec serving at the bar, leaving his wife with friends. However, there was nothing they could do about it, so joined Susan and Dr Peter and his wife for supper.

Their anxiety increased after supper when they saw Alice dancing with Alec. It was not the fact that they were dancing together, but that Alec was holding her in a very intimate way. Margery, who was sitting with friends, looked thunderous.

Later, Mary went to the cloakroom and rushed back looking very upset, asking for help. She said Alice and Margery were having a furious row and Margery was threatening to come up and expose Alice publicly for stealing her husband. Alice, in trying to prevent Margery from leaving the cloakroom, had taken hold of Margery who, in retaliation had grabbed hold of Alice's hair. Mary was unable to part them and rushed upstairs for help.

Celia and Susan went with along with Mary while David went to fetch Alec. He told him he must take Margery home immediately as they didn't want to spoil the evening with a public scene.

Alec said he couldn't drive because he'd had too much to drink - but he would order a taxi to take them home. David insisted he called for a taxi straight away. While they waited, Susan and Celia sat with Margery in the hall, while Mary took Alice into a small sitting room just off the hall.

Alice said she knew David and Mary were aware of her affair with Alec through seeing them in the pub before Christmas. She said both their marriages had been unhappy even before they'd met on the appeal committee. Her husband had accepted the situation, albeit reluctantly, but Margery had tried to hang on to their marriage. She'd made Alec promise, as they'd paid so much for the tickets, to stay until after the ball, and she would then consider a divorce. Margery had apparently threatened that, if he didn't agree, she would come and tell everyone what a shit he was. Alec, reluctant to have his name publicly besmirched, had given in. What had tipped Margery into rage was seeing Alice dancing with her husband in such an intimate way.

'So what's going to happen now?' Mary asked.

'Heaven knows,' said Alice. 'I think once Alec's got Margery home, he'll want to come back to me. I'll just have to wait here till he gets back.'

'Don't you think you should leave now as well?' Mary asked.

'No. I want to wait till Alec gets back. But,' she added, seeing Mary's anxious face. 'I'll sit quietly in a corner and I promise not to make a scene.'

Mary re-joined David and relayed what Alice had said. With Alec and Margery safely bundled off in a taxi, David was determined that this upset was not going to spoil their evening. Fortunately, apart from Celia and Susan, only Pamela, Mick, Stuart and Betty had been involved and he felt relieved that neither Lord nor Lady Marston was aware of what had happened.

Mary was deeply upset by what had happened and David could see that she was shaking a little. He trundled her off to the ballroom and held her in a tight embrace as they danced a foxtrot. Knowing that it was, on the whole, the older age group who could afford to come to the ball, they'd asked the band to play some of the old conventional dances. They also asked them to keep the volume down as they knew people would want the chance to talk as well as to dance. This was something he was to discover, in the many fund raising events they were involved in later, one of the most difficult things to achieve. It seemed that the young and the bands liked music to be played at maximum volume, while the older people wanted to be able to hear and enjoy conversation. It was a battle they never won. Bands would obligingly turn down the volume for a couple of dances, and then surreptitiously raise it again!

After Mary had relaxed a little, David felt the time had come to auction the car. One of the guests, a friend of Mark, was an auctioneer, and he introduced the auction with great aplomb – telling them all that the car had been donated for a very good cause, and by someone who had died in a hospice. She had instructed her son to give the car in thanks for the wonderful care she had received.

The car was worth £9,000 said the auctioneer, and he proposed to start the bidding at £7,500. David felt worried that that was too low, but in a short time the bidding had reached £9,000 and then to his amazement went up to £11,500 – purchased by a local businessman. 'He can afford to buy it. It'll come off the firm's expenses,' murmured Mark, a little cynically, in his ear.

Lord Marston then drew the raffle which had been as well supported as the tombola because the prizes included an airline ticket to somewhere in Europe, a stay in a holiday cottage in Devon, and membership of an exclusive golf club in the area. People had been very generous.

The rest of the evening passed smoothly. The tombola continued right up to the end. As people departed they all said what a wonderful evening it had been. Some were even so bold as to say to Lord and Lady Marston, as they left, that they hoped they would do it again. Lord Marston was non-committal!

As Lady Marston had suggested, they left the clearing up to the following morning. They were grateful for the suggestion, as they were all exceedingly tired. It had been a long day and added to all the work was the stress of worrying whether the evening would be a success. The incident with Alice and Margery hadn't helped. But they left feeling that all their efforts had been worthwhile.

They arrived back at Celia and Dan's house to find that Mary's parents and Jamie had gone to bed and were fast asleep. David fell into bed, and slept the sleep of the dead until gone eight when Celia brought him in a cup of tea.

After breakfast, Mary and David went back to Storrington Park to clear up. With the help of Bert, the handyman, the house was soon restored to pristine order. Just before midday Lord Marston appeared with a tray of glasses and champagne to toast the success of the evening. They expressed their gratitude for his hospitality and said they'd let him know, as soon as they'd sorted out the money, how much the evening had raised.

David stayed for lunch with Celia and Dan and Mary's parents, then went to see Stuart who'd agreed to be the treasurer for the event, and had taken the money home ready to be banked on the Monday. They spent the late afternoon counting money, writing cheques for all the costs, and working out what the event had raised. Together with two substantial donations which had been given to Stuart during the evening, they realised the evening had brought in nearly £50,000. Stuart decided this called for a celebration, and opened a bottle of champagne. They thought they ought to share the good new with all the helpers and spent the next hour on the telephone. Susan produced supper and wanted to hear all about David's wedding plans. He told them it was to be a church wedding – the wedding Mary had never had – and hoped Stuart would do him the honour of being his best man. 'I'm not sure about the 'honour' bit, but I'd be very happy to give you my support,' said Stuart laughing.

They spent a happy evening talking about old times and the future, and David had a feeling of euphoria, content about his private life, and confident the Ball had been an auspicious beginning to their fund raising activities.

But the evening ended on a sour note. When Stuart decided to put on the late news it shattered their happy mood. There was a report of the arrest of three Muslims in London on terrorist charges. Though no names were mentioned it immediately took their thoughts back to Jamal and the trial, and the suspicion that Al may have been implicated.

'Will we ever be free of this?' muttered David

'No, I don't think we ever will. I think the terrorist threat is here to stay.'

'They don't mention names. I'm always half expecting Al will be identified.'

'Yes, me too. But I don't suppose we'll hear any names until the terrorists are actually charged.

'Whether or not Al is involved, it's not going to help Jamal when the trial comes up again.'

'No, I fear not. '

It seemed to David that though terrorism was something they would never in the past have thought had any personal relevance to them, Jamal's arrest had changed all that, and he knew that in the future every report in the media about terrorist attacks would resonate personally.

They parted in a sombre mood

-58-
Hopes for Jamal's acquittal

A week after the Ball David was in his office when a call came through and a voice asked, 'Is that David Gardner?'

'Yes,' he replied.

The voice said, 'I have a call for you from Sir Ralph Delaney.'

David's immediate reaction was to put the phone down. He still felt very angry with him but, knowing that discretion was the better part of valour, he said 'Yes'

'Putting you through,' said the voice, and Sir Ralph came on.

'Is that David?'

'Yes.'

'Are you still in close contact with Dr Khan?'

'Yes. I visit him regularly in prison.'

'What I'm about to say is in strictest confidence.'

'We've been there before,' David muttered bitterly.

'Forget that, David. I want to help. If you want to try and establish Dr Khan's innocence I suggest you tell his lawyers to ask to see the transcripts of the emails sent by the three Muslims arrested last week on terrorist charges.'

'Would access be granted?' David asked, surprised.

'Yes,' said Sir Ralph. 'I will give you a telephone number for Dr Khan's solicitor to ring. He must ask for William Littleton. If Mr Littleton is not there, he must put the phone down and try again later. He must, I emphasise, speak to no one but Mr Littleton. When he gets through to Mr Littleton he must quote the following reference. Have you a pen handy?'

'Yes,' David replied, puzzled.

'It is 3JK020607. I repeat 3JK020607. Tell your solicitor that on no account must my name be mentioned. Mr Littleton will tell him what to do next.'

David started to ask questions but Sir Ralph said, 'I can tell you nothing more, David, so don't ask. But I'm glad your love life seems to be on track.'

With that startling comment, he put the phone down. David was astounded by the call. If he interpreted Sir Ralph correctly, he was trying to help them establish Jamal's innocence. It felt bizarre after all the trouble he'd taken to use him as a channel for information about Jamal and Al. Sir Ralph hadn't mentioned Ali Mansour, and as he thought about it, it was one more step towards confirming his feeling that it was Al who was the villain of the piece. He just wondered what information would be conveyed in the emails if they were able to get access to them.

David phoned Julian straight away and arranged to go over to his office later that day. Up to that point he hadn't confided in Julian about his involvement with Sir Ralph and what was obviously counter-terrorism, but in the light of this new development, he told him the whole saga.

Julian was what David thought of as a very upright man who always insisted on doing things by the book. He was over sixty and was greatly respected in the area, and Mary felt lucky to be articled to him.

He was astonished by David's account of his contacts with Sir Ralph. The suggestion that he himself should go up to London and look clandestinely at some files which were obviously highly confidential, threw him.

David agreed that the whole thing was bizarre, but argued that if it helped prove Jamal's innocence they ought to follow it up.'

Julian was eventually persuaded and next morning made the call as instructed. After three attempts, he got through to Mr Littleton. He quoted the reference number Sir Ralph had given David, and Julian was cross-questioned about his credentials. Then Mr Littleton said, 'I will get back to you later. You mustn't mention this conversation to anyone!'

In the afternoon, Mr Littleton phoned back. He suggested Julian came up to London as soon as he was able, and wondered whether he was free the next day. Julian said he wasn't but that one of his trainee solicitors was available. 'No, it must be you,' he was told.

Julian finally agreed to cancel his appointment and arranged to visit London the following day.

When he got back he looked extremely pleased. 'I've been given information that I'm sure will persuade the prosecution to drop the case.'

He told David and Mary what had happened. 'It was all rather bizarre. I arrived at the house and the door was opened by a stern looking man who asked me for the password and then let me in. He told me to hand over everything I had with me except my pen. Then he showed me into a room with just a table and a chair. There was a large blue file labelled 'Operation Jackdaw' sitting on the table, and a few sheets of lined blank paper. The man told me that if I needed the toilet, I was to ring the bell by the door.'

'All rather cloak and dagger,' commented David.

'Yes, I felt a bit spooked. But I sat down and opened the file. On the first page was a list of names headed 'Primary Suspects', and there were the names of the three men who'd been arrested last week which as you know were reported in the news. But also on the list were the names Ali Mansour and Suleiman Ahmed. On the next page was a much longer list headed 'Associates.' Among these names was Dr Jamal Khan.'

'So he was implicated!' said David unhappily.

'No. Just be patient. As I read on, there were biographical details of the five 'Primary Suspects' and briefer biographies of the thirty or so 'Associates.' Each of the five Primary suspects was given initials. Ali Mansour was referred to as AM and Sulieman Ahmed as SA.'

'Suleiman again,' murmured David.

Julian said, 'I was astounded by the information about Ali Mansour. He'd obviously been involved with terrorist groups for a considerable time. He'd visited Pakistan and Waziristan on a number of occasions, and had been observed associating with known terrorists there. Apparently his business interests were concerned with the chemical industry. The information Jamal gave about Ali was accurate only in so far as it related to their time together at university in the States.'

'But surely Jamal would have known about Al's other life?' said David.

'Well, not necessarily. It seems that Al's life was cleverly wrapped in a cloak of secrecy. I asked myself whether Al had completely deceived Jamal, or Jamal had very cleverly concealed his knowledge of Al's activities. As I read through the emails which were in the file, I came to the firm conclusion that it was Jamal who had been deceived.'

'How come?' asked David.

'Well, I copied down all the information that I thought relevant. It was a laborious task! I'm not used to using a pen these days as I use the computer all the time. I copied down everything I thought relevant - the biographical details of the five 'main suspects, and the details about Jamal, which were largely accurate – though the intelligence services rather surprisingly didn't seem to have picked up Jamal's involvement with the charity to de-radicalise young Muslims.

The folder was flagged in several places, and I assumed the flags were there for my benefit. When I opened the file at the first flag, I found a copy of an email. This, and many of the other emails in the file were all codes but there was a transcription below each one. The emails referred to meetings and consignments of goods. Quite a few of these emails were related to a planned event which I felt could be interpreted as involving bombs. Many of the emails referred to SA and AM, and others were addressed to them. One email talked about a consignment of goods being sent to Glasgow by 'AM.'

'How on earth did they manage to pick up these emails?' commented David.

'Who knows? It's all rather scary. But to go on. I then came to emails which seemed directly relevant to the chemicals found in Jamal's flat. These were emails sent in October, a few weeks before Kim's disappearance. The first said, 'Equipment ordered. AM to find a home.

Will notify where.' Then followed a series of equally terse emails. One, ten days before Kim's disappearance, read, 'Climping. 4 am tomorrow.'

The next day, another email said, 'Weather forecast bad. Holiday postponed till Friday. Same venue.'

On the Friday morning, another email said, 'Equipment safely collected. AM finding a home.'

An email on the Saturday at 8 am, sent by AM said, 'Medical equipment delivered to doctor.'

Then at 9 am there was a further email, sent to several different people, including SA, which said, 'AM a fool. Doctor not one of us. Remove equipment immediately from doctor's flat.'

This was followed by an email which said, 'Abort. AM now on holiday.'

Julian then said that he'd combed through the next few weeks of the file but could find no further references which might in any way be connected with Jamal, apart from one a couple of weeks later from SA which said, 'AM sleeper in F'.

Having copied all the entries he thought relevant, Julian said he rang the bell and a man he presumed to be Mr Littleton, though no names were mentioned, asked to see what he had written down and said he would photocopy the papers before Julian took them away.

When Julian got back and showed them what he had copied down, they felt that though the messages were coded, there was a good chance the prosecution would accept that they referred to Jamal and Ali, and that the one saying 'AM a fool. Doctor not one of us …' would exonerate Jamal. Julian arranged with Jamal's barrister to visit the office of the Crown Prosecution Service as soon as possible.

Mary had already promised to visit Jamal and tell him about the Ball, but they decided at this stage to say nothing about the emails as they didn't want to raise his hopes only for him to be let down.

Mary became more worried about Jamal's health every time she visited. He was keeping himself occupied by reading everything he could get hold of on terminal illness and palliative care, and hoped to take some qualifying papers so that, if he got out of prison he could work in that area of medicine. But the weight was falling off him and he looked ill. From what he said, she thought he was very lonely and hadn't made any meaningful contacts among the other inmates – though, fortunately neither had he received hostility from any of them.

When Mary told him about Jane, she said he was very upset, feeling he'd lost a very good friend.

Julian received a non-committal response from the Crown Prosecution Service, and they had to wait several weeks before hearing anything further. While they were waiting, they continued to keep the news from Jamal.

Meanwhile David felt he should honour his promise to Jane to look out for her husband Colin and arranged to take him out for lunch. Colin said his bishop had told him to take a month off, and welcomed meeting with an old friend of Jane. He told David he'd decided, after he'd sorted out Jane's affairs, to go up to Durham and spend a week or two with his son and family.

They went to the country pub where he and Mary had first lunched together. With its tastefully furnished dining room overlooking a small garden with a fountain, David thought it would be the ideal place to go for a quiet lunch.

He didn't know Colin very well, and was rather apprehensive about the meeting, but Colin proved to be very easy to talk to. He started by asking about Jamal, and told him what a touching letter he'd received from him after Jane died. Jamal had said what a wonderfully caring person Jane was, and that everyone loved her, and that she'd been a great support to him in his early days at the hospital. She'd helped him with some of the more difficult relationships he struggled with when he first arrived back in England. She was one of the few people he could talk to, and she'd understood the predicament of law-abiding Muslims who were unjustly associated with the disaffected and militant young Muslims and were constantly pilloried in the media.

David told Colin that, following some new information they'd got hold of, they were hopeful it might lead to Jamal's acquittal. 'I do hope so,' said Colin, 'Jane had a great regard for Jamal, and was distressed when he was arrested so soon after Kim's disappearance. She passionately believed he was innocent.'

They talked about Jane and her work and how she'd been able to get alongside people and give them encouragement. David said he felt her funeral must have been a great comfort for him – to know that so many people cared and wanted to say farewell. Colin said how very hard it was for him to accept – her illness had been so brief - though they'd both had suspicions for some time before the actual diagnosis of cancer.

David said, 'It must be difficult for you as a priest to cope with her death.'

'Yes, it's extremely hard. You have to try and balance your grief with your role as a priest. You feel your parishioners, however caring, are watching you to see how your Christian faith will help you to hold up. What not everyone realises is that grief needs to be expressed. Though I believe that Jane is in the hands of our loving God, and that we will meet up again in heaven, it doesn't lessen the grief of parting. This is not something everyone understands. Nor do people understand the need for the bereaved to talk about the departed – so many people avoid talking about the dead perso. I always tell people never to stop talking about their loved ones and to try and gain comfort from remembering the good things they shared.'

David nodded. 'I understand exactly what you're saying. I know how helpful it was to talk about my father when he died.'

'I'm very grateful to my bishop for suggesting I go away for a few weeks, so that I can express my grief in my own way. He said he knew the eyes of my parishioners would be constantly on me.'

Colin then talked about the very different reactions to death and funerals he received from Christian and non-Christian families. He glanced at David keenly and said questioningly, 'I've never seen you in church with Mary except on Mothering Sunday?'

'No. I am, what you might say, exploring the Christian faith. It matters so much to Mary.'

'When I get back from Durham you must come along to one of my Alpha courses. They explore the whole basis of Christianity, and many people come to faith through them.'

Taken a little by surprise, David nodded. He warmed to Colin, and felt that his parishioners were lucky in their priest.

-59-
Marriage Plans

Julian had a positive response from the Crown Prosecution Service saying that it was pursuing all the information he'd provided but that it would take some weeks to process.

David and Mary decided the time had come to tell Jamal about this development but warned him not to be too hopeful. Jamal's reaction was surprising – almost negative. The further confirmation of Al's involvement was something that seemed almost too difficult for him to accept. He felt that life had thrown so many bad things at him he couldn't believe in the possibility of ever being released from prison and returning to a normal life.

While waiting for the Crown Prosecution's response, Mary and David made several visits to the prison. Afterwards, Mary seemed to talk of little else which irritated David as they had so many other things to think about preparatory to their wedding in September.

The first thing they had to decide was where to live. They discussed staying on in David's house, but eventually decided it would be a good idea to make a fresh start, although they both thought they would like to stay in the same village. They decided to put David's house on the market straight away and to their amazement got a very quick cash sale with the purchasers willing to exchange as soon as they'd found a house.

This meant that any free time they had was spent in looking at houses. As Mary was busy studying for her law exams, their time was limited to weekends. They made a point of taking Jamie with them. Young as he was, they felt he was old enough to be part of the search.

David had always hankered after an old house, and to his delight, found Mary shared the same ambition. 'Though I had a happy childhood,' she said, 'I'd hate to go back to a suburban house in a suburban street. I've always hoped to have a cottage in the country.'

They very quickly found an old cottage at the edge of the village with an acre of land, abutting onto fields full of cattle. Mary fell in love with it straight away, as did Jamie. David felt a little more reticent, as it belonged to an elderly lady who had clearly done nothing to the cottage for many years. Mary insisted it would be a great project which they would enjoy doing together.

Their offer was accepted and the whole process of the sale of David's house and the purchase of the cottage went through quickly and smoothly. David realised how lucky they were - he'd heard so often of people who had been let down at the last minute because the chain had been broken.

The cottage, once empty of furniture, proved to be in a much poorer state of repair than they'd realised. David moved in with all his furniture, but he was not very happy living alone in the semi-derelict house, and wanted Mary to move in with him straight away. She refused, saying she wanted to wait till after they were married. It was their first major disagreement.

-60-
Jamal released and stays with Celia and Dan

Some four weeks after Julian had passed on the information to the Crown Prosecution Service, they received the news that Jamal was to be acquitted. Julian had a telephone call from the prison to say he was being released at 3 o'clock the next day. They were amazed at the speed of his release once the charge had been withdrawn, but absolutely delighted for Jamal. They decided that one of them should go and collect him. David had an important meeting at the hospital that afternoon, so Mary and Julian arranged to go.

A TORTUOUS PATH

They didn't know whether he would want to go straight back to his own home and thought he might like to spend a few days elsewhere. Over the months he'd been in prison, they'd discovered that Jamal had no Muslim friends other than Al, and that he seemed to regard Mary, David and his hospital contacts as his real friends.

When Mary told Celia and Dan about Jamal's imminent release, they were delighted and Celia, always very practical, thought that Jamal might find it very difficult going back to a flat which had been left uninhabited for months, and which would have no food in it. She suggested he might like to come and stay with them for a few days. Mary said that was a great suggestion, and would put it to Jamal when she collected him. David, to his shame, felt an immediate twinge of jealousy at the thought of him staying under the same roof as Mary, and hoped Jamal would opt to go back to his flat!

For Mary Jamal's acquittal somehow felt a vindication of Kim's trust in him, but at the same time it caused all the horror and sadness of Kim's disappearance to come flooding back.

There was no question in Mary's mind that it was she who should be collecting him from prison. She'd agreed with Julian and David that when they got there she would leave it to Julian to ask Jamal where he would prefer to go – back to his own flat or accept Celia and Dan's invitation

Mary wasn't sure what to expect when Jamal emerged from the prison carrying a bag of books, a laptop, and a rucksack of clothes. He seemed to have shrunk though he still looked clean and tidy and in command of himself. She felt happy at seeing him emerge from prison but found it difficult to keep back the tears, She rushed towards him and put out her arms to hug him. He put down his bags, and held her close. Then he turned to Julian who said 'David wanted to come but he had an important meeting at the hospital which he couldn't get out of. He sends his love and hopes to see you later.'

'It's so good to see you,' he said, smiling. 'I owe you all so much. You've been such wonderful friends – I don't know how to begin to thank you.'

'All that can wait,' said Julian. 'The first thing is to get you home.' Then he explained the options. Mary could see that Jamal was overcome with emotion when he heard about Celia and Dan's invitation.

It was eight months since Jamal's arrest and Mary suspected that no one had been in the flat while he'd been in prison. She warned him that they might find it in a very poor state as it had been empty for so long. 'We could go back to your flat first and see what sort of state it is in,' she suggested, 'and then go back to my home to recover.'

Jamal nodded agreement. Mary's stomach lurched as they entered the flat. The last time she'd been there was when she and David went to find out whether or not Al had returned the book Kim had lent him. Memories of Kim came flooding in – but she refrained from saying anything to Jamal.

As she'd feared, the flat was in a terrible state. It smelt musty and cobwebs were everywhere. Books and files were strewn over the floor just as the police had left them in their search for information. When they entered the kitchen, there was a smell of decay and mice droppings on the floor. The police had turned off and emptied, the refrigerator but had forgotten to leave the door open. The sink which Jamal had been using just before he was arrested was grimy, and the bath was full of large spiders and flies. Apart from some dried goods in the pantry, there was no food in the flat. Even the bedroom was in a mess. Bedclothes were stripped from the bed, and mattresses sat unevenly on their bases where the police had moved them, hoping to find information hidden underneath.

It was a dispiriting sight and Mary could feel Jamal's sense of desolation at seeing his normally well-ordered home in such a state. As it was a warm sunny day, the first thing they did was to fling open the windows, and let the sun flood in. But it was obvious there would be much to do before the flat was habitable again.

As they hadn't been sure whether or not Jamal would want to stay in the flat straight away, they'd decided not to get in any supplies for him.

Mary told Jamal she would help him tidy up straight away if he wanted to stay or alternatively he could come back with her to Celia and Dan's house, and they could tackle the job of getting the flat back to some semblance of order later. She could see that Jamal was shocked by the state of the flat, and suspected that, while in prison, he'd been dreaming of returning to his home just as he'd left it. She thought the best thing was to give him a little time on his own to decide, so told him that Julian had to go back to work, but that she was free. She suggested that while he thought about what he wanted to do, she would slip out and collect some supplies. Jamal agreed.

Mary popped into the nearby corner shop and purchased some dry goods – tea, coffee, biscuits, sugar, cereal and some coffee mate. She didn't want to get any perishables in case he wanted to go back with her.

When she returned half an hour later she found a number of pressmen outside. The news of Jamal's release had obviously just got out, fortunately too late to photograph him leaving prison.

She pushed past the press and managed to get into the flat and shut the door without them gaining entry. She found Jamal slumped in a chair looking utterly exhausted, 'I don't think I have the energy to tackle the flat just now. I feel too emotionally exhausted. If you're sure Celia and Dan would be happy to have me, I'd love to go back to their house. It's such a very kind invitation, and I haven't the energy to decline it.'

'That's great,' said Mary. 'Let's close all the windows and leave the flat just as it is for today. You'll need some more clothes. Why don't you go and pack some things while I make a cup of tea.'

'Always the British panacea!' said Jamal, smiling.

'And perhaps you should bring some books and your laptop in case you feel like doing any work while you're with us.'

Jamal nodded agreement.

After they'd had a cup of tea and biscuits she warned Jamal that the press were swarming outside. 'Do you want to speak to them now or would you prefer to leave it till tomorrow?'

'Oh God, I don't think I could face them now.'

'I'm afraid you'll have to face them sometime – but I can put them off for today,' she said, aware that it was going to be more difficult than she'd let it sound. 'I'll bring the car right up to the front of the flat, and we'll have to push our way through. When we're in the car shall I tell them you'll be willing to speak to them another day?'

'I'd rather not speak to them at all.''

'I know. But the press can be helpful in easing you back into your old life if you co-operate with them!'

Jamal smiled wearily and nodded. 'OK. I'll leave it to you to organise.'

Mary telephoned Celia and Dan to tell them they were coming and left a message for David, suggesting he came over after work. She went out to bring the car up to the front door and the press crowded round, asking her whether Jamal was coming out. She told them where he was but that he was very tired and was going to stay with friends. They all said they wanted to speak to him but she told them he would give them an interview tomorrow when he was less tired.

She went back into the house, shut all the windows, collected some bits and pieces, and then made a dash for the car. Needless to say the press took a number of photographs, and Mary realised she too would be in the paper the next day, and it struck her that people might speculate about her relationship with Jamal! It didn't worry her, as she felt so happy about his release.

When they got back to the Manor Celia and Dan were waiting to greet him. Celia said, 'It's wonderful to see you, Jamal, out of that horrible prison. May I give you a kiss?' and to Mary's surprise he responded without hesitation.

Dan shook his hand and said, 'It's been a terrible ordeal for you. We hope you'll try and relax while you're here and recover some semblance of normality. Celia's got your room all ready for you.' With that, Celia escorted Jamal to his room while Mary went to find Jamie who was having tea with his nanny.

When Celia came down she told them she'd suggested Jamal should soak in a long hot bath to shake off memories of the prison. Ever practical, she told him his clothes were likely to be damp after sitting in an unaired flat for so long, and suggested he put them on a radiator to dry.

It was a good hour before Jamal came down – looking much more alert. They sat in the conservatory enjoying a pre-dinner drink. As soon as Jamie saw Jamal, he went up to him and solemnly held out his hand. 'Hello Mr Jamal.'

'Hello, Master Jamie,' said Jamal laughing.

David arrived soon after. They talked a little about prison life and then Jamal, clearly not wanting to dwell on prison for the moment, asked what they'd all been doing during the last eight months. He wanted to hear about Mary and David's wedding plans, and where they were to live, and said, with a catch in his voice, how happy Kim would have been to know they'd got together.

Mary sensed that just a brief mention of Kim was all he could cope with at the moment.

Celia had prepared a chicken casserole, preceded by a smoked salmon mousse. Dan said he thought champagne would be in order if Jamal was happy drinking it.

'Of course,' said Jamal. 'I have no Islamic scruples about drinking alcohol – in moderation,' he added, laughing.

They spent a pleasant evening – watching the news at ten when Jamal's acquittal and release from prison was mentioned, and there was a picture of Jamal and Mary emerging from the flat. 'Fame at last,' she laughed.

Jamal excused himself immediately after the news ended, saying he was very tired.

'Stay in bed as long as you like,' said Celia. 'I'll bring you up a cup of tea – but not before nine.'

David departed soon after. When they kissed goodbye and expressed how happy they were at Jamal's release, Mary felt a sort of tension in him which she couldn't quite explain.

As she lay in bed that night, her mind went back over the traumatic events of the last year. It had been in June, twelve months before, that she'd first met David and Jamal – and little did she know then what lay ahead of them. She'd just been coming to terms with Ben's death, accepting the fact that she had to build a new life for herself and Jamie, and hadn't long started back to her career, thanks to Dan's encouragement, when they were faced with all the trauma of Kim's disappearance and murder, and Jamal's arrest.

'And here we are,' she thought with amazement, 'looking after Jamal whom we scarcely knew a year ago, and treating him as a sort of family member, while I'm engaged to be married to David!' She realised how fortunate they all were to be embraced by the love of Celia and Dan who lived out their Christian faith in such a warm and hospitable way. As she said her prayers, she gave thanks for Jamal's release, for Celia and Dan, for David and Jamie, and prayed for guidance during the coming months. She also prayed for all those who were less fortunate, for the prisoners Jamal had left behind, for all those who were sleeping rough that night, for the sick and the bereaved, and then decided to round off her prayers by saying the office of Compline.

She left next morning long before Jamal was up, and spent a busy day at the office. She and Julian spent some time discussing whether they should encourage or discourage Jamal from suing for compensation for wrongful arrest. They both felt that was going to be a tricky issue – especially as there was no sign of Ali's whereabouts, nor had Kim's murderer been found. They agreed that if Jamal raised the question, they would caution against any immediate action.

Julian left the office immediately when he received a call from Celia mid-day saying the press were outside and could he come and be with Jamal.

When Mary got back that evening, she found Julian had left, and Jamal was in the conservatory, playing snakes and ladders with Jamie. After giving Jamie a hug and chatting for a little while with Jamal, she went to find Celia. She was in the kitchen preparing dinner.

'How's the day been?' she asked.

'Well, fine really – except for the press. I took Jamal a cup of tea at nine as I promised, but he was fast asleep. He didn't emerge till nearly twelve. He was very apologetic but said he hadn't woken up till gone eleven. He said it was the best night's sleep he'd had since he'd been arrested. I gather the prison beds were very uncomfortable, and it was at night that his situation hit him the hardest, and he found it very difficult to sleep.'

'I'm not surprised. I'm so glad he's agreed to come here. I hope we can get him back on his feet before he goes home – of course, that is,' she added hastily, 'if you don't mind keeping him here.'

'You know I don't,' said Celia. 'This is a large house, I've lots of help, and as I'm already cooking for all of us, it's only one more person to feed. No problem at all.'

'So tell me about the press.'

Celia pulled a long face. 'Well, they arrived en masse at midday. As you know Julian came out as soon as I called him. I don't think Jamal could have handled the press on his own. But thanks to Julian, I think they went away fairly sympathetic'.

At that moment David arrived and they went to the conservatory to find Jamal. When they got there, Jamal stood up and greeted David with a handshake. Jamie, not jumping up into David's arms as he usually did, merely looked up, and said proudly, 'Mr Jamal and I are playing snakes and ladders and I'm winning.'

Mary could see David was a little put out, and said quickly, 'Jamie, aren't you going to kiss Uncle David?'

'Oh, of course,' he said, and went up to David for a hug.

During dinner David said he'd asked his cleaning lady if she would come over and help clean the flat. 'She's free tomorrow, and as it's Saturday I did wonder whether you would like us all to go over and help sort out the mess?'

Jamal's face lit up at the suggestion and they arranged that David would collect them about 10 o'clock the next morning. Celia and Dan said they would look after Jamie

The papers always arrived early at The Manor, and next morning, Saturday, they scanned them eagerly to see whether the press was hostile or sympathetic. Dan always took three papers – the *Guardian*, The *Telegraph* and the *Mirror* 'In order to get a cross section of public opinion,' he said.

They contained lengthy reports about Jamal's arrest, the discovery of bombs at his flat, and a lot of detail about Kim's murder. The *Telegraph* and *Times* were, on the whole, sympathetic but the *Mirror* guardedly hinted at its difficulty in believing a man could be innocent who had bombs in his garage. They felt it could have been worse.

When David arrived to collect Mary she had a bit of a scene with Jamie. Seeing David, he expected to go with them, and was enraged when he saw Jamal, David and his mother, as well as David's cleaner, Rose, driving off without him. Celia said he had quite a tantrum but they'd soon managed to calm him down.

Rose tackled the dirt, Mary tackled the bedroom and the clothes that had been thrown onto the floor putting aside those that needed washing or ironing, while David helped Jamal sort out the papers that were strewn across the sitting room floor. They had coffee half way through the morning but were still not finished at lunchtime. As they were making good progress it seemed pointless to give up before they'd finished, so Mary popped out and collected rolls, ham, cheese and fruit to keep them going.

By 3 o'clock the flat was back to some semblance of normality. It was tidy and smelt fresh. They'd put the water heater on, and were relieved to find the system hadn't been damaged by being turned off for so long.

The most difficult part had been sorting out the papers. Jamal left several piles on the dining table which, he said, he would sort out later. He looked absolutely exhausted.

A TORTUOUS PATH

Rose bundled up all the clothes that the police had pulled out of drawers, and said she would take them home and wash and iron them. Jamal was very grateful.

David drove them back and after having a cup of tea, said he would take Rose home and see them the next day. Stuart and Susan had invited them both to dinner that evening, but Mary excused herself saying that as her law exams were coming up in less than six weeks, and with all that had been happening during the last few months, she'd had very little time for revision and was beginning to panic. She felt she just must keep her evenings free.

She could feel that David was upset with her but knew it was really important that she passed the exams before their wedding. She didn't relish the idea of having exams hanging over her once they were married and was realistic enough to know that life was going to be very different and much more demanding, once they were living in their own home - having to look after David and herself without all the support she'd received from Dan and Celia during the last few years. So she kissed David goodbye and said she'd see him after church. David said he would come over mid-morning to keep Jamal company.

Mary felt very concerned about Jamal. He looked drained, and slumped down into a reclining chair in the conservatory where he fell immediately into a deep sleep. Celia woke him when dinner was ready, but he said he didn't think he could eat anything, and would like to go up to bed straight away.

The next day they realised that Jamal was suffering from more than exhaustion. He became seriously ill and to start with the doctors couldn't find out what was wrong suspecting it was nervous exhaustion. But he continued to be ill, and blood tests revealed he had an unusual virus infection. The doctors were so concerned they contacted the prison to see if there were any similar cases there, and discovered there were two prisoners with the same symptoms.

Despite being so ill, Jamal was concerned that he was being a burden to Celia and Dan, but they insisted he remained at The Manor. His illness was such that he needed little real nursing care. Sleep seemed to be the main requisite to start with. His appetite was much diminished, and he could only cope with occasional very light meals.

After a fortnight he began to recover physically, and actually dressed and came down and sat in the conservatory where he said he felt happiest – looking out on the garden instead of onto prison walls. But they were all worried by his mental state. He seemed to be in a deep depression and they wondered about counselling. They wished Jane had still been alive because they felt confident she would have helped him.

Though none of them were in any way knowledgeable about counselling, they felt they could help a little by encouraging Jamal to talk about all that had happened, and get it out of his system. Mary talked to him about Kim but it was Celia who really got through to him. He confided in her his utter feeling of loss – not only of Kim. He told her about the loss of his first girl-friend in America whom he had planned to marry before his parents intervened. And then he talked about his family – another loss. They'd failed to support him while he was in prison because of the disgrace he'd brought down on them. He talked about the loss of Al, the friend whom he'd trusted, which he thought was almost the most difficult thing he had to bear - betrayal. He told her that, other than the friendship offered to him by David and Mary, and she and Dan, he felt utterly alone in the world.

Mary could have wept when she totalled up the number of losses Jamal had suffered over the years, and just prayed that by talking about them, he might find some peace.

He opened up to Dan about some of the harassment he'd encountered in his early days in England. In the northern town where he'd been brought up, there were so many Muslims he never felt in the least alienated. But when he came back to England and lived in a town in the south where there was only a small ethnic presence he'd been made at times to feel an alien, and had suffered quite a lot of harassment – in the shops and public places as well as in the hospital.

David talked to him about coming back to work. He assured Jamal that he would receive all his back salary and was also entitled to up to six months sick leave, but very much hoped he would be back at work well before then. Jamal expressed his anxiety about returning to work. He was afraid that, though the charge had been withdrawn, there would be people at the hospital who would say that there was no smoke without fire, and felt he would always be under scrutiny. David urged him to think positively and to at least return to the hospital for a time while he sorted out what he wanted to do in the future. David was aware that Jamal's medical interests were turning in a new direction towards palliative care and thought that that ultimately that might be the way forward for him.

Julian gave Mary two week's leave before her exams which she spent at home. It meant that she saw a lot of Jamal as he slowly recuperated. This didn't please David though he never said anything – just glowered. Mary felt he was feeling jealous and did her best to reassure him, but being so engrossed in revision, she realised she was not sufficiently sensitive, and one day he erupted, accusing her of being in love with Jamal.

-61-
Mary and David quarrel

The comment led to their first major row. She was very angry. David had touched a nerve. She declared he was jealous, that she couldn't stand jealous people, and she wasn't sure she wanted to marry him after all. David went off in a huff.

David's accusation forced her to analyse her feelings. Despite her denials, she knew she was becoming increasingly fond of Jamal, and realised that, if she hadn't been engaged to David, she might have considered getting involved with him had he wanted her. She found him extremely attractive, considerate, well-read and interesting to talk to. She'd got on well with him ever since their first meeting, and during all the visits she'd made to the prison she'd felt very close to him.

The row occurred just before her exams. Celia said it was all due to wedding and exam nerves and told Mary firmly to concentrate on her exams before doing or saying anything she might regret.

David kept phoning and it was Celia who answered the phone. Mary refused to take his calls. 'Just be patient 'til Mary's exams are over. Then you can discuss the situation sensibly. If you push her now, you'll find she won't be rational, and you might lose her altogether. I don't want that to happen, David, I'm very fond of you both and think you're well suited.'

Jamal, sensing there was a problem, though not knowing quite what it was, announced that he was now feeling much better and would like to go back to his flat.

Celia phoned David to tell him Jamal was leaving and hoping to return to work very soon. David felt it would help Jamal if, before he came back to work, people understood why he'd been released from prison and why the charge had been dropped. He called together a group of senior staff at the hospital and told them a little of the story – asking them all to be considerate when Jamal returned.

He telephoned Aunt Judith who was overjoyed to hear the circumstances of Jamal's release. He also wrote to Charles, telling him more than he'd told the staff at the hospital. He received a long letter back, saying how relieved he was, and telling him that if ever Jamal was in difficulties or needed a job, David was to get in touch with him.

It struck David how many people believed in, and liked, Jamal, and realised he'd been a fool letting jealousy get the better of him. He felt ill with anxiety, thinking that here was yet another relationship going wrong, but decided the best thing to do was to get on with the work of renovating the cottage in the hope the relationship could be mended once Mary's exams were over.

When Jamal said he was leaving Mary realised she felt bereft at the thought and tried to persuade him to stay longer, but he insisted it was the right thing to do – that he needed to get back his normal life even though he knew it was going to be very difficult. She offered to go back with him to help him settle in but he refused saying she needed to get on with her revision.

David stayed away, and Mary forced herself to concentrate on revising though it wasn't easy. The house felt empty without Jamal and David's frequent visits. But she knew it was important to pass the exams and get the necessary qualifications to continue her legal career. She felt she owed it to Dan and Celia as much as to herself, so when she came to take the exams a fortnight later she was well prepared and felt fairly confident she'd pass.

With the exams behind her she had time to stop and think carefully. She realised she'd been somewhat naïve about relationships. Because she and Ben had been so instantly attracted to each other, there'd never been any question of competition. They just belonged from the moment they met. But with David the relationship had developed much more slowly. They'd had a longer period of getting to know each other before there was any intimacy at all. She knew David to be a warm, caring, and loving man, and knew he would be a wholly dependable and constant husband. She hadn't thought over much about what sort of lover he would be – but wasn't expecting the sort of passion she'd felt for Ben. And now, here she was, at the age of twenty-five, mother of a three year old son, finding herself for the first time aware of the complex emotional situations people can get themselves immersed in.

She didn't know how to handle her emotions. She realised she was very attracted to Jamal and that he'd been constantly in her thoughts while he was in prison. She'd been deeply concerned to see him looking ill and gaunt, and had felt distraught when he'd been so ill. And now that he'd moved out, she couldn't stop thinking about him and wanting to be with him. But then she thought about David. She felt angry and fearful about his outburst of jealousy, but then remembered all his good qualities and the feeling of safety and comfort she felt when she was with him. Then she thought about Jamie who loved David (but then, she told herself, he'd taken to Jamal too). It had never before occurred to her that she could possibly love two men at the same time.

She knew David had been phoning regularly but couldn't bring herself to speak to him. She decided she must get away, and arranged to visit her parents with Jamie.

A TORTUOUS PATH

When she got there she looked so pale that her father thought she was ill. Her mother could see there was something bothering her, but couldn't get her to talk. She was fearful Mary was about to have a breakdown. After a few days Mary said she must get back to work and left without telling her parents about her problem.

Dan who'd been her guide and mentor ever since Ben's death realised Mary was deeply unhappy and guessed what might be the trouble. He bided his time about talking to her, but the day after her return from her parents, said, 'Mary love. I know you're very unhappy and confused about the future. Can I help?'

Mary knew at once that Dan had guessed, and bursting into tears told him about her mixed feelings. A very wise man, he suggested that what she was feeling for Jamal was as much sympathy and compassion as love. He said he'd observed her and David together over many months and felt they were wholly compatible. 'David's a good man,' he said. 'I know he would make you a good husband and Jamie a wonderful father. You would never have given Jamal another thought if he'd married Kim. You would all have been good friends.'

Mary nodded.

'You've been through the most horrifying and difficult time. Not many people have had to suffer the trauma you've been through. I believe your emotions are all mixed up and you can't really think straight. You ought to talk to David. It's only fair. And perhaps you ought to go and see Jamal and find out how you really feel about him now he's back in his own home.'

'Dan, I feel such an idiot. Don't tell Celia will you. I've got to try and sort myself out.'

'I know,' he said, and gave her a hug.

She needed an excuse to visit Jamal and when Celia said that he'd left some books behind, it provided the excuse she needed. She phoned Jamal and told him about the books and offered to pop over with them sometime.

Jamal immediately said, 'Come to supper tomorrow - and bring David. I'm not much of a cook but I'll get a takeaway.'

'I'd rather come on my own. David's extremely busy at the moment.'

'Oh,' said Jamal sounding surprised. 'OK. If that's what you want. I saw David this morning. I thought he looked very tired and rather depressed. I hope he's not overdoing things. I'll look forward to seeing you tomorrow.'

When she arrived she felt embarrassed. Jamal greeted her affectionately and said, 'I'm sorry David can't come. Perhaps next time.'

After he'd poured her a drink, he asked about her exams and when she was going back to work. She told him she thought she'd passed, and was returning to work the following week.

'And what about you?' she asked. 'How's the flat?'

'Well, you know ….. It's not easy. The flat seems empty without Kim. When I was arrested I thought there'd be some explanation for her disappearance and she'd be here when I returned. Being here brings it all back. I keep thinking about her and wishing she'd walk into the room smiling like she always did. I can't stop wondering who killed her and why. She was the kindest, sweetest person you could ever know – never harmed anyone.'

She saw tears well up in his eyes. In the prison she'd have given him a hug but somehow didn't feel able to in his own flat.

'I sometimes wonder if I'll ever be able to build my life again.'

Mary took his hand and squeezed it. 'I know just how you feel. The feeling of loss is almost insupportable. But at least Ben wasn't murdered. Knowing how Kim died must be even harder to bear.'

Trying to change the subject Mary asked how he was finding it back at the hospital.

'Difficult. I feel everyone's watching me all the time. A lot of my colleagues are very sympathetic but I sense there's still a doubt in some people's minds about my innocence. It's not easy. I've decided to look for another job somewhere far away from both the hospital and this flat. There's nothing to keep me here - though of course,' he hastened to add, 'I've got lovely friends in you and David, and Celia and Dan. I'll miss you all when I move. Your David's been a wonderful support. He's always been there for me when I needed him - as have you,' he added. 'I think you're very lucky to have each other.'

Unhappy at the thought he was planning to move she asked him a loaded question, 'Surely, given time you'll find someone else?'

'No, I don't want to get involved with anyone again. It's too painful.'

Mary asked herself whether this was the answer she wanted or needed.

After supper Jamal talked mainly about Al and how deeply upset he was by his betrayal.

'It's almost impossible to come to terms with – especially with someone you've known for a long time and trusted completely. What I find so difficult to understand is how one can know so little about a person you've been living with in the same house. I had absolutely no idea he was involved in terrorism. He never gave any indication that he hated the west. I always thought he was interested in humanitarian aid – not bomb making. His betrayal is almost as difficult to bear as the loss of Kim. I don't think I'll really trust anyone again '

'It's surprising how little one really knows about the people around us. Perhaps it's a good thing.'

Mary left soon after nine and when she got home she went straight up to her flat without talking to Celia or Dan. She lay in bed thinking about the evening. She felt very upset that Jamal felt he had no roots in the area and was planning to move away; she felt guilty when she remembered what Jamal had said about David looking tired and depressed, and knew it was almost certainly due to her refusal to speak to him; and she took on board Jamal's comment that she and David were lucky to have each other – a remark which didn't indicate that Jamal had any special feelings for her other than warm friendship.

Mary realised she played no part in Jamal's future plans and chided herself for being so foolish.

She fell asleep resolved to get in touch with David the next day.

-62-
Marriage

When they got together the next day, there was a constraint between them at first. David apologised for being jealous and said 'I've been through hell, wondering if you'd have me back. If it hadn't been for Celia telling me to bide my time, I don't know what I'd have done.'

Mary explained that though she loved Jamal dearly and felt close to him because he'd been through such a harrowing time with Kim's death and his imprisonment, what she felt for Jamal was nothing like what she felt for David.

'So the wedding's still on?' he asked. '

Mary nodded. Then David took her in his arms and held her close. Not for the first time, Mary felt near to tears.

They talked about what they'd been doing in the weeks they'd been apart.

'How did the exams go?'

'Better than I expected. I think I'll pass. I did a lot of revision in the last few weeks so I'm hopeful. What have you been doing with your spare time?'

'Working on our cottage. It's in a right mess, I'm afraid. I've had the builders in and they've fixed the bathroom and the kitchen but there's still a lot to do. I've also prepared a nice room for Jamie. I think he'll like it.'

'Jamie's room before our bedroom?' said Mary laughing. 'I know where your priorities lie!!'

'You must bring him over to see it soon. After all, the wedding's only three months off.'

David looked at her closely for a few moments and said, 'We must never again part after a quarrel without talking about it.'

Mary nodded and when she left later to return home, both felt reassured

The time went by in a flash. David was unusually busy at the hospital, and wanted to get everything out of the way before the wedding.

Following the Ball the hospice appeal started taking off at an alarming rate with supporters organising a variety of events in their local villages – some of which David, as Chairman, felt he had to attend. Pamela, now happily pregnant, started a monthly newsletter for The Friends – listing all the events that were planned both centrally and in the villages around, and all the donations, large and small that were coming in.

Mary knew that now they had land for the hospice and plans were being drawn up for the building, she should be approaching the charitable trusts, but felt this would have to wait until after the wedding as she knew filling in application forms entailed a lot of work.

David attended several church services with Mary, and felt comfortable about having a conventional church wedding. Colin agreed to marry them in the church where Mary worshipped but asked them to come to some pre-marriage sessions before the banns were read. 'I think you're both too mature for me to talk to you about the responsibilities of marriage, but I would like to talk about the sacramental nature of marriage. I know Mary is aware of this, but I am not sure you are, David.'

David found the three sessions enlightening, and it helped him to know where Mary was coming from. He promised Colin he would attend his Alpha a course in the autumn – a course which Colin said was proving very popular both in England and world-wide.

Celia and Dan insisted on hosting the wedding reception at The Manor and decided to have it in a marquee in the garden.

When they made a list of who should be invited, Mary and David found they had listed more than a hundred names. Though Mary had no brothers or sisters, she had a number of close relatives while David, as well as his family in Scotland, had many friends in his village and at the hospital. They decided to invite all the members of the Appeal Committee and their spouses, though were uncertain what to do about Alec and Alice. Eventually they sent them each an invitation which said 'and friend', and wondered which, if either, would come.

Jamal was another person they were uncertain about, worrying that he might find it too upsetting when it was at about this time that he would have been getting married himself.

Both Aunt Judith and Charles were invited. Aunt Judith said she wouldn't miss the wedding for 'all the world', but Charles wrote that though he would have liked to come he had to attend a major conference. But he invited Mary, David and Jamie to visit him in the States the following year.

A TORTUOUS PATH

Mary was so busy with wedding preparations she didn't see much of David. She kept her promise to Jenny and Susan to be her bridesmaids, and she and Alison decided that Jamie and Jack were just old enough to be pageboys.

David invited his brother-in-law, James, and Celia and Dan's son, Anthony, to be ushers, and half-jokingly asked Mick as well. Mick, a twinkle in his eye, said, 'Thanks for the compliment, David, but I really think that's a young man's job. I'll certainly be at the wedding though to wish you well.'

Just three weeks before the wedding, the terrorist who'd been arrested in Frankfurt was identified as a Muslim called Ali Mansour who'd been living in Frankfurt under the name of Quesif Fayyad. The papers reported that he'd often visited England under the name of Al Mercer; that he was a friend of Dr Jamal Khan, a hospital doctor in the midlands, who'd spent time in prison on a charge of terrorism but had been released some months before; and that Ali Mansour was to be charged with terrorism and the murder of Dr Khan's fiancée, Kim Anderson, a nurse in the hospital where he worked.

The papers went on to say that nurse Anderson's body had not been found for many months. The paper then had a field day describing the curious circumstances which led to the discovery of Kim's body – a one in a thousand chance - and ended by saying that the police were still looking for the older boy.

Inevitably, the raking up of the story put a damper on the wedding preparations. David and Mary both felt they must spend time with Jamal to ease him through the confirmation of Al's involvement, and Mary wondered whether they would ever be free of the horror of Kim's death. Celia and Dan urged them to put all thought of what had happened to the back of their minds and concentrate on the wedding. 'You don't want to spoil your wedding. You need to have happy memories of the day.'

Al was brought to England and came before the magistrate's court on a charge of terrorism and murder. He pleaded not guilty and was remanded in custody to await trial

There was a time of panic three weeks before the wedding when Mary's father was taken ill and rushed into hospital. They drove down hastily to see him. He'd had a mild heart attack and was kept in hospital for a week. He came out armed with pills, and was determined to be at the wedding. They'd asked him to read one of the lessons Mary had chosen – a beautiful passage from the New Testament which Mary said came from 1 John 4 which started by saying 'My dear friends, let us love one another because the source of love is God.' David found the passage challenging.

Alison, James and children arrived from Scotland a week before the wedding and David was able to accommodate them all in the cottage which he'd worked hard to make habitable. Steven slept in his tent in the garden, Jack and Susan occupied Jamie's room, and Jenny, who, in the six months since they'd seen her, had grown into a beautiful and poised young lady, was to sleep on the sofa until the night before the wedding when she was to stay with Mary at The Manor.

The day after they arrived, Celia and Dan invited them all over for dinner. Jamie had been excited all day waiting to see them, and no sooner had they arrived than he took Susan and Jack into the garden to see the marquee.

Alison and James were made to feel very welcome. They had drinks in the conservatory before dinner. The garden looked particularly beautiful as Dan had imported a quantity of bedding plants especially for the wedding. He and James, both lawyers, soon started talking about Jamal and his court case. 'So unusual to have a hung jury,' said Dan, 'but it was very fortunate for Jamal – otherwise it would have taken more time to get him out of prison.'

As James had been interested in Jamal and all that had happened to him, David invited Jamal over to dinner one evening so they could meet. They established an instant rapport, and Jamal invited James to visit the hospital and have lunch with him the next day. Alison, Mary and the children had a happy day visiting a local castle where the children walked the walls and dressed up as mediaeval knights

The night before the wedding David spent the evening with James, Stuart and Anthony as well as a couple of doctors from the hospital. As they sat round talking, enjoying a convivial but sober evening, David thought wryly that he was rather older than most grooms-to-be and that had he been younger, the evening would have been much more boisterous. They returned home well before midnight.

The wedding day dawned bright and sunny. David felt very nervous waiting in the church for Mary to arrive, but as she walked down the aisle, David's heart lurched seeing how beautiful she was and feeling how lucky he was to have her.

Colin in his address talked about the quality of relationships, the importance of friendship, the necessity for humour and tolerance, and the need for constancy in times of adversity. It touched them all. Many of the guests were aware that this was a difficult time for him so soon after Jane's death, but he managed to introduce humour into his address, and left everyone feeling that what he said was as relevant to them as to the bride and groom.

After the service, they returned to The Manor where Mary's parents, David's sister and husband, and Celia and Dan stood in the line-up to receive the guests. It had always seemed to David one of the happiest moments at a wedding when all the friends and relatives who hadn't met for a long time were greeted. Their wedding was no exception with hugs and kisses, and introductions all round. The question about Alec and Alice was answered when they arrived together saying they were both getting divorced, and were going to get married as soon as the divorces were finalised. David and Mary expressed their good wishes, and the hope that all would go smoothly for them. Jamal arrived in the line-up with Colin, looking tired, but he said how very happy he was for them both and what wonderfully supportive friends they'd been while he was in prison.

The reception was in the marquee which friends of Celia had decorated with garlands of flowers. It was set out with round tables and a 'top table' on a raised stage. Mary and David had spent a lot of time beforehand organising the seating plan as they knew sitting with congenial people enhanced the enjoyment of formal occasions.

Mary told David that Dan and Celia had insisted on paying for most of the reception, and David was in awe of their generous spirit – knowing that, but for the accident to Ben, this would have been the wedding day of their son.

When it came to the speeches, David was at pains to express the love he and Mary felt for Dan and Celia, and their gratitude for all they'd done for Mary and, more recently for him. He didn't neglect to include Mary's parents in his speech and said how very relieved they were that her father was able to be with them after his recent time in hospital. He also expressed his love and gratitude to his sister and brother-in-law who, he said, were the only family he had left. Their love and care had supported him through many difficult times over the years and he was only sad they lived so far away.

Stuart's speech as best man was amusing and thoughtful, and Mary's father's solemn. Dan was persuaded to get up and say a few words – mostly about Mary who was like a daughter to him and Celia. He said how much they were going to miss her, and Jamie, when they moved out. 'But David,' he said, 'I insist that you bring them over to see us often. Otherwise you'll be in great trouble!' Everyone laughed.

After the formal proceedings the tables were cleared to the side. Mary and David were called to take to the floor for the traditional twirl round the marquee. They left soon after nine.

They spent the first two nights in a luxurious country hotel a few miles away. When David took Mary into his arms and made love to her he had a feeling of deep contentment, of coming home – something he'd never felt with Joanna who had been a reluctant lover, or with Samantha who had been so sexually voracious.

After two days, they went back to The Manor, collected Jamie, and drove up to Scotland. There they spent two nights with Alison and family before going off on a week's tour of the Highlands, leaving Jamie to be looked after by Alison. They returned to the hotel where he'd proposed to Mary, and spent two days there before heading off to the rugged and beautiful west coast.

When they returned to collect Jamie he was happy to see them, but Alison told them he'd been quite at home playing with Jack and Susan, and hadn't been worried by their absence.

They returned to Mary's flat at The Manor instead of to their new home as Celia and Dan had both suggested that if they took Jamie immediately to a new and strange house straight after he'd spent a week away in another house, he might feel extremely unsettled. This seemed a wise suggestion so they stayed on at the Manor for a week.

They started taking Jamie's toys a few at a time to the cottage and on several visits the nanny came too. As she lived half way between their new home and The Manor the move didn't affect her beyond the fact that the cottage was a much less prestigious place to work in than The Manor. After a week they felt Jamie was ready to move. They borrowed a van and took all the furniture Mary had acquired over the years

Even in the midst of moving they couldn't get away from Jamal and all that had happened during the last year. The first Saturday they were in their new house David opened the papers to see a report of the trial of Jamal's cousins who had threatened him and Kim just before she disappeared. There was no suggestion of terrorism, but they were tried for intimidating behaviour and were sent to prison for eight months.

David had felt anxious that Mary might find the cottage claustrophobic after living at The manor with its tall and spacious rooms. But she seemed happy from the first night she spent there.

Jamie, too, settled in quickly though they had a few disturbed nights to begin with. Mary had extremely sensitive antennae because she seemed to be awake and out of bed almost before Jamie cried out.

One night she was in a deeper sleep than usual and David crept out to see what the matter was. Jamie was crying and said he'd had a bad dream. David took him on his lap and cuddled him for a while. 'Where's Mummy?' he asked.

'She's still asleep. Do you want me to get her?'

'No, you stay,' he said, and put his arms round David's neck. David felt overwhelmed at that simple gesture and found it difficult to hold back his tears.

When the next day Jamie asked, 'Can I call you daddy now?' David felt their bond was complete.

Once they'd got the cottage in some semblance of order, and with only a few weeks to go before Christmas, they decided to start inviting some of their friends round. Celia and Dan, and Stuart and Susan were their first formal dinner guests. It was a good evening, and gave David and Mary an opportunity to express their appreciation for all the support Celia and Dan had given them over the last two years.

Their next guests were Pamela and Patrick. Pamela looked radiant, and when they left Mary said, 'It's wonderful how happy they are. I'd begun to think Patrick would never get married. And when Dan asked me to invite a few of my friends to his sixtieth birthday party, I never imagined that he and Pamela would get together. Yet, seeing them so happy, it's obvious they were made for each other.' David agreed.

Knowing Jamal was still very depressed, they organised a dinner party for him with Julian, and Geoffrey and Eric, two doctors from the hospital, who'd been at his engagement party. He thought it might help Jamal to feel part of the hospital family again.

When they invited Colin Masters, they invited him on his own, feeling he would prefer a quiet evening. They talked about Jane and her work, and he told them that his family in New Zealand was coming over for Christmas – that Jane had inherited some money from an aunt and, thoughtful as ever, had left some of it to the New Zealand family so that they could come over at least once a year to visit their father.

Colin had an aura about him that conveyed warmth and understanding, despite the underlying sadness he was suffering. As he left, he said with a smile, 'David. We're starting an Alpha course after Christmas. It would be good if you would come.'

David said he would.

It seemed incredible to Mary and David that Christmas was upon them. A year ago David had been with his family in Scotland and had rushed back south to Dan's birthday party, looking forward with excited anticipation to seeing Mary, while at the same time wondering whether what he felt for her was the right basis for marriage. Now, here he was, one year later, married to a warm and caring woman, and with a stepson who felt like his own. He was happier than he'd ever been in his life.

They spent their first Christmas at The Manor with Celia and Dan, Mary's parents, and Anthony and his family. Well before Christmas, they'd posted their Christmas presents to David's family in Scotland, promising to go up and visit them at the earliest opportunity.

It was a magical Christmas. Anthony and family arrived at The Manor at the same time as they did, and Jamie was off with his cousins within minutes. They all stayed right through to the day after Boxing Day. Jamie, like Jack and Susan the previous Christmas, got very excited about the arrival of Father Christmas, and before bedtime, placed, with great care, a glass of sherry and a mince pie by the fireplace. David was pleased to note that the cousins didn't try to persuade Jamie that Father Christmas didn't exist, as some older children do.

After Jamie was in bed, he and Mary filled his stocking and Mary said, 'You know you won't be able to sleep in tomorrow. I suspect he'll be awake by five, if not before.'

True to her words, Jamie came into their bedroom at five o'clock, carrying his stocking, his little face lit up with excitement. They'd only put small items in his stocking – the main present, a sit-on truck and trailer, was for later - but he took everything out of the stocking one by one, and kept saying, 'Isn't Father Christmas kind.' Eventually they pulled him into bed with them, and he snuggled down, and they got another two hours' sleep.

After breakfast, they went to church. They felt for Colin as it was his first Christmas without Jane, but were delighted to see his family from New Zealand were there giving him support.

They went back to The Manor for a light lunch and afterwards sat round the fire while Dan, dressed as Father Christmas, distributed all the presents that had been sitting under the tree.

They had their Christmas dinner in the evening – the children all sitting up for it. Dan, who was in very good form, told them about 'the old days' when they would put on the wireless and listen to the Queen's Christmas message and then would all stand solemnly when the National Anthem was played.

Celia, knowing he would be on his own, invited Jamal to join them for the evening. He arrived bearing generous presents for them all while Mary and David gave him books and a smart jumper, and Dan and Celia presented him with CDs as they'd discovered he enjoyed classical music. He stayed over until Boxing Day afternoon, and then went on to spend the evening with one of the doctors from the hospital.

Heavy snow fell after Christmas which delayed Jamie's start at nursery school. When it cleared, Mary took him and stayed with him for the first three times. He settled in quickly partly, David thought because of the time he'd spent with Alison's children in Scotland. The nanny stayed on and said she'd be happy doubling up as their cleaner on the days Jamie was at nursery school. This was a happy arrangement for Mary.

Soon after Christmas, David had a call from Colin saying the Alpha course was starting the following week and he hoped he would come. As he'd half promised Colin he would attend, he very reluctantly went along. He'd no idea what to expect and was surprised when he arrived to find the church hall crowded and tables laid for a meal. It was a relief to see that Colin was present, though David knew he wasn't the speaker for the evening. They sat in groups of eight at small tables, and were served a meal before the business of the evening began.

The speaker gave a historical presentation of Christianity and the sheer quantity of early manuscripts of the gospels and epistles that existed.

He pointed out that the earliest manuscripts of the Roman historians, whose authenticity people accepted without question, were some two or three hundred years later than the Christian documents. David found this very interesting and quite convincing.

After the talk, they got into groups, each chaired by someone from the local church, and had a lively discussion about what they'd heard.

During the next few weeks David, encouraged by Mary, attended the course and though not entirely convinced, felt more sympathetic to Mary's belief.

It was during the Alpha course that the news came that the boy who'd stolen the silver and buried it in Kim's grave had been found and arrested. David found himself the centre of attention as the whole story of Kim's disappearance and murder and Al's arrest was discussed at length during supper. Colin, realising that it would be almost impossible to divert the discussion and questioning, decided to use it as an opportunity to talk about the whole subject of forgiveness and reparation.

David knew it would upset Mary so, although he had discussed the earlier sessions, he didn't tell her about this one, saying it had been 'rather boring'.

Mary passed her exams with flying colours, and Julian started giving her legal cases that were more interesting and demanding. Life was settling down into a happy routine when they found themselves involved once again with the terrorist drama.

-63-
Ali Mansour

Mary was in the office talking to Julian when he received a surprising phone call from a Mr Sullivan who said he was Ali Mansour's solicitor. He said he believed Julian had acted for Dr Jamal Khan at his trial

Julian replied, rather curtly, 'Yes. That is so.' He gestured to Mary to pick up the other phone.

'My client, Mr Mansour, has asked me to persuade Dr Khan to visit him in prison.'

'Why? I'm sure Dr Khan has absolutely no intention of visiting Mr Mansour.'

'Well, Mr Mansour had some information he would like to impart to Dr Khan.'

'Why can't he write to Dr Khan and tell him?'

'I think Mr Mansour is afraid to put anything in writing and wants to talk to Dr Khan in person. He urged me to ask him. He thinks it's very important and in Dr Khan's best interest.'

'I'm very reluctant to speak to Dr Khan.'

'Please!' begged Mr Sullivan.

Julian finally agreed to ask Jamal but reiterated that he was sure Jamal would refuse. He told Sullivan that, as his solicitor, he would advise Jamal against visiting someone who was accused of terrorism – especially as Jamal himself had only recently been exonerated and released from prison.

Julian discussed this surprising request with Mary and they agreed that Julian should speak to Jamal but would advise him to decline. As expected, Jamal vehemently refused to have anything to do with Al, and Julian phoned Sullivan to tell him.

Julian thought that was the end of the matter, but Sullivan was persistent. A few days later he phoned again 'If Dr Khan won't come, has he a friend who might be persuaded to go in his place? I really must emphasise that it would be in Dr Khan's best interest if Ali Mansour was allowed to tell his story.'

Julian discussed the request with Mary before asking David whether he would consider going. David refused saying the last person he ever wished to see again was Al.

'What on earth has he got to say that would be of interest to Jamal now?'

'Well,' said Julian. 'I've been thinking about it and I just wonder whether Al has some information about how Kim died that he wants to tell Jamal'

It was this possibility that made David wonder whether he should change his mind. He decided to discuss it first with Sir Ralph before going to see Al. Though he'd been angry about being used, he realised there was a good reason why Sir Ralph had used him as a possible source of information, and he was grateful to him for being in part instrumental in Jamal's release. So he phoned Sir Ralph to discuss whether or not he thought he should visit Al as requested.

Sir Ralph immediately encouraged David to go, but said he should take with him a hidden tape recorder in case Ali said anything that might help in the fight against terrorism. So, a week later, he found himself on a train to the prison in Manchester.

Arriving at the prison he was shown into the visiting room. Looking round at the assembled prisoners he couldn't at first see Al. Puzzled, he asked the prison officer where Ali Mansour was. He pointed David to a man with a black beard, wearing the long grey shift one sees on Muslim men in the Middle East. It was Al. The last time David had seen Al he was wearing a British lounge suit.

Shocked, he went over to him and said, 'Al?'

'It's Ali, not Al!' he replied. 'Allah be with you, David.'

David was so taken aback he just nodded and said 'I didn't recognise you!'

'Well, now you see the true me. How's Jamal?'

'How do you think he is?' David said, unable to hide his anger. 'His fiancée is dead. His best friend is accused of murdering her, and he has been accused of terrorism and spent eight months in prison as an innocent man - and you want to know how he is!'

Al stared at David for several minutes before saying, 'I regret what happened to Kim - but nothing else. I am going to plead not guilty at my trial though I know all the evidence is against me. It will give me an opportunity to tell the world about the perfidious west, about the atrocities and injustices suffered by Muslims throughout the world. I will tell them about the horrors being perpetrated by the British and Americans in Iraq and Afghanistan, about the insults suffered by Muslims in so-called civilised countries, about the constant references to 'paki scum', and the jeers at women wearing the burkha, the harassment on the street of young blacks and Muslims. I rejoice in all that Jihad is doing. We have justice on our side.'

David was scarcely able to contain his anger. 'You call it justice? Murdering innocent people?'

'Innocent? No, you're all guilty – living your comfortable lives and hiding yourselves away from the truth.'

'The truth! Do you think hurling bombs and killing people is going to bring about change? All it will do is cause hatred and division. You're crazed. I thought of you as a civilised man when we first met.'

Ali gave a supercilious smile and said, 'You're mistaken my friend.'

'You're no friend of mine.'

Not wanting to continue the discussion, David said, 'Why have you asked me to come?'

'Because Jamal is my friend.' said Ali.

'No longer,' said David.

'So be it,' said Ali, shaking his head sadly, 'But I wanted him to know about Kim.'

'You admit to murdering her?' David asked.

'The police have what they think of as proof. My fingerprints were found in her car. I know I will be found guilty. But I want Jamal to know that I didn't murder Kim.'

'Then who did?'

'It wasn't planned. Jamal told me that he was working all night, and Kim was away for the weekend, so we thought the flat would be empty.'

'Who's 'we?' interrupted David.

'My business partner,' he replied.

'Suleiman?' David asked.

Ali looked startled, 'How did you know that?'

'Jamal told me.'

Ali's face fell. David realised he'd touched a nerve.

'So you thought the flat would be empty and took your evil bomb making equipment and dumped it in Jamal's garage without asking him,' David said angrily.

'It was only supposed to be for a day or two. Unfortunately Kim turned up.'

'But you knew she lived there?'

'No. I thought she lived in her own flat. We were in the garage sorting out the equipment when we heard the front door open. Kim found us straight away, and asked what on earth we were doing. She was a bright woman, and seeing our equipment, guessed straight away. She turned quickly to go back to the flat, but I grabbed her arm, and she slipped and fell down the steps, hitting her head and knocking herself unconscious.

We debated what we should do. I suggested to Suleiman that he load the car with the equipment and find somewhere else to leave it, while I took Kim to the hospital. He was against the idea. He said it was far too dangerous to let Kim go free as she would almost certainly tell the police.

We argued. Suleiman's much stronger than I am. He got out a knife and threatened me, then plunged it into Kim. She died instantly. I was appalled. I didn't like Kim, but I wouldn't have wanted to kill her. I knew we would now have to get away as soon as possible. We drove Kim's car into the garage and put her in the boot. Suleiman said we would need to concoct a story about Kim's disappearance to give us time to get away, so he came up with the idea of leaving a note to say Kim's mother was ill.

There was only a very small pool of blood in the garage, which we wiped up. We were about to load the chemicals back into Suleiman's car when we saw the milkman coming along the road. We were frightened he would be able to identify Suleiman's car if we stayed, so we decided to drive off straight away, and come back for the chemicals later. We put the chemicals on the shelves at the back of the garage where there were a lot of old containers of garden pesticides and fertilizer – knowing that Jamal, who never took much interest in gardening, was unlikely to notice them. I grabbed a spade that was hanging on the wall, put it in the car, and drove off. We drove to the forest, where we dug a hole, and buried Kim. For Jamal's sake, I laid her out as carefully as I could, though Suleiman thought I was mad. He wanted to get away as quickly as possible. We then dumped Kim's car, and drove off up north in Suleiman's car.'

David sat stunned, unable to make any comment,

'That's why I want to speak to Jamal. I want him to know it was an accident, and that I didn't murder Kim. I wasn't happy about him marrying Kim. She wasn't a Muslim and I felt he was betraying his faith. But I would never have wanted to kill her or hurt Jamal. He was my friend – though I didn't agree with his views.'

As David looked doubtful, he went on, 'You must believe me. You know I went along with his engagement – even came to his engagement party and entertained everyone.'

'And yet you risked compromising him by planting your terrible bomb making equipment in his garage!'

'I never thought they would be discovered,' he said, feebly.

David looked at him speculatively and then asked, 'And what did you do after you dumped Kim's body?'

'I went abroad.'

'With the hospice appeal money!'

He nodded,

'And why are you telling me this?' David asked. 'If you're pleading not guilty, why aren't you giving your account in court.'

'Because I can't betray Suleiman – even though I hate him for what he did.'

'But you've told me!'

'Yes. But your account wouldn't stand up in court'

'I'm not so sure,' said David. 'The intelligence services are on to you and your cell.'

David didn't think that comment resonated very well with Al. He looked alarmed, but pulled himself together and said, 'I wanted Jamal to hear it from me – and if not from me, then from a friend.'

There was nothing more David could say so he got up, appalled by what he'd been told. Al tried to say more, but David waved him aside and left.

On the journey home David was in a state of shock and kept going over what Al had told him. He had to acknowledge that however unpalatable were some of the accusations Al had made about the west's treatment of Muslims, they could not be denied. But, at the same time, David knew there could never be any justification for terrorism.

He wondered what Jamal's reaction would be to the information about how Kim had come to be murdered and hoped Jamal might find some consolation in knowing it was Suleiman not Al who had killed Kim. He hoped that as Al had wanted to get Kim to hospital it would lessen his feeling of betrayal.

He kept going over his conversation with Al, and the phrase 'paki scum' nagged him. He tried to remember where he'd heard it before. It seemed to him that it was somehow significant. He dozed a little, and when he woke up, it came to him. Suleiman, the young man in their group at the Symposium in the summer, had used the phrase 'paki scum' - his face, suffused with anger – accusing the west of corruption and intolerance. As he thought about it he began to wonder whether this same Suleiman was the man he'd seen with Al, walking along by the mosque with their arms round two young lads.

David thought it was strange how one memory triggers another. As he continued to think about it, he remembered the little incident at the theatre when he and Samantha had seen Al with a group of Asians, and as he was about to walk over and say hello one of them had said, 'Oh, here's Suleiman,' and they'd all walked away. Then he remembered the conversation between Samantha and Jamal at the hospital when she asked him if he'd come across a Suleiman Patel when he was at university in America. Everything seemed to click into place.

David was shocked by the revelation – for that is what it was. He was convinced that his supposition, intuition, call it what you will, was correct, and that this was the Suleiman who'd helped Al plant the chemicals in Jamal's garage.

He realised he ought to report his suspicions to Sir Ralph. That is what they'd all been asked to do at the Symposium. But what if, by reporting his suspicions based on such tenuous connections, he put an innocent man in jeopardy?

For the rest of the journey he agonised about what he should do, but by the time he arrived home, he felt certain that he'd identified Al's companion and decided to get in touch with Sir Ralph straight away and tell him of his suspicions.

Sir Ralph took down details and thanked David for the information. A couple of days later, Sir Ralph phoned back and said that they were grateful for the names David had supplied; that his identification of Suleiman was correct and that he had been under surveillance for some time but had now disappeared abroad. He said David's information was the missing piece of the jigsaw and when they found him, they would be able to arrest him.

When David told Mary about the circumstances of Kim's death she burst into tears and said it was all her fault. David couldn't understand where she was coming from until she said, 'If I hadn't been so keen to read *Charlotte Grey*, Kim would never have gone back to Jamal's flat that morning.'

David couldn't deny that what she said was in essence true, and it took several weeks before she could be persuaded not to feel guilty. David, Celia, and Dan all pointed out that if Kim hadn't gone to the flat and disappeared, the police would never have had cause to search the garage and the bomb making equipment would not have been found. They pointed out that bombs would very likely have been made and detonated, causing even more deaths.

For many years the thought was to haunt Mary and she would often wake up in the night, crying.
David hadn't told Jamal he was going to visit Al in prison, but the morning after he got back from Manchester he called Jamal into his office and related what Al had told him. He told Jamal that Kim's death had been swift and, being unconscious, she would have known nothing about it; that Al had wanted to take Kim to hospital when she fell, but Suleiman killed her because he was frightened she would go to the police.

Though Jamal accepted that it was a slight consolation to know it wasn't Al who'd killed Kim and that her death had been swift, it didn't make it any easier to bear and he left David's office more depressed than ever.

-64-
Jamal goes to Scotland and the appeal progresses

David was very concerned about Jamal's mental state, but felt happier about him when, a few days later Jamal popped into his office and said he'd been invited up to Scotland for a few days by David's brother-in-law, James. David hadn't been aware that he and James had kept in touch since the wedding and had been playing regular games of chess online. Hearing about the circumstance of Kim's death, he and Alison had invited Jamal to go up and stay with them in Scotland. David thought it was a wonderful gesture, and was delighted for him.

It was not until Jamal returned that David realised there'd been an additional reason for the invitation. The position of Medical Director at the hospice where both his parents had died had become vacant and James, hearing of the interest in palliative care that Jamal had developed in prison, thought he might be interested in applying. He took him to see the hospice, and Jamal decided immediately that this was a place he would like to work in. As James was one of the trustees, he arranged for Jamal to be interviewed while he was still in Scotland.

When Jamal returned south, he told David what had happened, and said that if he were to be offered the post, he would accept it. According to James, there were other applicants who were interviewed later, but Jamal had been the outstanding candidate and was offered the job.

In view of all that he'd suffered in the last year, the Health Authority agreed to release him straight away. David organised a farewell party for him at the hospital - and there were many who felt sad at his departure though understood why he would want to get away from a place that held so many unhappy memories for him.

Celia and Dan hosted a small gathering for him, and told him he would be welcome to stay whenever he came south.

His departure left a gap in their lives and they missed him, but Mary and David knew they would be able to see him whenever they visited Susan and James in Scotland. They learnt from James that Jamal was settling in happily in his new role, and was popular with the staff and volunteers.

Mary and David settled down into a happy and fulfilled life though Al's impending trial was a constant reminder that the terrorist saga was not at an end as Mary would be called as a witness.

Much of their spare time was spent working on the hospice appeal. Though David had said he would only stay on for a year as Chairman of the Appeal, whenever he tried to retire, he was inveigled by some ruse or other to stay on. He was never able to distance himself from what was going on and one Saturday, thanks to Betty, David found himself rattling a collecting box in a Street Collection. He returned home exhausted but felt he'd notched up a new experience to ponder upon.

A hospice shop was set up in the town and numerous events were organised both centrally and by the small cells that were being set up in the villages around the town.

Mary, now her exams and the wedding were behind her, and the promise of land had been confirmed, started approaching a number of charitable trusts, most of which responded positively. Everyone realised that having a hospice for the town was now a reality, and an architect was appointed to design the building.

The Mayor adopted the hospice appeal as his charity for the year and David was invited to attend the Mayor's Annual Dinner as his Guest Speaker.

As the funds started coming in and they were nearing their target, two separate committees were set up, comprising medical and professional people, to plan the building and the staffing of the hospice once it was built. The Chairman of the Health Authority, Sir James Lambert, was recruited as an observer, and the Authority agreed to fund some of the running costs of the hospice.

It was at this stage that they decided they needed a patron and invited Lord Marston to take on the role. He accepted and suggested they recruit some sponsors who would be asked for an annual donation of at least £500 – 'gift aided of course!' He suggested Margaret and her husband be asked to help him. He offered to host a dinner at Storrington Park when they'd signed up thirty sponsors.

-65-
Ali Mansour's trial

It was the beginning of May when Ali Mansour was tried at the Old Bailey in London. The trial was in two parts: first the charge of terrorism, and then the charge for the murder of Kim Anderson.

It emerged fairly early on that Al had been under observation for many months before he became involved with the hospice appeal. The owner of the Tandoori restaurant in London where David had first seen Ali, told the court that Ali and his friends had met there regularly and that their behaviour had been unusual. He felt suspicious and having a friend who was a policeman told him of his suspicions. His friend had passed on the information to someone in MI5.

The first few days of the trial were spent examining Ali's movements abroad. The main witness was a Doris Penrose, a middle aged woman with silver grey hair rolled into a bun, thick spectacles, a knitted black beret on her head, and wearing an old fashioned shabby brown coat which hugged her overweight body. It was when she started speaking that David sat up straight in his seat, realising the witness was Samantha.

His heart started beating fast with shock. Mary realised something was wrong and looked at him enquiringly. He mouthed back, 'I'll tell you later.'

As she was taken through her evidence by the prosecuting barrister, he understood what Samantha had really been involved with when she kept refusing to see him because she had to go abroad or had meetings to attend to. The fact that her work was so important somehow lessened his feeling of anger and betrayal.

Through Samantha's evidence the court learnt that Ali Mansour and his friends had been kept under constant surveillance and four of them had been arrested some months before. She said that Ali and his friend whose name she didn't know, had managed to escape abroad without being detected.

Samantha, if she had seen David in the gallery, gave no sign of recognition and when she left, David felt that that was the end of a chapter.

Jamal was an early witness. Both Mary and David accompanied him to the court as they knew what a strain it would be for him going over the nightmare again. Once in the witness box, he resolutely avoided looking at Ali. Jamal was cross questioned about the bomb making equipment found in his garage, and how Al came to be staying in his flat that weekend. The prosecution was at pains to state that Jamal had been charged but acquitted of all involvement with what had been found in his garage, but this didn't stop the defence questioning him at length about his relationship with Ali, about the events of the weekend Kim disappeared, and the arrangements he'd made with Ali about staying in his flat.

Penny and Nigel, Jamal's neighbours, were called to tell the court what they had witnessed the night they were leaving to go abroad on holiday. They produced passports to verify that it was the same night Kim disappeared. They told the court how surprised they were to see a car draw up at 3 am and saw two men get out, one of whom they recognised as Dr Khan's friend Al Mercer whom they'd met. They had watched them unload several large canisters into Dr Khan's garage.

Cross questioned, they said that as they had a plane to catch, they'd left almost immediately. They said their garage was at the other side of the flats so they'd seen nothing more, and it was only when they returned some months later and learnt of Dr Khan's arrest that they recalled the incident and told the police.

Later in the trial David was called as a witness.

'I understand,' said the defence barrister, that you visited Ali Mansour in prison after he was arrested.'

'Yes,' said David.

'Why is that? Is Mr Mansour a friend of yours?'

'No! Far from it. I went because he begged either Dr Khan or a friend to visit him as he had important information to impart.'

'So you went?'

'Yes, very reluctantly.'

'And did you discover why he wanted to see you?'

'Yes. He wanted to tell me how Kim Anderson had died. He said he hadn't killed her.'

'Can you tell the court what he told you?'

David then recounted the conversation as carefully as he could.

'Did he tell you the name of the colleague who he said had killed Kim Anderson.'

'No, not in so many words.'

'What do you mean by that?'

'I suggested to Mr Mansour that his name was Suleiman. He looked very surprised but he didn't deny it.' As he said this David looked toward Al and saw his face was suffused with anger.

The defence said this was just supposition and should be scrubbed from the record. The judge said it should stand.

David and Mary were not in court when the prosecution asked a question which gave Ali the opportunity to rant against 'the perfidious west' as he had told David he would. It was widely reported in the press and on the news

When it came to the charge of murder, Mary found herself an early witness. She'd been very nervous about standing up in court, but the prosecuting barrister reassured her by telling her that her evidence was of great importance in obtaining Al's conviction. She was taken carefully through all the details - that she'd spent the evening with Kim the night before she disappeared; that Kim had lent a book to Al Mercer that he'd promised to return that weekend; that despite the fact that people thought Al had not been to the flat that weekend, the book had been found on a shelf in Jamal's flat proving that Al had been there; that Kim's last words to her were that she would collect the book next morning so she could bring it to Mary when she and Jamal came to lunch on the Sunday.

The defence tried to rubbish her evidence by suggesting Al had returned the book some time before, but Mary stuck to her story.

The prosecuting barrister then established the circumstances of Kim's disappearance – the letter about Kim's mother in hospital; the discovery that it was a hoax, the efforts to trace the address of Kim's mother; the discovery that she'd never been in hospital, and the eventual discovery of Kim's body through a set of bizarre circumstances.

David was then called again to tell the court what Ali had told him about Kim's death. Ali corroborated what David had said, but refused to mention the name of Suleiman despite repeated attempts by the prosecution.

The trial lasted two and a half months in all, and at the end of it Ali was found guilty of conspiracy to terrorism and a party to the murder of Kim Anderson. He was given twenty-five years in prison.

Though Al's trial brought some sort of closure to what had happened, they knew that there were several issues still not resolved - one was the fact that Suleiman had not been found and the other that the money that had been stolen had not been recovered.

But their thoughts were diverted to the hospice appeal where it had all started. Excitement grew as the building slowly emerged. Most of the original committee continued to work hard to ensure sufficient funds came in to pay for it. Staff were recruited including a medical director, a matron and an administrator, furniture, equipment and medical supplies were purchased, and invitations were sent out to all those who had raised money for the appeal to come to an Open Day at the hospice before the first patients arrived.

It was a few months after Al's trial and conviction that the police announced they had recovered £210,000 of the £390,000 stolen. The rest had been spent on purchasing the bomb making equipment found in Jamal's garage. Though the members of the appeal committee were delighted with the recovery of some of the money, they felt very bitter that £180,000 raised through hard work and generosity to help the dying, had been used for potential death and destruction.

-66-
Married life

With the trial behind them, life began to return to some sort of normality. David and Mary had been married for a year when two major events in their family occurred. They'd delayed having a baby until they were sure Jamie was really settled. It was when he'd been at nursery school for a couple of terms that he came home one day and said, 'I want to have a sister or brother like Melanie!'

Mary and David looked at each other and found it difficult not to laugh.

'Why?' they asked.

'Cos it would be fun. Melanie helps to bath her baby brother, and they play in the bath, and they sleep in the same bedroom, and ……' he couldn't find the words to express what he wanted

Trying to suppress a laugh, David said, 'Well, you know, old fellow, we can't get a baby just like that. We'll have to wait a little while. But if you really want a baby brother or sister, we'll see what we can do.'

'Will that be next week?' asked Jamie eagerly.

'No, I'm afraid you'll have to wait longer than that. Perhaps by your next birthday.'

As he'd only just had his fourth birthday, they felt that would be a marker for him. He turned to Mary and said, 'Well, it looks like we've got a busy time ahead!!'

She laughed, swept up Jamie, and came into his arms.

Nine months later, almost to the day, their first baby arrived – a little girl they christened Felicity – a name they felt appropriate as she'd been so much wanted by them all.

Mary's father, who had been ill on and off ever since their wedding, lived to see his granddaughter. He came up for the christening, held Felicity in his arms, and blessed her. He died a few weeks later – peacefully, at home.

Mary was anxious about her mother staying on in her home so far away, and persuaded her to move. The flat that Mary had lived in at The Manor was empty, and Celia and Dan suggested Mary's mother came and lived there. Over the years, the two families had got to know each other well, and though Celia and Sybil were very different, they'd became good friends.

'Your mother has stayed here so often,' Celia pointed out. 'She already knows a lot of people in the village and at church. And you'd be only a few miles away. It's not like trying to persuade her to move to somewhere unfamiliar. She's still in good health and energetic and I'm sure there are lots of voluntary organisations locally that would love to have her.'

David and Mary helped move Sybil, feeling this was the beginning of a new stage in their lives.

A year after Felicity was born they had their second child – a boy called Thomas. It was amusing to see Jamie's reaction. He'd been delighted with the arrival of Felicity, but the thought of a baby brother was even more exciting. He started setting aside special toys for Thomas when he was big enough to play with him – all concept of time completely beyond him.

-67-
Hospice opened

Two very generous donations to the appeal enabled the hospice to be built sooner than expected, and the first patients were received.

A Formal Opening of the hospice was arranged by the newly appointed staff, and a member of the Royal Family agreed to do the honours. Just a week before the event came news of the arrest of another terrorist. When details were published the terrorist was named as Suleiman, the associate of Ali Mansour. He was to be charged with both the murder of Kim Anderson and with possessing bomb making equipment. This was the closure everyone had needed and they all felt it had come at a most appropriate moment.

As he waited in the line-up waiting for the Royal personage to arrive, it struck David that the only other volunteer invited for the line-up was Jamal. David had had to work hard to persuade the hospice admin staff to invite Jamal, and it made him realise how quickly concern with the present can obliterate the past. He felt it ironic that inside the building was a line-up of the newly appointed staff, waiting to curtsey and be formally presented, while the volunteers who'd put in four years of toil and sweat to raise the money for the enterprise, were standing outside in the rain, waiting for their moment of recognition after the main ceremonies were over. Life seemed to David unfair.

He thought about the volunteers. Over the time he'd been involved with the appeal, he'd had the opportunity to get to know people from all walks of life and realised that people get involved in charitable work for a variety of reasons. For some, it was the altruistic desire to do something for others; for those alone or widowed, there was a need to find friendship, support, and a listening ear; for the retired, a need to be affirmed; for others a way of keeping intellect and abilities alert and in trim; while for many it was their Christian faith that drove

He reflected on the dramatic events that had taken place in the years running up to the building of the hospice, and the people who had died during the course of those events – his father, Kim, Jane, Ben, and Mary's father. And then he thought about Jamal who was now happily working in a hospice in Scotland and, according to James, involved with a young and attractive member of the hospice staff.

Then he thought about himself. He was happily married with three lovely children, and he felt fulfilled and at peace with himself. But the experience of the years leading up to the present made him realise that life is fragile, and that the most mundane of lives can suddenly be turned upside down. It was the hospice appeal that had brought Mary into his life, and the hospice was now up and running, thanks to all their hard work, and was providing a valuable service for the terminally ill and their families. But though he rejoiced in what they had achieved, and in his own happiness, he was painfully conscious of the fragility of life, remembering the totally unexpected event that had affected so many of their lives and made them aware of the dangerous world in which they now lived.

Lightning Source UK Ltd.
Milton Keynes UK
UKHW022021150721
387226UK00004B/215